Chauncey Wright

Letters of Chauncey Wright

With some account of his life

Chauncey Wright

Letters of Chauncey Wright
With some account of his life

ISBN/EAN: 9783337136284

Printed in Europe, USA, Canada, Australia, Japan

Cover: Foto ©Andreas Hilbeck / pixelio.de

LETTERS

OF

CHAUNCEY WRIGHT

LETTERS

OF

CHAUNCEY WRIGHT

WITH SOME ACCOUNT OF HIS LIFE

BY

JAMES BRADLEY THAYER

Privately Printed

CAMBRIDGE
PRESS OF JOHN WILSON AND SON
1878

TABLE OF CHAPTERS.

Chapter		Page
I.	1830–1861	1–46
II.	1861–1865	47–63
III.	1865–1867	64–94
IV.	1867–1868	95–136
V.	1868–1870	137–156
VI.	1870, January–October	157–198
VII.	1870–1872, July	199–238
VIII.	1872, July, — 1875	239–319
IX.	1875, January–September	320–361
X.		362–384

THIS book has been prepared, and privately printed, for certain friends of CHAUNCEY WRIGHT in this country and in England. In making selections from the letters, I have not considered what might please the indifferent reader, but rather what would interest those who knew Wright, or who had already been drawn to his essays; being, however, not without hope that others into whose hands the book may fall will find here much that will seem worthy of their attention. I wish I might believe that anybody will have as much pleasure or as much benefit in reading the volume as I have had in editing it.

Even in so slight a sketch of life and character as is here undertaken, it has seemed well to omit nothing within my knowledge which might help to a just estimate of the man. The rule for such attempts, whether large or small, is that of the Roman author: "Cum exprimere imaginem consuetudinis atque vitae velimus Epaminondae, nihil videmur debere praetermittere, quod pertineat ad eam declarandam."

J. B. T.

CAMBRIDGE, December 21, 1877.

LETTERS

OF

CHAUNCEY WRIGHT.

CHAPTER I.

WHEN it was first proposed by a few friends of CHAUNCEY WRIGHT to collect into a volume his principal papers, it was intended to add to them, as a part of the same book, a selection from his letters. But afterwards this plan was changed. It seemed best, for the present at least, to respect the privacy of his letters, and to print them only for the reading of his friends.

Accordingly, at the beginning of the year 1877, the volume entitled "Philosophical Discussions" was published, with an Introduction by Professor Norton; while the letters were placed in my hands. The present volume consists in the main of selections from them. But it has been desired that some sketch of Wright's personal history and characteristics should accompany the letters, and this I have undertaken to give. Professor Norton's purpose, in his excellent "Biographical Sketch," was not so much to state with any degree of fulness these personal details, as to indicate Wright's characteristics as a thinker, and to furnish a key to his philosophical opinions.

My own qualifications for speaking of Chauncey Wright are those of a friend who had been intimate with him from boyhood to the day of his death. We went to the same school from the time we were twelve years old; we entered college together, and had there a close friendship; and, after leaving college, although our callings were different, and others for most of the time saw more of him than I did, yet I saw much; I was for a time his room-mate; we travelled in company during the summer holidays for several years, and were often together on the most familiar footing. When his death came, although it brought to me the sad reflection that I had been for many years near a wisdom and sweetness which I had but imperfectly appreciated, I yet felt very keenly that it was my oldest and most intimate friend that had gone.

CHAUNCEY WRIGHT was born at Northampton, Massachusetts, on September 20, 1830: he lived there until 1848, when he entered Harvard College. All the rest of his life he passed at Cambridge, and died there on September 12, 1875. He was never married.

From the time he graduated, in 1852, until the year 1870, he was employed in the office of the Nautical Almanac, and in this way supported himself. While thus occupied, he took now and then a private pupil; for a year or two, he taught in the school for young ladies, maintained at Cambridge during some years by Professor Agassiz. In the year 1870, and afterwards, he was for a short time one of the University Lecturers, and again an instructor in the College. During the last fifteen years or so of his life at Cambridge, he was in the habit of writing occasionally for the reviews or newspapers,—principally for the "North American Review" and "The Nation."

Such is the sum and abstract of his uneventful life. Let me now undertake, in presenting a selection from his letters, to add such details as may serve to explain them, or to illustrate his character.

On his father's side, Chauncey came of a family which had lived at Northampton ever since the foundation of the town in 1654. Samuel Wright, the first of the line in this country, was also the ancestor of Silas Wright, Governor of New York. He had emigrated from England in 1630, had passed with others from the neighborhood of Boston to the Connecticut River, and after staying for a longer or shorter time at Hartford, Windsor, or Springfield (where he was a deacon), had been one of the little company of thirty-eight who finally went higher up the river and settled at Nonotuck, now Northampton.[1] One after another succeeded in the family line of the Wrights, living and dying in the town where his fathers had lived and died before him.

Chauncey's grandfather was a private in the Revolutionary War. His father was Ansel Wright, a substantial, well-known, respected citizen, a deputy-sheriff of the county, and a prosperous dealer in those miscellaneous articles which are known in our country towns as "West India Goods and Groceries." He was a man of very simple ways, laborious in his business, seeing little of his friends, and not much of his family, but cheerful, kindly, known and liked by everybody in the town. No object was more familiar in the streets of Northampton than the stout, short figure of the deputy-sheriff carelessly seated in his mud-bespattered, open buggy, as he drove with loose-hanging reins his ill-harnessed, ill-groomed, hard-used, but rapid horse. Quiet and kind as the deputy-sheriff was, he was also quick-minded, wise, and shrewd. Many a story is current in Northampton now which illustrates his good-natured wit and a skill that he had in entrapping rogues which must have amused even the victims themselves. He was a man of

1 "Men of enterprise, of good sense, and truly Christian men: they combined industry and prudence, patient labor and economy." — *Rev. Dr. Allen's "Second Century Address," delivered at Northampton,* Oct. 29, 1854.

irreproachable character, and a constant attendant at the little Unitarian church in Northampton, which he remembered in his will.[1] He died in the year 1872.

The name of Chauncey's mother was Elizabeth Boleyn, or Bullen; for the name here as well as in England was spelled both ways. With a sister who is still living at Northampton, she came from Enfield, in Connecticut, when they were small children. She died on September 10, 1848, just after Chauncey had entered college; she is remembered as a woman of sober character, good sense, and reserved habits.[2]

Of Chauncey's early days, he himself has furnished an amusing account in his "Life," written in 1858, in the "Class-Book" of his class at Harvard College.

"I was born," he says, . . . "near the autumnal equinox, just as the sun was about to enter the Balance. To this circumstance and to my equable temperament I ascribe the subsequent monotony of my life. My father Ansel Wright is . . . doubtless himself descended from a series of English Wrights, who in their day and generation were well known to their friends. . . .

"My memory of the earliest events of my life is nearly uniform; but, as years advanced, a few salient events stand as landmarks, with no particular propriety that I can discover,

[1] A friend tells me: "Mr. Wright was always a pleasant man in his family, and very indulgent to his children, giving them more than they asked for, fond of joking with them, and allowing them the largest liberty in that way. George [the oldest son] liked to practise little tricks and catches upon his father, who always took them kindly, — for instance, getting his father to stand in a chair, and telling him that when he should ask him the third time to come down he would certainly come, whether he wanted to or not. Mr. Wright good-naturedly stood in the chair, and George called upon him twice to come down: he didn't come down, — and he waited in vain for a third call."

[2] Of Mrs. Wright, a friend says: "Chauncey's mother, unlike him, had dark hair and eyes and a dark skin: she was a quiet woman, and, as —— says, hadn't a particle of fun in her."

except perhaps the fact that they happened at moments in my life when I was unusually conscious, and serve to indicate this state of mind. The baby on which I was founded was, I suppose, like other babies, except in respect to its destiny, of which, however, its friends knew nothing at that time. At an early period in its life, its grandmother discovered on its head, which was born without hair, a light down, from which she predicted the present color of my hair.

"This child, though unusually sober and good-natured, was in no way remarkable, except at the time, as being *the* baby; but this I have observed is ever a source of wonder. I bear at the present moment upon my forehead the mark of a wound which this child received in its first attempts at walking, and by which among other features I was afterwards distinguished.

"My father was a Democrat and an ardent supporter of Andrew Jackson, then President; and I escaped only by the skin of my teeth (not then grown) from receiving the name of this statesman. Fortunately, the Fates and my mother interfered, and gave to this infant the name I now bear.[1]

"The first day at the infant school I distinctly remember as one of the saddest in my early life, a day of grief inconsolable. My teacher, or the lady who, I suppose, afterwards became my teacher, endeavored to comfort me by offering me something to drink, — what, I do not distinctly remember. It may have been milk or some sweet beverage. My fainting spirit with all its tender rootlets, rudely torn from home, could find no sustenance in earthly fluids; and so I came to my letters in tears.

"From the earliest period of my conscious life, I have shrunk

[1] This name, by which he was so generally and so familiarly called, even by friends who were not intimately acquainted with him, was not a family name: it was selected by his parents because they happened to like it.

from every thing of a startling or dramatic character. I was indisposed to active exercise, to any kind of excitement or change. I was never remarkable at any kind of sport; never could see the value or significance of any kind of formality. In illustration of this, I remember a circumstance in my earliest school-days. The school-mistress wished to introduce the custom of kneeling at morning prayer. This I obstinately refused to do, or at least obstinately did not do. The penalty for my disobedience was to kneel by the teacher's side, — a position of dramatic interest by which my spirit was broken.

"I was in general a very tractable boy, and never was flogged at school, though I remember some slight corrections.[1] I had some little ambitions, such as all boys have, but they were for the most part of a solitary nature. I never aspired to be a leader among boys, and never cared for their quarrels and parties. If I aspired to a place, it was to a solitary place and a peculiar one, not within the general aim of the boys. At one time, however, my ambition took a social turn. While I was still in the district school, I conceived an ardent attachment for one of the school-girls, which I have never men-

[1] A friend writes from Northampton: "Chauncey first went to school to a Miss Burt, with whom he was a great favorite, — he was such a good, gentle little boy. She used to teach the children to repeat hymns, but could not get Chauncey to learn them, or the alphabet, or any thing out of a book. He would sit still and listen to his mates, and after a time the teacher was surprised to find that he was learning all that she was teaching the others. In this way, he had learned some thirty hymns before he had mastered the alphabet. . . . His aunt tells me that he was the best little boy she ever saw. The only mischief she ever knew him to be guilty of was upsetting a pan of squash prepared for pies: it was on an upper shelf, and he was curious about the contents of the pan, and, in pulling it down to look in, it went all over him from head to foot. He said not a word to any one, but took off his jacket, and hid it away in a loft, cleansed himself and his trowsers as well as he could, and went to his father and asked for a new jacket. His father expressed a mild surprise, but gave him the jacket."

tioned before this writing to any living soul. I did not even intimate it to the young lady herself, but rather built small castles, or very diminutive houses in the air, wherein I dwelt in fancy with her I fancied, — I will not say adored. Such was the character of all the attachments or fancies I have subsequently had.

"Another social turn of my ambition was at the High School, where I studied hard for one of a series of prizes. I obtained one, not the first of the series, but the first and last in my past life. I carried to this school and retained the character of *good boy*. I was never flogged; and, on the occasion of receiving the prize I have mentioned, I was publicly praised as the only boy who had received, in that term of the school, no marks for tardiness or bad behavior. This virtue of punctuality I have since lost in college, principally in the Senior year, in which I received two private admonitions for cutting prayers. In this respect, then, the boy was not father to the man; though I think this can be explained, when we consider that I was not tempted like other boys by their sports, and that I was carefully trained to punctuality at home. Tardiness is the natural result of an indolent disposition, and this I have always had. I had in my boyhood a violent temper; but I was not quarrelsome, nor did I ever cultivate pugnacious qualities. My indolence has since completely mastered my temper.

"At the age of ten, I formed a liking for the study of astronomy, and my zeal in this easily overcame all the fondness for those surprises which had previously constituted the great attraction of New-Years' gifts, and so I asked my father for that puerile book, Burritt's Geography and Atlas of the Heavens; but I afterwards lost my interest in this study."

The first letter that Chauncey ever wrote has been preserved. It was written to his grandmother and his aunt, then in the State of New York, when he was twelve years old. I will give it, omitting only a name, just as the boy wrote it, with all its imperfections on its head. The sending of a letter in those days had not ceased to be a rather important transaction in a pecuniary way. The postage on this letter is marked in red ink on the outside — for it was before the day of postage-stamps — as "18¾."

To his Grandmother and to his Aunt, Mrs. Clarke.

NORTHAMPTON, April 29, 1843.

DEAR GRANDMOTHER AND AUNT, — As this is the first time I ever wrote a letter you need not expect much, but as I understand writing letters does not consist in telling what I never have done before, but in telling about the family and other things, I will begin by telling you that we are all well. I have had a sore throat two or three days back, but now have nearly got over it. About three or four weeks ago George took our cutting machine up in town and got it sharpened. He had not had it much more than a week afterwards when he cut his first two fingers off in the middle of the nails. He lost one of the ends in the hay and threw the other in the fire. They bled for some time, and after a while he began to faint. Father and mother led him to the bed. Father then went to the door, where he fainted away, and fell full length upon the platform, but we soon brought him too. George's fingers are now healing very fast. We have had a queer season for spring, but it is more like spring now. We have some snow on the ground but it is now going very rapidly. The school is now out and also the school in South St. When the last begins, Fred is going. Frank has got done working for us. He has moved up in South St. and has set up Soap and Candle business by himself, and has his shop in the old Dye House, between Mr. Davis'es shop and Mr. Kingsley's house. Fred says he wants to see Grandma. Asahel has got over his last summers disorder. He can now talk very plain. Aunt Polly's folks are all well. They have moved in with Sam'l. Jr. Aunt Electa's foaks are all well. Mr. Rust has bought a monkey for the shop. The day after he bought it George brought it down hear where he bit Ansel on the head. They carryed him to the shop again. There is one girl born in Maple St. Mrs. Dexter Clark is the claimer thereof. Ansel and I are going to lose one of our school-teachers, for Miss Alden is going to get married to Josiah Parsons of this town. Father keeps the black horses a going, and is as much hurried as ever. —— has been stealing from his Grandmother, and has gone to the state's prison for one year. Since writing the above, Frank's babe has died after being sick about five days with the scarlet fever. We have had a higher flood hear than the Jeferson flood, as I suppose you have read in one of our Northampton papers. Our hatchway wall fell in. The water was so high that it ran over our front yard fence. We have had a hard storm and the water is rising very fast, and there is some prospect of an other such a flood. Un. Sam has hired the mine farm. I believe I have wrote all I can think of, and will stop by requesting you to write: We all send our love to you.

Yours, &c.

CHAUNCEY WRIGHT.

In this letter, Chauncey speaks of a great flood. His father's house stood (and still stands) on Maple Street, near Mill River, and on the southerly side of it, — just at the edge of that great unfenced Northampton meadow which stretches away on both sides of Mill River to the Connecticut, and spreads into the Hadley meadow beyond the larger stream. A mile and a half to the south-east, in full sight, just across the Connecticut, Mount Holyoke rises suddenly out of the plain. This Mill River is the same which became so tragically famous in the spring of 1874, by a flood which came from the breaking away of a dam. The flood to which Chauncey's letter refers was of another sort, — such as often comes in the spring, when the Connecticut, swollen by the melting of the snows in the upper country, overspreads the meadows and fills the channel of Mill River with "back water." Mr. Wright and his neighbors used not seldom to be flooded, and sometimes cut off from all their usual means of communication with the town. Now the waters are shut out by a dike. Chauncey was fond of speculating on the phenomena of these streams; and it is probable that he found in them his earliest provocation to those studies in natural science which always had a special hold on his attention.

In the next letter will be found some amusing illustrations of an early habit which Chauncey had of writing verse. He continued it through his school-days, but then wholly abandoned it. It seemed odd to the rest of us at school — confounding, as we did, the form of poetry with the substance — to find Chauncey writing his compositions in verse, for he exhibited in his dealings little sentiment or emotion: indeed, his habits were rather marked by an unusual amount of that reserve in such matters which passes with boys for good sense. It is not difficult now to see that what attracted Chauncey to this form of writing was the exercise of ingenuity which he found in it. He continued always fond of ingenious modes of expression: the clinching of an argument by a happy phrase always gave him a peculiar pleasure. The reader of his letters, as well as of his graver writings, will notice this not seldom.[1]

[1] His wit also may properly enough be mentioned here: many will remember the excellent quality of it. Since I have been preparing this book, I have accidentally, at a public table, overheard a saying of his quoted as Charles Lamb's, — his description of that bookish creation, *a lad*. "A lad," he said, "is a boy with a man's hand on his head." Some of his friends will remember that he had a favorite amended reading of certain lines in Shakespeare, after the manner of the commentators.

It was the same mental characteristic which led him in later life to his experiments in legerdemain, of which Mr. Norton has spoken in his Biographical Sketch. As for his youthful verse, it was, indeed, often "ingenious;" but it neither claimed nor possessed any other merit. One of his schoolmates writes: "I have no recollection of him as a boy except that he astonished us all one Saturday, shortly after entering the High School, by reciting, in the way of declamation, a piece of poetry of his own composition. I remember consoling myself for my measureless inferiority in not being able to write a single line, by thinking that, after all, the verses were not remarkably good."

To Mrs. Clarke.

NORTHAMPTON, April 18th, 1844.

DEAR AUNT, — My last letter was clouded by the mournful event of Asahel's death, but those gloomy clouds have broke away and the sun now shines with resplendent glory. We are obliged to acknowledge that he who taketh also giveth, yea, and twofold also. On the morn of Wednesday, April 3rd to the great delight of all we were presented with a sister, and at eve with a brother.

We now look forward to the future
  And humbly wish them future bliss,
And may they live to age mature,
  They will if heaven will grant our wish.

The boy weighs six and the girl five pounds. They now enjoy good health. I shall not go very far into detail,

A much-quoted passage in "As You Like It," he insisted, is manifestly corrupt, and yet needs only an astonishingly simple transposition to bring it right. It should read, —

"And this our life, exempt from public haunt,
Finds . . . *stones in the running brooks,*
Sermons in books, and good in every thing."

but simply say that the girl resembles Fred. and the boy Asahel.

Mother is comfortable and the rest of our family are all very well. Father requests me to tell you that he has seen Mr. Searl since I wrote before, and Searl said that he thought that he could pay one hundred dollars on that note, about the first of June next.

Yours affectionately,
CHAUNCEY WRIGHT.

THE TWINS.

United by one strict relation
They do unbroken keep,
A concord suited to their station,
Togeather eat and sleep.

And may they grow and prosper well
And soon their use display,
Keeping one harmonious spell,
Togeather work and play.

And may they, when in old age prime
Look back upon the past,
Repenting all the misspent time,
Togeather die at last.

CHAUNCEY WRIGHT.

Chauncey was the second son and the third child, in a family of nine. Two of the children were girls: both of these, and three of the boys, died young. Neither of the twins, whose birth came on with such "resplendent glory," lived to see the old age which the poet invoked for them. There remained four sons. George, the oldest child, — four years older than Chauncey, — grew up to share his father's business as a grocer, became, like him, a deputy-sheriff, and died in November, 1865. He was an upright man, and widely beloved. His wife and several children survived him, and now live at

Northampton. Next younger than Chauncey was Ansel, who also succeeded to both branches of his father's business, and who lives now at Northampton, the last survivor of the household. Frederick, a younger brother, born in 1839, entered the army as a private in the Tenth Massachusetts Regiment at the beginning of the war of the Rebellion, was made successively second and first lieutenant of the Twenty-seventh Massachusetts Regiment, and was mortally wounded at Cold Harbor while acting as adjutant of his regiment. He died at a hospital in Washington, on June 27, 1864.

My acquaintance with Chauncey began when we were about twelve years old, he being my senior by a few months only. My father had moved to Northampton in 1841, and then lived for a little time quite near Mr. Wright's house. I do not recall Chauncey distinctly at this time, but remember well his brother George, who was the hero of all the small boys of the neighborhood, — a great swimmer, a wonder, in our eyes, of physical strength, and as kind as he was strong. I must have met Chauncey often in the train that followed our leader; but our eyes and thoughts were all fixed on him, and not on each other. We were together also at the High School, and, a little later, at what was called the Select High School, where twenty or thirty of the more advanced scholars, both boys and girls, were for a few years brought together by themselves. This experiment at co-education was soon given up; but we upon whom it was tried were most fortunate, for it brought us under the care of an admirable teacher, Mr. David S. Sheldon, now a professor in Griswold College, at Davenport, in Iowa. The development of Chauncey's mind owed much to the kindly influence and the wise and original methods of instruction of this thoughtful, refined, devout, and excellent man. One of his pupils, in a published notice of Chauncey's death, writes: "Mr. Sheldon led his pupils out into the fields and woods, and taught them to observe the facts of nature, — the life of plants; the life and habits of birds, animals, and insects; the movements of the heavenly bodies; the phenomena of the clouds, — and very soon it happened that one and another were absorbed in some special study of nature. The boy Chauncey took to watching the stars by night and investigating the phenomena of natural philosophy by day. He made himself a rude measurer of the distances of the stars; and the neighboring boys at times gathered about him to watch with open-mouthed wonder his simple experiments with the humble apparatus of his own contriving." Chauncey always remembered Mr. Sheldon with grateful appreciation.[1] Nothing could have been more consonant with his own nature than the gentle and sympathetic methods of his teacher: very novel they were to us in our experiences at the public schools.

A friend[2] who knew Chauncey at school, but hardly met him again until the last year of his life, writes: "Chauncey was a peculiar boy, somewhat reserved, and still not reserved in the sense of bashfulness, so common in boys of that age. He was very quiet, and much given to what is called 'brown study.' I think his most noticeable peculiarity was his abstractedness, amounting to absent-mindedness, espe-

[1] In his Class-Book "Life," he says, in a passage which immediately follows that I have already quoted: "In the higher English and Classical branches of the Northampton High School, I came under the care of a most kind and zealous teacher, Mr. David S. Sheldon, now a Professor in Iowa College. I was inspired by him with a zeal for natural history, which I have also since lost. I tramped in his company and under his guidance through most of the wilds of Northampton, collecting, preparing, and naming specimens of plants, bugs, birds, and reptiles. We drew into our pursuits nearly the whole school, and founded a museum of natural history, which, I think, is still in existence. My private collection of plants was partly destroyed by fire a few years before I went to college, but not till my whole interest had perished, never to rise from its ashes."

[2] Dr. Thomas Gilfillan, of Northampton.

cially in the school-room. Often have I seen him sit through a whole school session with a sheet of paper before him, and with pencil, ruler, and compasses, fill the sheet with curves and circles, squares and triangles, and all manner of figures, overlapping and underlying each other in apparent mathematical chaos, — whether of any significance to himself no one knew, certainly of no significance to any one else. Some looked upon this as evidence of something wrong, — a screw loose somewhere. When the class in Latin, Greek, or what not, was called, Chauncey sometimes failed to hear; and one would be sent to rouse him from his brown study, only to find that he had entirely forgotten to look at the lesson. On this account, he was not an apt scholar, except in mathematics, in which he always excelled, and with which he was always delighted. Out of doors, he was a quiet boy, seldom joining in the boisterous school-boy games, preferring to wander away by himself and within himself, yet always companionable and pleasant, ready to chat with any one who would chat with him, and always well liked by all his mates. He was very observing of every thing about him, making quaint remarks, and philosophizing upon it. To any one who sympathized with him in his study, or rather observation, of nature, he was a rare companion. It was my good fortune to be intimate with him in those earlier days; and pleasantly did we spend many happy hours together roaming about, — nutting, swimming, playing; sometimes talking, sometimes silent, but always with pleasant enjoyment."

It was, perhaps, in some of those "brown studies" at Mr. Sheldon's school, to which Dr. Gilfillan refers, that Chauncey, then fourteen years old, arrived at the "theories" which are so oddly sprung upon his brother George in the following letter. I am careful to reproduce the misspelling and the want of punctuation that set off so quaintly the conceits of the wise little head.

To his Brother George.

NORTHAMPTON, Mass., July, 1845.

DEAR BROTHER, — This sunday morning it is so hot that I have to take my seat in the jail shed[1] to *keep cool* while I write to tell you what ways the wheel of fortune has turned since last sunday. You need not expect that it has made many revolutions any way for it is as lazy as any of us this hot weather

We are all as well as the weather except baby who is a little down. He fell down the cellar stares the other day. Father hurt his foot the other day

We have had no prisoneres here who are going to Springfield or have gone since we wrote last

We have had no new prisoneres since father wrote except —— committed for debt.

Theories

In the begining God existed a mind like us who are made in his image or as we shall be in the future life and the qualities which characterise us and are finite in limit characterised him and were infinite in limit he created the earth ages before man with all the heavenly bodies now in existance except may be a few[2]

During this period it was void like the comics[3] at present and afterwards when it was fully formed the great changes were wrought in the space of six days. It was clothed with verdure, and was set perfroming its foremost and eternal work, of nourishing living beings of giving enjoyment to millions upon million times millions of minds. The pesent world is

[1] At this time, for a single year, the deputy-sheriff was keeper of the county jail, and lived in the jailer's house, then at the lower end of Pleasant Street.

[2] Here the philosopher had his doubts. After saying "except a few," he inserted "may be" with a caret.

[3] This spelling preserves the local boyish pronunciation of *comets*.

divided into three parts Animals Vegitables & Minerals the latter being but the raw materials the others transformations of minerals into that which is capable of containing and giving enjoyment to living minds Animals and Vegitables are destinguished from each other by performing the same office in different ways the former directly and the latter indirectly by giving nourishment to the animal. Minerals comprise all solids and fluids except those comprised by the other two and are of infinite duration vital perishes and needs renewal this nature produces. It is known that a graft from and old tree in a new one dies of old age before the other parts the potatoe being but the root dies in the course of time and new is raised from the seed. Nature efects this in the animal by the sexes. In the vegitable by the same thing in a different form. In the vegitable the sexes are unite in one plant with some exceptions the office of the female is to give the seed form of the male to give it youthfullness otherwise it would die of old age as soon as the female.

Thus much of theory. Please give your opinion.

Love from all to you and your's

Your's affectionately

CHAUNCEY WRIGHT.

Mr. Norton has remarked of Chauncey that "no strong personal influence seems to have affected the development of his intelligence." This was peculiarly true of his boyhood. There was little about him to attract the attention of persons outside of his family, and his life at home was unusually withdrawn from the agitations of society. But, even if circumstances had been different, it would have taken much to make any strong impression upon his invincible quietness. To say of him that he was mentally sluggish at this time would probably give a wrong impression of one who in some directions was gentle, sensitive, and easily moved, and whose mind, throughout his life, was always in its own way exercising itself upon some problem or other. But he certainly developed slowly,[1] and in boyhood one of his main characteristics was a placid, cool mind, which it was impossible to ruffle. Northampton at that time was very much under the influence of the Orthodox churches; and in the spring of 1846 there came a "revival," which swept in most of the scholars of our school, — for even so early was it thought well to agitate violently the religious sensibilities. Chauncey, however, was not to be moved, but kept throughout an attitude of amused observation, — a state of mind which had in it not merely the distrust or indifference of a Unitarian, but the cool curiosity of a philosopher.

In 1847, Mr. Wright's house was burned down. It was now found expedient that Chauncey should take some part in his father's business; and so he used, before going to school in the morning, to drive his father's ice-cart about town, and deliver ice. In March, 1848, he finally left the school, and was for some time employed in his father's shop. But it was soon determined that such a position was not the best one for this thoughtful boy. There was at that time an admirable woman in Northampton, who was a strong power in the community, who took, indeed, — within the little limits of the town, — all human affairs for her province, and who, in casting her eyes over the town, had observed Chauncey, and marked the ungenial region where his lot was just now cast. This was Mrs. Lyman, the wife, and about that time the widow, of the Hon. Joseph Lyman, who had been in former years the Judge of Probate, and later the high-sheriff, of the county. In the privately printed Memoir of Mrs. Lyman, written by her daughter Mrs. Lesley, of Philadelphia, the writer says: —

[1] "Bashfulness and apathy," says Mr. Emerson, "are a tough husk, in which a delicate organization is protected from premature ripening."

"Scarcely ever did Chauncey's father, the deputy-sheriff, drive past her door, that she did not hail him, to impress on his mind, with all the earnestness and pathos of her nature, that Chauncey *must have* a collegiate education; and I think, if he did not want her to be a thorn in his side until this dear wish of her heart was accomplished, he must have made a circuit to avoid her. But he was a kind-hearted man, and valued her sympathy and interest; and she never forgot the day when he came to tell her that Chauncey should go to Harvard, nor the sweet smile of the shy youth, who timidly thanked her for using her influence in his behalf. That day made a high festival for her, and, to use her own expressive phrase, 'was worth a guinea a minute to her.'"

In May, 1848, Chauncey was sent over to the Williston Seminary, at Easthampton, four miles away, to fit for college. The time was short — only three or four months — before the examination, and, in some particulars, the candidate was very backward. He found the preparation a tedious business; he had no friends at Easthampton, and he hated the study of the classics, to which he had now to bend. In August, he and I went to Cambridge together to be examined. Our friend, Mrs. Lyman, was already there, and had done what she could to prepare the way. "I have seen the President,"[1] she wrote early in August, "and said all I could for Chauncey, and I have no doubt he will get in." He did get in, but not without conditions.[2]

The minister of the Unitarian parish in Northampton at this time was the Rev. Rufus Ellis, now of the First Church, in Boston. Dr. Ellis has kindly sent me his recollections of Chauncey: a portion of his letter I reserve for a later page.

[1] Edward Everett.

[2] In the Class-Book, Chauncey gives a brief account of the end of his school-days and the beginning of his college life, which is, I believe, inaccurate as to some of the dates.

"As you know," he says, "my knowledge of our friend goes back to pleasant Northampton days, and to his boyhood. My two most vivid pictures of the youth present him first in his father's shop, and again as he stood before me translating from some Latin text-book and from Felton's Greek Reader. The days in the store were an intercalation, and I must have had a dim sense of this; for I recall my thought about him as out of place behind the counter, and not a person to buy groceries of. He stands before me, in the picture that comes up before me now, — with his light hair and pale face, — as one who was not there to stay, — a kind of visitor and temporary person in the shop. His garments, I distinctly remember, were not like those of the rest, and would have answered well enough for an Easthampton student or even a Harvard Freshman of the period. It could not have been long after this time, when he came to me with his school-books, to see how much he could recall of his High-School Latin and Greek, and whether it would suffice to tide him over the examinations for admission to Cambridge.

"And I have him before me again in the little room which opened out of the Doctor's office, where I was then accustomed to hear the recitations of two pupils who were preparing for college. He had forgotten a part of the little which he had learned, and made poor work of it. Would it be worth while for him to try? I must confess that I said no. I could not see how with such a meagre outfit there could be any thing but a disappointment. But he was like the boy who, when asked if he could read Greek, said in reply that he did not know, for he never *had* read Greek, but would try. He made the attempt; and thanks, it may be, to something which he *could* do, or to the discerning spirit of one and another examiner, he was admitted."

Before passing on to Chauncey's college days, let me find a place here for a note relating mainly to the period of his school-life, written by a lady[1] who was his schoolmate. "My school-girl reminiscences," she writes, "have not sufficient clearness of outline to be of value; for the powers of his mind, which afterwards were developed in the direction of mathematics and philosophy, made no adequate impression upon a fellow-student in Latin and the common English branches of the Northampton town school. I recall, however, the manliness of his character, which was all the more striking from the modesty and reserve with which it was associated. I believe the first party he attended was given at our house. In the winter vacations, he returned to the work of helping his father, and was accustomed to drive his cart about the town, in fulfilment of orders that were left at the store. He came into our kitchen during the morning of the party to distribute groceries, and showed the instincts and dignity of a gentleman to no less advantage than in the evening, when he mingled with the guests, and took his part in games and dances that were quite new to him. This may seem a small matter, and yet it showed a frank self-respect, a certain breadth and strength of bearing which are seldom to be found in one so sincerely modest as our friend. Another remembrance of Chauncey was at one of the pleasant conversation parties of Mrs. Charles Lowell.[2] There he carried off the honors of the evening, with the same quiet self-possession with which he discharged the humblest offices connected with his father's business."

During his Freshman and Sophomore years, Chauncey roomed in the third story of "Massachusetts," at the southwest corner, No. 25. This was not a Freshman room, and he had obtained it by buying out a Senior. My brother was a Junior, and we roomed for a year directly across the entry from Chauncey. During this year, we saw each other con-

[1] Mrs. Josiah P. Quincy, of Quincy.

[2] At Cambridge, about ten years later.

stantly; indeed, Chauncey passed the greater part of every day in our room. He seldom had a book in his hands, for neither at this time nor ever was he addicted to books, or much devoted to the regular studies of the college. When a recitation was immediately impending, he grew busy and sometimes agitated; but, for the most part, he was content to sit about and talk if anybody was ready to talk, or keep silent if others were busy. He had never much to say, but was always comfortable and a source of comfort to others, even in silence. It grew more and more surprising to us to see how little he read and how much he knew. His coming was always welcome: it was like the coming of a familiar member of one's family,—nay, rather like that of some pet animal; it seemed the effect of mere gregarious instinct. He had generally, as I mentioned, little or nothing to say; he *appeared* to be thinking of nothing: certainly, he was not preoccupied by any thing that called for solitude or silence. He was always sympathetic, ready to listen, ready to talk, ready for an impulse in any direction. He was oddly impersonal, and his presence was as natural, as welcome, as little marked as the sunlight or the air. When strangers came near, he was very shy and silent, but among his intimates as playful as a child. Upon his singularly amiable and compliant disposition, some of us used occasionally to play, —to invite him, for instance, to take a pail and go down two flights of stairs to the college pump for our water. This experiment upon his good-nature was often tried; and I doubt if he ever held out in refusing. Sometimes, indeed, he gently resented the outrage, but he would soon yield to our clamorous reproaches, with a sweetness to which not even the young ruffians who abused him were quite insensible.

During a part of the Sophomore year, Chauncey shared his room with Mr. C. C. Langdell, then a member of the class just ahead of us, and now the Dane Professor in the Law

School, — during so much of the year as Mr. Langdell remained in college; for, having entered as a Sophomore, he left early in his own Junior year. They had met as strangers in the course of some negotiations about the room, and Mr. Langdell remained in college too short a time to form any intimate relations with a room-mate of a lower class; but he still recalls the ease with which Chauncey dealt with certain difficult matters in the Junior course in astronomy and physics which had puzzled him, although he was the best scholar in his class. He remembers also the trouble that Chauncey had in getting up his Latin and Greek. I was in the same division with Chauncey, and was often a witness to the poor results of his labors in these departments. There was indeed something comic in Chauncey's helplessness and distress at a Latin, and especially a Greek, recitation. Small had been the work of preparation, and even disproportionately small was the harvest. He could neither translate nor pronounce respectably. But in mathematics he was easily master, and so in the physical sciences; while in moral and intellectual philosophy he was always good, and grew to be excellent. His themes and forensics also were good, and sometimes of unusual merit.

Chauncey never aimed to take high rank in college, but his standing was respectable;[1] and under the rules of that day, which gave a part at Commencement to the first half of the class, his name appeared on the Commencement Programme for an essay on "Ancient Geometry."[2]

When Chauncey came to college, he knew nobody except

[1] He was at his graduation the twenty-seventh scholar in a class of eighty-eight.

[2] "At the close of our course," he says in the Class-Book, "the world was deprived of the results of my learning, as embodied in my Commencement part, by an accident, which for a time disabled me as to my power of walking. When I recovered, I limped from Holworthy to the Nautical Office; and I have remained in its employments to the present time (July 24, 1858)."

four of his Northampton schoolmates who were there. For a good while he was hardly known at all out of this circle, but during the last two years he grew rapidly in the acquaintance and good opinion of his classmates. He was a member of the Rumford Society, the Natural History Society, and several others. He was not a member of the Institute of 1770. Of the Hasty Pudding Club, he became an honorary member after he graduated. In distributing the class honors, Chauncey was awarded the jack-knife. This dubious testimonial used to be given to "the homeliest man" in the class. I doubt if it was ever honestly awarded. Sometimes it was made the vehicle of ill-will, and sometimes of good-natured banter to a favorite; and the sum of money voted for it varied accordingly. In a later class, they disliked a man, and voted him the knife, with fifty cents to pay for it: in our class, they liked him, and voted him twenty-five dollars for it, — an amount which, as I well remember (for I helped in the search), Chauncey found it impossible to expend upon any single knife to be found in Boston. He took the vote of the class as it was meant, and was good-naturedly proud of the handsome gift.

But certainly Chauncey was not the homeliest man in the class, and nobody thought him so. He was not, indeed, handsome: he had thin, rather long, and very straight red hair, somewhat light blue eyes, and a complexion which grew painfully red with any unusual exposure to wind or sun. His head was large and well formed; but his features at that time had little about them that was marked, and his expression then was often dull and inanimate. He was rather large in person, and about five feet ten inches in height. Although not precisely awkward, he was without grace, and slow and heavy in his movements. He had also at this time little knowledge, care, or taste in dress. No popularity could come from his mere appearance and manner. Although there was nothing whatever in him that could offend one, yet there was, as I have said before, little to attract a person who did not know him. Those, however, who did know him, found often a sweetness and composure in his face, — a steady thoughtfulness in the look and a light of quick intelligence in the eyes which held them fast. He was one whose face for a long time grew handsomer and nobler as he grew older, and those who saw him in his later years are aware how thoughtful, how expressive, and how fine a presence he had.

I can best complete the picture of Chauncey as he appeared to his classmates by quoting from the letters which some of them have sent me.

One with whom he was very intimate, who had been for a little while a schoolmate at Northampton, and was at one time his chum in college,[1] writes : —

" He was so retiring and so little self-asserting that it was long before he was found out. We used to think he was irregular in his way of studying. But the fact is he was always studying, without going through the usual forms and appearances of it. The commonest occasions and incidents always set him thinking and philosophizing.

" Although we were chums during the Senior year [at Holworthy 15], I did not see much more of him than other classmates, on account of a way he had of living wherever he happened to be. This disposition was more easy of gratification, because he was always so warmly welcomed wherever he came. The idea of ever seeing too much of Chauncey Wright never entered the head of anybody. If his host was occupied for the moment, Chauncey had a way of sitting quietly, musing, or reading what happened to be handy, always carrying away something from it. He never seemed tired or sleepy, except in the mornings about prayer time, — rarely rousing till the last bell.

" Of course, it was well understood by the time we gradu-

1 George H. Fisher, now a member of the bar in Brooklyn, N. Y.

ated that he had remarkable talents. When we left college, there was no one more respected or better liked. He was, I believe, literally without any unfriendly antagonisms of the slightest kind. His gentleness, good-humor, kindliness, self-forgetfulness, were as universally recognized as his thinking power."

From the letter of another classmate,[1] I take the following extracts: —

"I first knew him well on taking a room (Mass. 26) opposite his.[2] I was fond of metaphysics; and Chauncey and I used to have long discussions. . . . His originality was shown by his frequent solution of some deep problem. His discoveries were not always very important; but they were worked out in his own mind, and were seldom helped by reading. I rarely knew of his reading a novel. One queer exception occurs to me. On a Saturday evening, in the winter of our Senior year, he came to my room with a paper-covered novel, — Pierce Egan's 'Quentyn Matsys,' a fearfully sensational romance, based on the life of the famous blacksmith and artist of Antwerp. It was written in the most gorgeous and melodramatic style. Chauncey seemed to have got the idea that he had something very fine, and so we sat down to read the book to each other. He began; then I took up the book. The alternation, I think, was kept up for some time; but, finally, as I was reading in the small hours, I found that he had fallen fast asleep. I finished the story for myself, and then woke him up. I believe this was the only partnership in the study of romance that we ever engaged in. . . . There is no member of our class of whom I have pleasanter recollections."

Professor Cary, of the Theological School at Meadville, — another classmate, who grew intimate with him in the west entry of Massachusetts, — writes as follows: —

[1] John T. Perry, now editor of the "Cincinnati Gazette."

[2] This was at the beginning of the Sophomore year.

"If I should describe my impressions of him by the use of negative epithets, I might seem to imply that positive qualities were wanting; and yet what I *feel* cannot be better expressed than by saying that he was not inordinately ambitious, not self-seeking, not envious, not suspicious, not critical of others' faults, not resentful of injuries, not one against whose rough corners his friends were constantly jostling. . . . His maturity bore fruit of which his earlier youth hardly gave promise. I always, even in college, looked upon him as a philosopher, yet more as a practical than a speculative one; and so was somewhat taken by surprise when I found how high a rank he was gaining as an original thinker in the line of the most abstruse discussions of the times. Even within the past few days, I have been made to feel how inadequate had been my previous estimate of his powers, by reading in the London 'Academy' of the 24th ult. [Feb. 24, 1877] the unhesitating affirmation that he was 'one of the finest philosophical minds which America or any country has produced.'

"His practical philosophy seemed equal to any emergency; and no strange or unexpected circumstances ever excited him to any more vehement expressions than the utterance of his sole exclamatory oath, 'By Zeus!' uttered with a tone of unmingled surprise."

Dr. Cheever,[1] now the Professor of Clinical Surgery in Harvard College, writes:—

"Chauncey Wright, Cary, Chase, and myself were very intimate in college. Wright roomed in Massachusetts two years, and I did three years. He was one of the most charming and genial of companions, and of wonderful conversational powers: this was mostly in the form of philosophical or speculative soliloquy. Many nights we spent listening to him until one or two in the morning. We planned to start him by irritative or skeptical remarks; and he would run like a good clock.

[1] Chauncey's chum in the Junior year at Mass. 28.

He was, in talk, like what we read of Coleridge, De Quincey, or Hamilton. He was shy as a hermit crab; and the entrance of one not in the set would send him to his hole for the rest of the evening."

Another view of Chauncey may be had through the eyes of the second scholar in the class:[1]—

"My acquaintance with Chauncey in college was comparatively little. Not being in the same half of the class,[2] I saw him only at the elective recitations in mathematics,[3] which he took to the end of the course. I remember my first visit to his room, where I found him boxing with F. H. All the paraphernalia of the pugilist seemed prominent, with, I think, the antlers of a deer, and some other objects of natural history, hung about his room. My impression remained a long time that the college studies were of wholly secondary importance in that quarter. In the mathematical elective hour, he would occasionally exhibit an original method of arriving at the same result with Professor Peirce; and there he grew greatly in my horizon. . . . Whatever he said or did, it seemed but the surface only of a great deep beyond. It was the sense of reserved power in him which gave one the idea of greatness. His gentleness and sweetness of nature seem to me almost unexampled. I never saw even a ruffle in the great sea of his placidity and goodness."

Chauncey, while in college, was not fond of letter-writing: it was with him a painful and elaborate exercise. I know of only a few letters written at this period, and these are of slight importance.

In November, 1850, he writes to his friend Fisher: "It will doubtless be a source of great satisfaction to you to hear of

[1] Addison Brown, now a lawyer in the city of New York. Brown entered Sophomore, coming to Cambridge from Amherst College.

[2] The classes then recited in two divisions made alphabetically.

[3] The electives then began with the Junior year.

the success of the Union meeting of yesterday [at Faneuil Hall, in Boston], which I had the pleasure to attend. Dr. Warren presided; and speeches were made by B. R. Curtis, Hallet, Choate, *et cæteri*, and demonstrations of enthusiasm by the audience, among whom your humble servant, sitting behind the great American Eagle, gave sundry manifestations of delight by beating the floor with the end of a broken umbrella. . . . Ten of our class are going to teach, and fifteen of the Seniors."[1]

In the winter vacation of the Junior year (January 20, 1851), he wrote from Northampton to me: "In my excursions about town to see the improvements, I notice a large church standing close beside the boys' school-house.[2] . . . Cigars have lost their flavor, and smoked in solitude increase my melancholy. Yet, as I have said on a former occasion, I mean to accustom myself to a solitary nook in this desert country, neither courting the favors nor tempting the frowns of Fortune; and then, if I am not content, I will say with the poet, —

> 'It is not grief that bids me moan:
> It is that I am all alone.'

To-morrow I shall commence the Homer,[3] and shall probably make it the spice of my life for the rest of the vacation; for I don't intend to hurry myself."

Doubtless, Chauncey did miss the society of his only classmate at Northampton; for during the vacations, while in

[1] This refers to a custom, now long discontinued. While there was a six weeks winter vacation, ending about the first of March, it was the habit of the college authorities to give leave of absence to such students as needed it, from Thanksgiving (the last Thursday of November) for the rest of the winter term. By this means, many students were able to command a solid three months for teaching in the country district schools.

[2] Situated at that time in the low land behind the "Old Church."

[3] This probably refers to a college "condition."

college, and for several years afterwards, we were constantly together. We walked to Mount Holyoke, and traversed the meadows in all directions; we explored the paper-mill, and cotton factories, and all the machine-shops we could find. We sat under the trees, and read and talked, and had many a long discussion. Chauncey would come up to my father's house, and sit all day and late into the evening; sometimes he went home twice a day for his meals, and sometimes he did not; but it was the regular programme that we were together every day and all day, in the same simple, affectionate, matter-of-course way that had gone on in the Freshman year. At this time, Emerson was a very favorite author with him; and, although his own habit of mind grew to be very different from that of Mr. Emerson, he never lost a cordial appreciation of the utterances which had stirred his early enthusiasm. As I have said, he read few books; but he had, in succession, certain favorite authors. The first in order was Emerson: he was a constant resource in the vacation-readings at Northampton. Then, soon after leaving college, he took eagerly to Bacon; and there was a time when his friends heard little from him that was not flavored by the wisdom of the "Novum Organum." At about the same time, and for a good while, he was a careful student and an ardent admirer of Hamilton. To him succeeded Mill. And then came Darwin and the literature to which the "Origin of Species" gave rise. Darwin was a thinker who fairly drew from him an unbounded homage; and this lasted till his death; I never heard him speak of any one with such ardor of praise. During his last days, he had returned again to Bacon, and was reading Plato with deep satisfaction. But, as to all his later likings, a sufficient guide is found in his correspondence, in Professor Gurney's letter, which I print on a later page, and in the articles which Mr. Norton has preserved in the "Philosophical Discussions."

When he graduated in the summer of 1852, Chauncey became immediately, during the vacation, a computer in the Nautical Almanac office, then lately established at Cambridge. The salary, although small, was enough for his outlay; and being increased from time to time, as he was promoted or as his duties changed, it continued through nearly the whole of his life to be his principal means of support. He added a little to his income by teaching; and, in the latest years of his life, he taught or lectured for a short time in the College. From these sources, or from the writing of an occasional scientific article in the "New York Evening Post," or from his other articles in the "Nation" and the "North American Review," came all his pecuniary income until the death of his father in 1872. This brought him a small amount of money; but he never was able to be very free in his expenditures, and at the time of his death he left but little property.

The work at the almanac office was very easy to him, and was of a kind which did not bind him to any particular hours. He invented new ways of computing, which shortened his labor; and I have heard him say that he could do his year's work in two months of steady application. But the duties were solitary, and grew to be very tedious. So long, however, as friends were thick about him, so long even as he could find some *one* with whom to pass his abundant leisure and share his teeming speculations, he was very happy; nay, if he could do no better, that affectionate and simple nature was happy enough if even any busy and preoccupied friend could be found, and he might sit with him, and smoke and think and ruminate in silence.

During all the early part of his post-graduate life at Cambridge, there was a good number of his friends at the professional schools; some became connected with the College, like Gurney and Chase. He formed also new friendships with others who became from time to time attached to the College. In later years, that acute and learned lawyer, the late Nicholas

St. John Green (afterwards a Professor in the Boston Law School), whom he had first known as a student at Northampton, and whose permanent home was in Cambridge, came gradually to be intimate with Chauncey.

The following letter to his friend Fisher was written within a year after they had left college: —

To George H. Fisher.

CAMBRIDGE, May 8, 1853.

If you were ever so culpably negligent as I have been, you can conceive the difficulty of beginning this letter. If it were not for adding to other difficulties an inconvenience of posture, I should write this letter on my knees.

Proverbs have condemned procrastination (and critics have condemned proverbs), and so I will only tarry a moment to remark what a fearful object a long-neglected duty gets to be.

Perhaps in your own experience you may have noticed what a magnitude a little duty will assume, after we have left it far back in the distance, and turn to look at it through the mists of a guilty conscience.

Thus this letter has haunted with its fearful front (which now lies nearly finished before me) those leisure hours devoted to laziness and smoking.

The warm weather has begun to remind me forcibly of those lazy but palmy days of last year when . . . Holworthy was the scene of Eden from which too much knowledge forced us to part.

Last year I have seen very little of the so-called real life of the world, for I have hardly got out into the world yet, and as I am now disposed I never shall; for though there is a weary feeling in hours of leisure, and a longing for something more active and inspiriting than my pursuits, still the satisfactions of a man of active business only compensate in my opinion for the jostlings and the conflicts of his life.

Upon reconsidering the above sentence, I can't see how it can be interpreted into a joke; and I must therefore inform you by way of explanation that I am *not* sentimental, but have written the aforegoing for want of aught else to say. . . . I haven't written much news, not knowing what is news to you; not knowing what you know, I can't tell what to tell you. If you wish to be enlightened, you must show your darkness.

On December 4, 1853, he writes to Fisher, correcting the statement of a friend that he had a salary of $1,500 at the Nautical Almanac office and a good chance of being appointed to a tutorship in college. "Discount a third," he says, "from the one, and a half from the other, and you have a fair view of the worldly advantages of your old chum. . . . Come to Cambridge, where many of our class still congregate. . . . In the Law School there is a vigor of thought and a stimulus to study which can't be found anywhere else."

At the beginning of the fall of 1854, after a short absence, I returned to Cambridge for seven years, and, entering the Law School, took lodgings with Chauncey. We were now chums for a year or more. There is little in this period that I can recall as worthy of special mention. Although I was very busy in my own occupations, I saw much of Chauncey and thoroughly enjoyed our arrangement. We read together on Sundays; and in our walks about the country, according to an old habit, we examined machinery, gas-works, factories, the glass-works at East Cambridge, and the like. After a while, the need of economy and the kindness of a friend drew me to other quarters; and in a few years Chauncey went to lodge — where he continued for a good many years — in Little's Block, at the corner of Main Street and Dunster. His classmate Gurney, then a tutor in the College, had been living in this building since the beginning of 1857, and remained there until the fall of 1863. During the whole of this period,

Chauncey had the advantage of constant intercourse with Gurney, — an opportunity which was of great benefit to him, and which he improved to the utmost, making great and almost unending draughts upon the hospitality of his friend by day and far into the night. Nor was Chauncey the only habitual visitor there. The evening light in the second-story, front-corner room on Dunster Street was now, for a number of years, the beacon to summon in as bright and goodly a company of young men as Cambridge could then supply.

During most of this time, up to 1861, Chauncey boarded with Mrs. Lyman, our old and most kind friend from Northampton, who had come to Cambridge in 1853. Here, in the summers that followed, Chauncey had the pleasure, more often than before, of meeting Mrs. Lesley and her husband Professor Lesley, of Philadelphia, with their two little girls, to whom Chauncey was devoted. Before this, the Lesleys had been his friends; but a more intimate acquaintance began now, which gladdened Chauncey's days to the end.

Mrs. Lesley has given me some account of her acquaintance with Chauncey, from which I take a few passages: —

"I first saw Chauncey a good deal in 1853, the summer before Mary's birth. I think he had then very few friends in Cambridge, and that he used to like to come and see my mother and me. It was a rare pleasure to listen to his conversation, at that time less assured than it afterwards became in tone, but full of a delicate tendency to speculation, always given with a modest hesitancy peculiar to his nature, and full of reverence and deference for the feelings of others. I left Cambridge the first of October.

"I think it was a very short time after I left Cambridge that he went to board with my mother. I spent the summers with my mother from that year until she went to the Asylum, in 1861; and I can hardly give you an idea how difficult those summers would have been to get through, but for his constant and considerate kindness. I was always in ill-health in those days, scarcely hoping to get the better of tendencies which all expected would shorten my life. But I recall with unspeakable gratitude how, in every way, he tried to make things easy to me. I cannot recollect his ever alluding in any way to my being an invalid; but there never was any thing more evident than that it was in his mind, and that he was resolved to help me through the weary days. He brought books and read aloud; he took the children off for hours, if he saw I wanted rest; and when my poor mother was overcome with restlessness, he either diverted her, or took me to some place where I should not mind it. . . . Of personal talk, I never had much with him, even in those days of closer intimacy than came afterwards; and sometimes I have regretted a little that I had not come nearer to his personal history, as it might have given me some advantages of friendship in aiding him in his later years. But at that time any approach to personal subjects, which he never invited, would have seemed indelicate and unworthy of that fine character. As I now look back, I can think of no one who seemed to me more distinguished for disinterestedness, singleness of mind, and purity of heart, and who, in little things as in great, more habitually considered other people. He stood to me then as a noble type of the Christian gentleman.

"You know all about his love for little Mary, and his deep interest in her education. He used to tell me that he always had her in mind when he wrote about education. I told him one day that I thought all the old-fashioned talk and stories about impulse and principle were very harmful; that children and grown people, too, ought to be taught that principles were not good for much until they became impulses; then they would do their work and unconsciously. He seemed greatly delighted at this very simple remark, and said, 'Well, we will have Mary brought up that way.'

"I felt that his life at my mother's was very hard for him in some ways, and it made me anxious. When she went to the Asylum, in 1861, I wrote him that the one thought that it would sign a release for him reconciled me to her going more than any thing else. Since then, how much we had to mourn, not dreamed of then."

In another letter, Mrs. Lesley writes: "I think very few persons can do entire justice to his sympathy and consideration for others. I can never recall without emotion a time when I had to go back from Cambridge to Philadelphia alone, — with Meggie, a baby in arms, — and so weak that I dreaded the journey, though I never said so to a living soul. At the last moment appeared Chauncey, saying decisively, but very quietly, that he was going with me. I shall never forget my sense of relief, as he took Meggie on one arm and my bags on the other, and assumed the entire care of us all. He scarcely spoke to me on the journey, because he divined I could not talk; but I think I never felt a kindness so deeply. And I found afterwards, by mere accident, that he had written or telegraphed to Mr. Lesley at different points of our route, my husband being then out surveying in Western Pennsylvania. When I think of his phlegmatic temperament, which always disinclined him to exertion, and his occupations at that time in the Nautical Almanac office, this incident rises before my memory with great force. It has often made me feel what he might have been in domestic life, and what that would have been to him."

The first letter to Mrs. Lesley which has come to my hands was written while we were rooming together: —

To Mrs. J. P. Lesley.

CAMBRIDGE, Nov. 16, 1854.

We take great pleasure in accepting your kind invitation to spend Thanksgiving with you. . . . I shall see, I imagine, little Mary walking very briskly, and rapidly coming to that period when, first becoming conscious of herself, she will see the fresh and bright forms of those intuitions (afterwards by experience turned into common sense) which will make her the little oracle we used to talk about. James and I have nearly finished the "Jesus and his Biographers" of Mr. Furness, and are very much impressed by it. The great doctrine of the book, however, is, it seems to me, a great step in philosophy; and it is because most men have too narrow notions of what is meant by "in the course of nature," and too vague notions of the Christian miracles themselves, that they do not think more like Mr. Furness. Many events that are so emphatically in the course of nature that they are enumerated in books of science, are events that have never happened more than two or three times, — events brought about by costly and careful experiments (as in the laboratory), and yet are regarded as more truly facts of nature than those of the ordinary course of events.

But this sounds more like an essay than a letter, and I hope you will excuse me for resorting to my old hobbies to fill a letter, for I am entirely out of the letter way of thinking.

In August, 1855, he writes pleasantly to his classmate Darwin Ware,[1] in reference to a plan for going to Northampton, whither I had preceded them on foot: —

"I should have answered your note immediately, if I had

[1] Ware was an intimate friend, from whose recollections of Chauncey I shall repeatedly quote. They were room-mates at Cambridge in 1856, and were companions in several summer journeys.

not been on the point of an expedition afoot, for the day, to Chelsea Beach, where I dipped and toasted myself to my heart's content. By Saturday, I shall be ready for another turn, so as to be sufficiently colored for my journey to Northampton.

"I found by my yesterday's experience that twenty miles per day, at least for the first day, is best enjoyed as a background to present ease; and as for the second day, — this being my second day, I am competent to judge that twenty miles on the second day isn't enjoyed at all."

To Professor Lesley.

CAMBRIDGE, March 25, 1856.

Mary Walker[1] has for a few days past been sick with a rheumatic cold, but is now much better. She will write to Mrs. Lesley very soon. Meantime, she gives me the box enclosed with this letter, and sends the following instructions: —

"Uncle Zack belongs to the Presbyterian minister Mr. Lā'sā [I spell it by the pronouncing dictionary], and is the sexton of the Baptist church.

"Willis Haywood, waiter at the largest hotel in the place, will direct to him; or any other waiter at any other hotel will direct to Mr. L.'s.

"If Aunt Lucy should be dead, inquire for Glasgow, one of the colored deacons of the Baptist church, who belongs to Mr. Saunders. Either he or Uncle Zack may be trusted."

[1] Mary Walker was an escaped fugitive slave, who had been aided by Mrs. Lesley in her flight. She lived with Mrs. Lyman, in Cambridge; and after Mrs. Lyman left Cambridge, in 1861, Chauncey lodged at Mary Walker's house. After her death, he continued until his own death at the house of her daughter. Mary Walker's "instructions" have to do with those secret agencies of communication between the slaves and the North, which used to be known as the "underground railroad."

I feel how little worth there is in a general acquaintance with any subject, when I consider how totally unfitted I am to undertake such a work as you so generously proposed to me. Why, I never used my senses for any thing finer than simple drawing and eating a fish dinner. And as to astronomical observation, I should as soon think of officiating at a sacrament as of offering my poor, untrained senses to such a service. I am very much obliged to you, however, and should like, if I can get an opportunity, to attend the survey as a student.[1]

Of late, I have been writing an essay, which I call the "Philosophy of Mother Goose," — very dry and dull. It is about infantile and juvenile education. I may hereafter expand it into a review of juvenile Sunday-school books.

I suspect that I had Mamy in my mind some of the time, though no one, I am sure, would suppose it in the reading.

My love to Mamy and Mrs. Lesley, — to Mamy first, because of her seniority, for she belongs to older time than the rest of us.

The essay of which Chauncey speaks in the last letter was read before his club on the evening of March 26. It was heard with a great deal of interest, and has always been remembered for its shrewd and characteristic wisdom.[2]

[1] Professor Lesley is unable to recall the proposition to which reference is here made.

[2] I find it preserved just as he wrote it, — a rough draft in lead-pencil, in the half-filled sheets of a college blank book. He had been drawn to the observation of children, as he intimates, by seeing often the little daughter of Mrs. Lesley at Mrs. Lyman's. The reader will probably be interested in seeing one or two passages of it: —

"If the venerable mother of nurses," he says, "had, in addition to her motherly tenderness and sympathetic appreciation of the juvenile mind, been endowed with dialectic powers, she might, in her protest against these abusive tamperings with her classic songs, have reasoned thus:

Before the same club, Chauncey read other papers in the course of the next year or two. On May 21, he read upon the "Real Difference between the Philosophy of Ancient and of Modern Times;" on November 19, upon the "Rest of Plants;" on November 27, 1857, upon "Winds and Storms;" and on October 13, 1858, upon "The Stereoscope," — an article in the form of a dialogue.

It was about the year 1856 that he was first drawn a little into general society, by means of those "Conversations" at Mrs. Charles Lowell's, on Quincy Street, to which Mrs. Quincy has referred in the letter already quoted. He was also a member of a Shakespeare Club which used to meet at Mrs. Lowell's house. Not only Chauncey, but many another young person in Cambridge, during those years, had reason to remember

'I do not aim to make a man of a child, for that is the work of Providence, but do I not know what a child is, and what are its wants, better than you, O most audacious Mrs. Science, and do I not believe in spite of your theories that the satisfaction of its natural wants is the best way to further the work of nature? . . . What is good taste to a child, — nay, what is the difference between the sensible and absurd, — before the discriminating powers are excited? Are not contrasts the means by which discrimination is provoked? Is not the pleasing most distinctly realized in the ugly, the true in the false, and the sensible in the absurd? I venture timidly into your own province, when I assert that the imitative dispositions of children, the perpetual make-believe and play of their tender years, and their ability to discriminate at the first dawn of intelligence the serious from the comic, are the means by which their common sense is nourished and the abstraction of meanings effected. Banish not then the grotesque, but set it off with the beautiful, that by the contrast the beauty of the beautiful may be realized. Tell them impossible stories, that the limits of the possible may be known. Talk nonsense and baby-talk, that good sense and correct language may be acquired. But in all this do not dissimulate: guard with religious care that first discrimination of intelligence, the earnest from the make-believe.'" — "It is wise," he says, later on, "instead of directing the tasks of children and neglecting their sports, to direct the sports, and let the tasks take care of themselves." — I wish it were practicable to quote the whole paper.

with gratitude the wise and kindly interest which this admirable woman showed in gathering them about her.[1] At the "Conversations," Mrs. Quincy has truly indicated Chauncey's position: it was found that he excelled us all; the others often saw themselves become little else than willing listeners at the keen and eager discussions that went on between Mrs. Lowell and him.

In 1857, Chauncey entertained the idea of going to the United States Naval Academy at Annapolis, and went so far as to allow his name to be mentioned as a candidate for a professorship there. At about this time, also, he was asked to go as professor to a Western college. But neither of these plans came to any thing.

In October, 1858, Mr. J. D. Runkle, Chauncey's friend and associate in the work of the Nautical Almanac, began the publication of the "Mathematical Monthly," a periodical which ran through three volumes, ending in September, 1861. Chauncey made several contributions to the first two volumes of this journal, as follows: Vol. I. p. 21 (October, 1858), "The Prismoidal Formula;" ib. p. 53 (November, 1858), "Extension

[1] It was to her that the poet, her husband's brother, addressed this beautiful sonnet: —

"Through suffering and sorrow thou hast passed,
To show us what a woman true may be:
They have not taken sympathy from thee,
Nor made thee any other than thou wast;
Save as some tree, which, in a sudden blast,
Sheddeth those blossoms that are weakly grown,
Upon the air, but keepeth every one
Whose strength gives warrant of good fruit at last:
So thou hast shed some blooms of gayety,
But never one of steadfast cheerfulness;
Nor hath thy knowledge of adversity
Robbed thee of any faith in happiness,
But rather cleared thine inner eyes to see
How many simple ways there are to bless."

of the Prismoidal Formula;" ib. p. 244 (April, 1859), "The most Thorough Uniform Distribution of Points about an Axis;" Vol. II. p. 198 (March, 1860), "Properties of Curvature in the Ellipse and Hyperbola;" ib. p. 304 (June, 1860), "The Economy and Symmetry of the Honey-Bees' Cells."

On January 25, 1860, he was elected a Fellow of the American Academy of Arts and Sciences. Of this learned body, he was the Recording Secretary from May 26, 1863, to May 24, 1870. And he contributed to its publications the following two papers: viz., on May 8, 1860, one "On the Architecture of Bees," — "Proceedings of the American Academy," Vol. IV. p. 432; and on October 10, 1871, another on the "Uses and Origin of the Arrangement of Leaves in Plants,"[1] — "Memoirs of the Academy," New Series, Vol. IX. p. 379.

To Mrs. Lesley.

CAMBRIDGE, Feb. 12, 1860.

About Thanksgiving time, I entered upon new duties, — the teaching of Natural Philosophy in Prof. Agassiz's School; and, as this school has no winter vacation but the Christmas days, you see how I have hampered myself.

[1] This paper is printed also in the "Philosophical Discussions," p. 296. In the "American Naturalist" for June, 1876, Vol. X. p. 326, a short paper was printed, at the instance of Professor Goodale of Harvard College, entitled "A Popular Explanation (for those who understand Botany) of the Mathematical Nature of Phyllotaxis. By the late Chauncey Wright." To this article the following note is appended: "This article was prepared by Mr. Wright several years ago, at Professor Gray's suggestion. In its manuscript form, it has been found of much interest and value to the botanical students in Harvard College. It is here reprinted, without change, from Mr. Wright's notes." The substance of the paper before the Academy, as I am informed by Professor Goodale, was incorporated in the English translation of Sach's "Lehrbuch der Botanik."

. . . I have received from Mr. Lesley his pamphlet on the gradations of words. I have looked over it, but not yet attentively enough. The idea of it is a very attractive one, and closely resembles the argument in that new book on "The Origin of Species," — Darwin's, — which I have just finished reading, and to which I have become a convert, so far as I can judge in the matter.

Agassiz comes out against its conclusions, of course, since they are directly opposed to his favorite doctrines on the subject; and, if true, they render his essay on Classification a useless and mistaken speculation. I believe that this development theory is a true account of nature, and no more atheistical than that approved theory of creation, which covers ignorance with a word pretending knowledge and feigning reverence. To admit a miracle when one isn't necessary seems to be one of those works of supererogation which have survived the Protestant Reformation, and to count like the penances of old for merit in the humble philosopher. To admit twenty or more (the more, the better), as some geologists do, is quite enough to make them pious and safe. I would go even farther, and admit an infinite number of miracles, constituting continuous creation and the order of nature.

My friend Darwin Ware, in answering a request for some account of Chauncey, as he saw him in repeated summer vacations at the period which we have now reached, says:[1] —

1 This extract from Mr. Ware's letter is preceded by a little sketch of the vacation journeys to which he refers. "In 1857," he says, "you and Chauncey and I were a fortnight together among the Franconia Mountains of New Hampshire, and again in the following year. Those days in retrospect are bright with sunshine. You will remember how we passed them, — taking long walks, climbing the mountains, following up the courses of mountain streams, and bathing in the icy waters of secluded rocky basins fed by waterfalls, and sometimes, in the afternoon, strolling into the woods, or in some quiet nook, in the shade of

"Chauncey was always ready for a long walk or a hard climb when it was proposed to him, although by nature disinclined to bodily exertion. The companionship on these excursions was the main thing he cared for; and his will offered little resistance in determining a day's plan of recreation. His sweetness of temper, the wide range of his sympathies and knowledge, and the incessant activity of mind shown in his conversation, made him a charming comrade. The highest regions of thought, in its search after truth, were the most habitual to him; but he could incline to mirth and gayety, and joined in quiet sports with genuine relish. A strong, companionable sense of humor in him was more open to its impressions than active in producing them. The pervasive heartiness of his laugh was contagious, — its tone deep and mellow, and in strong contrast with his ordinary voice, which was on a high key, and almost feminine in refinement. When he was happy in his social intercourse, his face, which was very sensitive to the play of feeling, fairly beamed with genial pleasure. His large

trees, reading aloud in turn the one poet, Shakespeare, we had brought with us.

"In 1860, we spent with Chauncey a vacation at Mount Desert. The little steamer that now carries so many to Bar Harbor then had only three or four passengers besides ourselves, and stopped only at South-west Harbor. We had learned the secret, however, before we started, that not at South-west Harbor, but at Bar Harbor, was the place for the true worshipper; and so, on landing from the boat, we took a wagon, and were conveyed directly there. At Roberts's, — then the only house that received strangers, — we stayed a week or ten days, furnished with the most meagre accommodations, and a fare of little besides fish, berries, and milk. I remember no other permanent visitors then at this place. Some of the time we were on the water, but more we spent in climbing the mountainous island, and exploring the grand sea-coast.

"In the following year, Chauncey, Gurney, and I passed a vacation together in excursions on foot among the Berkshire Hills. Chauncey and I walked from Pittsfield to Stockbridge, where Gurney joined us. About Lenox, Stockbridge, and thence to Bash Bish Falls, we had many a pleasant jaunt."

stature, rather heavily moulded, was graced with the manner of the gentlest and most amiable of men. Such personal characteristics helped to inspire the sense of perfect fellowship which friends felt in his company.

"In these vacations, Chauncey talked most about what he was then most thinking; and I never knew the time when he was not pondering some deep learning in Science or Philosophy. This was the mode of his extraordinary intellectual growth. In the apparent absence of the means of nutrition, it was like the growth of a tree within which powerful processes are continually going on, by which, from the proper germ, is reared a giant oak. A few authentic books gave him the history of science and philosophy. The key of all the sciences, mathematics, he held with an easy grasp. Through meditation, he wrought out deductions that were knowledge, and framed those intelligent questions that are half the answers of truth. Comparatively little observation and research enabled him to make those answers whole. The naturalist has been able, from a single fossil scale, to describe the structure of the fish from which it came. In the same way, from the fragmentary segment of a system or a theory, Chauncey seemed able to reconstruct the full orb of thought. Such methods would not been been attended with large results, without the wonderful power he had of long-continued, concentrated attention, and of steadily holding in his imagination the realities upon which his thought was fixed.

"And yet, as a companion, he was not abstracted or self-absorbed. His highest thinking was never permitted to separate him from his friend. He made his meditations part of the common stock of the social partnership. With undivided interest and sympathy, he entertained another's thought, and returned it with generous increase. In a mind so trained by great studies, and purified by the love of truth, there was no place for prejudice or intolerance: there was only entire impartiality and kind appreciation.

"The direction of Chauncey's studies in 1857–58, and again in 1860–61, as I remember, well represented the twofold discipline of his powers, which enabled him afterwards to compose the two essays on subjects so diverse as 'A Physical Theory of the Universe' and the 'Evolution of Self-consciousness,' published in his 'Philosophical Discussions.' At the earlier period, I recall his comments on the successive theories in geology; the nebular hypothesis; the undulatory theory of light; his explanation of the formation of mountains and their disintegration; and of other science familiar to one who knew

'What land and sea, discoursing, say
In the sidereal years.'

At the later period, the experience philosophy, the utilitarian theory of morals, natural selection, and kindred doctrines, were the most frequent serious topics of Chauncey's conversation. For a good while after our visit at Mount Desert, they passed, with us, under the humorous name of 'The Mount Desert Philosophy.'

"These vacation rambles, under summer skies, through the most beautiful and impressive scenery of New England, I shall always cherish among the tenderest and most delightful of memories."

CHAPTER II.

THE beginning of the war of the Rebellion had now come. Chauncey's youngest brother, Frederick, a brave and thoughtful boy, had volunteered as a private in the Tenth Massachusetts Regiment, and passed the summer in camp near Washington. In the fall of 1861, he was sent home to take part as a second lieutenant in enlisting the Twenty-seventh Regiment. On October 30, 1862, he was made first lieutenant. He was at home on leave in the early part of the year 1863, and again a little later. On June 5, 1864, he was fatally wounded at Cold Harbor, and was removed to a hospital in Washington, where he was attended by his brother Ansel. He died three weeks later, on June 27, and was buried at Northampton, on July 3.[1]

[1] These details, which are of interest as explaining some letters which will be inserted under their proper dates, I take from a brief sketch of this brother, written by Chauncey in 1865. From this account, I will add one or two passages which are worthy of attention here for the moderation and just feeling with which they are expressed, and for the light which they throw on Chauncey's own character.

"Accustomed from boyhood to responsible duties, his character was not less mature than that of most New England youths at twenty-two. His predominant feelings in volunteering for the war, though controlled and concentrated by a sense of duty, — such as had become a settled habit of his life, — were still those of a young man with whom sympathy with his fellows and an enthusiasm for a great popular movement made the path of duty appear more attractive and the sacrifice less burdensome. The novelty of so great a change in life had, also, doubtless a considerable influence in determining him to take this step; but, in every subsequent step, the sense of duty was uppermost, — that plain,

To Lieutenant Wright.

CAMBRIDGE, Oct. 29, 1861.

I was greatly relieved this morning by George's letter, telling of your discharge. Your letter received a week ago was every way pleasant, except in being written at Camp Brightwood instead, as I had expected, at Northampton. Then came the news of the battle at Ball's Bluff, which kept me anxious all the week lest the Tenth Regiment should be ordered on some military expedition before you were discharged. But the hard thoughts which I was beginning to entertain against the tardy officials at Washington are all happily dissipated now, and I most heartily wish you joy in your new dignities and duties.

Believe that you deserve your commission, but believe still more that you ought to deserve it; and don't let your ambition rest here. There are several ranks higher than that of second lieutenant, you know, which you will no doubt deserve, if you keep in mind that you ought to deserve them.

Yesterday, in Boston, I attended the funeral services held in honor of young Lieutenant Putnam of the Twentieth Massachusetts, who fell at the battle of Ball's Bluff.

He was the nephew of the poet Professor Lowell, a fine fellow about your age, and very accomplished. I had the

every-day, enduring habit which had become a second nature with him. . . .

"On his second furlough, at the end of two years' service in the Twenty-seventh, he returned to his home on a short visit. These years had wrought great changes in him. His character had reached maturity: a weightier sense of the responsibilities to which he was about to return appeared in his bearing and conversation, and by a natural association of feeling made the last parting from his friends seem sadder and more tender than any former one had been. Apprehensions of new dangers to be encountered, were heightened by a deeper sense of the value of the life again offered to the cause which had ennobled it."

honor of being his tutor in Mathematics for a short time last winter. Several others of my friends and acquaintances, officers in the Twentieth, were wounded in that battle, and behaved very bravely. Young Putnam received his death-wound while supporting another wounded man.

I shall try to see you before you go with your new Regiment.

To the Same.

CAMBRIDGE, April 29, 1862.

You were unlucky in not being in fighting trim for the battle at Newbern, but I think you did well in not risking another fever. I hope to hear of your perfect recovery of health and strength by the next accounts.

I almost envy you the excitement of the active uncertainty of the camp and your picket duty. To be a mere looker-on. leading a very dull life and finding nothing of interest but the newspapers, and these very meagre and tantalizing, is a condition of passive uncertainty in which it is very hard to be cheerful. I tried the theatre last night, and got quite waked up. A little comedy in these tragic times is a healthy stimulant.

You will have heard from home about the flood and the dike being washed away.

There is one thing in which I hope to interest you, if you have the leisure to attend to it, — a little "contraband" business. You remember Mrs. Mary Walker whom you saw at Mrs. Lyman's last summer. She is a native of Raleigh, North Carolina, and once the "property" of a Mr. Cameron, now deceased, — one of the wealthy first men of the place. Her mother and her children (some of them) are still in the possession of the old gentleman's heirs, — a Mr. Cameron, Jr., and a Mr. Mordecai in Raleigh. If you can make it convenient to inquire of any escaped "contrabands," who hail from

Raleigh or vicinity, if they know any such people, and where and who they are, and all that is known about them, — whether any have escaped or are likely to escape; and if you can find it possible to communicate with them and inform them of what you know about Mrs. Walker; or if you can find it possible and convenient to befriend them in any way, you will do a good thing, and put me and all concerned under great obligations to you; and please write me all that you find out as soon as your leisure will allow. I intended long ago to write about this business, but have neglected it till now. An agent at Newbern keeps a list and an account of all the "contrabands" that come into your lines.[1]

The next letters were written while Chauncey was suffering from a slight injury. The injury had been slight, but the consequences were serious. On the 28th of March, he had bruised the instep of his right foot. A physician was called the next day, who found him feverish and suffering much pain from this hurt. A mortification of the skin soon followed, and for some days the symptoms were threatening. But the danger was checked, and before long he moved about on crutches. The recovery, however, was very slow; and it was nearly five months before the injured part was healed. On October 1st, the memorandum of Chauncey's physician, who has kindly given me these details, states that the patient "walks six miles a day."

During this period, Chauncey suffered much from his confinement, and from depression of mind at finding how sluggish

[1] It was one of the results of the war that Mrs. Walker and her family were reunited. This happened through the efforts of a high official who accompanied General Sherman in his memorable visit to Raleigh in 1865, and who in a short stay of two hours in that city found time personally to make certain inquiries which resulted in so much happiness to this excellent woman. Her mother had died; but her children were found, and they afterwards joined her at Cambridge.

were his powers of recuperation. Now and at other times, he suffered the evil effects of some imprudent habits, — a too sedentary way of living, the practice of excessive smoking, and extremely irregular hours of sleep.

To the Same.

CAMBRIDGE, May 26, 1863.

It is more than eight weeks since I lost the use of my right foot, as you have doubtless learned from home. I began about a week ago to use crutches a little, and have ridden out twice.

Now in all this time I have had plenty of leisure to write you, and the disposition to do so also, but for some reason — I think from sheer laziness, I have hitherto neglected this as well as all other kinds of effort, living on in the serenity of nothing to do.

You have doubtless also heard how your man Henry has become my man Henry.[1] In fact, I have all the external appearance of a veteran soldier, with my wound, my crutch, and my contraband. . . .

To the Same.

CAMBRIDGE, June 15, 1864.

I was very thankful to learn, with the first news I received of your mishap, that — thanks to tender care and a good constitution — you are doing so well.

Ansel writes that you expect to be on crutches in two or three weeks. Hope is a good medicine, but don't let it stimulate you to impatience.

[1] This was a fugitive slave who, coming into our lines, had become the servant of Lieutenant Wright, and been brought to Northampton. Chauncey's father had sent him to Cambridge to take care of the invalid.

But it will hardly do for one like me to attempt to counsel such a brave and noble fellow, as you have shown yourself to be, how to bear his misfortunes, though I had also to exercise the courage of patience last summer with my inglorious wound.

I was very glad also to learn from Miss Ware that you had come under the care of so good a friend.

Before long — before you have had many weary days to count — I hope to be with you for a short time at least. Meantime, I shall hear frequently from you through George and Ansel.

To Ansel Wright, Jr.

CAMBRIDGE, June 16, 1864.

I have just received your letter: your news is quite satisfactory. I wrote to Fred and to Miss Ware yesterday.

In less than a fortnight, I shall be able to get off, without taking with me work which it would be inconvenient to do away from Cambridge. Perhaps, with good luck, I may be ready sooner.

To the Same.

CAMBRIDGE, Tuesday, June 21, 1864.

Your good report of Fred came this morning. He is doing surprisingly well. I am making all haste to get ready. At almost any other time, I could have got off sooner; but as we are on the point of getting out the Almanac, and putting the last work in the hands of the printer, I cannot pick up my tools and break communications with the office as soon as I desire to. I shall be ready, however, sooner than the time I set. At my present estimates, I shall start on Saturday the 25th. I left an order in Boston this afternoon for a quantity of California wine and brandy to be sent to Fred. If he does not need it, some one else may. My love to Fred, and tell him to keep up his spirits. I regret that William Ware will be unable to come with me.

Chauncey reached Washington on June 28, but his brother had died the day before.

In the next letter is found the first mention of Chauncey's acquaintance with Mr. Charles Eliot Norton and his family, and of his visits to their summer home at Ashfield, Mass. This acquaintance had begun at Cambridge a few years earlier. It will sufficiently appear hereafter how greatly it contributed to Chauncey's happiness throughout the rest of his life.

To Miss Catherine I. Ireland.

CAMBRIDGE, Sept. 1, 1864.

I went to the little heaven of Princeton, and had a splendid time with Mr. Lesley and his beautiful family. He had come from a meeting of the wise ones at New Haven for a few days' vacation, but I fear I didn't leave him much time to rest his thoughts. Long walks absorbed in the oblivion of longer talks (stories without an end, Mrs. Lesley called them), beautiful landscapes, — appealing in vain to introspecting eyes, — and invigorating airs, brought us health and inspiration and strength, all unconsciously.

Looking from the mountain, I always think faster and freer and better, but about any thing rather than the landscape. It seems so much better to talk *from* the beauty than *of* it. Perhaps I don't properly appreciate it, but value it like meat and drink, the pure air and (may I add?) my cigar, only for the excitement it gives.

Mr. Gurney joined us for a day, and I returned with him to Cambridge after a short visit, but went again in a few days to escort little Mary to Cummington, the little hill-town in Western Massachusetts where she has spent most of her summers. This journey involved visits to Springfield and Northampton, and finally a visit of two days to the Nortons at Ashfield, a town joining Cummington. These towns are higher than Princeton; and so, instead of the scientific conversations I had with Mr. Lesley, I rose to the heights of metaphysical and moral questions in my talks with Mr. Norton, and suited the topic to the altitude, — having risen from murky practicals, through the clear certainties into airy speculations.

To ——.

[October, 1864.]

I was pleased to receive your letter yesterday, putting in definite form the points which it is necessary to clear up, in order to come to a common understanding. Our conversation at the party left the matter in a very unsatisfactory condition; for I regard a misunderstanding as the most annoying, if not the most pernicious, form of error. I am conscious now of having attended too exclusively to what I should have regarded as inaccuracies of language and the misapplication of terms, so that I failed to comprehend the points of view from which they probably arose. But mathematicians are the most exacting of purists, since, having none but perfectly definite ideas, and for the most part a perfectly adequate nomenclature, they are intolerant of, and, as one may confess, also insensible to any thought not set forth in exact form. It behooved me, therefore, instead of understanding your language in a strict mathematical sense, and thus misunderstanding you, to endeavor to find your true meaning, and to put it in what I conceived to be a better form.

In 1864, Chauncey was led into an important correspondence with Mr. Francis E. Abbot, then a Unitarian clergyman at Dover, N. H., now editor of "The Index" newspaper at Boston. The occasion of it was an article by Mr. Abbot in the

"North American Review" for July, 1864, on "The Philosophy of Space and Time." With the metaphysical ability shown in this article, Chauncey had been much impressed. The half dozen letters, running through several years, which make up his share of this correspondence, furnish a good illustration of his cordial appreciation of the labors of a younger man, and of the candid temper and largeness of mind with which he could conduct a discussion. Some who find his published essays difficult to read will follow him here with comparative ease. These letters, also, throw light on his opinions upon certain important subjects not much discussed by him.

To Mr. Francis E. Abbot.

CAMBRIDGE, Dec. 20, 1864.

I received a few days ago your essay on the Unconditioned from the "North American Review," with your request for thoughtful criticisms of the views presented therein.

I am greatly obliged to you for this favor and gratified by your invitation. Your essay has pleased me much by its beautiful philosophical style and admirable clearness, and it seems to me to evince very great metaphysical ability. I have not, however, given that studious attention to it which will warrant me in undertaking an elaborate defence of Hamilton's doctrine against your strictures, or in attempting more than an indication of the objections to them which I felt rather than clearly excogitated in a cursory reading. Indeed, I should now hesitate to say any thing, but for my desire, in acknowledging your favor, to comply as far as possible with your request, and because I shall not be better prepared for a long time to come.

Your doctrine is founded on the position of a distinct faculty of knowledge, — the supersensuous reason, — which Hamilton, so far from having overlooked, expressly rejects, as not warranted by an analysis of the mind and its contents; and the difference between his doctrine and that of all his opponents rests ultimately in their psychological analyses.

In order to establish his exclusion of reason as a faculty of knowledge, or as any thing more than the sum of the necessary limits and conditions of knowledge, it behooved him to account for the fact of a *belief* in unconditioned existence, and to show how a belief is possible without a knowledge, either intuitive or inferential. He was opposed to the rationalists, on the one hand, by denying that the negative proposition, "There are no limits," or the equally negative proposition, "The limits are absolute or unconditional," — can be either proved or positively made known by intuition. He differed from the empiricists, on the other hand, by not overlooking or rejecting the fact of a belief in the unconditioned in general, or the fact that unexperienced and unprovable negative propositions may yet have valid claims on our credence. The positive part of his doctrine maintains against empiricism that such a belief is valid, and the critical part examines the explanations of this validity given by the rationalists; and he rejects even Kant's *quasi* faculty of reason or regulative faculty, as assumed simply for the sake of this explanation and as being unnecessary to it.

It seems to me, therefore, that the justness of your criticism of Hamilton turns on the correctness of your preceding psychological analysis of Space and Time as rational ideas, in which you assume a faculty capable of attributing to these relations the negative notions of infinity and incomposite unity.

The existence of such a faculty is the only real question between you and Hamilton, and you yourself allow that the validity of a part of your criticism rests on the accuracy of your analysis of Space as necessarily illimitable. I ought to notice here, in passing, that Hamilton uses Space and Time as illustrative examples of the attribution of the negative notions "infinite" and "absolute," and not to defend any doctrine about space and time as metaphysical objects. He says in his letter to Mr. Calderwood, "that there is a fundamental difference between *The Infinite* (*τὸ ἓν καὶ πᾶν*), and a relation to which we may apply the term *infinite*. Thus, Time and Space must be excluded from the supposed notion of *The Infinite;* for The Infinite, if positively thought it could be, must be thought as under neither Space nor Time." I am especially desirous to call your attention to this point in Hamilton's very interesting letter, because it agrees with your own conclusions on the danger of reasoning from quantitative infinity. But Hamilton does not so reason, as you seem to suppose.

Space and Time only enter as essential elements into the discussion through your analysis of them. And if the negative notion "infinity" be derivable, as you maintain, from a positive faculty of knowledge competent to vouch for the proposition, "There are no limits to space or time," then these ideas, as the source of the notions, may become essential to the discussion, and Hamilton's illustrations may be shown to be absurd. But the discussion really goes back of this, and tests the correctness of such a psychological analysis.

Again, before coming directly to this discussion, I must notice, with reference to your analysis, that Hamilton himself insists upon a distinction between Space and Extension, which, however, is different from yours, and he proposes the names Extension and Space to designate the two notions, which are, as he supposes, derived from two sources; namely, the primary intuitions of sense, in virtue of which we actually and immediately apprehend the extension of objects, and the intellectual form of Space through which we are necessitated to conceive of every thing as in relation to extension; but this form is not in Hamilton's Philosophy an object of thought. It is a determinant, but not a constituent of knowledge.

Indeed, a Form, in Kantian phraseology, is neither a knowledge nor a faculty of knowledge, but rather a determinant of the limits of knowledge, though regarded by Kant himself as something more than a negation of knowledge.

While you denote by Extension the same thing that Hamilton proposes to designate by that name, your Space, as a positive datum of a distinct faculty, the supersensuous reason, is different from, and even a contradiction of what Hamilton proposes to call by that name, or that which compels us to think always in relation to extension. That which you call Space seems to me to coincide in part with the empiricist's abstract space, or the mere notion, which like any other general notion is supersensuous or unimaginable, simply because imagination or representation is always of the particular possible in experience. But you pass beyond the empiricist's abstract space, when you assume a faculty competent to connect the notions of space and infinity, and to vouch for the truth of the proposition that "Space is infinite;" and in fact you thus assume the real point at issue.

I do not propose to undertake a counter analysis, but shall limit myself to pointing out Hamilton's exposition of the meaning of the judgment "Space is infinite," — a judgment for which you have, with the rationalists, felt obliged to assume a supersensuous positive faculty of knowledge. It is really a statement somewhat elliptical of the fact that space extends beyond our power of knowing or conceiving it. The statement involves the subjective fact that the all of space is incognizable and inconceivable by us, though this fact is expressed in an objective form, as if this inconceivability were a property of the object itself. The abstractive power of the understanding cannot aid us, for this adds nothing to our knowledge. Disregarding the picture, then, and thinking no longer of that colored expansion, the sky, we do not come to any object in our experience of which we can positively think that it is infinite. All that we can positively think of the abstractest conception of Space is, that we are unable to conceive it at the same time as the abstractest and as definitely bounded. But this is neither thinking nor implying that space in itself is unlimited, much less does it imply a knowledge that Space is unlimited; and Hamilton not only denies the possibility of such a knowledge, but denies that we can even conceive the possibility of such a knowledge. "Space is limited;" "Space is unlimited," — these propositions, so far as they express any thing which is actually in the mind, are each the recoil of thought from the other, and we finally rest on unlimited space as the least obtrusive and staggering inconceivability, and the one for which we can most easily substitute a pseud representation, — namely, an indefinitely great extension. But this negative proposition is not only insusceptible of proof or of intuition: the synthesis of its terms is impossible in thought, or, as Hamilton says, is inconceivable.

This leads me to speak of Hamilton's use of the words "conception" and "conceivability," which, I think, you have misapprehended. If there be any term in the vocabulary of Philosophy which our author is especially anxious to use in a single, unambiguous sense, it is the word "conception," which he alone among British philosophers used, throughout his writings, as the name of the act of the understanding or of the elaborative faculty, though sometimes it stands for the product (more properly *concept*) of this faculty. He never uses the word as synonymous with imagination, or to denote an act of imagination, except where, as in the present discussion, the act of the two faculties coincide. To understand or conceive a house on fire, and to imagine or picture it, are essentially the same act, but the terms direct attention to different aspects of this act, and this difference becomes an essential one, when we consider abstract and general terms applicable equally to many objects; for here the particularity of the acts of sensuous imagination makes them inadequate to determine the sense of a general term, which may, nevertheless, be understood or conceived; and it is only in this meaning of the word "conception," and in the cognate senses of the derivative terms, that Hamilton ever employs them. Infinite Space, if it be an object of thought at all, is a single particular object; and hence, if it cannot be imagined, it cannot be conceived. Hamilton also points out, what is quite as essential to this discussion, another ambiguity in the use of this word, which he himself carefully avoids, and of which he convicts Dr. Reid. It is generally incorrect to speak of imagining a proposition, as you seem to accuse Hamilton of doing, but even when we speak of conceiving a proposition we are not out of danger; for Dr. Reid says that he can conceive of the proposition that two sides of a triangle are together less than the third side, though the proposition is absurd, and hence he concludes that the possibility of conceiving is not a test of truths. But Hamilton points out the fact that conceiving the terms of a proposition and the logical form by which they are bound together is not conceiving the proposition itself, which he renders, in order to avoid this ambiguity, by the phrase, "conceiving the *possibility* of the propositions." If the proposition is not a general truth, this is the same as imagining, or representing in the phantasy, the synthesis of its terms. We must not suppose even in case of a possibly true proposition, of which neither proof nor intuition is possible, that the supposition of its truth, and an understanding of its terms and its logical form, constitute any thing more than what philosophers call a symbolical conception; which, indeed, is no conception at all.

The propositions in question in the present discussion are not general truths, but particular ones; and if imagining and conceiving are the only kinds of thinking, these propositions cannot be thought. We should not regard that as cogitable of which we only have symbolical conceptions, since we have symbolical conceptions of absurdities. The supersensuous reason as a faculty of thought and knowledge is an invention of the rationalists to account for the belief we have in an unconditional, unimaginable reality; but this invention Hamilton regards as unnecessary, and therefore unwarranted. The laws of thought are alone sufficient, he thinks, to account for this belief. For if it is possible to frame concerning any nature two propositions in each of which there is no incongruity of terms, but which contradict each other, then, since one must be true, we have evidence of the existence of this nature in the laws of thought themselves. We have no means of knowing which of two mutually exclusive inconditionates is the truth, but we have evidence that something inconceivable is true, and therefore "that the capacity of thought is not to be constituted into the measure of existence." This is the gist of Hamilton's arguments; and it is opposed equally to the scepticism which would limit faith to the domain of real knowledge, and to the dogmatism which would extend knowledge to the horizon of a legitimate faith.

Herbert Spencer has totally misconceived the purport of the reasoning, and he supposes Hamilton to have argued in the interest of empiricism. Mr. Mansel, on the other hand, has sought to shield ecclesiastical authority from the assaults of rational criticism, and, by a wholly gratuitous application of Hamilton's doctrines, to place absurd and meaningless dogmas in the same category with inconceivable reality. This of course begs the question; and indeed any positive doctrine of faith begs the question, is incapable of proof. The test of a true faith is emotional and moral, not intellectual. Our respects must decide what is worthy of belief. Not what claims our respect, but what gains it, is our true faith, and the basis of our religion; and nobility of character is the sole end and criterion of its validity.

Your treatment of Hamilton's definition of the conditioned

as "a mean between two extremes, two inconditionates, &c.," seems to me to be a little captious. He of course does not regard it as a logical mean, else, as you say, the law of excluded middle would not apply. The expression is obviously metaphorical, or perhaps we may say he uses the word in a psychological sense, to denote the only effective effort to conceive, in which the mind rests from efforts ineffective in directions logically opposed to each other; but we must distinguish between the logical opposition of these supposed objects of knowledge and the mental acts by which we attempt, but without success, to comprehend them. These acts are still of the conditioned; and, being inept and irrelevant, they are in a sense opposed to both the logical extremes, which they fail to comprehend.

According to this interpretation, which has always seemed to me to be Hamilton's meaning, your diagram of oppositions, which is simply logical, is quite misplaced. The first part of Hamilton's paragraph, ending in the italicized words "*can be conceived as possible*," is the statement of the psychological difficulty. The last part, ending in the italics, "*must be admitted as necessary*," is the solution, — the only solution which the laws of thought can give of this difficulty. It is not a real solution. The difficulty is not removed, but it is reconciled with a belief in unconditioned existence. At least, Hamilton and his followers believe it to be so reconciled; and this is the purport of his philosophy, which, so far from being a defence of empiricism, is a defence of faith against empiricism, — not by denying incontrovertible facts on the one hand, the limitations of sense and understanding; nor yet by assuming an indefensible dogma on the other hand, the position of a faculty of absolute knowledge; but by showing how the limits of thought may disclose themselves as such, or prove that thought is limited not simply by ignorance and inexperience, but by the conditions of its positive activity.

Hamilton's list of "Contradictions Proving the Psychological Theory of the Conditioned," which he gives without comment, was given, I suppose, to illustrate by a wider induction the absurdity of attributing infinity to any thing cognizable; and your comments only carry out the obvious intent of the author. You explain the absurdities by showing that the notion of infinity is inapplicable to the several cases supposed, and so far you agree with Hamilton; but he would go farther, and regard these examples as affording inductive proof that the notion of infinity is inapplicable to any thing conceivable.

I regret that this restatement of such portions of Hamilton's doctrine of the conditioned as seemed to me, after reading your valuable criticism, to require elucidation and emphasis, is all that I can do in answer to your request. A more detailed examination would have required a more careful reading of your essay than I have had time to give it.

CHAPTER III.

THE reader will have noticed the warmth of Chauncey's regard for the Lesley family. He had found with them not only sympathy and affection, but a great intellectual stimulus. Mr. Lesley, now Professor of Geology and Mining in the University of Pennsylvania, and the official geologist of that State, had formerly been a minister in the Orthodox Congregational Church; nor has he, I believe, ever relinquished the distinctive part of his religious opinions. Chauncey could hardly have found a keener or more original thinker, — one more eager to welcome a new thought, more competent for the discussion of it, or less disposed to accept it unchallenged. Professor Lesley, in the midst of a hundred pressing occupations, has found time to send me some reminiscences of Chauncey. I insert them here, and do not omit the frank and characteristic expressions of his dissent from some of the opinions of his friend: —

"My first acquaintance with Chauncey Wright was made nearly thirty years ago, and continued under the inspiration of the most cordial friendship, without a break, to the time of his death. We loved each other dearly, and with good reason. His best friends were also mine. We passed days and weeks together under the same roof. It was his kind practice for more than a dozen years to spend his Christmas holidays with my wife and me at our house in Philadelphia, and we looked forward through each autumn to his visit as one of the great events of the year. One of my pleasant recollections of Chauncey is of his habit of carrying my daughter Mary in his arms around the garden of Mrs. Lyman's house in Cambridge. She was never so happy as when he held her. Their mutual attachment was beautiful to look upon: it long outlasted babyhood on her part, and on his part never failed. His heart was of pure gold. His generosity to the young, the weak, and the aged, bore the stamp of a refined nobility. He was in truth one of Nature's noblemen: incapable of a meanness, unselfish, passionately fond of pure and true people, and holding himself aloof from those who fell beneath that standard. He vouchsafed his friendship to few, but from these he withheld nothing.

"Such was my friend for me from first to last, and as I believe still is and always will be. For death is only a longer voyage to Europe or to China. We cease for a while to see and hear the departed, but they are as real and living to us on board ship on a far-off sea, as on the wharf at home. If letters fail when sent by post, that is no sign of death; nor is the lack of communication with Chauncey Wright now a sound argument on *his* side of the discussion respecting a future life. I firmly believe and joyfully look forward to the renewal of his visits in some future Christmas holidays.

"What weeks were those! What eloquence flowed from his lips and eyes as he walked up and down the parlor floor, now and then turning and standing to enforce his views, or leaning half in revery against the mantel-piece, while some superfine illustration flowed softly and evenly from his imagination in language singularly choice and elegant. His writings are hard for the inexpert to read; but women and children could understand all that he said, even when he was in his highest moods. There was neither tedium nor uncertainty for his hearers while he spoke. Many of his positions I accounted philosophically untenable, because I did not accept all of his premises. But no exception could be taken against his logic; no misunderstanding of his train of thought was possible; and never was English spoken more delightfully by a scholar and a gentleman.

"One thing always impressed me: he never lowered the tone of a conversation. I never heard him use a slang word, or any expression approaching the limits of vulgarity, — by which I merely mean the stupid and inelegant. It required genius of no common mould to maintain perpetually such elevation above the commonplace without becoming a bore to common people or wearisome to his companions in philosophy. He was indeed a genius of the higher world; and this it was that made him in other respects, — in all respects, — as I have already said, one of Nature's noblemen.

"During most of the years of our intercourse, I was myself as fond of metaphysical discussions as he was; and you may better imagine than I describe the delights of our meetings, the regrets of our partings, the brilliancy of our evening parties, the earnestness of our walks together, the depth of our friendship. But of late years I became absorbed by affairs, and disuse of the tools and weapons begat in me indifference to the arts and exercises of metaphysics. For several years before Chauncey's death, I saw less of him than before; and our correspondence also fell away; for business obliged me to neglect the art and exercise of letter-writing also. He only shared the fate of all my other friends. Then, when we met, we found ourselves intellectually travelling in opposite directions. His tendencies were all towards that New City which men are building on the fens of Mattershire, and I found him speculating in its water lots. For my part, I preferred to keep house in the Old Jerusalem, where it was dry, and where I could, at least now and then, sniff a breeze from the Everlasting Hills. He traversed my opinion that phyllotaxis is merely a well-bred habit of the *soul of the plant;* that however many creators the infinitely numerous organic formal inventions of the world may call for, and however subordinate (in a hierarchy perhaps) these subordinate creators may be to a God of Gods and Lord of Lords, — to try to disinspirit matter is to make Berkeleyism a necessary refuge for the philosopher. He called for proof of the invisible, and would accept of no half proof.

"It is the old story. Friends love and leave each other; usually because one stays and the other goes. But being eternally friends, they meet again; usually by the return of the traveller. It is my belief, my dear friend, that the school of the Darwinists is in this fashion on its travels. It resembles, I think, Sir W. Thomson and his crew in the 'Challenger,' sounding the depths, and collecting the form-treasures of all seas, — only to come back and enrich books and museums, but by no means to change Metaphysical Science in any noteworthy degree."

To Professor Lesley.

CAMBRIDGE, Jan. 19, 1865.

Thank you very much for your objection to one of my theological arguments, as well as for your expressions of approval. The theological arena is a new one for me,[1] and I am painfully conscious of being poorly armed for its contests. The study of exact sciences, where one cannot go astray without falling into absurdity and incomprehensibility, is not so good a discipline as is commonly supposed, for preparing the mind against inaccuracies of thought and expression in matters full of darkness and pitfalls. I have seen many illustrations of this in the arguments of mathematicians when out of their element.

The above confession must not be understood, however, in any other than that soothingly general sense in which con-

[1] The reference is to an article on "Natural Theology as a Positive Science," in the "North American Review" for January, 1865; Philosophical Discussions, p. 35.

fessions are made in church, — "O Lord, we have grievously sinned, but not by this, that, or the other particular act, of which our uncharitable neighbor thinks us guilty." My error is only that of being misunderstood, — a great and dangerous error, it is true, in a literary aspirant, — but then it comes also from a confusion which is in the readers as well as the writers of theological discourses.

In mathematics we attend principally to the reasons, and let the conclusions follow if they will; but in theology the conclusions are of the first importance, and the reasons are dragged after them. Now I erred in not pointing out with sufficient distinctness that my aim was to examine the arguments and not the conclusions of Natural Theology, — to examine the reasonings from physical facts to certain conclusions, and not the interpretation which might be legitimately put upon these facts, if the conclusions were granted or otherwise verified.

It is doubtless true, granting the conclusion, — the existence of a law-giver and designer, — that the laws and apparent designs which are discovered by science are the signs or symbols of final cause or purpose; but how, then, can we use them as proofs of what we have assumed in thus interpreting them? My argument against Paley is *ad hominem*. He says a law implies power, and so it does; but it does not determine the nature of that power, saving only that it is a power which acts according to law, or is manifested by an order.

Design, which is an antecedent in the order of human production, is illegitimately assumed to be a real and essential and not an incidental, phenomenal antecedent, unless intelligence is shown to be essential to all order. But this is the point in question. The materialist assumes just as validly that design is an incident to the order of human contrivances, or is what the logicians call an "inseparable accident," but not an essential antecedent to this order as such, and therefore is not implied in order generally. When Paley and other theologians conclude that "the works of nature proceed from intelligence and design" on the ground of scientific evidence, they pervert language just as much as the materialist, when he argues that they proceed from law, — always supposing, of course, that we do not grant the conclusion of either side. To the theologian, who begs the question, law and design are the obverse and reverse of the same fact, — the objective and subjective aspects of the same nature, — intelligence. To the materialist, who also begs the question, design is the characteristic of the anticipating, reflective action of the human mind, rehearsing in its little world, the imagination, the acts by which it modifies the course of nature. The form of order which it thereby impresses on the powers of natural agents is not essentially different from the order which pervades the whole of nature, — the order of law, — the origin of which he does not profess to know or even conceive, but calls it substance, of which the type to his mind is the substance of the bodies which manifest this order or matter, and when he refers the order of nature to the "agency of law," he means the agency of the power of which law is the manifestation, — just as the theologian, when referring any thing to design, means to refer it to a personal cause. The materialist refers the order of nature to an unknown and as he believes unknowable origin; and as far as physical evidence is concerned he is warranted in doing so, quite as much as the theologian is in drawing his conclusions from the same source, — unless, indeed, it be an axiom that "all order is designed order."

But, if this is true, what need of argument? We do not prove axioms by argument.

But the conclusions of theology so fill the mind, answering to other than rational interests, that any one who would hold them in abeyance, and strictly follow the argument *a posteriori*, seems to doubt or reject them, or to yield to motives other than rational ones for disbelief, while he is only examining their grounds as he would the reasons of a conclusion in physics or mathematics.

Starting from religious conclusions and interpreting nature in accordance with them, the theologian discovers "law" and "design" as symbols, and his proofs amount to pious circles, like those of the whirling dervish; and it seems to me he would perform a more substantial service to religion, if he would look straight at the origin of his faith, instead of such pious exercises, by which he gets so dizzy as to bring science and faith into conflict.

But I must stop lest you think me giddy, too, from so long a contemplation of such gyrations.

A glimpse of Chauncey among his associates at the office of the Nautical Almanac may be had from the following passages of a letter from Professor Simon Newcomb, late of the United States Naval Observatory at Washington:[1] —

"My acquaintance with him," he says, "began in 1857, when I became a computer for the Nautical Almanac, and hence a sort of scientific colleague. He had then an abominable habit of doing his whole year's work in three or four months, during which period he would work during the greater part of the night as well as of the day, eat little, and keep up his strength by smoking. The rest of the year he was a typical philosopher of the ancient world, talking, but, so far as I know, at this period, seldom or never writing. His disciples were his fellow-computers on the almanac. He regarded philosophy as the proper complement of mathematics, — the field into which a thinking mathematician would naturally wander. Philosophic questions were our daily subjects of discussion. . . . My favorite subject was that to which the

[1] Since this was written, Professor Newcomb has been appointed Superintendent of the Nautical Almanac.

enclosed correspondence relates, — the compatibility of free-will with absolute certainty regarding human acts, and the absence of any reason for supposing that human actions are any less determinate than the operations of nature. Wright was at first inclined to claim, in accordance with popular notions of free-will, that these propositions were not well founded, but at length was led to maintain that, considered simply as phenomena, they were correctly formulated; that is, that we have no reason to believe human acts, considered simply as phenomena, to be any less determinate than the operations of nature. This is the ground which you will see that we agree upon in the enclosed correspondence.

. . . "When Darwin's 'Origin of the Species' appeared, it was the subject of a special discussion, extending over a considerable time, before the American Academy of Arts and Sciences. It was in following this discussion that his views of the philosophy of natural selection first seemed to assume a definite form in his mind. The fallacy involved in the popular arguments respecting the cell of the honey-bee was long his favorite theme, and at length led to his communicating a short note on the subject to the American Academy."

The correspondence referred to by Professor Newcomb consisted of a letter from him to Chauncey, asking that he would suggest proper Greek or Latin phrases for certain philosophical discriminations, and of the following letter in reply: —

To Mr. Simon Newcomb.

CAMBRIDGE, May 18, 1865.

. . . Much more thought and care than I have yet given to it would be necessary to a final and valuable decision on so important a matter as the invention of a nomenclature, — which is to ordinary metaphysics what the construction of a machine is to the working of it.

I have examined only one book at all likely to contain any terms suited to your purposes. A little work of Burgersdyck on Metaphysics contains innumerable scholastic subdivisions of the genus *potentia*, but none to the purpose; and I am inclined to believe that you are right in thinking that the ideas you propose for baptism have never before been analyzed, or at least signalized, with any distinctness. At any rate, such a conviction has been the more readily accepted by me, in that it saves me the trouble of continuing research in this direction.

I accordingly appealed to the classical knowledge of a friend for the proper Latin equivalents of the phrases "possibility for aught that we know" and "possibility for aught that we do not know," or "for aught that exists;" and I had the good fortune to find that the Latin idiom is well adapted to these meanings, and renders them in phrases which have quite a scholastic ring. *Quod*, with the subjunctive, does the business.

Potentia quod sciamus and *Potentia quod ne sciamus*, or *Potentia quod vere sit*, express your P_1 and P_2 quite scholastically. For your P_3 there is a choice of phrases, — *Potentia quod velle possimus*, or *Potentia quod valeat voluntas*, — which seem to me to hit the mark.

You do not, of course, wish that the nomenclature should decide whether P_3 is included under either P_1 or P_2 as contradictory opposites, dividing, as they seem to do, the universe of potentiality between them; but you wish a term by which the problem can be stated and discussed without ambiguity or confusion; and these phrases seem to me to be sufficient for this purpose.

The sense of freedom or of liberty to choose, is the consciousness of a power to choose in a different way from that we actually follow, or of a possibility for aught that we can will, or for aught that the will avails. That is, the particular act of the will does not represent all the determinants to action which we contemplate in deliberate choice.

Hence I propose for your

P_1 . . . *Potentia quod sciamus;*

P_2 . . . *Potentia quod ne sciamus, vel quod vere sit;*

P_3 . . . *Potentia quod velle possimus, vel quod valeat voluntas.*

Potentiality is not contrasted in scholastic language with *determination*, but with *actuality;* existence *in potentia* with existence *in actu* or *in esse*. But it does not seem to me essential to adopt technical phrases for your C_1, C_2, C_3, in so far as they are the negations of your P_1, P_2, P_3, though it is obvious that a distinction should be made between actual causal determinations and the logical determinations of thought, — between what is determined without reference to our knowledge and what is determined in our knowledge.

Determination and indetermination seem to me to be the best terms, taken by themselves in their broadest sense, and excluding the use of the vague and ambiguous terms "possibility" and "potentiality." And if we also exclude the words "liberty" and "necessity," as Mr. Mill proposes, we shall simplify the problem of voluntary actions very materially.

The question will then be, whether there are any elements, known or unknown, which enter into volitional determinations not in accordance with the law of causation, or other than the regular consequents of conditions and determinations previously existing in our characters and circumstances.

I contend that no evidence of the existence of such elements can be distinguished from ignorance. All testimony in the matter must be negative. Dr. Johnson says: "We know our wills are free, and there's an end on't;" but I contend that we do not know that our wills are not free, and there isn't even a beginning of a solution of the question from the testimony of consciousness. With reference to the possibility of any other evidence, the only practical problem is whether, in considering human actions, we ought or ought not to presume that they fall under the law of causation, just as all other phenomena in nature are presumed to do. This problem is quite distinct from any anticipation we may have that we may become acquainted so intimately with the springs of human action as to be able to predict with certainty the course of an individual's conduct. We do not hope to predict the weather with certainty, though this is probably a much simpler problem; but we nevertheless believe the complex phenomena of the weather to be made up of elementary regular sequences.

That our conscious volitions are not so compounded, we certainly can never know; and the only presumption in favor of this doctrine is its seeming dependence upon our sense of moral freedom and responsibility. But I contend that this seeming reason is only an illusion and a misunderstanding of the question. The world has been deceived for more than sixteen centuries by metaphors invented by some Alexandrian Platonists speculating on the nature of virtue. Sects, schisms, and strifes have been the consequents of these unfortunate metaphors drawn from Roman law. While everybody recognizes as real those feelings which we describe as a sense of moral freedom and the feeling of responsibility, few attend to the metaphorical character of the names which are given to them. "The virtuous man is free," said the Platonic philosopher. "He is, like a Roman citizen, uncontrolled by a master." "A vicious man is a slave." Such is the metaphor: now what is the real character so described? This freedom is internal control in place of external control; centric or self control, which, so far from making a man free, in the scientific sense of the word, makes his life regular and his conduct calculable. He has a freedom like that of the solar system or like that of a normal growth. Again, moral responsibility was so named from legal responsibility in Roman law; and the sense of it is only the sense of dignity and trustworthiness which is characteristic of moral feeling, a sense of being intrusted with interests not his own. This sense is also proportional to the virtue of a man, though it is not absent from any one capable of sympathetic and reflective action. Minus the metaphor, it has nothing to do with the question of philosophical liberty.

From all these considerations, I conclude that, if the terms in which the problem of philosophic liberty is discussed be freed from ambiguity and metaphor, there will be little or nothing left to discuss; only the idle question, in fact, whether in the world of the unknown, and the arcana of ignorance, there be not such things as undetermined beginnings, real, finite, first causes; — an idle question, because no affirmative testimony can be adduced except our ignorance; and, as this is insufficient to disprove the law of causation in other cases, how can it be of weight in this?

To Professor Lesley.

CAMBRIDGE, May 31, 1865.

. . . If any thing could diminish the sympathy I feel with your disappointment in being obliged to give way to invalidism and to take a vacation, it is the pleasure I anticipate from your promised visits. They will be more grateful to me than sea-shore or mountain, and I look forward with impatience to the days when you will come with your budget of "things to discuss."

We may find the mountains or the seashore good grounds for our rational picnic, though we only go to them for the pleasure of losing sight of them. No day of last summer comes more distinctly and pleasurably to my recollection than that on which we climbed Wachusett together, — and greater heights than that, in discourse.

To Mr. Abbot.

CAMBRIDGE, June 26, 1865.

I trust you will not consider the long time I have allowed to pass before responding to your friendly challenge to a philosophical tournament, as any indication of hesitation or unwillingness on my part to undertake the correspondence you propose. I had much rather you would regard it as time required to consider the difficult problems, — involving, as they do, so many knotty points and grounds of diverse opinions; but in fact the time has not been so employed. I have had few opportunities and fewer occasions of inspiration; and nothing but comparative leisure at present and a desire to express the pleasure and gratification I received from your letter and your request for further correspondence, excuses the present attempt to respond to them.

The clear summary which you give of your argument for the infinity of space, and the questions which you propose as containing the chief issues between us, help me to bring my thoughts at once to the discussion. You ask first, "What is the origin of the idea of space simply considered, as the absolute correlate and condition of matter irrespective of its infinity?" In answer, I propose to give, as briefly as I can, the empiricist's interpretation of the admitted facts of space, and his explanation of what he conceives to be the origin of the idea. "The idea of space as the *necessary and absolute condition* of matter," as "the *receptacle of matter*, without which as an extended object it could not exist," includes, it seems to me, a confusion of two distinct propositions, on the discrimination of which the empiricist bases his criticism of the absolutist's philosophy. He denies that any necessity is cognizable except the necessities of thought; and he would consequently say of the idea of space, that though it is necessary to the representation of matter as an object of thought, yet it cannot be known as the necessary and absolute condition of matter *per se* or as underlying noumenal existence. Things and their relations known as phenomena, and their laws, include all that is known to us, except bare existence. Space and Time, distinctly known by abstraction and generalization, are none the less relations of things, merely because they are the absolute conditions [of thinking] of things; the *conditio sine qua non* of their existence [to us]. And there is not any true or unavoidable antithesis between "abstractions, generalizations, or relations," and the "absolute correlates of things," as thought. Relations may be necessary as well as contingent; and because things cannot be conceived out of certain relations, it does not follow that these relations have any other existence than in the things in which they are cognized. To postulate the order, which experience determines in our thinking, as also the order of ontological dependence, is to assume at once and without adequate discussion the position against which the empiricist protests.

The conception of Time and Space as primarily any other than those relations which are universal in our experience of things comes from confounding the truly abstract Time and Space with their abstract representations. I mean by abstract representation the imaging in the phantasy of as few of the properties and relations of sensible objects as can be represented, excluding or leaving in the background all else. Such syntheses of all the relations necessary to the conception of things in general give the abstract ideas of space as the "receptacle of matter" and of time as the continuum of events. These are not primary intuitions, but constructive synthetic representations made up of the elementary abstract relations of things and events. What we really and immediately know are phenomena — objects and events — with their relations. Proceeding to know them better and better, we first class them by the ultimate and truly unanalyzable principle of "likeness and unlikeness." Resemblances and differences of all degrees are cognized, and those phenomena in which resemblance is as perfect as is consistent with their plurality are still found to differ in what we call Space and Time; and this is all we ultimately know of space and time. They are the abstract genera of differences which exist between all phenomena as plural, however great resemblances they may have. An identical object is known by phenomena differing in time only. The universality of the relations of space and time in our experience, and their consequent necessity in our thoughts, united with the notion of identity in an object, gives the notion of *continuity of existence* both in space and time. We are not immediately cognizant of this continuity as such. What we know are discrete phenomena and their relations of resemblance and difference.

I do not believe that Space and Time are pure hypotheses posited to account for the relations of phenomena. I think they are really cognized as ultimate differences in phenomena; but the continuities of Space and Time must either be of the nature of hypotheses, or else I think we must grant your position of a faculty above sense and understanding capable of cognizing them. As hypotheses and as the only hypotheses we can form to account for or rationalize our experiences, they may be regarded as truly necessary to thought and universal, like the relations on which they are founded.

That time continues between any two events, and that space extends between any two objects cognized by us is inferred as being simply necessary to thought, since we cannot imagine any quantitative difference which is not divisible nor any parts which are not different in space and time. The relations of space and time are intuitions of sense; but as receptacle and continuum, or as conditions of these relations, they are hypotheses. The conception of continuity involves that of quantity, which I think is primarily cognized as a relation of the relations of time and space — and, I may add, of intension in sensation or power. Two events are conceived quantitatively as separated by other events or the possibility of other events which still differ in time. And similarly of objects in space and of sensations. Objects, events, and feelings are related in space, time, and power, and these are related in quantity. Out of the vague apprehension of quantitative relations in these, we form precise abstract conceptions of quantity, which we cannot however separate entirely from these relations. We have therefore three species of quantity, — quantity in space, time and degree.

But you may object that a rationalizing hypothesis, which, you will say, is not, and cannot be, given by sense or understanding, must come from a faculty above these, which is also the source of the validity of the hypothesis; but I contend that so far as such an hypothesis is apprehended at all, and so far as it has any validity, it is apprehended and vouched for by understanding and sense. The process is perfectly analogous to the formation of general ideas, which it is now admitted on all hands cannot be apprehended by sense or represented in imagination, yet is the proper function of understanding dealing with the data of experience. In the same way, the hypothesis of a receptacle or continuum, so far as it is apprehended at all, is apprehended in and through the relations of the phenomena which it reduces to rational order. As well contend that mathematical formulas and processes which convey no meaning in themselves, but develop implicit relations of quantity, are given and vouched for by a special faculty, as contend that space — the receptacle — is a distinct datum of intelligence.

The distinction between Space and Extension is thus to my mind only that which subsists between an abstract synthetic hypothesis and the elementary relations which it reduces to order and harmony in thought. The latter alone are properly apprehended by any faculty of knowledge. Space is really apprehended in the relations of extension in bodies. All bodies — the whole non-ego of sense, embraced in one intuition, with the exclusion of all which is non-essential to representation in general, gives us the space of imagination. Rational space is that which is essential to clear, distinct, and rational thought, or is necessary to understanding. It excludes color and tangible properties, and includes the hypothesis of continuity. Sense by itself does not give continuity, but at the same time does not exclude it. All the data of sense are in accordance with it; and hence they verify or give validity to it, so far as it has validity or is capable of verification. The impossibility of thinking contrary to it, is not regarded by the empiricist as a distinct kind of proof. This only expresses the degree of the proof which experience affords.

I come now to your question concerning the infinity of space. This predication, though it cannot be understood, cannot be denied, since it involves no contradiction. At the same time, it cannot be affirmed as an hypothesis necessary to account for any cognizable fact which is not accounted for by the idea "that space extends beyond our powers of knowing or conceiving it." What infinite space includes, more than this, is unnecessary, and therefore unwarranted; and it is only by sublating the contradictory proposition, as you propose to do in your proof (p. 94, N. A. Review), that it can be posited.

But what is the contradictory of infinite space as distinguished from indefinite space? Not finite space simply, as you propose in your proof. The truly infinite is the unconditionally unlimited or indefinite, and its contradictory is the unconditionally limited, — not merely the finite, which may be conditionally limited. What you really sublate in your proof is only the conditionally limited as predicated of abstract space. You say: "For suppose it [space] limited, it must be limited either by matter or by vacuity [that is in either case conditionally limited]; but Space is presupposed by matter, and is itself, in the absence of matter, vacuity, consequently, &c."

But this dilemma does not include an alternative which is the real contradictory of infinite space. Unconditionally limited space is neither limited by other space nor by matter, but *per se* or by itself. This is inconceivable, of course, — obtrusively and staggeringly so; but it does not involve any logical contradiction, and is not therefore repugnant to reason any more than its equally inconceivable contradictory, infinite space.

Since therefore I must disallow your demonstration of infinity, I come to your third question, "What is the reason why the infinity of space is a less obtrusive and staggering inconceivability than its [absolute] finitude?"

The clause following the words you quote from my letter, though connected only by an "and," contains the reason. I should have said that "we finally rest on unlimited space as the least obtrusive and staggering inconceivability, [since it is] the one for which we can most easily substitute a pseud representation, namely, an indefinitely great extension." The suffering senses are quieter, but the understanding is still frustrated. Æsthetic considerations — or perhaps I should say *anæsthetic* considerations — decide, where reason is balanced. The decision is the other way — and for the same reason — in the case of the infinite and absolute of causation. An absolute beginning is preferable to an infinite non-beginning, because we can easily substitute for it a pseud representation; namely, a beginning in knowledge or in consciousness, such as, in the case of our own volitions, seem like new creations, self-determined. This satisfies sense and imagination by deceiving them, but the understanding is still baffled.

Infinite space, as an hypothesis to account for any thing of which we are truly cognizant, not only transcends our powers of conception, but also the necessities of thought. A simpler hypothesis is competent to do all that it can do. We need only space which includes all that we can know, and extends beyond our powers of knowing or conceiving it.

The infinite and absolute are therefore both inconceivable and incognizable by us in the relations of space and time. How much more so out of relation to these! The Infinite and Absolute of pure Being, transcending time, space, and phenomena, are only names to us, but names which, nevertheless, as mutually contradictory, says Hamilton, stand, either the one or the other, for an inconceivable reality. This which is Hamilton's peculiar doctrine is to my mind the weakest point in his argument. As an empiricist, he was not competent to draw such a conclusion. He was not, however, a thorough-going empiricist; and he can be convicted of inconsistency, if it be showing that he was not competent to affirm for the laws of thought an absolute validity independently of experience, while he denied any such thing as an absolute knowledge.

I imagine that this is the flaw which Mr. Mill has discovered; but as I have not yet read Mill, and do not know what his line of argument is, I set down this anticipation at a venture.

I hope that my argument will not prove unanswerable, and that I may hear from you at your earliest leisure.

During these years, Chauncey had grown intimate with the family of Mr. Norton. I am able to give some account of his acquaintance with them from the pen of Mr. Norton himself. He says: —

"I first heard of Chauncey Wright in 1857, soon after returning to Cambridge from a two years' absence in Europe. The 'Atlantic Monthly' was just established; and Mr. Lowell, its first editor, printed in one of the early numbers [1] a striking and interesting paper by Wright, called 'The Winds and the Weather.' I remember that Mr. Lowell spoke to me of it in high terms of praise, and told me of the modesty and shyness of the writer, and of his apparent promise as a scientific thinker. I heard of him occasionally from other friends; but some time passed before we met. In the winter of 1858 or 1859, a little club of men of various interests was started in Cambridge, and I think I first saw Wright at one of its meetings. He was generally very silent; but, when he spoke, his words were to the point and worth listening to. We did not meet often, but our acquaintance slowly ripened into friendship; and when, in the autumn of 1863, Mr. Lowell and I became editors of the 'North American Review,' Wright was one of the men whom we both desired to engage as a contributor to its pages. In the winter of 1864, I saw much of him; and he began to be a frequent visitor at my house. At first, except when alone with me, his shyness made him silent, and gave him the appearance of reserve; but this gradually wore off, and he became before long an easy and familiar friend with all the members of the household. His mode of work by continuous stretches, with intervals between them of freedom from regular occupation, gave him leisure during those intervals for frequent walks with my wife, my sisters, or myself, and for loitering days, spent in winter in the parlor or my study, and in summer on the piazza or the grass. During these days, he shared in the common domestic interests, — in talk or reading, in the amusements of the children, in discussion of affairs, of characters, of education,

[1] Vol. I. p. 272, January, 1858.

of the conduct of life, &c.; was full of ready sympathy in small concerns, of wise suggestion and service in important matters."

To Mr. Charles Eliot Norton.

CAMBRIDGE, July 23, 1865.

The time you name for my visit will be a convenient one for me. I wish I could be as sure that Gurney will be able to come with me. I propose to go on Tuesday to Mount Desert Island with Thayer, to revel for a week near the seas and mountains.

I have read Mill's Hamilton once, and I find it much more difficult to say what I think and feel about it than I anticipated. I feel at present more in the condition of a learner than a critic, but it wouldn't do to tell the public so. I rebel, nevertheless, against much that Mill says, though I do not feel confident in my opinions. He appears to make sad havoc of Hamilton's opinions and arguments, and on the latter topic he is certainly strong, and I willingly acknowledge him victor.

This is the way with metaphysics, which are for the most part false, — even clearly false arguments for opinions vaguely expressive of some ill-apprehended truths. The chief merit of Mill's book is in the clear exposure he makes of the fallacies of the metaphysical school which Hamilton represents.

In my second reading, I am taking notes so as to get a summary view of the points which interest me; but these, I fear, will not interest the readers of the "Nation."

In August, 1865, he writes to Mr. Norton that he has sent to the "Nation" "a very tough and profound criticism," — an article entitled "Mill on Hamilton." This was the first of his contributions to the "Nation:" the last appeared only three days before his death.[1]

In the fall of 1865, his brother George died. It is to this event that the following letter makes reference: —

---

[1] A full list of these contributions is as follows: —

Vol. I.	No. 9, p. 278,	"Mill on Hamilton."
	20, p. 627,	"McCosh on Intuitions."
II.	27, p. 20,	"Mill on Comte."
	55, p. 724,	"Spencer's Biology."
	60, p. 804,	"Martineau's Essays."
III.	72, p. 385,	"Masson's Recent British Philosophy."
IV.	80, p. 27,	"Mansel's Reply to Mill."
	90, p. 231,	"Ennis on the Origin of the Stars."
	102, p. 470,	"The Reign of Law."
V.	116, p. 238,	Note to "Mathematics in Court."
VI.	148, p. 355,	Bledsoe's "Philosophy of Mathematics."
XIII.	335, p. 355,	Two Notes on Mr. C. S. Peirce's Review of Berkeley.
XVI.	412, p. 351,	Notice of Mill, from the paragraph beginning, "The standing of Mr. Mill," to the end.
XVIII.	467, p. 381,	Lewes's "Problems of Life and Mind."
XX.	503, p. 113,	Two Notes in answer to a request for information about books relating to the theory of Evolution.
	505, p. 146,	"Sir Charles Lyell."
	508, p. 208,	Note on Bastian.
	512, p. 277,	"McCosh on Tyndall."
	518, p. 379,	"Speculative Dynamics."
	520, p. 405,	"Who are our Ancestors?"
	p. 409,	Note on Professor Winlock.
XXI.	522, p. 9,	Two Notes on Sir Henry Maine and the "Greatest Happiness" principle.
	524, p. 43,	Blackwell's "Sexes in Nature."
	532, p. 168,	"German Darwinism."

To Mrs. George F. Wright.

CAMBRIDGE, Nov. 28, 1865.

A week of busy occupation has passed very rapidly, but makes my recent sad visit to you seem distant. Here in Cambridge, removed from the associations which must constantly at every turn force the grievous reality of our loss upon you, it comes to me as a dream which I can hardly realize; and when I realize it, I feel the additional affliction of the fact that I am not in a position to realize it *fully*, by being able to make it a part of my special care and daily life. For a sorrow such as ours is worthy not to be put aside by impertinent businesses, but to be ennobled by a life of duties which are consecrated by the sorrow. But this is your own true consolation, to know that you have many things to do which he would have wished you to do, and which you have to do because he can no longer do them, — duties now more sacred than ever to you. The nobility of such duties takes away the pain of loss, and makes life the more worthy, since in a sense he still lives in them.

How much better to feel the lost one's presence in the work we have to do, than to think of him as removed even to a happy life remote from ours. The life that survives death, so far as the living can comprehend it, is in the feeling that we have gained new motives, new inspirations, new sanctions to carry on another's life of duty in our own.

To the Same.

CAMBRIDGE, June 28, 1866.

. . . I did not tell you, I believe, that we were engaged on the business of removing the Nautical Almanac office from Cambridge to Washington. My share in the business was to get my present work forward as far as possible, so as to begin on the first of July a new arrangement, by which I am to be allowed to reside in Cambridge, Northampton, or the North Pole, if I please, and to take work "by the piece," instead of a salary. This will be much more profitable to me, as it gives me more to do.

To Mr. Norton.

CAMBRIDGE, July 24, 1866.

A few days after I received the manuscript following your last note, I entrapped Gurney into listening to the new philosopher. It was a hot day; and, after I had read a little more than half, I desisted, — Gurney looked so weary and bored. And so we returned to worldly affairs and common thoughts, letting the philosopher lie in my drawer for three weeks or more. To-day, Gurney submitted to hear the rest, that we might, if possible, qualify our very unfavorable opinion of the first half. Long before I had finished it, the old expression of weariness came upon our friend, and made me pause to ask if he found it dreary. "A howling wilderness," he answered. As we were emulous of godlike qualities, we persevered to the end, but have our redress in the following report: —

Utterly without method, the article is very deficient in mere literary excellences; and, though freer than is usual with transcendentalists from astonishing expressions, it lacks at the same time the genuine transcendental merit of suggestiveness. It is the mere dry husk of Hegelianism, — dogmatic, without the only merit of dogmatism, distinctness of definition.

I am not so much a positivist as to deny that mystical and poetical philosophies are valuable products of human genius; but then they must be works of real genius, — of a Plato, a Hegel, or an Emerson. No being is prosier than the uninspired disciple of the mystic. All that is stimulating — all the glorious vision — has melted away. Instead of clouds, we have left mere idiocy; blank staring at emptiness.

To the Same.

NORTHAMPTON, Aug. 9, 1866.

Arrived here on Tuesday evening. I have attended one of the conferences of this amiable body [the American Association for the Advancement of Science].

To a listener who permits the free play, and has room for the happiness, of the malevolent affections, it was tolerable. What greatness of mind and character such debates force upon the attention — by contrast! I shall drive up to Ashfield, bringing Lesley and his little girls, who will visit their friends in Cummington. Lesley has consented to be my companion in a visit to you for a day; and I have no doubt you will extend to him the hospitality which Gurney forfeits by his ill-arranged engagements and occupations.

To the Same.

NORTHAMPTON, Aug. 10, 1866.

. . . I find the *savants* much more reasonable and sensible in private conversation than in debate. In private discourse, they are much more apt to give you the result of mature thought; but the interest of debate depends too much on the illusory charm of new and crude ideas. Among the superstitions of America, please mention the admiration and ambition of public speaking. I have assured several *savant*-struck ladies that enthusiasm in speech is very apt to be proportioned to crudeness in ideas. But this does not explain ———, who repeated yesterday what he has said at every scientific meeting at which I have heard him speak; and he said it with as much animation as if the world were not weary of it. I never heard him mention it in private; and so, notwithstanding its age, I class it with new and crude ideas, — with the difference that it is a chronic case of public speaking, — a brilliant idea which occurred to him once upon a time, and has been a standing marvel of inspiration ever since.

To the Same.

CAMBRIDGE, Aug. 31, 1866.

. . . This evening I start with Lesley and Thayer for a few days' trip to Mount Desert. I expect to learn a good deal of geology, with so good a teacher and in a region so rich in geological interests.

In driving away from Ashfield, on our first turn to the left, about half way up the hill and on the right of the road, lay a great rock, much worn and with a quartz mass exposed on its surface shaped like a letter S. Lesley said that this was an excellent specimen of what Hitchcock calls compressed pebbles. In your next drive that way, you should look for it. I hear that the Buffalo meeting was a great success. I think the National Academy ought to satisfy ——'s ambition for control. Why is pettiness always ahead and so active; and why is magnanimity so stupid and slow? In short, what is the origin of evil? These problems, geological and spiritual, will last you a fortnight, when I hope to make you a visit and hear your answers.

It was during this promised visit to Ashfield, I think, that the excursion took place to which Mr. Norton refers in the following passage of a letter from which I have already quoted: —

"In 1865, I think, and again in 1866 and 1867, he spent some days with us in our summer home at Ashfield, where he learned to know, and became strongly attached to, our friend and summer neighbor, Mr. George William Curtis. I remember well an excursion in the autumn of 1866 or 1867, which we three made together from Ashfield to North Adams, where Mr. Curtis was to deliver a political address. The days were among the finest of the year, the country through which we drove was as beautiful as any part of Massachusetts, the landscape was in its full autumnal glory, and the incidents of the little journey were various enough to give animation to the days. Wright was in excellent spirits: he was open to all the influences of the time, and, quickened by them to more than usual vivacity, he displayed, in a way not to be forgotten, the large resources of his thought, the wise conclusions of his mature judgment, in discussions of politics, of religion, of philosophy, and of practical life, and in his shrewd and kindly estimates of men. He often afterwards referred to these days, and especially to the scenery and the talk in harmony with it, on the morning of our return, as we crossed the Hoosac Mountain.

"The quality," adds Mr. Norton, "of our relations with Wright, was unique. It was of complete, easy trust. There was no possibility of a misunderstanding, or of even the most transient irritation. His sweetness was absolute, his obligingness never at fault, he had no sharp points to be watched for and avoided. There were no intermittences of confidence. The only drawback on intimacy with him lay in one's own liability to physical exhaustion. His powerful physical and intellectual frame prevented him from always recognizing the comparative feebleness of his companions. He could talk well, too long for average human nature, and sometimes when he was fresh for a new start at midnight others were weary; but he was not tyrannical, and, if not always perceptive of the moods and conditions of his friends, he was not vexed by being asked to conform to them. A man freer from pettiness of all sorts, freer from the sensitiveness of self-reference, I have never known."

Among the friends whose acquaintance Chauncey especially valued were Miss Catherine Howard, of Springfield, Massachusetts, and her sisters. He first knew them at Cambridge. Miss Howard taught there at one time in Professor Agassiz's school, at which Chauncey was himself at the same time a teacher. From time to time afterwards, as he passed through Springfield on his way to and from Northampton or Ashfield, he was in the habit of passing some hours with this most agreeable household.

The following letters to Miss Howard are good specimens of the kindly humor with which he used to answer the questions which his friends often saved up to ask him :—

To Miss Catherine L. Howard.

CAMBRIDGE, Dec. 6, 1866.

. . . But I wander into moral philosophy: your question is one in natural philosophy: "Why does molasses-candy grow whiter from our working it?" This admits, it seems to me, both of a poetical and a scientific answer. After the manner of our countrymen, it might be answered by asking other questions. Why does the sea grow white when the winds work it into foam? Why are beaten eggs white? Why is snow white? or, to descend to bathos, Why is soapsuds white?

In the three cases where fluids are concerned, the sea, the eggs, and the soapsuds, the admixture of air with them is the property common to them all. Let us believe, then, that a pure aërial spirit enters into, and purges these gross fluids of their dark and evil properties. This might satisfy the poetical imagination, and every good Christian conscience.

But the sceptical, scientific understanding demands to know more about it. That which is common to all the five cases (the sugar and the snow, as well as the three fluids) is the fine mechanical subdivision of these substances,—which in the case of the fluids is effected by the admixture of air, but in the case of the solids is independent of this circumstance.

Solid ice is not white, but pulverized ice and snow are; and a large list of substances might be added which grow white, and many others which become lighter in color, on being pulverized.

But what has this all to do with molasses-candy? Just this: the process of working it is one by which it becomes finely subdivided by the admixture of air with it. Melt the worked candy, and it becomes a thick, creamy foam, from which the heat would soon expel the air, and it would then relapse into its pristine dark and evil state. Fine mechanical subdivision in the worked candy, or breaks in the continuity of its solidity by the interposition of minute particles of air, is, then, the condition in which molasses-candy agrees with all the cases analogous with it in respect to the property in question. (I am following the Baconian method, — perhaps I ought to tell you.)

But the sceptical spirit is not even satisfied with this. Why should minute mechanical subdivisions, interruptions of the continuity of a solid or fluid substance, produce whiteness? Here optics comes to our aid. In a finely divided substance there is a correspondingly greater number of reflecting surfaces. Every minute bubble of air makes such a surface. The amount of white light, or sunlight, which is reflected near the surface of such a substance, bears a much larger proportion to that which is reflected from greater depths, and after transmission through the substance, than when the substance is continuous in its texture. A continuous substance, like undisturbed water, reflects principally, almost exclusively, from one surface. But foam reflects daylight, or white light, from innumerable surfaces, and reflects light which has penetrated only a little way into it. The color of any substance is composed of light from two sources, — of the light which it reflects and the light which it transmits, either directly or by internal reflection. Directly transmitted light, as in the case of colored glass, is that which the substance does not absorb. In all other cases, we have a union of the two kinds of color, — the color which is reflected unaltered from the outmost surface of the substance, and that which is reflected from the interior of the substance. The proportion of these two sources of color depends chiefly on the mechanical constitution of the substance. In homogeneous, continuous substances, internal reflection predominates. In heterogeneous, discontinuous substances, like the worked candy, external reflection predominates. Snow and refined sugar are white because their light is chiefly that which is reflected from innumerable crystalline surfaces. In unrefined or brown sugar, the crystals are covered by a film of treacle or molasses, which is washed off in the process of refining. The internally reflected light from the treacle gives the brown color, the other constituents of white light being absorbed by this substance.

Molasses-candy, therefore, grows whiter from our working it, because the working introduces air into it, and thereby increases the number of reflecting surfaces near its exterior, from which white light is reflected without the loss, by absorption, of any of its constituents.

In your note, you come very near to this explanation: you say, "I have bothered you so many times before this" (so far you are wrong, — but you add) "to get a few rays of light thrown into the depths of my ignorance, &c." I am surprised that you did not see in this the answer to your question! It is because light is thrown into the sweet depths of the unworked candy, and is not reflected, that it looks so dark. It is only by reflected and superficial light that it grows in whiteness.

. . . I shall be pleased to answer, if I can, any other questions — *not metaphysical* — which you may still have in reserve.

To the Same.

CAMBRIDGE, Dec. 11, 1866.

Is it not a pity that, after having written at such length, I should be obliged to rightly earn your thanks by a supplement!

In attending too exclusively to the general principles involved in the solution of your problem, I overlooked a circumstance of main importance to the special question about the candy.

I have nothing to retract as to the principle that a fine mechanical subdivision of the mass is the cause, on the optical principles which I explained, of the whiteness of the worked candy. But the admixture of air with it, though one of the means of effecting this subdivision, is by no means the most important. A breaking up of the mass, as it stiffens or becomes of a vitreous consistency, is effected by the working. This is analogous to the effect of pounding ice or cakes of maple-sugar, when the pounding does not pulverize, but simply cracks the mass into minute but coherent fragments. You know that in freezing ice-creams the constant stirring prevents solid congelation, and breaks the freezing mass into minute crystals of ice. Something similar to this takes place in working the candy. For though the candy does not crystallize, it is still vitrified, and the working prevents it from vitrifying into a continuous, translucent body.

This explanation can be tested in practice; for, according to it, the critical time for working the candy to its utmost whiteness is when the whole mass is nearly stiff, and when the parts which become quite stiff or vitreous break and mingle with the still pliant mass without being remelted by it.

CHAPTER IV.

WE reach now the first of Chauncey's letters to the sisters of Mr. Norton. These continue down to the end of his life, and it is in them that we shall find, after a little time, a large expression of his character and his wisdom. In the family of Mr. Norton, he had found culture, repose, and a degree of sympathy and of just and catholic appreciation which entirely won him. He grew very intimate with them all, and not only visited them at Ashfield, but at Cambridge also was on terms of very familiar friendship; so that at times, towards the end of his life, hardly a day passed without his being at their house. How great a service this was to him will appear farther on. He cherished for them all and to the end an affection which warmed his nature into beautiful expression, while it did not disturb, but rather deepened, that intellectual repose which was always characteristic of him, and which continued to give an increasing charm to his correspondence.

To Miss Grace Norton.

[1866 or 1867.]

. . . I beg you will not believe that I understood your objection to being called a "positivist" as an expression of serious dissent from the doctrine, and, indeed, I was but half in earnest in propounding the question; for I should myself be averse to accepting the name, except in the spirit in which many other appellations have been received by thinkers from their opponents, — as reproaches willingly borne for the sake of truth, or else humorously assumed as really harmless.

Besides, "positivism" is not a catechizing faith, and allows large latitude for beliefs, so far as they are professed as personal convictions, and are not imposed on all minds alike, on the penalty of forfeiting respect for intelligence or character.

Such a penalty properly applies only where the evidence is common to all minds, or where all admit the same fundamental facts of experience, as in physical science and in the elements of moral science. All observers not laboring under hallucinations of the senses are agreed, or can be made to agree, about facts of sensible experience, through evidence toward which the intellect is merely passive, and over which the individual will and character have no control. Such evidence is not the only kind which produces belief; though positivism maintains that it is the only kind which *ought* to produce so high a degree of confidence as all minds have or can be made to have through their agreements. And positivism maintains (to give the obverse of your formula) that, if the existence and character of God are to any mind *not* proved, they cannot be proved. If one cannot help believing it, then one has arrived, through other evidence than what can compel all minds, to a state of belief, perhaps fortunate, which is dependent on individual characters and experiences rather than on universal experience. Every mind has many similar beliefs, on many subjects beside theology, and holds them with various degrees of confidence. All that positivism demands in regard to theological beliefs is that they be put, intellectually and morally, on the same footing with others of this class; that the education, the experiences, and the type of character which produce such beliefs, shall not be regarded as intellectually and morally superior to those which fail to produce them. In other words, positivism holds that the intellect and the moral character, which ought to be the measures of each individual's proficiency, rest in the concurrent, unquestioned experiences in nature and in human life of all minds and hearts;

for this is the widest experience. . . . Considerations which practically amount to proof — that is, actually do "determine the intellect to give or withhold assent" — are not regarded by positivism as on this account of equal weight with those by which unquestionable beliefs *ought* to be determined. But positivism does not demand that we should question to the extent of ejecting from the mind all questionable beliefs; for this would be to accept the equally questionable contradictory beliefs. It only prescribes that we shall try continually to test and correct our beliefs by the particulars of concrete experiences of a kind common to all, when this is possible; and, when it is not possible, that we shall hold our beliefs in a spirit which recognizes the absence of the most perfect proof, however great the interests or the hopes may be which our faith sustains.

Diversities of mind and character, resulting in differences of practical belief or faith, are not to be altogether deplored, but rather welcomed as parts of the riches of human life, provided they be subject to principles, which, whether we call them liberal or positive, are, I am sure, both yours and mine.

To Mr. Norton.

[Feb. 18, 1867.]

Being this morning inspired with certain reflections, which were suggested by our talk on your paper about religion, I have written out a "brief" of them; and as I am impatient to submit it to you, and cannot come this evening, as I should prefer, I enclose it in this note.

Religion (subjective) means a man's devotion — the complete assent and concentration of his will — to any object which he acknowledges to have a right to his entire service, and supreme control over his life. Religion (objective) means the object or objects whose claims to this supremacy are acknowledged. An irreligious man is, then, first, one who acknowledges no supreme ends or objects; or, secondly, one who, though he acknowledges, does not habitually submit his will to such a power.

Morality, as contradistinguished from religion, is, subjectively, the habit of observing certain rules of conduct, deemed worthy or conducive to generally desirable ends, whether with or without an acknowledgment of the supremacy of these rules as injunctions, or the supremacy of the ends which they are believed to subserve. Morality (objective), as contradistinguished from supreme ends, means the rules of conduct deemed worthy or subservient to any generally desirable ends, whether these are acknowledged as supreme or not. An immoral man is, then, one who does not observe habitually and consistently any principles of conduct: either, first, from infirmity of purpose or want of discipline; or, secondly, from pure selfishness or a disregard of generally desirable ends.

Religion and morality are both realized in the practical nature of man, in character, in the fashioning of his volitions and desires. Both are concerned with "duty" in the broadest sense of that word; and religious and moral duties are often indistinguishable. But religious duties, or acts which are believed to be religious duties, come to be distinguished from others by the predominance of two marks: first, their absolute or unconditional character; second, their inutility, or the immediacy of the relation of act to object or end.

Besides such immediate and unconditional or religious duties, civilization creates a host of others, and many other motives to their observance. Partial, relative, conditional duties, with which morality in the narrower sense of the word, or casuistry, has to deal, may be enforced by meaner motives than the acknowledgment of unconditional obligations as the grounds of all right conduct. Hence, the possibility of an irreligious morality.

The above discriminations are independent of any theory, utilitarian or other, of the source of moral and religious convictions and truths, and are designed to show that religion and morality are definable and distinguishable independently of creeds and codes. This is the same as Mill's position.

To the Same.

CAMBRIDGE, June 13, 1867.

My visit to Northampton was only a short one, and was mainly filled with business. But I found it very pleasant, — almost as pleasant as living in Cambridge at this season. The town itself was even more beautiful. Cambridge has, however, the supreme advantage to me of having one spot in it where I can attain, at will, the greatest beatitude, — that of complete abstraction from the external world, even in a day in June. My room has become so familiar to me, that my knowledge of it has ripened into oblivion. I live here a disembodied spirit, undisturbed by the distractions of any thing foreign to me.

. . . It would have been very pleasant to have made my journey a vacation, and to have included in it a visit to you; but the "sweet nothing to do" is a luxury for which I fear I shall never have the means, since I spend my time here as unskilfully, and with as little forethought, as the New York capitalists do their money. I have not yet "learned the fine art of spending" *time.*

To Miss Jane Norton.

CAMBRIDGE, July 4, 1867.

. . . The only effort I have made lately, of much account, is a long reply to Rev. F. E. Abbot's letter, in which I have rather plainly spoken my mind on the practical bearings of our debate. I have not yet summoned the courage to copy it for him. Perhaps when I do, I may send it first to you. I scribble (perhaps I ought to tell you) my more deliberate thoughts in pencil on scraps of paper; for I cannot think deliberately in ink. It is too much like the captious office of the recording angel, making indelible the spontaneities of the moment, rather than the sincere principles of a lifetime.

To Mr. Abbot.

CAMBRIDGE, July 9, 1867.

. . . The long intervals in our debate add to it a certain dignity, let us believe. The discussion is one which reaches across the centuries, and rises above the conditions of time, space, and circumstance, by at least having these for its objects.

I was much interested to learn from you, also, that your views have undergone considerable modifications in the form of concessions to empiricism. My interest in the questions between us has always been much less practical than yours. It has been almost entirely speculative, because I have always believed that the really *essential* positions of morals and religion could be sustained on the "lower" ground of common-sense, — on what men generally understand and believe independently of their philosophical theories; and I have always felt that philosophy was concerned with matters of theoretical interpretation rather than with practical matters of fact. Indeed, the history of philosophy hardly ever exhibits any divergence in opinion as to simple questions of practice, as to what should be done next in any given state of social circumstances, — though it is one of the weapons of the orthodox to deduce the direst practical consequences from their opponents' theories. It is upon the *causes* of the admitted state of facts, or upon the *grounds* of the allowed desirable changes in them, that thinkers differ practically. The distinction between "conservative" and "progressive" in practical matters, has hardly ever been coincident with fundamental differences in philosophical opinions; and in proportion as men become absorbed in practical questions do the old party lines of philosophical thought disappear. Witness the entirely distinct personalities which Mr. Mill presents as a speculative thinker and as a practical statesman. Few who have come to know and respect him in his later public capacity know or care about his theory of cognition.

I accordingly regard the duty of liberality in speculative matters as a disagreeable and compulsory one, only towards those thinkers, of whatever school, who maintain that their theories involve exclusively the welfare of mankind, — who accuse their opponents of denying some admitted and obvious facts in practical matters. Any one whom we are bound to respect is bound to know such facts, and to know how to act accordingly. If he does not, we put him in an asylum, — out of respect for the humanity which he has, nevertheless. Men conclude in matters affecting their own welfare so much better than they can justify rationally, — they are led by their instincts of reverence so surely to the safest known authority, that theory becomes in such matters an insignificant affair. How weak theory is in general, can be judged by the slow progress men have made in knowledge foreign to their immediate wants, — in scientific knowledge. And the explanations which they have hitherto given of their beliefs in practical rules of conduct afford the best possible evidence of the practical weakness of theory even in the most important matters. To stake any serious human concern on the truth of this or that philosophical theory seems to me, therefore, in the highest degree arrogant and absurd, as coming from a confused begging of some philosophical question, — from taking for granted that something is important practically which is in theory problematical; from taking for granted, for example, that our duties would be different, or be more or less binding on us according as our faith in a future life should be well or ill founded.

My interest in philosophical and disputed matters is, therefore, almost entirely speculative. It is not quite so, because clear, scientific knowledge has important practical consequences. The truths of astronomy and chemistry, for example, have conferred great and unforeseen benefits, and so may the truths of philosophy when fully ascertained; but, so long as there is room for dispute and enlightened doubt, there are no practical applications which can rightly prejudge theory, though it is common enough in philosophical disputes to make an illogical *reductio ad injuriam* of an opponent's views. When errors are really exploded, as in the case of the false religious philosophy of the "inquisition," we see clearly what enormous practical consequences are involved in philosophical theories. And it is an interesting question, how much injury may be done by the influence of false views of philosophy, in the aims and methods of education now-a-days, — whether many poor bodies are not tortured to their deaths by a tax put upon them through an over-stimulation of the mind and conscience, by a tax which is philosophically credited to the supposed inexhaustible powers and undying nature of the soul. But to accuse a creed of such consequences, until scientifically proved, would be to commit the error in speculation which above all others I reprobate.

Your movement toward empiricism interests me the more, because I suspect that no genuine thinker can remain long in the position of an eclectic, such as M. Cousin held so many years. Eclectic systems have rarely outlived the vanity of their authors, who would be priests and philosophers at the same time. If, then, your conscience does not deceive you with illusive evidence, I am almost confident that you will come out in what you call "empiricism," — in what Mill calls the experiential philosophy, or what Comte called positivism.

This philosophy denies nothing of orthodoxy except its confidence; but it discriminates between the desirableness of a belief and the evidence thereof. Faith is in this philosophy what it was with St. Paul, a sentiment, not a faculty of knowledge. A man who has invested all his goods in a mine believes the more readily in its hidden wealth, and is not so likely to suspend his judgment on the question, as he would be on the question of the habitableness of the planet Saturn. He will, nevertheless, if he remain of sane mind, admit that the judgment of an unprejudiced geologist, who can so suspend his judgment, is better than his own, and that the geologist's report is a better guide than his own hope. So it is with the positivist. So far are his positions from leading to heterodox conclusions in religion, as they are constantly accused of doing, that it is only by a hitherto unrecognized formula of logic that they can possibly be conceived to do so; namely, "that sublating the reason sublates the consequence, and posits its contradictory," — that to reject the authority of revelation and the validity of the arguments of natural theology is to prove atheism! A positivist in the pulpit would thus be no anomaly. He would only be a preacher who knows how much better the dignity of the highest moral character is than any excellence in a life common with that of the beasts, — whether it endure longer or not; who knows that duty is as real and as binding on all men, in subserving the real ends, which God is supposed to care for especially, as it would be if the evidence of God's existence were a hundred-fold more cogent, and duty were really known to be his commandment.

But I have run a great way off the track in following the reflections which your apostasy from the orthodox philosophy has suggested. I meant, in writing to you, only to acknowledge your letter, and to resume, then, the thread of our debate.

You infer from my exposition of the empiricist's doctrine of space and time that I "deny them all *independent* objective existence." I would modify a little this deduction. I regard them as objects, — phenomenal objects, — and not merely as forms of sensibility. As to their "*independent* objective" (if you mean by this, noumenal) existence, I can deny or affirm nothing, — only that space and time, as we know them, and, consequently, as they are, to us, are relations among phenomena; and, as we know, they depend, or "are conditioned on the existence of phenomena themselves." Your conclusion, that "could we conceive the annihilation of phenomena, the relations subsisting between them would also be annihilated," is, therefore, in substance, correctly deduced, though it should be more explicitly stated that the phenomena and the relations here spoken of are also "conditioned on the existence" of a knowing mind; and that the annihilation supposed is the annihilation of thought as well as of its object. What would remain we know nothing about. Things in themselves and their relations to one another, whether real or not, are not real to us, — are not objects of our knowledge; though, if they exist, they may be the causes of our knowledge.

I assent also to your inference that, in my opinion, "relations are objective realities;" but I would not be understood as allowing by this that I regard them as noumenal realities. Whether the latter exist, and whatever they may be, the relations of which we are treating are relations of objects, which are only known as objects to us, and as conditioned on our cognizance of them. I believe that the relations between such objects belong to them, — are objective, — and are not moulds or forms in us into which objects fit.

When I spoke of the relations of time and space as "intuitions of sense," I ought, perhaps, to have explained that I did not hold the abstract cognizance of them as possible in sensuous, or, indeed, in any other intuition. Such cognizance implies, it seems to me, the abstractive action of the attention in understanding, — not any intuitive power at all. More correctly, I should have said that the grounds of relations (*fundamenta relationum*) are intuitions of sense; the relations themselves, as distinct from their concrete terms, being cognizable, not intuitively, but only by abstraction, and being representable only by the reproduction of such and so many sensuous data as are implied in them. The cognizance of relations is, indeed, an abstractive grouping of phenomena. The *twoness* of two hats (to take your example) is as much in the hats as their color, texture, or form; but the cognizance of it in the abstract is not an intuitive process at all. It adds no content to the concrete cognizance of the group. It subtracts rather the texture, form, use, and all other attributes of the manifold object, — leaving to our attention only difference in space and a species of plurality, which, by similar acts, we have generalized under the name of "two." I, "who admit the objectivity of relations, and hold them to be *immediately* known [in the concrete], can deny that here is logically necessitated a higher intuitive faculty than sense," because to me intuition signifies a concrete addition to the content of our cognitions. I admit that space, time, and number are peculiar, — unlike most other apparently simple notions which we generalize from the manifold of sensuous intuitions. They are not referable to simple and unanalyzable sensations, such as give us the color and texture of the hats; nor are they analyzable into a plurality of simpler relations, such as is implied in the *use* of the hats. They resemble the latter notion in being distinctly cognizable only by abstraction. They resemble sensations in being apparently simple. It may be admitted, until an analysis has been proposed, that number, and perhaps also time, are simple, unanalyzable properties of things in general *as objects of knowledge*. That they appear only in acts of abstraction and understanding does not prove, however, that they are intuitions of a supersensuous faculty, unless it can be shown that the understanding adds as well as subtracts in its discursions.

With space, the case is different. Our apprehension of it may in one way be analyzed. Introspective analysis cannot, it is true, resolve it into simpler elements ; but we can easily conceive of it as an *idea of sensation* (as Locke called it), as consisting of an unanalyzable group of sensations cemented by insoluble associations. On this hypothesis, the universality of space in our cognitions comes from its invariable association with other and really simpler sensations, and its simplicity comes from the limit in our powers of introspective analysis.

It appears to me that Kant's division of our knowledges into the *data* of experience and the *conditions* of experience (the one being the intuitions of sense, and the other being the forms of sensibility and understanding) came from a mistaken deference to the philosophical prejudice that that must belong intrinsically to the mind which we cannot by abstraction extrude from thought. It doubtless does belong to the *reflective* and *developed* mind, and belongs to it as contrasted with *further* acquisition, or as contrasted with *additional* experience ; but this does not prove or imply that the forms of sense and thought were not determined by experience in the first instance, or were not then, as ever afterwards, as much the data of experience as what is called "contingent knowledge." I cannot therefore subscribe to Kant's distinction of the "conditions" and the "data" of experience as fundamental ones ; nor can I admit that there is any better ground for your distinction in similar terms. By intuition, I understand, not what we cannot analyze into simpler elements by introspection, but, generally, what cannot be supposed to be composed of simpler elements even in the infancy of the mind. Mr. Mill's psychological method is supplementary to the introspective method of the thinkers of your school ; and, until its resources are exhausted, I cannot believe that the questions of philosophy are definitively settled.

To Mr. Norton.

CAMBRIDGE, July 24, 1867.

. . . I have been on the point, on several occasions, of writing to you, but my unconquerable indolence has prevailed, along with the claims of various duties (which I have not done), — enemies which I propitiate, after a barbarous fashion, by sacrificing to them all my nearest relations, with the exception of my ease. I have unintentionally taken a long and uneventful vacation, parleying with the thief of time, and giving myself up to ponderous amusements, such as reading the last "North American Review," and writing fragmentary essays and criticisms. Do not expect me ever to finish any of them for the Review, for they are only notes of thoughts which seemed to me at the moment better cut and dried for future reference than allowed to resolve themselves into the humus of a fertile oblivion, — for fear that weeds might come up instead of better ones. Among my more serious diversions is the study of ——'s metaphysics in the Review. I can only take small quantities at a time, both on account of the density of the matter and the pungency of the style. I have read your general views on translation with great interest. . . .

I have had the pleasure of meeting Mr. Abbot, my metaphysical antagonist, personally, and debating in a pleasant conversation the various points of our controversy. I find him as able in talk as in his writings. I also met Mr. White of the Cornell College last week, and hope to meet him again before he leaves these parts, for I had but a few words with him after the dinner on Thursday.

Gurney and Lowell go to-morrow to Manomet, near Plymouth, for a few days by the seashore.

To Mr. Abbot.

CAMBRIDGE, Aug. 13, 1867.

Thank you for "the Radical's Theology," which I have read with great interest. I think it all excellent in style; and the first part (up to the "Grand Postulate") admirable, compared with most that is written on the theme of religious freedom. On the "Grand Postulate" I am aground, and cannot go on with you.

Geometry is, I suppose, responsible for the idea that science in general must have some postulate to start with; since from the earliest times geometry has presented a misleading type to philosophy. A completed science, thrown into a synthetic form, has of course its postulates, taking for granted that certain things can be done, the demonstration of which would lie outside of the synthesis, or form no part of its organic structure. A postulate proper is a *practical* axiom determined by the *end* in view; and so far as science in general has any other end in view than simply to know every thing it can learn, it may have postulates, which are not, however, undemonstrable truths, though they are in general undemonstrable *deductively*. The law of causation may be looked upon as a postulate in science generally, since our search, as soon as it becomes systematic, implies the general fact that the explanations we seek are possible, — that some law or laws, after the general type we have ascertained already, exist among the unexplained phenomena, and give a unity to the universe of knowable things corresponding to the unity of knowledge sought in science. And so of the postulate or canon of induction, that a generalization is good and is to be accepted as a universal truth, provided there are no contrary instances, and that no other generalization can limit, condition, or qualify the first or show how it may not be universal.

But by what right are such postulates used in scientific reasoning? Is it by their own *a priori* validity? They certainly cannot be proved deductively, since they are the broadest of generalizations, — but why not proved inductively? Are they not, in fact, simple statements of the summary results of all our experiences in the past, and the practical axioms of our expectations in the future? Are they other than truths coextensive with *our* universe at least, and with our conceptions and anticipations. The answer to this is, of course, that a limited experience cannot prove an unlimited proposition. But there are two issues to this objection, and the one commonly overlooked is, that propositions which, in form, are unconditioned and universal, still ought not in fact to be believed beyond their application to the known universe; nor yet to be disbelieved or doubted; because about what we really know nothing we ought not to affirm or deny any thing.

The position that an axiom cannot be proved, which the *a priori* school maintains, seems to me preposterous, — or else a mere quibble; for, to be sure, it might be said in defence of the doctrine, that an axiom, being avowedly a starting-point in deductive science, has implied in its very name that it cannot be proved. But all that is really implied in the name is that truths when *called* axioms are *used* for the deductive proof of other truths, and that their own proof is not involved in the process. This does not deny, however, that they may be, as truths, the conclusions of other processes; to wit, the inductions of experience. If they are, then the only ultimate truths are the particulars of concrete experience, and no postulate or general assumption is inherent in science until its proceedings become systematic, or the truths already reached give direction to further research.

But, waiving the "postulate," you say that the principal question of Theology is this, "Is the mysterious Power which fills the universe a conscious spirit or an unconscious force? Is it Love or Fate that holds the throne of Being?"

And, again, "The question is simply between consciousness and unconsciousness, — which is the higher mode of being?" To my mind these questions are analyzable into still more fundamental ones. What is meant by "higher mode of being"? Higher relatively to what? If it means "best calculated to move and interest conscious beings," then the conscious mode of being is undoubtedly the highest, but not necessarily the first in time. That conscious modes of being are at least a part, and the most interesting, morally and religiously, of the manifestations of "the mysterious Power which fills the universe," there can be no doubt. Mind is at least manifested in man, the animals, and perhaps in some degree in all organic beings, and these belong to the universe. But when you ask whether this "mysterious Power" be itself a conscious spirit or an unconscious force, the alternative you present, if insisted on, would resolve the mystery, whichever branch you might take. Or perhaps you call this Power mysterious simply because we do not know which alternative to take? Is it resolvable into either the mystery of consciousness or the mystery of force?

But there is no such opposition between consciousness and force, between Love and Hate, as you appear — in common with nearly the whole religious world — to assert. This phraseology is probably descended from the barbarous doctrines of the earlier Christian centuries, the old dualism of the Manicheists. The supposed opposition is involved in the doctrine of free will, which finds, of course, a fundamental contrariety between the freedom of consciousness and the necessity of force, but the free-will doctrine is in fact a pure assumption, which ignores all just scientific method, and even contradicts some of the results of science. This "mysterious Power" manifests force, law, fate, if you will, — everywhere, in mental and spiritual, as well as in the merely physical phenomena of nature; and it manifests consciousness, in varying degrees, throughout the whole organic world, reaching its highest manifestations in man. But man, however conscious, is none the less a part of fate, — though not compelled by an external fate to act by laws which are not his, or by determinations which are not in himself. No *real* fate or necessity is indeed manifested anywhere in the universe, — only a phenomenal regularity.

Such, it seems to me, is the scientific answer to so much of your question as submits itself to scientific comprehension. In another form, the question of the hidden nature of "the Power of the universe" may be more fairly brought before the tribunal of science. Does the production in nature of the phenomena of consciousness, and the various instrumentalities by which consciousness is developed, — such as organs of sense, the human eye, for example, — does this imply the existence of an independent and superior consciousness, which, being able to see without eyes, could provide vision for his creatures? That "the mysterious Power of the universe" actually manifests vision in the eyes of men and animals, there can be no doubt; but the question is whether, prior to the existence of living creatures and the laws of their growth, some other form of consciousness was not required for the "contrivance" of the organs and vital conditions of consciousness?

Not from any truths of creation which science has yet reached can she answer this question. What, indeed, do we know about the creation of organic beings, except perhaps that they began to exist on the earth within a limited time, and that various races have succeeded one another? So long as men compared, after a childish imagination, creation to the *making* of any thing in the operation of various human handicrafts, so long there could be no doubt or mystery about this question. The Maker of the eye must, of course, be able to see. So long as vision, so important *to man*, was regarded as a divine power, and so long as he allowed his reason to be governed by such empty maxims as "that the greater cannot be produced by the less" (whatever this may mean), so long the problem admitted of an easy solution. "The Creator must have powers equal at least to those he creates." Yes, certainly; but what is here meant by "equal," "less," or "greater"? A man with sight has a supreme advantage over the blind man, from a human point of view, and with reference to various human needs and enjoyments; but is God superior to a man in this merely, — that he has superior powers to compass his various ends? To ascribe to creation the possession of various powers as means to ends is to put an anthropological interpretation upon it, — is to describe creation as a manufacture. To escape such a crude imagination, the consciousness that is ascribed to "the mysterious Power of the universe," by those who really recognize it as mysterious, is supposed to be only the *essence* of consciousness, an "abstract entity," the metaphysical consciousness; not the powers of the five senses, with memory, imagination, reasoning, which are only powers relative to weakness and limitation, but something common to them all, and transcending them all, which in fact gives being to mental powers in men and animals.

That "the mysterious Power of the universe" really does manifest mental and spiritual powers at least in men and animals, is a fact which science fully recognizes; and that these powers are by far the most interesting, to the moral and religious nature of man, of all the phenomena of nature, is the fact with which religion is chiefly concerned.

I have tried in the above to sketch briefly the method in which true science should approach these questions, avoiding as far as possible the terms which have attached to them *good* and *bad* meanings, in place of scientific distinctness, — terms which have a moral connotation as well as a scientific one.

Such terms and arguments are constantly employed in questions like these, — "which is the worthier, which the 'higher' of two conceptions," or "which is the more elevating, the less degrading belief?" This is really to argue as much on "the principle of authority," as the Romanist, the Protestant, or the Unitarian; for the Church, the Bible, and the Christ have fashioned human language, — have tied meanings and feelings together in words, which science has the right to separate. All older authorities are represented in the authority still exerted over human reverence through the moral associations of words. You say that science has rejected the "principle of Authority." In fact, true science never knew it, — wholly ignores, instead of rejecting this principle.

Those thinkers whose beliefs are mainly determined by the moral tone of their times and by as much of pure science as they can attain to, — still adhering in their questions and definitions to the use of *good* and *bad* words, — reject the older authorities, indeed, in the concrete, but do not reject the principle of authority absolutely. They substitute for the dogmas of the Church, and the sacred Scriptures, and the teachings of Christ, the teachings of *good* and *bad* words, which retain the unction of all effective past authority. Words have "reputations" as well as other authorities, and there is a tyranny in their reputations even more fatal to freedom of thought. True science deals with nothing but questions of facts, — and in terms, if possible, which shall not determine beforehand how we ought to feel about the facts; for this is one of the most certain and fatal means of corrupting evidence. If the facts are determined, and, as far as may be, free from moral biases, then practical science comes in to determine what, in view of the facts, our feelings and rules of conduct ought to be; but practical science has no inherent postulates any more than speculative science. Its ultimate grounds are the particular goods or ends of human life.

To Mr. Norton.

CAMBRIDGE, Aug. 18, 1867.

. . . Since our talk last summer on what religion is, and the subsequent development of our ideas on this subject, I have meditated more and more, impelled by a dissatisfaction with the state in which we left the distinction between moral and religious duties. The idea that the one consists of the obligations of the highest expediency, while the other is concerned with absolute obligations, has come to seem quite trivial, and inadequate to distinguish the objects of feelings so different as our religious and moral sentiments. But I think that the true distinction is discoverable in the classification of duties which Mill adopts from the Catholic casuists.

The Calvinist, regarding this life and the next as all one and part of a grand moral scheme, in which obligations, duties, rights, and sanctions are completely balanced and mutually fitted to each other, conceives three different classes of virtues as essentially one, — as all on the type of legal duties, that is, of duties of "perfect obligation," with corresponding rights either in human beings or in the Divine Being. This identification of religious and all other obligations with legality is the characteristic of the extreme Protestant or Calvinistic creed. But such an identification confounds these distinct elements: namely, 1. The truly legal duties, which have corresponding rights in other human beings and real sanctions in the punitive powers of the State, — such as duties of refraining from various forms of violence, for example; or paying one's debts, and keeping other legally sanctioned contracts; 2. The positively moral duties, which are without legal sanctions, and are not enforced except by depriving the delinquent of voluntarily, or freely rendered benefits, and by the consequent evils of such deprivation; 3. Those duties which are above the sanctions of fear or favor, and have their rewards and their sanctions either in another life or in themselves, — or in the evils of the absence of the requisite motive to them.

These last seem to me to be the strictly religious duties, as distinguished from legal and merely moral ones. Over and above what society requires and enforces by its power, and beyond what individual consciences demand of others and obtain by the power of opinion, or by moral means, there are other *duties*, in the modern religious sense of the word, which the individual conscience recognizes, and to which the individual conscience is constrained by sanctions either wholly self-subsisting, or sustained by a superstitious faith in another life. From doing a religious duty there are no visible benefits to the agent, and from neglecting to do it no visible evils, evident to any but himself. If his imagination of a future reward or punishment determines this invisible restraint, his religion is superstitious. But if immediate happiness in doing his duty, or misery in not doing it, is the ultimate sanction, then his religion is real, or a part of his character.

The earliest recognition of this idea, the intrinsic happiness of duty, is the Socratic doctrine, — that to suffer injustice is better than to do it. The later Stoic doctrine, that virtue is its own reward, is an affirmation of the same essential principle. This is the religious idea of duty, as distinguished from those acts whose sanctions are external, either in the legal exercise of power or in the free exercise of opinion and favor. Neither force nor favor, neither negative nor positive external sanctions, are the adequate grounds of action to the truly religious soul. Whether the doctrine of a future life (rewarding by external benefits and punishing by external evils) is true or not, the true idea of religious duty is independent of it. This idea rests wholly on the value of the act, *per se*, to the agent, — on the happiness it gives him, or the misery he suffers from omitting to do it.

This, according to Mr. Grote, was a novel idea in the

time of Socrates. Up to that time, the pagan world had no feeling of duty other than to deserve exemption from punishment or else the favor of other men or of the gods. The invisible restraints and sanctions of superstitious beliefs were the only ones which deserved the name of religious motives. The most enviable man — the happiest man — was he who possessed the most power to secure the visible goods of life, without fear or favor. In our time, the religious idea of duty has grown so prominent, through the influence of Christianity, that the novelty of it to the childish mind of the Greeks can hardly be realized.

With this change in the moral feelings of the world, the distribution of duties into the three classes has also changed, and is progressively changing as the world moves on. Moral duties become legal ones, or are peremptorily required by law. Religious duties become moral ones, or are demanded of us by the consciences of other men; and with intellectual progress (which is the fundamental one), duties of which men were ignorant become known, and the extent of what good we can do (ideally meritorious, without being either morally or legally binding on us) is constantly growing.

But nothing is properly called a duty which has not some sanction; that is, some real motive, in fact, to do it; and it is by their actual sanctions that duties are distributed into the three classes. Religious duties are not a merely negative class, a class without sanctions, or real motives to do them. The peculiarity of this class is that their sanctions, not being external or independent of the religious character, cannot directly produce this character. Men may take on trust the fact of the superior happiness of a supremely virtuous life over a merely moral one, or may be persuaded by external and non-religious motives, such as a superstitious respect for superior authority, or a belief in future rewards and punishments; but the true religious sanction is the real superiority of disinterested rational actions as a source of happiness to the agent himself. His actions cannot be disinterested in the absolute sense of the term, — cannot be independent of the happiness of the agent in the widest sense of happiness. He may observe his religious duties, because he is happier in following the authority he respects or in the anticipations of a future happiness, than in following the momentary impulses of his lower nature; but his conduct is strictly religious only when determined by the immediate, peculiar, and supreme happiness, which the acting for universal ends, without fear or favor, causes in the mature religious character. This is the sanction which determines, not, indeed, what really are religious duties, but which of our actions are done in the truly religious spirit.

The whole question of what are our duties in general is dependent on wholly different considerations from those which determine the classification of them under legal, moral, and religious duties. The question is fundamentally a scientific one (the question of Deontology), of what ought to be done, whatever the sanctions may be by which a principle or rule of conduct is enforced. The classification of duties according to their sanctions is not scientific and permanent, but historic and subject to change with the moral and intellectual advance of the race. The science of duty decides what ought to be done, on principles which may or may not be effectively appealed to as the motives to right conduct. But the distinction we are considering is properly one of real sanctions, — the distinction of duties according to such sanctions. From the scientific point of view, there is but one fundamental sanction, to wit, the test of all right conduct (for the test of conduct is fundamentally the warrant of it), namely, the "highest good." To act from this sanction, from the love of the "highest good," is to act religiously, disinterestedly, and "on principle."

The unity which the Calvinist sought by reducing all virtue

to the legal type is an end really to be sought in the philosophic type of utilitarian morality; for this is the only truly philosophic scheme, the only one which does not base itself arbitrarily on opinion, — on the shifting, historic ground of the so-called "moral sense." There is no other test of what duty is in general, and no higher or more religious motive to it, than that it conduces to the highest good of the greatest number.

I have yielded one point to you by using the words "religion" and "religious" in their unhistoric, though not conventional, sense, against my last summer's protest. I felt then a prejudice against these words, as falsely uniting the noblest feelings with the meanest ideas; as being of those *good* words through which one of the subtlest forms of tyranny is exercised over freedom of thought.

The practical lesson of this sermon is that there are many actions which, though they may be recognized as obligatory by the conscience of the one who does them, ought not to be imposed as such on any one by any other human being. But, so far as such actions are really beneficent, and are recognized as such by others, they should be classed as positively meritorious, as works of supererogation. We should not seek to make them obligatory simply on the ground of their positive worth. For, by this reasoning, the more worthy an act is, the more obligatory the act would be, and saintliness would be imperatively demanded of us, — the Calvinist's paradox. It is not by laws and legal sanctions, nor yet by opinion and moral sanctions, but only by worship, — the positive reverence due to the highest even of human virtues, — that such virtues have a foothold in the world.

But I may be guilty myself of violating the great principle of religious liberty by compelling you to read so long a sermon. A sermon never naturally comes to an end. It is a series of endless evolutions of thoughts and sentiments, with but little help from art, and no help at all from the great art of making an end. It is necessary to arrest such discourses *flagranti delicto*, in the very act of starting on another theme, — which I do.

To Miss Howard.

CAMBRIDGE, Sept. 18, 1867.

. . . Your question (the best book on psychology for the young ladies) has just recently been considered and debated by Professor Gurney and me, with reference to the wants of a young gentleman, recently graduated, who also proposes to teach philosophy to young ladies. . . .

We have concluded that as good a book for this purpose as can be found, among many poor ones, is Dugald Stewart's "Elements of the Philosophy of the Human Mind." An edition of this work, abridged and annotated by Professor Bowen, has been used as a text-book in this college in past years; and Professor Gurney proposes to continue the use of it as an introduction to the college course of philosophy. This reprint has passed to a second edition, published in 1864 by William H. Dennet, of Boston. But your Springfield booksellers will know all about that. What they may not know about the book is that, in my opinion, it is an elegantly shallow treatise, not difficult to understand, because superficial; and it ought to be rather interesting to beginners. Professor Stewart was a good man, and is doubtless now in heaven. He wrote on philosophy in the interest of all that is lovely and of good report. There are no heresies in his book.

I hardly think you will need any other book to help you understand this one. But you might get some useful hints from Sir William Hamilton's "Lectures on Metaphysics," of which Professor Bowen has also edited an abridged edition. And, if you want to have all the ideas which you will get familiar with in these books completely upset and overthrown, read Mill's "Logic" and his "Examination of Sir William Hamilton's Philosophy." I can hardly conceive of a more wholesome discipline of the human understanding than an interested study of Hamilton's Philosophy, followed by a reading of Mill's criticisms of it; but I think Stewart's book the best to begin with.

I venture to volunteer the advice that, in teaching philosophy, it is well to call in question and refute every thing you can, with the aid of collateral reading, in order that the young ladies may never forget that they are not studying their catechisms, — not merely studying to acquire true and settled doctrines, but mainly to strengthen their understandings, to learn to think, and doubt, and inquire with equanimity. To help you teach this is the chief advantage of a parallel course of study. Still better, perhaps, since you would not have leisure to do all this reading, would it be to set those zealots of the class who are not satisfied with the length of the lessons in Stewart to reading other books for the sake of discussion. Let each come armed with some confounding objection to the doctrines of the text, and the recitations will be lively and profitable exercises. But this is rather an ideal advice, not founded on my own experience.

I am glad to hear from you that you have had so pleasant a summer. You only dread the coming work because it is strange. My dread of mine is because it is so dreadfully familiar. I have treated it all summer with a familiar neglect.

As this is the last of the letters to Miss Howard, I will add here some passages relating to Chauncey, from a note which she has kindly sent me: —

. . . "My remembrance is of the sweetest courtesy in explaining often very abstruse or scientific matters to very incompetent people, and he never even looked surprised at any thing you did *not* know. He often went to Northampton to spend Thanksgiving, and always came here to tea on his way back, with the faithfulness which marked his friendships; and we were in the habit of storing up difficult questions which came up in our classes for Mr. Wright's annual visit. The late train to Boston left Springfield at two o'clock at night; and you know how oblivious he was of the lapse of time when he was talking on subjects that interested him. With labors behind and before us, and the subject not unfrequently above our heads, we often felt shivers of sleepiness; but Mr. Wright would seem unconscious of every thing, and placidly say, as he rose to go in the small hours, 'I see you keep the same late hours you always did.' — Once we were talking about the disintegration of the rocks in Conway, and S. said, 'If rocks go to pieces, what can you trust in?' Mr. Wright replied, with his inimitable serio-comic manner, 'Truth!' — He wanted to tell me about some book on one occasion; and I told him I was going to pass my Christmas vacation in Roxbury, and asked him to come there and see us. He said he would; and shutting his eyes, as if he were studying a problem, he said, 'By what system of mnemonics can I recall that?' and he did not invent a system, for he did not come.

"—— was on the conservative side always, in religious talks with Mr. Wright, and once told him she believed implicitly that the world was made in six days. He looked at her as if she were a new order of being, and I never shall forget the tone of his exclamation, '*Is it possible?*'

"We saw him constantly during a little visit which he made at Nantucket in the summer of 1871. You know how apt he was to lead the conversation to religious subjects. —— was really pained by the turn the conversation took one evening, and she said most earnestly, 'Mr. Wright, don't you believe in the immortality of the soul?' I felt almost nervous at this direct question, for fear what his direct answer might be, but it has been my sheet-anchor since: 'I think there is more reason to believe it than to disbelieve it.'

"You remember that Professor Peirce gave a course of lectures at the Lowell Institute. Mr. Wright had a seat near the front, and was always there till Mr. Peirce referred in a very complimentary manner to Chauncey Wright. He seemed utterly overwhelmed, and never appeared at the lectures again.

. . . "But the sweetest thing I remember in him was the way of advancing these ideas: there was nothing in the least aggressive about it, and a something that was almost tender in his way of trying to see your side of the question."

In the last letter to Miss Howard, Chauncey humorously speaks of "dreading" his work because it is so "dreadfully familiar." President Runkle of the Institute of Technology at Boston, who was for years associated with him in his work upon the Nautical Almanac, has sent me some information as to Chauncey's habits of work, from which I will here quote: —

"His Almanac work," he says, "always seemed the greatest drudgery, and he never did it till the last minute. When he could postpone no longer, he laid all else aside, and worked, almost literally, day and night till it was done. But it was done most conscientiously. For the sake of system, and to reduce the mental tax as much as possible and also to secure accuracy, he was willing to make many additional figures; and he rested his mind by changing from one part of the work to another. For instance, if he had a long series of numbers to convert into logarithms or the converse, he would lay these aside, and perform additions for an hour or two, for the sake of rest. I have known more rapid workers for a short time, but never one who could do such a vast amount of work on a long stretch. . . . For many years I knew Chauncey intimately, and I am certain that I have never known a man so little influenced by external circumstances. He lived almost wholly in an ideal world.

. . . "After my coming to live in this town, Chauncey often came over to spend an evening.[1] He arrived late, and it was always early morning before we were ready to separate. He never would accept a bed, always saying that he liked the walk in the early morning. He probably felt that, once in his own room, he could prolong his nap without interfering with any one's household arrangements.

"If he had had the ambitions which spur many men, he could have won almost any place, and I once felt sorry that he did not have them; but now I am thankful to have known one soul above the petty motives which actuate common mortals, — whose only aim was to discover the truth, and who was never even conscious that there could be any reason why he should not state it, no matter what private or public opinion might be upon the subject in hand."

To Mr. Abbot.

CAMBRIDGE, Oct. 28, 1867.

I was very glad to hear again so soon from you on the subjects of our debate, and to know that you still retain so fresh an interest in them in spite of your recent losses and perplexities.[2]

Your letter interests me very much. It is so full of sug-

[1] Mr. Runkle's house was at Brookline, and about three miles from Cambridge. Chauncey's visits were made during the years 1866 and 1867.

[2] Mr. Abbot was at this time a Unitarian clergyman at Dover, New Hampshire. The allusion is to difficulties which arose out of a growing divergence between the opinions held by him and those commonly held by his denomination. These controversies culminated in litigation of a very interesting character, of which an account may be found in the case of Hale *v.* Everett, 53 New Hampshire Reports, p. 1.

gestive points, and affords so much light to me on the real grounds of our differences, that I hardly feel able in the limited space of a letter to say all I wish to on its various topics. The most profitable discussion is, after all, a study of other minds, — seeing how others see, rather than the dissection of mere propositions. The restatement of fundamental doctrines in new connections affords a parallax of their philosophical stand-points (unless these be buried in the infinite depths), which adds much to our knowledge of one another's thought.

Concerning the foundation of experientialism, I agree with you "that experience includes more than a heterogeneous mass of particular sensuous impressions, and cannot be explained by a mere 'law of association' among such impressions." Our cognitions are indeed more than the mere chronicles of a sensuous history. There are orders and forms in them which do not come directly from the transient details of sense-perceptions. Indeed, without the constant reaction of the mind through memory upon the presentations of the senses, there could arise nothing worth the name of knowledge. If our memories were only retentive and not also co-operative with the senses, only associations of the very lowest order could be formed. We should not each know the same world, but only each his own world. It is only by the accumulation, the perpetual shifting, and the thoroughgoing comparison of impressions, associating, dissociating, and reassociating them according to laws of understanding, that the order of true cognition is finally brought out of the chaos of sensuous impressions. This order, once established to any degree, exercises a constant control over the senses, and governs our attention in perception. This ferment of the mind, giving rise to an intellectual order, establishes the strongest associations among its elements, and some associations which are insoluble.

This process is not determined solely by the laws of association among the elements of the primitive impressions. There is always an *a priori*, or mnemonic element involved. Associations, either original to the mind or early established, control the formation of new ones. Of the manifold of a presentation, only parts are retained in the mind and remain adherent to one another; and this selection is determined *a priori*, by the orders of impressions already experienced, or else by an order inherent in the very nature of the intellect.

The "*a priori* theory" holds that this final order of cognition belongs to a pre-existent *intellectus ipse*, and is, in some respects at least, independent of the primitive orders of sense-associations. It holds that the final products of understanding contain elements not contained in the primitive impressions and educible by the permutations of them in reflection. It holds, in other words, that the higher faculties of knowledge are like the organs of sense, already existent and equipped for action prior to the occasions and independently of the matter of knowledge; that thinking is a process performed on the impressions of sense by powers which are not in any way determined by the matter of thoughts, and which consequently add to the result elements not contained in the sense-impressions.

If I understand the form in which you hold to this doctrine, it is that the elements added by understanding are objective ones, not forms of understanding, but facts of experience, which the understanding intuites in sense-impressions. As the material forces of light, heat, sound, pressure, and chemical change, could not of themselves, without the organs of sense, produce the sense-impressions, so neither can these pass on of their own inherent powers into abstract thought, but must come into the form of thought through a pre-existent organ of thought, acting by laws peculiar to itself. The *relations* of sensible objects — the *twoness* of two hats, the *superposition* of the book *on* the shelf, and the like matters of thought—are not, according to you, intuited by sense, any more than the color of a sonorous body is intuited by hearing or the tone of a colored body by sight. If we could not be conscious of the two hats without being conscious that they are *two*, or conscious of the book and the shelf without being conscious that the book is *on* the shelf, this would only prove that the understanding acts simultaneously with the sense, and that only the vaguest sense-impressions can be cognized without an action of the understanding upon them, to discover their relations.

To this I fully agree. In fact, I would go further, and maintain that there is no cognition by the senses in contradistinction from the mental powers generally. Instead of allowing two orders of independent cognitions, those of the senses and those of the intellect, I would maintain that all cognitions alike involve understanding in some degree, or some relation of the new impression to the previous content of the mind. An impression is cognized only when brought into consciousness; that is, into relations with what we have previously thought or felt or desired.

Nevertheless, I regard as valid the distinction of intuitive and abstract cognitions. The first we have without any consciousness of its cause; that is, without any other mental facts preceding and generating it in a recognizable general process, of which we may be reflectively conscious. Abstract cognitions we have as consequent upon others, and may attend to the process of their generation. In both, there is a sensuous basis, though not one separately cognizable. I can realize in thought a relation, like superposition, only by imagining things in this relation, — that is, by having subjectively determined sense-impressions of some things superposed on other things; and I arrive at the abstract notion of superposition by attending to compound objects which resemble each other in this respect, like my hat on my head, the book on the shelf, the inkstand on the table, &c. I maintain that relations which can by abstraction be thought as in objects, must exist in objects as intuited, and also that the intuition must be more or less understood, — brought under classes, or associated with previous experience, in order to be properly cognized at all.

You would regard the *color* and the *shape* of an object as intuited by two distinctly different modes of mental action. The sense of sight cognizes the color, the understanding the shape; for the shape can only be cognized by comparison with abstract forms, which "brings the object into relation" with other objects. But I maintain that the color of the object is cognized in precisely the same way, as being like or unlike the color of other objects. The color announces itself, — is presented to consciousness, by rousing all the colors of memory which similitude or contrast can by association connect with it. This is a process of which we are distinctly conscious only in its effect, as when we name the color. Without some movement towards this reasoning, there is no attention to the color, no cognition, no effective intuition. When this movement is also cognized as a process of thought, the cognition ceases to be intuitive, — is the result of conscious understanding, — but is none the less a movement of impressions, either objectively or subjectively determined, which are as sensuous as color. It is true, as you say, that "in the book singly, or in the shelf singly, there is no relation of superposition;" but the fact that you can attend to them singly, abstracting the relation, does not prove that, after being presented, they need to be "brought into relation" by an act of understanding. It is by an abstractive act, indeed, that you attend to them singly and out of the relation which is as much in the sensuous intuition of them as their colors or shapes. It is a favorite formula with me that there are two kinds of memory or reminiscence, — the memory of representation and the memory of judgment. In the first, we recognize singular facts of experience individually; in the second, in their generalized results. In the first, through the pictures of imagination; in the second, by the language of abstract thought. Every item of experience adds to the cogency of a common-sense judgment, though not distinctly recognized or consciously added to the weight of evidence. But, if it is recognized as a ground of evidence, it must be as an instance of a rule, or as a fact similar to other facts. For what is it in the intuition which is cognizable, unless it be its likeness or unlikeness to other intuitions? The book on the shelf, the hat on the head, the inkstand on the table, are similar compound or plural objects in respect to the relation of superposition. This similitude is not apprehended by the senses independently of mental operations; but neither is the color nor the weight nor the texture of these objects apprehended by the senses, independently of memory, imagination, and abstraction.

What you call intellectual intuition, I should regard as belonging to all cognitions alike. Indeed, the distinction between the intuitive and the non-intuitive knowledges is rather a logical than a psychological one. Cognitions which cannot be analyzed by introspection are called intuitions. These are the data, the axioms, the premises of logical processes, and the conclusions of such processes, being distinctly exhibited as consequent on other cognitions, are non-intuitive, derivative knowledges. But no amount of introspection can analyze a cognition down to the bare, unrelated data of the senses, strictly speaking; for this would be to dissolve all the links which bind the sensuous impression to consciousness, and to extrude it from the mind altogether.

But we may hypothetically descend to such a basis of knowledge. In accordance with physiological science, we may suppose, with Mill and Bain, that the higher mental faculties are formed by experience, that consciousness is a growth out of such primitive elements, a growth governed by laws of association, at first wholly chronological, or by the association of contiguity, — and afterwards more and more dependent, through memory, on associations of likeness and unlikeness. Though this theory has not yet shown itself competent to explain all mental phenomena satisfactorily, it has not been shown to be incompetent to this end, and seems to me in all respects a legitimate hypothesis.

It seems to me that the experiential philosophy is far from ignoring, as you affirm, the distinction of the "must" and the "is," though it doubtless makes less account of the distinction than the *a priori* school. The fact itself, that some of our beliefs are unconditional and do not admit, so far as we can conceive, of any exceptions, is recognized fully and explained by this school on their principles. The range of our beliefs is determined in its capacity beforehand, by the range of our conceptive powers. But our conceptions are not limited to the range of beliefs in general, though in some matters we cannot conceive the contradictory of what we believe. The belief is then said to be necessary. This is the phenomenon to be explained. The doctrine that our conceptive powers are acquired by experience, as well as our beliefs, does not ignore this problem, though it makes it a less fundamental one in philosophy. If the testimony of all our experiences, including those which have fashioned language and our conceptive powers, be in favor of any proposition, this has all the marks of what is called Universality. "The universal is more than the general," as you justly say, since conscious generalization must form a predication in terms which have previously been separated in our conceptions of them. Thus, in "all matter has weight," the term "matter" connotes attributes which we can conceive without thinking of weight. But "all bodies are extended," unites terms each of which would be inconceivable without the other. Bodies may have other properties besides extension; but these cannot be conceived of, separated from extension. When language is exactly adequate to express a fact which is invariable and unconditional in our experience, it expresses what is called a universal truth.

You say that, in reading such explanations as this, you are "continually conscious of an unsatisfied expectation." You wish to know not the "how," but the "why" of the matter; that is, I suppose, you demand to know why you *must* believe certain facts, not simply how such beliefs are generated. But it seems to me that the "why" of the "must" is a contradiction of terms, when the "must" is an ultimate premise. There are two kinds of necessity in propositions, — a deductive necessity which contains the "why," and a logically fundamental necessity which excludes any question of fact. The Pythagorean proposition is as necessary as any axiom of geometry; but reasons for it are required to compel assent. Assent to a belief can be compelled only by other beliefs, in themselves irresistible, and brought to bear on the proposition by the irresistible connection of beliefs or by logical laws. The *a priori* school founds philosophy on such beliefs and laws, maintains their eternal and indestructible existence as mental facts, and refuses to listen to any explanation of how the mental facts might be generated as an inductive consequence of the actual orders of concrete, sensible experience, and be made *apodeictic* by the limits in the conceptive faculties, which are also determined by experience.

I do not understand that Mr. Mill accepts the distinction of phenomena and noumena as a valid division of real existences. On the contrary, he only accepts the question implied in the distinction, and decides that noumena are non-existent *to us.* The discrimination is a valid one, even if noumena do not exist at all. To say that phenomena are all that exists is to say that, in knowing phenomena, we know all the natures that exist. To affirm the existence of noumena is — at any rate to the positivist — to affirm that something exists of an incognizable nature. Mr. Mill is surely not guilty of accepting "that pernicious theory of *Dinge an sich,*" in simply entertaining a question of them, and dismissing them to the limbo of incognizability. On the contrary, he thereby signalizes that important doctrine of positivism, — the relativity of knowledge, — that the only objects immediately known are really mental states, effects in us which we attribute, according to their connections, either to a self or to an external world, without further capacity for knowing more about their subjects.

You appear to me to use the words "noumena" and "objects" in rather unusual senses, when, in the first place, you say that "noumena are known *in* phenomena, which are their manifestation." You define a noumenon as the something which appears, the phenomena being "only appearances." I had supposed the phenomenon itself to be the something which appears and disappears, and the noumenon to be a supposed permanent reality, which, if known, could not be known by the occasional appearance and disappearance of phenomena, but only by the "pure intelligence." Hence, their name. Noumena should not be confounded with 'the permanent possibilities of phenomena," which are determined by the general laws of phenomena, and represented by our expectations and anticipations; for, by definition, noumena are actual permanences, which, if known, are known absolutely, — that is, immediately as they are, as permanent immutable entities. Laws are permanent, and are really the grounds of our expectations; but laws are *abstractions,* not "things in themselves." If the laws or relations of phenomena were immediately known, — that is, independently of the frequency of occurrence and the individual likenesses of phenomena, — then we should have an *a priori* and immediate knowledge of the immutable and the necessary, or a knowledge of noumena.

Secondly, you surprise me by asking if Idealism is not "the very negation of objective science?" By objective science, I understand the science of the objects of knowledge, as contradistinguished from the processes and faculties of knowing. Does Idealism deny that there are such objects? Is not its doctrine rather a definition of the nature of these objects than a denial of their existence? There is nothing in positive science, or the study of phenomena and their laws, which Idealism conflicts with. (See Berkeley.) Astronomy is just as real a science, as true an account of phenomena and their laws, if phenomena are only mental states, as on the other theory.

You say that "the facts and laws of the universe recorded in Humboldt's 'Cosmos' were in no wise conditional on the existence of Humboldt's mind, or of any other human mind." I readily admit that little or nothing characteristic of an individual mind like Humboldt's would be likely to appear among the recorded facts and laws of the universe; yet these facts and laws are accounts of things seen and heard and weighed and smelt and tasted. They are the orders of invariable and unconditional sequences and coexistences among the sensations of colors and sounds and pressures and odor and savors, none of which could exist without a mind. These facts and laws, you say, "survive the death of generation after generation of scientific men;" but, as they describe what only eyes can see and ears hear, some sort of minds, human or other, scientific or vulgar, are essential to their continued existence. What would be those aspects of the heavens which astronomers observe and predict, if no minds were in existence? Nothing surely but a potentiality. A statement of what can be seen under given circumstances must surely include the circumstances of the presence of eyes with a mind to see.

You ask to be admitted to my confidence by learning from me my speculative beliefs concerning the existence of a God and the immortality of the soul, and promise not to be shocked by any revelations I may make. The verdict of "not proven" is the kind of judgment I have formed on these matters; but not on that account am I warranted in taking up a position against the general opinion of my fellow-citizens, for this would be to become as illogical as the most confident among them. Atheism is speculatively as unfounded as theism, and practically can only spring from bad motives. I mean, of course, dogmatic atheism. A *bigoted* atheist seems to me the meanest and narrowest of men. In fact, practical considerations determine that a state of suspended judgment on these themes is the state of stable equilibrium. I have no desire to wake into a strange, unknown future life, and I can discover no valid reasons for any confidence in such a waking. As purely speculative or scientific doctrines, these demand assent no more cogently than a theory that some distant planet is inhabited, or, better still, that the planet is largely composed of granite or some other stated substance, — for we might have a sentimental bias in favor of an inhabited planet.

Practical grounds are really the basis of belief in the doctrines of theology. The higher moral sentiments have attached themselves so strongly to these traditions that doubts of them seem to the believers like contempt for all that is noble or worthy in human character. This paralogism even goes so far as to declare man's life utterly worthless, unless it is to be prolonged to infinity; that is, I suppose, the worth of any part — say a year's life — is infinitesimal, even if filled with the purest enjoyments, the noblest sympathies, and the most beneficent activities. In whichever conclusion respecting a future life I might seek at last to cease from questioning and to wilfully resolve my doubts, I should never cease to repudiate such a view of the value of the present human life.

You perceive that on practical grounds I openly dissent from orthodoxy, but I may appear to you to evade the speculative questions. I do not think that I do; for though I may not consistently hold on all occasions the even balance of judgment and the open mind, which I think as proper in such matters as in all others, it is at any rate my design to do so. Whichever way we yield assent, we feel ourselves carried, not by evidence, but by the prejudices of feeling. We fall into one or another form of superstitious belief. Suspension of judgment appears to me to be demanded, therefore, not merely by the evidence, but as a discipline of character, — that faith and moral effort may not waste themselves on idle dreams, but work among the realities of life. Practical theism, if it means, as it ordinarily does, the exclusion from the mind of all evidence not favorable to received religious doctrines, seems to me to put religious sentiment in a false position, — one incompatible, not only with intellectual freedom, but with the soundest development of religious character, — with that unreserved devotion to the best *we know*, which tries all things, and holds fast to that which is good.

Very few men could confess a belief in a God or a disbelief in one, without expressing more than their speculative convictions. So far from being like their opinions on the law of gravitation, it would almost necessarily be with feelings of exultation, enthusiasm, and hope, or with bitterness, contempt, or despair, — so strong are the associations of feeling attached to this word. Nevertheless, it is a doctrine of positivism that the real interests of moral and religious culture, no less than those of scientific knowledge, are quite independent in fact (and might be made so in education) of these doctrines and associations. And this is also my belief.

I sincerely regret to learn from you that your views have brought you into such difficulties as to render it necessary to give up your profession. Would teaching private pupils, fitting boys for college, be an employment you would like? It is one of the most remunerative to those who are in the way to get it; and, although I am not in that way, I think it would not be difficult to find such employment. I should be happy to use all my influence to this end. I am told that there is a good opportunity at present to start a school for young ladies in Boston; for, though there are several excellent schools kept by ladies, there are none equal to Professor Torrey's, which he gave up when he came to Cambridge.

But I hope that I have misunderstood you, and that you will be able to continue, as a religious instructor, to exemplify how irrelevant metaphysics really are to the clergyman's true influence, — quite as much so, I think, as to that of the scientific teacher. The pursuit of philosophy ought to be a side study. Nothing so much justifies that shameful assumption by ecclesiastical bodies of control over speculative opinions as the inconsiderate preaching of such opinions, in place of the warnings, encouragements, sympathies, and persuasions of the true religious instructor. The lessons which he has to deliver are really very easy to understand, but hard to live up to. To help to live up to the true ideals of life seems to me the noblest, if not the only, duty of the preacher.

To Miss Jane Norton.

Sunday morning [November or December, 1867].

I am not so sure as you seem to be that ——'s "house *must* fall," especially if the "overwhelming agents" are as scrupulous as you think becoming in the "perfected philosopher." I am not one of those who believe that truth will prevail by its own inherent force, — that is, the weight of evidence. The force by which truth will prevail, if it ever does, is the force of flat contradiction, undermining and beating down inveterate prejudice. Unless the floods and the winds beat upon that house, it is just as secure on the sand as on the rock. The temptation there is for assaulting a reputation like ——'s is the obvious one that such personal reputations are the strongest props of the prejudices we oppose. Almost all false dogmas gain currency through the reputation for wisdom of their authors and promulgators; and, as prejudice is more than error, so it must be met by a force more soul-compelling than evidence. A just indignation is not inconsistent with such a "balance of *abstract* wisdom and justice" as can be maintained in the presence of *concrete* folly and wrong. Simple truth will outweigh *mere* error (else it would not be truth); but it requires the strains and blows of passion to overcome the resistances and tenacities of prejudice, and, if the passion be subject to justice, compassion for the enemy is weakness.

But passionate opposition is no more likely to be just than is tenacious prejudice to be true; and any appearance of such feeling is likely to lessen the effect of just criticism. Consequently, I am greatly indebted to you for your suggestions touching certain words and phrases in my article, which you have promised to note for me.

Forgive the aphorismatic emphasis of these remarks.

CHAPTER V.

FOR more than a year now, I find nothing from Chauncey's pen. During this period, or probably a little earlier, it was gradually brought to the knowledge of the friends who then saw him oftenest that he had yielded to an infirmity which afterwards caused him much unhappiness.[1] Irregular habits of work and sleep, physical inactivity, and the practice of excessive smoking, had brought on sleeplessness and physical suffering, from which he sought relief in stimulants. The breaking up of old haunts and habits, resulting from the departure or marriage of friends,[2] and the solitary and monotonous nature of his ill-adjusted tasks upon the almanac, induced a great depression of mind. At about this time, the Nortons went abroad for several years;[3] and, in losing them, he lost one of his chief social resources and supports. His work now fell greatly in arrears;[4] he excused himself from

[1] After anxious consideration, I think it best to speak of this subject openly and fully.

[2] In the fall of 1868, Professor Gurney, his most intimate companion, was married. Mr. Gurney had removed from Little's Block in 1863, yet he continued to see much of Chauncey until near the period which we have now reached.

[3] In the summer of 1868.

[4] President Runkle writes: "On July 1, 1866, the whole of the work upon the Lunar Ephemeris was given to Chauncey and myself. We divided this work evenly between us. As nearly as I now remember, Chauncey did his work the first year. The second year, he fell behind, and I helped him out. The third year, he delayed his work till late, and then told me that he could not do it, and gave up the contract."

all invitations of friends, absented himself from his clubs, and took little satisfaction — indeed, had little, if any, power — in writing, or in his favorite speculations.

This state of things was a cause of the greatest surprise to his friends, and of no little alarm. At last, they communicated with him on the subject through one of their number, and with happy results: after one ineffectual endeavor to recover from his weakness, he made a second attempt, with good success. His friends gathered about him, and, without his observing it, engaged him more actively in correspondence, in visits, and in social occupations; and he gradually recovered his spirits and the full vigor of his mind. In a year or two, they had reason to think that he occasionally fell back, and there is no doubt that afterwards he yielded at intervals to this evil tendency as long as he lived; but these lapses were not frequent.

Through it all, he seemed like one who was the victim of a disease: there was no baseness about him, and no love of low companions or low habits. Sad it was, beyond description, to witness the temporary wrecking of that fine intelligence; to see his suffering, his heroic efforts to recover himself, his imperfect success: that he was blameworthy, I shall not deny: that he was permanently injured by these habits, I believe; his judgment was a little less serene, — he was a little less faithful to the catholic tenets of his philosophy. But it was a good thing to see how small was the injury to the best part of him, — how simple, sweet, and wholly uncorrupted his character and his heart remained, how soon the freshness of his intellectual interest revived, and how largely he regained his old power in the exercise of the balanced and masterly faculties of his mind upon the most important philosophical questions of his time.

A very little thing would have saved him. Had his employment been one which demanded a daily conformity to rules and hours of work; had he been married, or had any social duties; had it perhaps happened that any one of his old intimates remained by him, with whom he might sit, either to talk or to speculate in social silence, as of old, — he would never have gone wrong. But it had fallen to the lot of this warm-hearted man — built, outwardly and inwardly, for the enjoyment of all that is best in human intercourse — to live, for the most part, the perilous life of a thinker, a life which was not cheered, supported, and admonished through the more intimate social relations, nor subjected to the wholesome influences that might *command* regularity in the daily ordering of it.

A letter from Mrs. Lesley which alludes to these unhappy facts has a reference to her satisfaction at this time in thinking of his intimate relations with the Nortons, — a circumstance in which all who cared for him rejoiced, as the chief source of happiness and safety for him in his later years. It would, indeed, be difficult to say too much of the delicacy and the assiduity with which these friends now sought to draw him away from the solitude which was his chief danger, into the sunlight of their sympathy. "From 1862," writes Mrs. Lesley, "I saw less of Chauncey. Our own work in life became more and more imperious and exacting; and though we now and then had a lovely visit from him, of which the remembrance will always be like a treasure laid up in heaven, yet many were the visits he promised and planned which never were made. We heard with rejoicing, however, of the friendship he had formed with the Norton family; and, when we met, he would read to me with delight his letters from them. I felt that my prayers for him were answered in the good influences that surrounded him from these sources, and that the appreciative friendship of others would give him all that time and circumstances had denied to us the opportunity to offer."

To Mr. Abbot.

CAMBRIDGE, Feb. 10, 1869.

I have had the proposition [1] of your letter of so long ago, so long in debate that I presume you have concluded ere this that my silence means dissent. This I am now persuaded is the true interpretation, though contrary to the current maxim.

I owe you an apology for this delay in answering your kind letter, to which you wished an immediate reply. But I really desired to see my way clear to meeting your wishes and my own, touching the essay on the positivists' religion; and I regret very much that I cannot count upon myself as good for so difficult and delicate a task. My pen has of late forsaken the paths of speculation; and I have not been able to persuade it back.

I do not feel competent, nor do I care, to address, unprovoked, a large promiscuous audience, the majority of whom judge by texts and phrases, and apply the touchstone of magical words, — and so think they think. Something more stimulating, like misrepresentation by an opponent, or like personal debate, must inspire me. A cold thesis, served in a book, does not incite the speculative appetite with me; and I confess to the heartiest sympathy with Plato's preference for a *man*, who can question and answer, rather than for a book, which must say much at random, or demand an artist's skill and imagination in the writer. One of the most important of the teacher's or preacher's qualifications, yet one of the rarest, is a knowledge of the hearer's mind, so that his discourse may answer to something, or else raise clear and profitable questions. Most philosophical books, lectures, and sermons seem

[1] A request that Chauncey would contribute an article on "The Religious Aspects of Positivism" to a volume which it was then proposed to publish.

to me either mechanical performances, or else the offspring of a subtile vanity and desire for intellectual sympathy. Let one persuade many, and he becomes confirmed and convinced, and cares for no better evidence. Men will not agree in the fashions of their dress, in manners, or "beliefs," till reduced to the naked facts of experience; and the precepts and methods of modern science, every day extended to new fields of inquiry, will, in these, I believe, do more to invigorate and correct the human understanding than all the essays of all the philosophers.

The old philosophy is ignored by science, not opposed by it, and must take its chance in the reconstruction of speculative thought without the aid of the traditions, the loyalties, and the patriotisms which now certify so much to so many. Why are we Protestants rather than Catholics, Unitarians rather than Orthodox, radicals rather than reactionists? Certainly, not for the kind of reason which makes us Newtonians.

Positivism, to be sure, so far as it pretends to be a philosophy at all, is more than the body of the sciences. It must be a system of the universal methods, hypotheses, and principles which are founded on them, and if not a universal science, in an absolute sense, yet must be coextensive with actual knowledge, and exhibit the consilience of the sciences.

But while positivism ignores religion in the narrower sense of the word, — that is, the body thereof, — it nevertheless, unlike the old atheism, does not reject the religious spirit. It is rather constrained — not for itself, but through the earnest, practical characters of many of its disciples — to yield some worthy object to religious devotion, which they think they find in the interests of humanity. But this is an affair of character, not of intelligence. If you define the end of philosophy to be the attainment of religious objects and truths, then positivism is no philosophy. The religion of positivism is no part of its philosophy, but is only a religion which consists with its rigid methods and restraints. Mr. Mill maintains that such a religion is not only possible, but has actually controlled the lives and formed the characters of men of this way of thinking.

I see that, after declining to enter into this discussion in your book, I have straightway been tempted to take it up in my letter; but my aim is only to show how such an essay as you desire would not properly come from one who is a positivist in spite of religion: it should rather come from some one who is religious in spite of his positivism. I could do better in the way of defending this philosophy from theological attacks than in adapting a religion to it.

I hope to hear from you soon, in spite of my ill-deserts, and to hear that you are prospering.

To Miss Jane Norton, in Europe.

CAMBRIDGE, Feb. 15, 1869.

I returned to-day from passing the Sunday with James Thayer, in Milton. The visit served as a temporary and partial diversion from the stagnation of Cambridge, or rather of this old room. Thayer has two of the brightest little boys that I have ever known, — vigorous, sensible, and full of frolicsome life from the beginning to the end of the day.

I am going as soon as I can, to take my work into town, and work with Mr. Runkle at the Technological Institute. This will involve the walk in or out of town, or both, every fair day. Walking without companionship or necessity or special object, is a dreadful bore; but you see I am going to make it a sort of necessity. Meantime, I am making a heroic virtue of it, for it goes much against the grain, like resuscitation from drowning.

I did not see Mr. Lesley during his short stay in this neighborhood; but I saw Mrs. Lesley and Mary and Meggy once before they went to Philadelphia, and found them well and happy. Mr. Lesley's health has very much improved, and he appears this winter, I hear, almost as well as ever; but he carefully refrains from hard work, and occupies himself chiefly with his duties as librarian of the Philosophical Institute. . . .

I went on Wednesday to hear Mr. Emerson read the poets and comment on them. Ben Jonson was his principal theme, and, on the whole, the discourse was interesting. At least, I did not get to sleep, nor even sleepy. This reading is the only one of the course that I have heard. Some former ones are said to have been much more interesting, especially the previous one on Shakespeare. There is, of course, a double interest in these exercises. To learn what pleases Mr. Emerson in a poet, is almost as interesting as it is to listen to his readings and comments.

I don't know when I have written so long a news letter, and all this without a sketch of an essay, or even a hint of one; and besides so incoherent and childlike! I shall certainly let you read my essay on political parties in manuscript, since you prefer it; but when it will be written is impossible for me to conjecture. I think that voluminous reading will be necessary for preparation; and meantime a dozen other fine theses will present themselves for reflection and study, — that is such study as an indolent leisure permits. When I stop dreaming and win back again the spirit of work, then the Muse may come also.

I have lately declined to write, at Mr. Abbot's request, an essay on the Religious Aspect of Positivism for a book of Essays to be published in the spring by the Free Religious Association; also reviews solicited for the "Nation" and the "North American Review." In short, there is no end to the catalogue of my delinquencies; but there is that sort of pleasure in confessing them, which confirmed invalids sometimes take in recounting their afflictions and infirmities to sympathizing friends. The sinner, when his faults are not malevolent or contagious, is a similar egotistical object of benevolent interest.

You must have read Mr. Goldwin Smith's paper in the "North American Review," on the English Revolution. It interested me very much, though I was inclined to question some of his estimates of men and events, — with no right, however, to dispute them. . . .

How fortunate we are, in this country, where the most radical changes are provided for, in our very organization, with no huge hulks of ancient privilege to block the way! This reminds me of a question Mr. Curtis proposed in one of our old walks in Ashfield: whether any privileged class, like a priesthood or an aristocracy or the slave masters, ever voluntarily resigned their powers. We could recall no instance in history. Such powers are always taken away by force or resigned from fear of it.

To the Same.

CAMBRIDGE, March 22, 1869.

I cannot believe that you designedly imposed on me as a punishment, the difficult task, which would require much reflection, of giving clear and satisfactory reasons for my refusal of Mr. Abbot's proposition about the Essay on the Religious Aspects of Positivism; but I feel myself in the condition of the school-boy who can only answer the demand to explain his misconduct by the summary but inexplicit reason "because," — an answer by which he enounces, at least, his faith in the universality of causation, or in the doctrine of "the sufficient reason" without which nothing happens.

It might possibly be easier to write the essay than to say why not do it. Both would be difficult expositions; and to attempt the essay would perhaps be the directest means of demonstrating my incompetency. There may appear but a shade of difference between a general essay on the religious bearings of positivism and a defence of this philosophy and its adherents, from the attacks and misrepresentations of theological opponents. But the difference is really material. I may be the swiftest racer on this course; yet to no purpose, since I lack rider and spur. If I were more of a Comtist than I am, — that is, had a proselyting interest in the direct practical bearings of positivism, — I should rush, I suppose, to a platform, or into print before the great and discriminating public. As it is, I have much greater confidence in the indirect influence of the causes which have made this philosophy prevail, for determining and exerting its religious effects, than I have in the discussion of themes, which, in the common estimation, are more specifically religious.

Our side cannot now help being heard on its substantial merits, and has no need of pulpits. The effect on the character and direction of men's faiths, which the possession of a large and extensive body of unquestionable and united truths is fitted to produce, is one which follows naturally, in whatever direction this body of knowledge has disciplined the philosophical dispositions to act, within the legitimate limits of speculation. To take in enough of natural philosophy to make one feel sure that the weather is not ruled by any free moral agents, though it diminishes many other assurances, much supposed weather-wisdom, is a great step in advance. To take such steps in social science must have the effect to turn men's attention to new social interests, no longer directly dependent on the social powers of the prayerful, the hopeful, the angry, the wilful, or the affectionate child, but on those of the foreseeing, contriving, intelligent man. Moral effort, though, as before, arising in the burnings of the heart, will then gain through its light a far-reaching influence, which its warmth does not possess. On this aspect of the subject, I might write to the verge of sentimentality; but this, I suppose, is not what Mr. Abbot wanted from my pen.

What positivism has to say about the great religious doctrines of "supernatural causes" and the "future life," is the question of the theologically trained mind; and, if positivism has nothing to say on these things, how can it justify its pretension to be a philosophy and a competent guide of life? In this question of authority, its not unskilful opponents strike at a vital point; but the blow can be parried, and in return positivism can more pertinently demand of the so-called religious philosophies *their* authority for saying any thing on these themes. To the reply that life would not be worth improving, that moral effort would be vain, without some such grounds of action as religion presents; that any questioning of these must be settled before life can have an intelligent interest for us, or human nature appear to be superior to the brutal, — to such replies, the kind of return which positivism is most naturally and charitably inclined to, is not polemical but hygienic. The formidable aspects of these themes, the associations of feelings which have grown up with them, are of the nature of diseases, infectious or transmitted, — but not unavoidable at the outset, as our ignorance and the limits of our possible development are. They are traditional distortions of development, which the natural man, even in attaining the most advanced moral growth, need not undergo. This view of the matter (the doctrine of distorted development) is the positive counterpart of the orthodox doctrine of "original depravity."

The cure should not be "heroic," since this method attacks the patient as well as the disease. Opening to his activity a mental and moral and even philosophical life, infinitely varied in objects which invite attention and incite to effort, and wide enough for a rational spirit of speculation (the pursuits of positive science and their various directions), — complete pre-occupation is the treatment. If this should be objected to as practically only a culture in "*mere* morality," it would be, as Mr. Emerson says, "much as if one should say, 'Poor God! with nobody to help him.'"

In my correspondence with Mr. Abbot about the direct bearings of positivism on the subject of religion, I was conscious of adopting, in a mild way, the heroic treatment, attacking under indirect forms not his opinions, but the still too superstitious spirit, in which he seemed to me to hold them, — in which he seemed to attribute still, in his understanding, the weight of valid evidence to the force of merely associated interests. To dissociate these interests, not to criticise his doctrines, was my only end in the debate; and I should not be willing to enter again into any such debate, except it be again with a person equally candid, unprejudiced, and intelligent, — certainly not with the public.

My regard for the social and political attitude of radicalism, as the extreme and yet the logically valid result of Protestantism, is very widely separated from my interest in the several philosophies, practical and speculative, which in the minds of the several radicals is so intimately (and to them so naturally) associated with this attitude. As a distinct body of religious thinkers, or as other than a few among liberals of many varieties, I have little sympathy with them, and not much respect for their intelligence. Perhaps you will think me a little prejudiced.

I have so little space left in which to tell the news, or even to make such a sharp turn and deep descent, that I am constrained to regard this as *the* essay in question (abortive and abbreviated though it be), instead of the letter I meant to write.

To Mr. Norton.

CAMBRIDGE, July 9, 1869.

I have got so much accustomed to contemplating vast wastes of time behind me, which are infertile not so much from the lack of cultivation as from the long droughts to which they are subject, that I look upon my delay in answering your letter as a kind of fatality, of which I regard and suffer the consequences without self-reproach. Nevertheless, I am not a fatalist; for conscience has its share in determining me this sultry July morning to break my long silence. What roused my conscience under such an unpropitious sky, it would be difficult to say, — unless, like a beleaguered power, it wakes to find the siege raised and its enemies gone. . . .

Commencement was certainly a much finer day than I remember at its old dates; and the return to something like the old rational festivities at the dinner was a marked improvement in the interests of the day. The old readings of the necrology were not revived, and even the printed list is at last reduced to bare names and dates. Harvard now counts among its honored children only its benefactors, and even these are regarded as only partly paying the debt due to the great interests of learning. Attorney-General Hoar pronounced over those rich citizens who were not benefactors of the colleges "that saddest epitaph ever recorded in history, 'And the rich man also died, and *was buried.*'" . . .

The change in the government of the College by the new mode of electing its overseers was much eulogized, and with justice; for each year shows more clearly the value and importance of the change. One incident of it, which has lately interested me, is the chance it affords for a fair trial by competent electors of a modification of Mr. Hare's scheme. The adoption of this modified plan at the next choice of overseers is now very probable. The committee of elections have been instructed to inquire into it, and to adopt it if they find it has substantial advantages. The modification of the scheme which this would involve — that is, the irresponsible choice of nominees by it, and the responsible choice of officers from these by plurality votes — has interested me a good deal during the past few days on account of its bearings on general politics, — a view of the matter which I think has not been considered in detail by any who have studied it. I cannot do better, I imagine, by way of ascent to philosophy, than to give you some account of my lucubrations on this subject.

Having studied the practical workings of this mode of counting votes, and found that it is made remarkably simple by certain practical devices for the roughly just distribution of the surplus and scattering votes to the candidates of second choice, my attention was called to the advantages of the proposed double election, — first of candidates by minorities, and then, from these, of officers by pluralities, — through which it is intended to prevent the virtual control of an election by a majority composed of minorities acting in concert. This is the main advantage of the modification, and has been duly considered; but there is also another advantage in it, through which majorities get their rightful power, and are made to assume their rightful responsibilities. To make this clear, I must go forward to the conclusions of my speculation, and regard the community as divided into two bodies, — although so far as the exercise of the suffrage is at present determined with us, these would be composed of the same individuals. The two classes ought to be, first, the governing class, who exercise government through the suffrage; and, secondly, those of the governed whose wishes and whose judgments of their own interests ought to be consulted. The functions and the implied qualifications and the consequent extent of these two classes, ought to be regarded as quite distinct, though both of them will and must include the same individuals, when these belong at once to the governors and the governed. In logical language, these classes are communicant in their extension, though distinct in their comprehension.

The right to decide upon the choice of public officers, and the enactment of public measures, implies more than self-government. It implies, as Mr. Mill has so clearly pointed out, the right to govern others, and it ought to go along with responsibility, and with the power to enforce these decisions even in the last resort, that is, by force. This power in democratic communities resides, therefore, in the majority of male adults, — the potential rebel or anarchical power of the community. On the other hand, the right to be consulted and heard with reference to such decisions, not merely through the courtesy of electors or by the moral force of free discussions, but also by the exercise of a legal or constitutional control over the will of majorities, — this right does not involve ultimate responsibility, but only an intelligent interest in public affairs, and it belongs justly to all whose wishes and knowledge can be of any real service to themselves or others; that is, it belongs to all intelligent adults of both sexes. In this division of rights and powers, we have a solution of the woman's suffrage question on what I conceive to be its real merits; and, by the proposed modification of Mr. Hare's scheme, we have the means of carrying this solution into effect. At the same time, without modifying essentially the responsible suffrage or the present laws of election, we can put a highly just and civilized scheme of nomination in the place of a grossly unjust and barbarous one, through which caucuses and conventions not only fail to represent the wishes of intelligent minorities, but practically usurp the powers even of majorities, driving and penning them like sheep. This reform might be effected even without legal or constitutional enactments, if party organizations could be induced to consent to it, and use their influence for it, so great is their power for good or for evil. That they would be the last to consent, is a proof of the evil.

Under law, the scheme would work in detail somewhat like this: Let the names of every intelligent adult, of either sex, who desires it, be registered at the nearest voting-place, and let copies of these registers be sent to a central bureau, and, between certain convenient dates, let each such person send to this bureau a list of nominations as long as each chooses, but written in the order of preference, — one vote counting in the final distribution for only one candidate. Newspapers, caucuses, and public meetings may aid in suggesting candidates, or candidates may offer themselves through any means of publication. Such extra-governmental agencies would still be of service, though without such a virtual usurpation of powers as now obtains.

Let the lists of nominations so made, and containing twice or thrice as many names as there are offices to be filled, be then sent to the voting-places, and let a choice be then made from this list by each elector, and the final decision be made by the electoral body at large, on the simple principle of pluralities. This will, in case of a division of the community on any prominent question, amount to a decision by a responsible majority, without neglecting or sacrificing minor questions or interests, as is so often done in our present political contests.

The scheme in this shape would not preclude the admission of women to the electoral body proper and to the legislature, when by practice in politics they shall have learned to make laws on other than parental and nursery principles. In native force and influence, they are not inferior to many non-militant men who now have the suffrage. But I have said enough to show the two principal advantages, — the prevention of "log-rolling" by minorities and the assumption of responsibility by majorities, — belonging to this modification of Mr. Hare's scheme, and to show the ease with which it could be put into practice, the cure it would effect of some of our worst political evils, and the solution it affords of the woman's suffrage question. Could any political device have more or more important utilities?

To Miss Grace Norton.

[July 17, 1869.]

. . . But I know you will forgive this trifling when I confess to you that I am debarred from any but the most serious and necessary *talk*, by the continuance of a cold which has begun to show unmistakable signs of being based on, and in league with, a whooping-cough, — caught, at my last visit to Milton, from the little Thayers. What a fall is this! To say nothing of the fate of livelier talk, — to have even the maturest utterances of experience and calm reflection, constantly interrupted by the loud and impertinent explosions and strangulations which I suffer in common with infants! Can you wonder that I do not preserve my wonted gravity with the unimpeded pen? On Monday, I mean to seek a remedy in a new treatment lately introduced in France, and also found very successful by Dr. George Hayward, of Boston, though long known, he says (in the "Medical Journal"), to the English; instead of flying to some watering place or to the mountain air, I shall seek relief in the exhalations of the lime-vats of the Cambridge gas-house. . . .

I felt [in reading Mill's "Subjection of Women"] what I suppose is a very common aversion to being completely convinced by cold logic, with only a little irony for sauce, — with not one word of persuasion, no warmth of eloquence. But, being convinced, I am now persuaded that I agreed substantially with Mr. Mill before. The main points of the argument are familiar grounds with a student of Mr. Mill's writings. First, his scepticism, — in the true Socratic sense, — his detection of opinions as founded on a false persuasion of knowledge.

He points out the impossibility of knowing, without such experimentation as the subject has never received, what the nature of women is, or of men either, as distinguished from the highly artificialized characteristics which are due to tradition and custom. I rebelled against his tracing historically the legal subjection of woman in marriage, and her other disabilities, solely to the worst dispositions of barbarians, — to their love of domineering. I fancied that I had seen in little boys and girls differences which guided them, as by instinct, to choose from the very first the means, and to exert the social powers and influences, which were calculated to gain for them their greatest successes as men and women. But, on reflection, I found, with only indirect aid from Mr. Mill, that I had probably overestimated the simplicity of the natures of boys and girls; that I had not considered what little heaps of traditions and customs they really are, after all; how subtly observant and sympathetic they are; how constantly, though unwittingly, parents and nurses, friends and teachers, are impressing them with artificialities of feeling and manner, thought and expression, — while they have nothing to unlearn, no *a priori* prejudices to stand in the way of the most rapid acquisition of whatever is not opposed to their simple common nature: so that, as soon as they begin to regard themselves as little men and women, — as they do almost as soon as they begin to speak, — they begin to command and to coax, to frown and to smile, and to play ruler or subject, according as their ample experience points the way to their advantage. How difficult to find, then, the nature that lies back of all culture, or to find the difference of sex, if any, which belongs to it. Indeed, we may define the human being as one whose nature, as we know it, descends mainly by other channels than those of the blood, — in the spiritual and invisible currents of an extremely complex, artificial life, without which the human nature is immediately lost in the brute, and with reference to which the original nature is more a receptive than a productive power; though, possibly, human life might spring anew from an untaught infant colony.

Next, we come to Mr. Mill's familiar position, "the law of liberty," — which is allied to his scepticism. Let this unknown nature, whatever it may be, make itself known through perfect freedom to work itself out; unless it prove on trial to be bad, that is, positively injurious, and not merely contrary to custom. The stupidity of not merely anticipating without trial, but also re-enacting, the supposed laws of human nature, is shown up in this happy way. "One thing we may be certain of, that what is contrary to women's nature to do they never will be made to do by giving their nature free play. The anxiety of mankind to interfere in behalf of nature for fear lest nature should not succeed in effecting its purpose, is an altogether unnecessary solicitude," &c. And so he challenges the marriage laws to show some better origin for their justification than the old barbaric dogma that *might* not only does, but should, make *right.*

He acknowledges that all other barbarities, like slavery and absolute government in their various forms, which have yielded to modern civilization, have been compelled to yield. The legal subjection of women is an anomaly in the highest civilization, the one barbarity which has had too much strength in it to be overcome by the forces of civilization. And it seemed to me at first that herein was a necessity which made any thing more than mere mitigations by civilized laws an Utopian project. The relation of a superior will to an inferior one might be rendered in a high degree attractive and the source of great happiness and great virtues. Indeed, the virtues of chivalry and generosity are founded on such relations. Will the world resign all its romantic virtues to the humdrum of loving equality and justice? The possession of tyrannical power, with the virtue to refrain from its abuse, is an attractive position and character, not only to those who have them, but also to those who are their objects; so much so that, as Mr. Mill says, "It is part of the irony of life that the strongest feelings of devoted gratitude of which human nature seems to be susceptible are called forth in human beings towards those who, having the power entirely to crush their earthly existence, voluntarily refrain from using that power;" and he adds that it would be cruel to inquire, "how great a place in most men this sentiment fills, even in religious devotion." Slavery, in its worst forms, exhibits fidelity and devotion in the greatest degrees. "These individual feelings nowhere rise to such luxuriant height as under the most atrocious institutions." So then, we must part with the devotion, fidelity, and gratitude, along with the chivalry, gallantry, and generosity, that depend for their existence on human institutions, — except in that last exercise of them, the abolition of the institutions. There will still be room enough for these virtues in the accidental and unavoidable inequalities of life.

But how are men to be forced or induced to make this sacrifice? Mr. Mill does not dwell so long or so clearly on the answer as could be wished. To prove the reasonableness and probable advantage of the sacrifice, is enough with him; but his hope seems to be this, — that adherents of the cause can be found in sufficient numbers in the powerful and offending sex to divide it against itself; that those who hate slavish worship, and the possession as well as the exercise of tyrannical power, will some day outnumber, or at any rate outweigh, the barbarians in civilized society, and will put such worship and power out of existence, — irrevocably out of their own, as well as the barbarian's possession; and out of men's religious ideas also.

You see that what I think on the question is so nearly like Mr. Mill's thought, that I have hardly done more than epitomize parts of the essay. . . . Radical positions on the details of policy, such as women's claims to the suffrage and to various professional pursuits, are far less solidly founded than general radical positions of principle, which, while disclaiming a profound knowledge or insight of human nature, yet demand a profounder inquiry into it and a freer play for it; which regard all legal and social restrictions, not founded in an ascertained necessity, as shabby impertinences. Indignant protests against barbarism and presumptuous ignorance from such radicals as Mr. Mill are far more efficacious than the undignified clamorous assumptions of another class. It is a characteristic quality of Mr. Mill, shown both in his speculative and practical writings, that he is far less solicitous to separate himself from those with whom he agrees in main tendencies, though differing in details, than most thinkers are. In philosophy, he is much less sectarian than Huxley or Spencer, and does not reprobate Comte; and in social reforms he is much more charitable toward silly radicals than I should be, but for his example. The main, and far the most important, division of opinion to him is the one which separates the modern from the ancient world in faith and practice. Probably, his more profound radicalism, beginning simply in the removal of time-honored obstacles, will ultimately work greater changes than any the silly radicals now dream of, or any I dare to predict. So I cannot yet treat "the whole question." No doubt, the scheming radical has his use, if in nothing else at least in this, that he familiarizes prejudiced minds with possible changes, and so makes them easier if they happen to be judicious. That they may be judicious, or at any rate worth testing in spite of their novelty, is the extent of my radicalism at present.

CHAPTER VI.

THE beginning of the year 1870 brought to Chauncey a proposition from the authorities of the College to deliver a course of University lectures. This gave him peculiar pleasure, and he accepted it at once. He announces it to his friends on the first day of the year.

To Mrs. Lesley.

CAMBRIDGE, Jan. 1, 1870.

. . . I must tell you of the New Year's present I had this morning, — a proposition from President Eliot, of the University, that I should give next year a course of lectures on Psychology in the new University post-graduate courses. The experiment this year is thought to be sufficiently successful to warrant a considerable extension of it for next year. I was rash enough to accept the proposition, being in the spirit of hopeful resolution appropriate to the day. Let us hope that I shall acquire by next September that sense of superiority to a learned audience which will be needed to make the task a pleasant one. My little experience in this line makes me remember most distinctly what a trial to the nerves such work is. It is, I imagine, almost as bad as preaching, which you should not let Mr. Lesley do too often.

To Miss Grace Norton.

JAN. 13, 1870.

It seems only a little time since I was in Northampton, waiting for bright days in October to cheer an expedition to

Ashfield and the hills. But Winter and I were both out of season, the one too early and the other too late; and we settled in the valley waiting for each other — or, at least, one for the other — to depart. If Winter had any motive in the matter, it was more persistent than mine; and, my patience being exhausted, I came back to Cambridge. The weather has since been equally unseasonable in the opposite direction, and not especially favorable to recovery from a chronic cough. Time, nevertheless, even of the officinal quality, is the panacea that cures all ills; and, with the aid of the normal forces of health, it has brought me to my present state of comparative salubrity, — with weaknesses, to be sure, an abnormal liability to take colds, and an invalid feebleness of the conscience which finds sophistical excuses for negligence and indolence.

. . . There is one romantic incident, however, — one rash act of heroic adventure which I have to confess or boast of. I had the temerity, on New Year's day, to agree to give a course of lectures on Psychology next year, beginning in September, in the new post-graduate University courses, which are to be greatly increased in number. Something like the German University lecture system is aimed at, by thus bringing out such special talents or acquirements as are to be found in a community like ours, but have hitherto been turned to no public account except unsystematically in our literature. Much that can be had only by personal intercourse between a man of learning and his audience, is lost where the press is the only medium of communication. Books and Reviews, even the "North American," cannot create that open and generous rivalry among scholars, which makes the standard of learning so high among the Germans. Indeed, the only way in which even the demand for learned books and reviews can be made as effective with us as it is in Germany is by a similar public attitude of our writers and scholars; by their coming, not before popular, heterogeneous audiences, but before classes. Admirable as cheapness in books and the power of the press are, yet they cannot create an interest in the subjects of the most valuable books, comparable to that which the authors of them might communicate personally. This is a value in the lecture system which cheapness in books can never supersede. It is a value which no art can cheapen; but it is a value which English and American appliances of education have simply thrown away, for the most part. Much culture and learning adorn the society of both countries, which ought in some way to be connected with public education, and chiefly by raising the standard of learning in the Universities. To these considerations the President of the College is wide awake. Nowhere else in America can a college command such assistance towards laying this foundation of a University, or creating an effective demand for one. Such is my understanding of the project in which I have rashly engaged to take part; but considering that it is only just begun, and is still in the experimental stage, proper modesty does not forbid that I should try myself by a little experiment in teaching, — with the possibility in view that I may prevail against the hosts of the enemy, and put to rout the forces which —— and —— and —— still continue to command for the subjugation of the human mind.

Of course, the University will recognize no distinction of sex. The classes are composed of men and women, though up to the present time no woman has been appointed lecturer. Let us hope that the question of women's rights will be so far advanced in this new order of things that it will be merged in the wider question of human rights in general. In fact, my sympathy with Mr. Mill's essay on this subject was rather, as I discovered on reflection, on account of principles which apply to the condition of women, emphatically, perhaps, but not exceptionally. I agreed with your estimate, both of the quantity and quality of woman's *influence*, the power she has over *unreason*, — in spite of her subjection; and I think it much more estimable than that which is equally peculiar to men, though this may be a prejudice of mine. And I regarded your writing to me as if I were a woman, as a compliment second only to being treated as one of the *emancipated*. Still, believing as I do, that human beings generally, even children, have hitherto been much more in subjection to authority than they ought to be (both directly and indirectly, or through the sanctions of punishments and rewards); and believing that the true standard of law and morality, the true well-being of all, is defeated by laws which infringe individual tastes, preferences, or sentiments, without being required for security or for compassing any obvious or important utility; and seeing that, so far as women are treated differently from men, it is mainly in consequence of some traditional and prevailing sentiments, which are not justified by any more obvious utility than an unreasoning conservatism, — I am in general ready to protest against this present state of things and in favor of larger liberty. The true standard, utility, is the basis alike of law and liberty. It requires laws with their sanctions in some of the relations of life, and equally requires the entire absence of restraints in others, both for securing the largest amounts of the most worthy enjoyments in the present conditions of human happiness, and as affording the only possibility of experiment, change, and future improvement in them. Undoubtedly, the world has greatly improved of late, in its legal and moral codes, by rationalizing the requisitions which are made on the individual through civil and popular sanctions; but it still stands in need of improvement. And it is only because woman's condition is less improved on the whole than man's, that her rights need to be signalized in a special manner.

As to the degree in which women are in subjection, it is true, as you say, that "greater force of character and wider experience" have more influence than sex in determining the ruler and the ruled, in all immediate personal relations. But then men have so arranged the affairs of life that, for the most part, they or their sex have the best opportunities for acquiring these qualifications for ruling. There can be no doubt that these are acquired. At any rate, whatever may be said of the origin of force of character, whether it comes, as is most likely, from the discipline of important truths and responsibilities, or not, — still it is certain that a "*wider experience*" cannot be innate. No doubt, a prince is better able to rule than a peasant, and therefore has a better right; still, society is just as responsible for the peasant's subjection, since it has made the inequality by the difference in their education. In like manner, many actual relations of inequality, in themselves proper and just, are yet founded on or grow out of arbitrary discriminations, and are in their origin unjust.

You say of American women "that their legal subjection has no perceptible effect on position or character, except among the lower classes." But does not this exception include that (much the largest) number of women who stand most in need of protection from just laws and just public sentiments, — for whom, indeed, and not for the others, a reformation of the laws is needed? I do not think that Mr. Mill has overlooked the existence of a class, — large even in England, I suppose, but much larger with us, — who are in advance of the laws and the general sentiments of society, and are practically independent of them. Such a class justifies, indeed, his hopes, but could not have justified his silence. It was not of them or for them, but rather to them, that he spoke. But whether in reality women in America are in subjection in any important respect or not, it is certain that in the estimation of nine-tenths of American men they not only are, but ought to be. That their subjection, however, is not of the nature of servitude, but rather of religious obligation, is a part of the arrogant opinion which springs from a sentimental estimate of "the fact of sex," and blinds men to the truths that personality is a still greater fact; that individuals embody the ends of all social institutions; that the agent is much more than a servant and is greater than any office, and should have the right to choose his or her duties, subject only to the limitations of real abilities. The needed reform is not so much a political as a social and religious one. The sense of the solidarity of interests should not rest in a slavish sentiment, which makes the servant subordinate to that superstitious object "society," but should be founded on a feeling of personal worth, identical with the interests of all, and, as far as possible, realizing in itself all the good which social institutions compass. Though individuals are indebted to society for the most worthy kinds, as well as for larger measures, of happiness, yet the abstraction, "society," has not in return any rights. Individuals only have rights. Whether Max Müller is correct or not in ascribing myths to a disease of language, by which words with forgotten meanings become personal or proper names, it is certain that a thousand other more important superstitions spring from that most pernicious disease, — afflicting the maturity as well as the infancy of language, — "realism," by which a general name becomes the name of a reality, different from the objects or the qualities which it denotes in common. It is in this way that "society" has appeared to have claims which the individuals that compose it do not have; and thus a reform in logic became necessary for the overthrow of many social and religious superstitions. In fact, the two warfares, the philosophical and the social, or the theoretical and the practical, have been carried on side by side from the days of the schoolmen; and it is not an accident, but an historical consequence, that Mr. Mill is the modern champion at once of nominalism in logic and of individualism in sociology.

It is under the rights of individuals, then, that I would place the rights of women; and it seems to me that those who agitate specially for the latter are not usually actuated by the true principle of liberty, since what they demand is not equal exemption of all persons from oppression, or at any rate arbitrary authority, but they ask an increase of the range of authority by conferring it equally on all. So far as this is really regarded as an indirect means to the end of true liberty, it may be justified; but the usual motives are, in fact, the love of power and a wish to share it, and a false notion that inequality is in itself unjust. What is properly meant by the equality which is essential to justice is only the *generality*, or the equal and strict applicability of its rules; but these rules may themselves consist of definitions of proper inequalities in rights and duties. An *arbitrary* inequality, or one which is founded on mere custom and unreasoning sentiment, will be unjust, provided, as is likely to be the case, it not only deprives individuals of powers which might be usefully exercised, but also interferes with those pursuits of happiness which belong more essentially to the individual.

The suffrage is originally based on the expedient rather than the just; though, when once acquired, it may become a right through considerations more essential to the existence and well-being of society than those of expediency. That the suffrage, as it now exists, is based on more important grounds than can be urged for any extension of it, is manifest from this consideration at least: that any important infringement of the existing right would lead to social anarchy, to something much more serious in motives and consequences than the war of words about its extension, which, so far from endangering the citizen's security, adds rather to his entertainment. I think, nevertheless, that the present limitation of the suffrage with us is a groundless impertinence. . . . To attempt to persuade women that the suffrage does not properly belong to their sphere may be well enough; but to take away all choice in the matter by positive enactments of law is inconsistent with the very principle of liberty. It is not, therefore, for the benefit of woman, but simply for liberty's sake, that I would demand for her this right.

To Mrs. Lesley.

CAMBRIDGE, Feb. 8, 1870.

I promise myself, if I am very good, that I shall go out to Italy next summer for a short trip, and while I am making final preparations for my lectures. But I ought to keep the promise, perhaps, to myself, since keeping it secret is the only way in which I can be sure of keeping it at all. I imagine that the interest of metaphysics and of travelling will make an agreeable variety. If I find introspection wearisome, I shall have a ready relief at hand, and shall not be in danger of losing my faith in the existence of an external world. If I find so great an extension of externality a bore, I can with profit and without loss of time turn my eyes inward. Isn't this a generous programme, — an excursion into two worlds at once? The great Kant recommends, for the study of anthropology, in lieu of foreign travels, a residence in some great city, situated on a great river or other thoroughfare of the tide of humanity; and, with an amusing *naïveté*, — remembering that he was never more than fifty miles away from Königsberg, and considering what must be the travel through that city, — he recommends *it* as peculiarly fitted for the study of human nature. Perhaps Philadelphia will serve my turn, if Cambridge and the commerce of the Charles have not brought me into sufficient contact with varieties of mankind. Still, Kant for himself advised rightly; for under his microscope there was doubtless more variety of human nature in his native city than *he* could, in the distant views of a traveller, have found elsewhere. The naturalist travels only to collect, not to examine, his specimens, unless they are by their very nature spread abroad, as in geology; but if they fly into his museum, all the better: the fatigues and expenses of travel are avoided. But even Kant might have been justified in travelling to visit his friends; and this is a motive which still induces me to hope to see you before many more days.

To Miss Jane Norton.

PHILADELPHIA, Feb. 26, 1870.

I received your last letter only a few days before coming here, where I am happily domesticated with my friends the Lesleys; and now, after the first absorbing interests of my visit, I can turn with the greater pleasure to old times and friends far away. I cannot recall the date of my last letter; but it was some time early in January, I think, and ought to have reached you before the date of yours. Perhaps it has been miscarried or lost, or it may be at the bottom of the ocean and not so happy as my last letter to you, or as the prophet Jonah, — to survive the floods and be delivered from the deep to teach you. . . . Why didn't you give me the promised moral lecture, instead of ironically charging me with being a Millite? For you see that I have so nearly attained that unsexed condition of mind that I have generalized like a man, and applied like a woman, your observation on not liking to appear to be a partisan of Mr. Mill. I suppose that such partisanship is as great a sin in me as it could be in you. . . . But all the personal feeling toward my philosopher of which I am conscious is founded on the fact that he is the least capable of being a partisan leader. There is the very least of personal power in his writings. He only wished, and is only fitted, to draw with him the co-partisans of truth; for, as Mr. Goldwin Smith says, "there is reason to suspect that his intellect is the inflexible and incorruptible servant of the truth." He had no such following as that of Comte, or other passionate and conceited lovers of what they conceive to be true. But enough of Mr. Mill. . . .

Though I did not have the pleasure of seeing Ashfield or the Curtises last fall, I had a partial substitute on Thursday evening by going with Mary, and as one of an immense audience in the great opera-house of this city listening to Mr. Curtis's lecture. The buttoned-up frock-coat and the well-known tones and manner, and the eloquence with which he set forth the perils and the folly of our American system of civil appointments, carried me back to the pleasant old days.

I find my friends here unusually well this winter, and as happy as good people can be. Mr. Lesley, having got educated into the care and conditions of his sensitive nervous system, keeps pretty well, though his enthusiasm still tempts him to over-exertion. Think of preaching eight Sundays in succession, with the week-days full of work! Still, he has learned to keep within certain limits which grim monitors set to his work. I consider myself quite a moral man, — so far as observing the laws of health is concerned, — compared with him. And the little girls, as we still call them, are as well and happy as if their parents were not the invalids they are. It is hardly a pity that —— has grown to womanhood; for she combines most attractively the charming unconsciousness of the child with the charming consciousness of the woman, and has such grace of nature as to bridge over the awkward chasm of hobbledehoyhood. It surprises me sometimes, and makes me doubt my theory of the great dependence of human beings for their characters and powers on the moulding influences of life and circumstances, to see how completely she seems the fulfilment of infantile prophesies; but, then, I reflect that she has always been in the same mould, strongly influenced by the same characters as those that she may have inherited. I think, certainly, that some are born good and some bad, in a certain sense; that is, the most fundamental conditions of virtue, or the absence of them, are, or may be, inherited.

Great sensitiveness or capacity for enjoyment or suffering, with a memory capable of recalling vividly past pleasures and pains, are natural endowments leading to prudence and power of sympathy. Socrates called virtue a kind of knowledge, and in one sense it is. It comes from adequately recalling past goods and evils, and therefore realizing vividly the present pleasures and pains of others through sympathy, and securing their pleasures and our own and avoiding pains through prudence. Infants in arms may show differences in these respects.

You see how cunningly I wander round to my favorite subject! I am easily persuaded that it demands a little further elucidation; and you know that it is easier to utter what flows freely from the moral consciousness than to cast about for those exceptional truths of fact that are called news; which, so far from representing the real life we lead, are, in fact, its monstrosities. "History is little more than a register of the crimes, the follies, and the misfortunes of mankind;" for in this way only does that great stranger, the past of our race, interest us in detail. We like the details, both good and bad, of our friends' and acquaintances' peculiar circumstances; but philosophy alone teaches us life. Let us, therefore, listen to philosophy. I will indite you a psychological lecture.

It may make the matter of our debate clearer, to state what may be admitted, according to the philosophy I profess, to be innate and heritable elements of character and mental powers. Every active and sentient being that is born has, independently of any predetermined channels of activity and sensibility, certain general capacities for them, the degrees and proportions of which may be regarded as predeterminations of character. A certain degree of both is essential to constitute that amount of mental life which is peculiar to the human race, and probably depends on the size of its brain. Certain proportions between the original activity and sensibility will constitute varying innate capacities, which are independent of education and of special organization. The boy strikes out into the world with greater innate force of spontaneity and strength of passion, — supposing the conditions of nutrition and general health to be the same. A greater nervous sensibility than his, combined with less nervous spontaneity, will make the nature more impressionable and receptive, less aggressive, and less impertinently or idly inquisitive. They will predispose to the education or growth of the emotional nature, and especially the tender emotion in its various relations, and to greater capacities for sympathy. Persons and intimate personal relations thus become, as we may say, *by nature*, the objects of a predominant interest, perhaps of an engrossing one; and objects which force themselves on the attention will constitute themselves the teachers of those who are so endowed as to be attracted by them. But it is clear that the purpose of a general and catholic education is not to exaggerate one-sidedness. It is all the more necessary that the education by inanimate things and impersonal affairs should be systematically prosecuted.

There are, no doubt, many other and more special predisposing causes to the choice of the mode of life, and the objects of study, in the original or physical constitution. But these are not to be regarded as divinely ordained or right, simply because they are inborn; for customs and circumstances of life accordant with, and constantly associated with them, must react to increase them, like other physical qualities, and render them more regularly heritable in the varieties or classes which custom thus determines. It may not be best for the human race, with reference to its future conditions and possibilities of happiness, to be constituted as it now is at birth, — any more than it was best to be as it was when born a less intelligent and social race, with fewer arts and social acquisitions. As to what is absolutely best for the human race, in its circumstances as well as in its adaptations, — in its heaven as well as in its fitness for it, — this is not known to us ; and, since the relatively best is not to be found completely revealed in the nature and inheritance of the race at any single epoch of its progress, — not at present any more than at any past time, — and since experience and experimental science is the last resort, the authority of all authorities, the largest scope should be given to their determinations. On this ground, the largest liberty consistent with the existence and the most obvious well-being of society should be left to nature ; that is, to the individual choice. Individualism is thus vindicated as a means to an end, — the end of social improvement. The possibility of monstrosities in nature is also the possibility of amelioration, — when what we need is enlightenment, and not merely a more effective motive to conform to known types and prescriptions. Living Nature is a never-ending experiment in the possibilities of her laws ; and I believe in regard to our race what you think, at least of the individuals, — that, in the possibilities of progress and development, natural charms can be attained which are by no means inherent in character, and qualities may become instinctive or inbred which are now only acquired through education. There is a nature above nature, a nature of infinite possibilities in which we wander, — as well as the powers that hem us in and guide our several steps.

To Mr. Norton.

CAMBRIDGE, March 21, 1870.

. . . The newspaper man is the type of the worst side of our modern civilization, — its shams and artificialities. It is he, and not the man of science, who presents the widest contrast to the poet. He deals with human interests in the gross, without delicacy. He numbers and paragraphs them, but never weighs them; and we, his readers, are apt to follow his lead. No discrimination of interests, no refining or artistic judgments, find place in his pursuit. To shock the nerves and arrest the attention of the busy multitude, whether agreeably or disagreeably, with facts or fictions, is his whole affair. The man of science often seems but little better, — not less a gossip but a more eccentric one, prizing a fact for a fact, with not even a correct judgment of whether it has any interest at all. Still, where he does not show imagination he is redeemed by a great faith of which the newspaper man has nothing. He may not be governed by a clear insight of remote though real relations: still, he is moved by a true faith in the possibilities of real but undiscovered ones, and so he prizes his facts genuinely.

My muse suggests that on this theme I might survey the great past of which you are a pious witness, when there were no newspaper men, and when men were governed, if not beneficently by reason, at any rate by great passions and noble devotions, so that Fine Art was possible. I am not overmuch inclined, however, to admire this old and now impossible concentration, or the kind of nobleness and the possibility of individual distinction, the incentive to individual ambition, which it implied. Humanity is conscious of too many and too massive interests to allow such concentration and singleness of purpose. It is utilitarian reason, and not religious passion, which must govern the modern world. "Fixed ideas," once controlling elements, are now subservient instruments of great purposes or characters. They are still needed for discipline, but are not worshipped as masters. Representative men are, to be sure, no longer possible: the identification of a man and an idea, so that personal and moral or æsthetic motives may reinforce each other, and history be presented to us in fine ideals of works and characters *intensively* grand but proportionately narrow, — in other words, perfection, under more or less arbitrary limitations, is not a leading modern aspiration. Our great men are the wise and painstaking promoters and guardians of extensive interests. They show moral greatness in fitness for great responsibilities which the needs of a highly organized society may impose upon them, and not merely in what their special genius, or combined taste and ability, define for them. They are lost, it is true, in the bright day they work in; yet they may be absolutely brighter than the religiously great artist or scholar or philosopher or reformer, who stands out against the surrounding darkness of barbarism. These personages present moral greatness in its elemental form, and in perfect correlation to the rudeness and violence of the ages to which they belong, in which all life was passionate. We cannot be too grateful for them; but this does not constitute them our types, — at least, not examples of what we would be perfect in, though types of perfection in their way. In the spirit of this distinction, we see in our day the great Christian type in the character of Jesus, studied as a phenomenon of a by-gone time, as an example to be imitated only "in the spirit," or in its most essential but least particular qualities, and as almost identical with moral greatness itself.

I find on reflection that, instead of being indebted to Spontaneity for my inspiration, I am really led into this train of reflections by the questions of Miss Grace's letter, and am anticipating what I should properly reserve for my answer to her. Nevertheless, all this is naturally connected with the suggestive thoughts in your letter on the conditions and prospects of modern society. I find it hard to admit that the future of Europe, which seems so dark to you, may have to pass, as you appear to anticipate, through phases like those of the first thirteen centuries, attractive as the brighter side of that picture may be and dark as the worse side of modern life may seem. From what you say (if you can recall it at this late day) and from Macaulay's observation that what modern civilization has to fear is no longer the incursions of outside barbarians but an irruption of the barbarism at its very heart, in the populations of its own great cities, we can see with sufficient clearness where the danger lies. The causes are, as you say, no longer political (at least in the modern historical sense of the word), but immediately social. To meet them, social science will have to amend essentially that fine Greek invention, the free city and its government. We have improved greatly on the Greek idea, and applied it with success to the government of empires through our representative system, but democracy is now the least successful in its earliest applications. . . .

The latest and best scientific explanation attributes the decline and fall of Roman civilization, not to the strength of outside barbarism, but to an avoidable governmental and financial mismanagement; and it would be a very improbable result of modern studies of social problems to find that the intrinsically weak inside barbarism of modern society is unmanageable, and must be permitted to undermine civilization in its turn. That the power of wealth, more firmly seated now than ever before in the history of mankind, must give way again to princely and military powers; that wars shall again be waged against it, instead of with its permission and aid; that all the mediæval train of horrors shall follow, — destruction not only of life, but of subsistence, followed by famine and pestilence, by diseases more fatal than warfare itself and unknown to modern life; and all this as the result of the ferment of social agitation, not peculiar to modern times, in a class, the offspring of cities and our defective city systems, subdued already in its rank and file by want and debility, and likely to be the first victims of such a state of things, — is to me incredible. Of course, our rulers may make fatal mistakes, as the Romans did. One fatal mistake would be in not sustaining the class of prosperous and independent yeomanry, the true backbone of civilized communities as now constituted. Yet the privileges of wealth ought to be — will have to be — circumscribed. The rapacity of wealth is, of course, the taproot of all these evils, the source of the hostility which threatens social revolutions. We have got to amend the great Roman invention, the laws of property, as well as the constitutions of large cities and the management of their populations. But a scientific study of the subject from the point of view of utilitarian political economy will, I am convinced, meet the demands of the revolutionists at a point far short of their programme. It would be easier for it to do so, but for the complication introduced by the city problem. Looked at rationally and from a utilitarian point of view, the rights of private ownership, the protection of the individual in the possession, accumulation, consumption, productive administration, and posthumous disposal of his surplus gain, — is founded simply and solely in the motives they afford to his making such gains, and adding them, as he really does (in spite of his seeming private appropriation of them), to the store of public wealth. Without these laws or their main features, society would fast relapse into barbarism and ruin, and the first to suffer and to perish would be the rank and file of the discontented revolutionists themselves; and revolution would be checked at the very outset, provided the better parts of the population were not previously and fatally weakened, as in the Middle Ages, by persistently injurious and short-sighted legislation. But so far as the laws of property are inherently, or through changed circumstances have come to be productive, not of increased gains, but of a large and permanent class of unproductive consumers, so far they are devices of legalized robbery, and must be abrogated or amended, if justice is ever to be effected by legislation, through whatever political powers. It is perhaps unfortunate that the problem will have to be solved through democratic agencies and the unavoidable ascendency of the will of the masses in political matters. But, after all, it is a real question, which is the more untoward instrument for the truly just and wise philanthropist to work with, — the ignorant and prejudiced masses whose benefit is sought, or the equally prejudiced aristocracies, blinded by self-interest, whose unjust privileges must be curtailed? I am not an ardent admirer of democracy; but at the same time I regard the anti-democratic Macaulayan doctrine (I may say misapprehension) of democratic tendencies as not less unphilosophical and sentimental than such stupid worship of mere numbers. It is an equally stupid spite. Macaulay showed his utter incapacity for dealing philosophically with political problems in speaking, as he does, of the privileges of wealth, as if they were absolute rights, with no ulterior foundation; and in treating democracy as if it were essentially hostile to what in fact are the very conditions of its ascendency over despotic powers. Democracies and aristocracies are both blind, and if led by men of their own sort must inevitably carry the state with them to destruction. But do not let us dwell despondingly on the powers and tendencies of the instruments we have to deal with. What if there is in our hammer nothing but heaviness and inertia?

I have little to add by way of news. I met Mr. Godkin last Saturday at our club dinner. He had the evening before given his lecture on "Rationalism in Legislation," which I did not hear, but hope to read in the "North American Review," where he has consented to publish it.

I am studying a little for my lectures, or lessons as I shall call them, in mental science. I do not intend to read written lectures but to comment on a text-book, to expound and explain the difficult topics and doctrines of Bain's book, and expatiate on the interesting ones. I do not see the propriety of proving my competency to teach, by rivalling all the authors, and taking a step in advance of the latest. In most of the courses hitherto, the teachers have chosen the more laborious, but less difficult, task of reading written lectures; thus sacrificing, it seems to me, what such exercises can afford peculiarly and in contrast to books. I shall, if possible, excite discussion in the class. Perhaps, if I can do no better, I may have confederates to give the exercises the vivacity and interest there is in actual debate, and such as even the most artistically written dialogues cannot emulate. The dullest will listen eagerly to real metaphysical discussions. But, as I began with saying, it is not rational to trust to Spontaneity, happy and inimitable as her inspirations sometimes are; so I shall prepare a few written nucleuses for occasional use. I have often thought of you in connection with the scheme of these University lectures, and the opportunities it affords for bringing cultivated people together; its freedom from the narrowness of mere pedagogism.

I hope that you fully understand that letters from Florence are marked events among "the immortal incidents of [my] Cambridge;" and that you will regard the fact from the point of view of Christianity rather than that of political economy. And give my kindest, most affectionate regards to all.

To Mrs. Lesley.

CAMBRIDGE, March 22, 1870.

It is more than a fortnight since I left you. . . . I really felt a little homesick when I arrived at this uninhabited room, where no one waited to welcome me, except the old books and the old work. I did not care to brush the dust from them, and they did not seem to care whether I did or not.

. . . What does Mr. Lesley think of Mr. Alfred Wallace's estimate of geological time in the last two numbers of "Nature"? I should like to have an evening's talk with him about it. I like the ingenious suggestion that in the past sixty thousand years species have changed at a comparatively slow pace on account of the comparatively equable climates which astronomy indicates for this period. It is somewhat like the exception he makes in a former paper as to the changes to which the human race has been subject, and tends in the same way to shorten the estimates of the previous ages of creation. But I don't feel so much confidence, as Mr. Wallace seems to have, in the limit of one hundred million years which the physicists set. The history of the solar system and the data derived from the mechanical theory of heat seem to me too much matters of mere guessing. The physical data are exact enough, so far as they go; but the physical history of the universe is known in too few of its elements to warrant such confident chronology, even if we leave miracle altogether out of account. To speculate exclusively on the little that we know, in place of speculating totally on our ignorance, is going to the opposite extreme. I should rather think the geologist himself entitled to the first word on the subject, or, at least, to as much *time* as he wants. To take the present rates of cooling and loss of force in the earth and the sun as typical and universal facts, and to calculate solely on them, is too suspiciously simple to be a probable account of nature. It smacks too much of cosmogonic theories.

I am still inclined to believe that the history of the solar system is not an entirely regular development or a simple specimen of universal progress out of an original "homogeneity" (as it is now the fashion to call the old nebula), and that science ought to free itself entirely from this unscientific prejudice which cannot be proven or tested any better than miracle, and is prompted chiefly by the impatient love of simplicity that characterizes all transcendental speculation (either abstract or concrete), *i. e.* theories of inexperienced phenomena. Only the facts of *life*, or the histories of living organisms, show decisively a regular external order, and this, so far from being typical, is found to depend, in the last analysis, on an almost infinitely complicated, but self-conserving combination of the internal, elementary orders of nature, or laws of matter, living and dead; and it shows itself decisively only in the development of the individual organism, and but vaguely in the development or history of species.

The physical laws of nature are thus to my mind the only real types of the general order in the universe. Life builds an order out of these, which, so far from exhibiting in its stages of development an epitome of the general order, ought to be regarded, so far as evidence can guide us, as an entirely exceptional and precarious state of things, lying within the compass of natural possibilities, but far from illustrating the general results of the interactions of natural forces. These results present themselves to my imagination as they did to old Aristotle's as an infinitely complex and confused movement, without apparent beginning or end or tendency, but showing at every turn the intimate play of action and counteraction in the balanced forces from which they spring. Gravitation and heat are the two most powerful and pervading causes of this movement; but the laws of heat are known only on one side, — its wasting action, its tendency to diffuse the mechanical energies of nature. Cosmogonic physicists, like Professor W. Thomson, assume that this is all that is to be known about it, and do not inquire what may become of it in the spaces through which it is diffused, or how a round of actions can be effected through it and the agency of gravitation which would not tend to uncompensated movements, or to that transition from one chaos to another which the modern cosmogonists assume as the general order of nature.

This scepticism of mine is now called "materialism." It is not the same as the ancient doctrine of this hateful name, since it is not opposed to the same orthodoxy; for even orthodoxy is subject to change! Perhaps I should say something like this in the evening's talk, if my eloquence were not checked before arriving at the last sentences by crushing objections. Now, I have it all my own way, and get safely through my peroration. Such is the privilege of letters — and sermons! but one has to imagine the applause.

I send in the same mail with this a slate for Mr. Lesley's editorials. I find that the lead-pencil flows on the surface of it almost as freely, if not quite, as ink. Give my true love to all.

To Miss Grace Norton.

MARCH 25, 1870.

The principles of this art [jugglery] are really very few, but their applications are manifold. And this is in the main true of the much more dignified and impressive shows, — the mysteries and problems of human nature. Forgive my drawing a moral, after all; but your studies in history and my studies in psychology, which happen to be nearly parallel, suggest it. While you have been studying types and theories of character in mediæval history, I have been reading how the finest, most amiable phases of human nature are consistent with the entirely selfish origin and nature of its fundamental elements. How the capacity for sympathy and disinterested actions and the foundation of the higher justice can come into our volitions, without being originally planted there, — as the sentimental orthodox psychologists maintain that they are, — is a problem which my author, Mr. Bain, has attempted; and, though his explanations do not seem fully adequate or on a level with their theme, yet it is true, as he says in reply to Mr. Martineau's criticisms of another of his theories, that "scientific explanations have often a repulsive and disenchanting effect, and the scientific man is not made answerable for this." We plainly see this in tricks. Why shouldn't it be so in more serious matters? Mr. Martineau and his school may prefer the enchantment to the explanation, as many do in regard to tricks; but do not let them rest under the further illusion that they compass both in what they are pleased to call philosophy, that fine composition of poetry under the forms of science, of which Hegelianism is the most notable modern epic. The tendency of an idea to become the reality, considered as a distinct source of the active impulses in the mind, and the tendency of "fixed ideas" to thwart the operations of the will, whose nature it is to urge us *from* pain or *to* pleasure in ourselves, where alone they really exist to us, — are the basis of his explanations. Not only the phenomena of ordinary and mesmeric or somnambulic dreaming, and the effects in waking moments of ideas in conjunction with states of excitement or under the influence of great passions, like that of fear, or of great concentration, as in the fascination of a precipice, or the depression of a painful recollection, culminating sometimes in insanity, and commonly exhibited by it, — not only these exceptional phenomena, but also facts of wider and deeper import in human nature, find their explanation in this tendency. "The only way," Mr. Bain says, "that I am able to explain the great fact of our nature denominated Sympathy, — fellow-feeling, pity, compassion, disinterestedness, — is by reference to this tendency of an idea to act itself out," through which the perceptions of the outward signs of pleasure and pain urge us to act as if they were our own. The utilitarian does not differ from other moral beings in this respect. He also must be irrational to the extent of being habitually urged in his conduct by ideal, in place of actual, pleasures and pains, by goods and evils which are not present except in idea.

Now, the natures which are the most capable of thus living

out of themselves are also those most prone to passionate as opposed to rational actions; that is, to act from motives which are not real and present pleasures and pains in themselves, but which replace them by a susceptibility to the excitement of ideas. This susceptibility goes even further in most cases. In all moral actions but those of the extreme utilitarian, whose motives or sanctions, as well as his standard of conduct, come through his sympathetic nature, and by an immediate reference of conduct to the goods and evils felt through ideas, — in all other cases, the excitement does not take the immediate form of sympathy, but has apparently an absolute character. Indeed, the motive power of moral ideas is not ordinarily, if it ever is, derived immediately from any connection between them and ideas of good and evil as ends; and it is regarded by most psychologists as a unique power, whatever may be the source of the ideas which exert it. The ideas of right and wrong are certainly not the same as those of good and evil simply. In the last analysis, they are a *commanded* good and a *forbidden* evil. The element of *authority* is essential to them. Hence, the introspective psychologists have naturally been unable to discover the moral nature in the mere capacity for sympathy. But they are mistaken in assuming that the "moral imperative" is unique as a motive power, or is underived. Indeed, in the more tractable intellects, allied to the human, as in the more intelligent dogs, the education of the conscience, both as an active force and as a power of judgment, is capable of being carried much further than the capacity for sympathy would account for, great as this is in these animals. Right and wrong in a dog's conscience may be supposed to differ from those of a more highly sympathetic nature, in having in much larger proportion the element of pure authority. They are, perhaps, the commanded and forbidden simply, — the connected ideas of good and evil being simply those of reward and punishment. So a dog could never be a utilitarian, or feel the "good of all" as a commanding motive, and as the warrant of his master's authority. "Conscience is an education under authority," and its force is primarily the various motives which authority addresses to us. These are not unique, but borrowed powers, — love, fear, and all the train of pains and pleasures under human control, the goods and evils of rewards and punishments, with their moral representatives, approbation and disapprobation.

But here, again, as in the case of pure sympathy or disinterestedness, the actual goods and evils or rewards and punishments, or even the reference to them through actual approval or condemnation, may be wholly replaced by the power of ideas, when these have acquired the requisite associations. And here, again, the utilitarian is like all other moral agents. He differs only as to the authority which he acknowledges as final, or as the test or ultimate authority of all proximate authorities. He simply denies an absolute, intuitive standard, and for an outward standard substitutes the good of all in place of the will of God; or, if he identifies these, it is by limiting his definition of the latter by his ideas of the former; and, if he is a practical utilitarian as well, then also his controlling motive to right conduct is the good it does, commanding him through his sympathies, since, as before, this is only present to him in idea, and is objective only through the excitement of ideas, or by the quality through which ideas tend to act themselves out.

Now, this quality, and the temper which conduces to it, in a perfectly sane mind, I regard as a chief constituent, when existing in a high degree, of what you describe as noble passion; and, when wrought into the character or the persistent and habitual tendencies of the will, it seems to me to be essential to the finest types of character. But, besides this, there is an element in what would commonly be understood by noble passion or energy of moral activity, which comes from without or is objective, and dependent not merely on fineness of nature, but on historical causes, — on the times, the manners, and the prevailing religious, æsthetic, and moral conceptions. We ought to discriminate in an historical personage between the admirable qualities which are intrinsic and excite to universal and genuine imitation, and other charms which give attractiveness to him and his times, yet are not the pure gold, but the ornaments, the images, the sacred vessels, or, it may be, the utensils which are wrought from it. The charm of the forms into which genuine excellence has entered may be easily confounded with their intrinsic worth, — especially since genuineness, not fearing singularity, nor yet seeking it, will fall naturally into a diversity of outward embodiments, in some of which falseness will seek by imitation to hide itself; and since imitation has thus gained by association a bad character, and individuality an equally factitious good one. But this is not worse than the utilitarian insensibility to association, as opposed to æsthetic feeling, which would estimate an antique coin, for example, solely by its weight and quality of metal.

There were times when the relations of men to wealth, to its acquisition and administration, were inconsistent with the highest types of character, and were instinctively shunned as an impertinence and a moral obstacle; but for the modern man to seek the kingdom of heaven by this road would be like seeking to resemble a man of genius by imitating his eccentricities. There may be cases, even in modern times, in which wealth is truly felt to be such an obstacle, — the instance lately of wealth in slaves, — but these are fortunately cases of casuistry or individual morality, and do not any longer demand that poverty shall be preached. Or, to come to the true theme of this discussion, there were times in which the problem of noble life demanded for its solution a greater concentration and singleness of purpose, — even an escape from "the world," — and the consideration of fewer objects of a universal and disinterested character than are embraced in the moral scope of to-day. These conditions gave to the controlling ideas much more the character of ruling passions, and even led to the insane forms of moral action or to fanaticisms. "It is easy to die for an idea when we have but one." Beyond the utilitarian or beneficent measure of an idea thus made effective, there is an æsthetic charm in this very intensity, provided we can forget the cost, or overlook the narrowness and the poverty of the conditions to which such wealth of character is related. Such refining or æsthetic views are easy in historical perspective. The grand cathedral hides the squalid hovel. But the refining process cannot be applied by the living to their own age. The meanness, the corruption, the vice of it, meet them at every turn. That these are really less than in past times, and that great resources of moral energy, less conspicuous, but not less real, are guiding it toward a better future cannot be made clear to the imagination, and can only be evidenced by dry comparative statistics to the utilitarian understanding. But if the monument of our age, the religious edifice on which thousands of busy hands and studious minds are laboring, be the future material well-being of mankind, dedicated to the worship of happier and purer lives, and to a like pious care for posterity, will it be a less glorious monument or less deserving of future admiration than the cathedral? We are apt to think of the old cathedral-builders as all animated by the "quality of noble passion and the finer sensibilities, faculties, and emotions;" but may not a future age see in our enterprises a similar elevation of moral purpose? Some of the leading spirits of our times are as disinterested and devoted, and find in their aims, whether in politics, industry, or science, as powerful a stimulus to noble passion as the leaders of that age. The masses in all ages are led by the few in all that raises them much above the level of animal wants. Their moral powers are chiefly comprised under the principles of imitation and authority, or in the faculties of following and obeying. There are also the selfish rich in all ages alike. Posterity will see the money of the rich and the labor of the poor, or all that remains of either, glorified in the monuments, whether religious or utilitarian, whether material ones dedicated to immaterial interests, or immaterial ones dedicated to material interests, that commemorate the nobly disinterested, or the few that really live for mankind.

The moral type of modern times, besides being familiar, and thus disenchanted, is more broadly based on ordinary and universal human interests. Its catholicity is its only distinction. Hence, an æsthetic charm is missed; but shall we on that account call it a lower type? Do not let us forget that the picturesqueness of past types is in great measure relative and an historical illusion, like the charm and attractiveness of some old fashions of dress or of architecture. The qualities which determine individuality or its charm, cannot be used for distinctions of rank. They are not, as the naturalists say, "ordinal characters." The orders of moral excellence cannot be made to depend on them: though individuality itself is a sign of genuineness, and in this has its charm, as when we judge from such characters in a painting that it is a faithful portrait. The intensity of the energy of moral feeling, provided this feeling rises to that stage of efficiency and steadiness of purpose which can justly be expected of it, is not in any higher degree the measure of its nobility, even though occasion should prove it equal to heroic action. It must also be rationally directed, else it may be insane rather than noble. The utility of its end, in which should be included the refinements of real life, must be this measure, though an absorption in ideas which spurns pleasure and wealth, and foregoes the innocent enjoyments and the goods of common human nature without feeling the sacrifice, must always be to us æsthetically fine. It is not moral, because it is inimitable. The *spirit* of it only touches our life. It does not demand our approbation, since it involves no real sacrifice ; but it commands our admiration, and appeals to æsthetic and religious emotion. Such types are to be prized, as all fine things are ; if they could be common, an essential element of their worth and attractiveness would be wanting. *They belong to our religious nature.* The condition of moral esteem is that the sacrifice should be real and felt to be such, both by ourselves and by the objects of our esteem. Such esteem, to be morally effective, cannot consist with a small estimate of the goods to be sacrificed. *This belongs to our utilitarian moral nature.* So also a religious type, to be morally effective, must be real. A purely fictitious ideal is morally inert. Hence, a myth which has ceased to command faith is morally dead also.

But I have moralized enough to prove at least that I believe in modern times and types, if not to throw any light on the problems of your letter. If I have been wandering in all these pages around the real questions without having touched them, the fault is in the monologue. The Socratic dialectic, or art of getting at clear issues and a common understanding, is, as you say, the better way. If we had been taking one of the charming walks [about Florence] which might have furnished hints and illustrations, our talk would have been less connected perhaps, but could hardly have wandered more widely or more at will. Don't take this moralizing as a specimen of a psychological lecture, but only as a letter. I can imagine the patiently attentive, somewhat puzzled look, expressive of "What is he driving at?" in the audience listening to such a "brief." Extemporizing and watching the faces of the audience, as lawyers do before a jury, may make up for a want of illustrative and expansive power in my pen. But this letter is long enough without — long enough to refute — any suggestion of a defect in the way of expansion.

To the Same.

JULY 16, 1870.

. . . A true morality does not forbid selfish pleasures, except so far as they, in the long run, inflict harm on others, or more harm than the agent himself would incur for them, if it fell on him instead of others. Comte's "altruism" falsely makes the good of others the sole end, instead of the restraining limit and proper guide of conduct. In the long run, the privileges of wealth — that is, most of them — conduce to the benefit of society; and so the law allows of prodigality, though morality marks debit against it in its unbalanced accounts. . . . Moreover, a certain social and moral rank, involving substantial dignities and privileges, is an order which society confers as a *quasi* means of payment of its debts; and whoever fills or aspires to this rank undertakes to act upon, and is therefore bound by, a stricter code of morals than mankind at large; and in this way I agree with you. I think that the privileges of wealth might and should be curtailed. A moral aristocracy among the wealthy should admit to its freedom no one who uses his claims on the public goods for costly and entirely selfish gratifications. I do not entirely like the figure of "stewardship," as defining the relations of the rich man to society. What he, in fact, possesses in our modern economy is the right to dispose, for his own gratification, of a certain portion of the property, the actual goods, which industry is constantly creating or employing. If he refrains from using this privilege, it is the same for the time being as if he had given all his possessions back to society. His money, in the hands of his banker, is circulated by loans; and his houses and lands are occupied and used just as if he did not exist. As a rich man, he is simply one who has the power to take of the goods offered for ultimate exchange as much as he pleases, up to the limits of his so-called possessions. He may consume these goods himself, or give them to be consumed by his beneficiaries; but he is not properly a steward simply as a rich man. He is more exactly a butler. As the creator of his fortune, or as a business administrator, through whom the wealth is increased by the appliances of industry, he is properly called a steward, and in that capacity is as useful and honorable a citizen as the merely rich man can be. Beyond that, his powers and means of doing good are very limited, nothing comparable to his apparent powers as a benefactor, or his real powers as a consumer. His peculiar duties to society as a merely rich man are chiefly negative, and are involved in the obligation not to do the harm he has it in his power to do, — not to waste the goods he has at his command, and not to diminish the productive use of his wealth by the industrious.

You ask to what times precisely I refer in saying that there were times when the relations of men to wealth were inconsistent with the highest types of character. I really had in mind conditions of society, rather than actual historical periods, but of such as history affords examples. When a title to property acquired by war, or by any form of violence, was regarded as equally honorable with the title of industry, or even more honorable, and when Cæsar reduced the value of gold one-quarter by the enormity of his plunder, — the possession of great wealth could not but be associated with conduct and traits of character which the highest ideals, even of ancient times, reprobated, and which early Christianity unquestionably associated so strongly with the things that are Cæsar's, that for a rich man to enter the kingdom of heaven was next to impossible. The same condition of society existed throughout the whole supremacy of Rome, and was the chief cause of the decline and fall; and the advent of the strictly modern era was marked by the change of relation of the wealthy and industrious to the state and to princely power, — the state henceforward, from being the brigand it was, becoming a borrower and an honorable debtor. In all this period, and even now in India, the noble passion for a better life is seen dissociated from wealth. But now, with us and in Europe, since feudalism and the slave-trade no longer confer titles of property, or none that are not countersigned by a more authentic and honorable authority, the rich man may feel that he is not of the company of those who owe their possessions to the victims of violence: he may feel, and be, of the company of the innocent. Still, his means of positive beneficence, even as a friend of the poor, depend upon possessions more strictly his own than worldly goods can be. If he has not the heart of charity, and the head too, he had much better give his money to be bestowed by those who have; otherwise, his munificence will be only a variety of prodigality. As giving leisure and opportunity for the culture of the mind and heart, wealth appears in the most honorable relation it can sustain to the problem of noble living. . . .

I do not think that the universality and the utilitarian or humanitarian character of the modern types of noble endeavor are at all inconsistent with that concentration of thought and feeling in individuals, which is the condition of hearty, earnest strength of action. When I spoke of the greater concentration and limitation of aims which characterized the middle ages, I was not thinking of the narrowness of individual pursuits, but of the narrowness of the range of pursuits within the conception of noble life. Offices, devotions, opportunities for noble effort, have multiplied since then, and have acquired a more distinct reference to the universal ends of human happiness; but it does not follow that the individual actor now, more than then, must scatter his energies fruitlessly over the whole field they cover. It is one of the constituent elements of the idea of progress that there shall be specialization as well as differentiation in the development: that is, offices or functions are multiplied and co-ordinated, or adapted as a system to some common end; and all the parts of the organism become more and more specialized or limited in their several functions. The lung-tissue becomes fitted for nothing but respiration; the skin-tissue for nothing but transpiration; the gland, the nerve, and the muscle are each a tissue of general inabilities, with one special proficiency; but all are determined in their agency by the ends of a common life. The common life in which the moral nobilities of the Middle Ages found their ends—in other words, the essential religion of the Middle Ages—was itself narrow, but capable of inspiring with heroic energy every special devotee. It brought heaven nearer to his work; but each workman was no more a specialist than now,—not so much so. The idea for which it is easy to die, if we have only it, is not the idea of our special service, but of its chief end.

I am curious, by the way, to learn from you whether the interest you have in knowing who said that "it is easy to die for an idea when we have but one," is from the merit of the observation itself, or from a vague consciousness of having heard it before? I remember, with the distinctness of yesterday, having long ago communicated that maxim to you as a saying of the sage Gurney; I thought when I quoted it that you would remember it, and need I say that I counted on the rhetorical effect of the association? Perhaps the vague memory which prompts your question, if that be the case, was just as effective for the purpose. Having shown you what a wily rhetorician I am capable of being, I will go back to the Middle Ages.

The difference between the essential religions of those and of our times appears, as you say, "not so much among the leaders of the world as the led." The masses of our times are essentially unreligious, or, what comes to the same thing, their religion is not that of the leaders. The imaginations of the uneducated are incapable of being animated by the enthusiasms that inspire our men of genius. The essential religion of the leaders is not sufficiently sensuous to reach them; and the only remedy I can conceive is the education of the masses.

As to Art, the love of it, except as the result of a special and systematic culture, and as an acquisition of the educated, must grow up in a people with Art itself, and with a sentiment of it as a distinction in which the people have a conscious pride. To be a persistent and effective sentiment, other than a love of the beautiful in general, it must be like a mother's love for her children, greater because they are hers than because they are beautiful.

And, speaking of the sensuous in religion, the Roman Church bases her power on its catholicity. Is not this "the power of bells and banners over the human soul," of which you speak, — the power, namely, of the senses over the human soul? The startling, vivid, pungent effects on the senses are connected by an original endowment of our natures with a whole circle of emotions. Terror, anger, mirth, enthusiasm, are in turn excited by them. The first essential psychological principle of the bell or the banner is that which causes terror in the birds or anger in the bull, mirth in the child, or enthusiasm in the devotee, according as other and subordinate sensuous effects and mental associations determine the specific character of the emotions.

You see that I have followed the question-and-answer system, or rather the answer system, in spite of your injunction, "that a letter should bear some impress of one's circumstances;" but I am not sure that I have in fact violated the rule, since the only voluntary reflections which I have to set forth are those inspired by your letter. Whether I have answered all your questions, or any, in a manner entirely satisfactory, I have, at any rate, dogmatized enough for one letter; and, to modify the otherwise unmitigated omniscience of my style, I will propound one problem in return.

Tell me, from your point of observation, what is going to be the result of the war announced in this morning's telegrams.

To Mr. Norton.

CAMBRIDGE, Aug. 10, 1870.

Letters grow more charming and interesting as our correspondences are lengthened out, partly, perhaps, because from the necessity of the case they become, in default of any better, the normal mode of intercourse, and become as precious to us as the sign language is to the deaf and dumb.

. . . I am sure you will regard charitably my evident disposition to review you, and will consider that you are in a measure responsible for this tendency from my training under you in the "North American Review," for which, by the way, I have not written for a very long time. I have just finished reading Mr. Wallace's book of essays on Natural Selection, which I may notice, if I do not lose my interest in it before coming round to it again. It is a very clever book.

I never told you of my acquaintance with Charles Salter,[1] formerly Unitarian minister in West Cambridge, who died very suddenly last spring, on a voyage to Europe. I came to know him quite intimately last fall and winter, and exchanged opinions on theological and kindred subjects quite freely. He was studying law, having given up the ministry on account of doubts on fundamental tenets in theology. This change was a matter of very serious concern with him, and was made from the most modest and conscientious motives, such as an unwillingness to dogmatize beyond the limits of his own assurance. He appeared to me to be a most accomplished

[1] See p. 199.

and sensible man; and unlike most radicals he had no philosophical substitutes for, or original proofs of, the religious doctrines he had undertaken to teach; but he seemed to be governed in his views of religious doctrines, much more than most men, by moods of feeling. He felt the force of sceptical objections most when it was his duty to remove or ignore them, but freedom from this responsibility restored his confidence. His mind and character interested me a great deal, though I am not at all sure that I have indicated the interest or can express it.

. . . The Gurneys are in Cambridge most of the time this summer, interested in the progress of their house. I occasionally see them, and share with them the summer comforts of Shady Hill.[1] I was for two days last week the guest of James Thayer, in Milton, and devoted most of one day to a call on the Lesleys at Brush Hill.

. . . What you say of the responsibility of the glittering generalities of our Revolutionary politics for the irrationality of political creeds in Europe seems to me quite true, though not the whole truth, or a complete explanation of the matter. As the revolutionists borrow from us, so we borrowed from the philosophers certain half truths, really founded in utility and in history, but needing the interpretations and qualifications of the philosophic reason. But the philosophic reason is out of place in a quarrel, and resigns its influence to the sentimentalist and the maximist, and these fight fallacy with fallacy. Against the fallacies of divine rights, whether in king or capitalists, the fallacies of liberty and equality are good thunder; and, so long as force is an efficient means of supporting or overthrowing convictions, they are legitimate arguments. But these are the staples of politics in Europe. *Ergo*, &c.

[1] Mr. Norton's place at Cambridge, then occupied by Professor Gurney.

Forgive my resorting to the emphasis of the syllogism as if I were arguing against any thing you say. I wish only to transfer part of the responsibility of Utopian politics to the hard necessities of the case. The ideal absurdities of Utopia are in part at least induced by the actual absurdities of Europe. Two of the causes you mention, the deep-rooted, religion-sanctioned, actual abuses in the social conditions of Europe, and the delusive aims and absurd expectations of the revolutionists, — are in a great measure responsible for each other, like the polar conditions, or the two electricities of electric induction. I am the more inclined to this opinion, since we have outgrown our old sentimental creed from the lack of opposition to it, which, I think, was the condition of its very existence; while it seems to me to remain still the creed of European republicans from the continuance of the opposition. But this is only an incidental point of your most interesting discussion; and, having performed my patriotic duty in respect to it, I fully agree with you in regard to the deplorable consequences of the facts, however interpreted. There seems no escape from them, only a mitigation by making the revolution as rapid and complete as possible. This will not achieve perfection, but will afford the only basis on which substantial progress is possible. Perhaps the best service France or Louis Napoleon could do at the present juncture would be to republicanize Europe, as some prophet has predicted he will do as a last desperate measure.

From this the transition is natural enough, though somewhat abrupt, to the consideration of the part which utilitarian reason has to play in such a tragedy. Reason is quite out of place in dealing with the idea militant, with passions or sentiments, in assisting their direct actual power over the human will; but it is ever ready, in moments of reflection and in peace, to harmonize conflicting passions and sentiments by the only certain and universal standard of well-being and duty. Utility does not oppose itself, as many intuitive or sentimental moralists suppose, to the proper jurisdiction of feeling, — to devotion or to the passionate love of the beautiful. Its philosophy does not contend for the sanction of utility as the sole and sufficing motive to conduct. It only proposes a standard as the proper test — a negative test it may be — of every motive. It does not propose to measure beforehand the positive elements of possible human excellences, the highest aims or the supremest delights. Its real enemy is *a priori* conviction, or prejudice asserting itself as its own justification, or sentiment born of strife and narrowness, and sanctioned only by custom and traditional religious authority. So far as a feeling is ultimate and an immediate source of human happiness or excellence, it is its own positive standard and sanction. Utility tests it only negatively in its consistency with other interests and feelings, and with the maximum of all in all sentient beings measured both by intensity and rank, — not moral rank, for this is a resultant, an acquired or conferred dignity. The inductions and criticisms by which this test is applied may be long and difficult, and may not be possible for an individual observer of social conditions, — being like the inductions of astronomy or other physical sciences; but, as the result of many centuries of observation, they are embodied in the best or wisest moral codes or exemplars, which come to us sanctioned by many associations, not in themselves rightly authoritative, but often more influential (and usefully so) than their rational grounds could be, except with the most refined and enlightened.

There is an antithesis between utility and beauty, between the useful and the beautiful, which is often mistaken for an antagonism. A useful thing is a means simply, and not an end in itself. A beautiful thing belongs to the class of ends in themselves, or absolute ends, to which also belongs every ultimate source of pleasure of whatever rank or intensity.

The beautiful thing agrees with the class to which it belongs in having no ulterior end, or only an incidental one, like Mr. Darwin's uses of color in birds and flowers; but it differs from its class generally in having a high rank, an intrinsic dignity or preferability in kind, which depends on its mental relationships and affinities. But whether the pursuit of the beautiful be right or wrong is not determined by its rank as a pleasure, although this rank, depending on its broad relationships, would be likely enough to insure that consistency with the maximum of excellence or happiness or pleasure or well-being, or by whatever name we call the true ultimate standard of moral excellence. Now so far is the pursuit of the useful from being inconsistent with the pursuit of the beautiful, that it really presupposes such ultimate ends as the grounds of its utility.

But it is not the beautiful alone or even pre-eminently, but the whole class of ends in themselves — all our pleasures and those of all sentient beings — that constitute the grounds of utility. It is a mistake, however, which all, or almost all the opponents of the utilitarian philosophy make, as well as many of its advocates, to suppose that the measure of a pleasure in this philosophy is simply its intensity as a feeling, and not also its rank or preferability in kind, or a certain dignity it has in the spiritual hierarchy independent of and antecedent to its proper moral rank. This moral rank is a derived dignity, and is determined by preferability or weight with the will on the whole and as compared with the *sum* of the pleasures or ends that are sacrificed for it, both in ourselves and others. But in this estimate the intrinsic value of a pleasure, independent of its intensity and depending on its extent in our natures and in our lives, should be taken into account. Thus, the intuitive moralist is correct in affirming intrinsic differences of dignity in ends, at least as motives in the developed will, or in any but the most elementary of mental natures; but he errs again in supposing that these are the same as moral differences or original distinctions of right and wrong. They are unquestionably the grounds, which along with the intensities of feelings as pleasures or pains, determine the moral rank of actions or rules of conduct.

To allow these original differences of rank in ends may seem to be granting to the intuitive moralist all that he demands, and leaving nothing distinctive in the utilitarian philosophy. But this is far from being the case, either theoretically or practically. In theory, this philosophy has still to insist distinctively that no rule or principle of conduct, except its own fundamental maxim of the greatest universal benevolence and disinterestedness, can be received on the authority of any sense or sentiment or properly intuitive power, or be ultimately and authoritatively determined to be right, except by the longest acquaintance with the conditions of well-being, and the general consequence or effects on well-being of acting on the rule. Some of the most fundamental and important rules of morality, chiefly negative in form, are, it is true, quite simple corollaries from obvious conditions of well-being and the fundamental axiom of the greatest good; and it is also true practically that more influential sanctions than utility are necessary to enforce its injunctions, and are therefore sanctioned by it. Moreover, what is called the conscience, or strong and controlling aversions to certain classes of actions and admirations or approvals of other classes, should be respected and carefully fostered, even though in some matters it leads wrong; since a faulty conscience is more useful or less harmful on the whole than unprincipled conduct, even in the best disposed natures. But practically, also, the utilitarian philosophy has a distinctive lesson to teach, or rather many lessons, — a whole world of abuses to correct, which subsist by the very same sanctions or the same kind of sanctions the intuitive morality adopts as the basis of right and wrong.

Such are the self-sanctioned prejudices, time-sanctioned iniquities, religious absurdities, all of which can claim the same grounds of justification as those on which the intuitive morality would base the ten commandments; namely, that most people, or at least somebody, *feels* them to be right. That *somebody*, say the pope, should be infallible in his feelings, is a necessary corner-stone of this philosophy, and most of the unorthodox or radical advocates of it claim this infallibility for themselves; but it follows from their principles that in cases of dispute some pope, — whether the Roman pontiff or not, — some holiest man, must be the final arbiter. The aims and lessons of the utilitarian philosophy are not, however, in any way opposed to, but are rather in alliance with all that is noble and beautiful and delightful in the possibilities of human nature. It is only incidentally, or perhaps by a mistake of its true scope and interests, that it turns attention away from æsthetic pursuits to the broader but perhaps on the whole not worthier interests of science or industry or politics.

I do not think that you at all overestimate the spiritual rank of æsthetic pleasures. They are intimately associated with the fundamental quality of moral nobility; they consist with generosity and sympathy, and are inconsistent with monopoly, thus differing from merely sensual pleasures, though like these they are ends in themselves. Again, they are refined pleasures. All that is disagreeable or loathsome is removed; and the special end of the fine arts is this refinement or abstraction of the beautiful. Moreover, they are pleasures of the higher senses, and have extensive intellectual affinities This is Mr. Bain's analysis, which, whether complete or not, is the best I have seen. Æsthetic pleasures doubtless belong, as you say, to the most sensitive, susceptible, and passionate natures; and they were doubtless more pursued, but I think for a different reason and not from temperament, by the men of the thirteenth century than by those of the nineteenth. There is nothing in the aims of our times inconsistent with them, except, perhaps, the catholicity and variety of modern interests, and a consequent want of concentration and general sympathy and of public patronage of them. Instead of whole communities devoting their surplus wealth to them, and re-enforcing them with the powerful sentiments of patriotism and religion, we have now, and probably can have, only schools or at best colonies of artists, who must inevitably seem narrow in their aims compared to the men with whom Art meant not only beauty, but the highest honors and public spirit and religion. A great general may be entirely absorbed in the problems of the art of war, but his enthusiasm for his pursuit cannot be said to be independent of the patriotic ardor of his soldiers. And so, though no doubt, as you say, the best Gothic artists were distinctly and consciously moved not through devout passion, but through plain æsthetic joy, yet the intensity and quality of their feeling must have depended on an appreciation of their work, which sprung from other than æsthetic motives, — from national or race pride, from patriotism or religious devotion. Indeed, as you go on to say, the happiness of the Gothic artists was "in the successful solution of problems they had to solve. It was the delight of beauty *joined with* the excitement of genuine scientific achievements;" but this adjunct is not an æsthetic motive, though it be the last infirmity of noble minds.

CHAPTER VII.

At this period, Chauncey, although far from well, was hard at work in the ineffectual endeavor to bring up arrears in his work upon the Almanac. Of his manner of life at this time, his interest in philosophical discussion, his happiness in the society of some of the ablest of the younger men at Cambridge, and his adherence to his old, dangerous habits of work, we may see something from a letter which a friend [1] has kindly sent me: —

"During the year 1869–70, I sat at the same table with Mr. Wright, Professor Cutler,[2] and Mr. Salter.[3] The two last-mentioned gentlemen talked much and very cleverly, and Mr. Wright was often drawn into the conversation, much to the delight and instruction of several of us younger men who were listeners. Often after dinner Mr. Cutler would invite Mr. Wright to his room; and there, with two or three young men for an audience, the conversation between them would be kept up well into the evening. When once fairly started, Mr.

1 Mr. J. J. Myers, a graduate at Cambridge in the class of 1869.

2 Elbridge Jefferson Cutler, Assistant Professor of Modern Languages at Cambridge, from 1865 to 1870. He had been made a full Professor just before his death, in 1870. Mr. Cutler had been a friend of Wright's ever since they were together in College; they were also members of the same Club. Professor Cutler had already become known outside of the College by his poems, which gave promise of an excellent future; within the College, his loss was deplored as that of one of the most brilliant and successful of its younger teachers. — Ed.

3 See p. 191.

Wright did much the greater part of the talking. He saw a great deal of Mr. Salter at this time, and they often took long walks together to discuss certain questions in which Mr. Salter was especially interested, which had troubled him much, and had even caused him to leave his profession, the ministry. He told me that his conversations with Mr. Wright were very instructive. Two or three times during that same winter Mr. Wright asked one or two of us around to his room to hear him read articles which he was at work upon, or had finished. If he found we understood them, he would leave them as they were; but, if we did not, he would sometimes rewrite or change them.

"His work on the 'Nautical Almanac,' which he was still carrying on at this time, was, I always thought, a great weight upon him. He would postpone it until the very latest moment, and then work upon it night and day until it was finished. I remember calling on him one morning, and finding that he had been up all night at his work, and had only rested for an hour or two the night before. In answer to my question why he worked in that way, he replied that he preferred to do this kind of work so. 'It is about as much work,' he said, 'to get my mind running in this regular, machine-like way, as it is to do the thing itself when I am once fairly started.'"

To Miss Grace Norton.

Oct. 16, 1870.

. . . I shall not launch forth, then, into any sea of philosophic disquisition, more especially as you have given me no commission for such an errand, and as I now have opportunities to decide and dogmatize on disputed questions and doubtful matters twice a week, orally. The long-meditated lectures have begun. I have talked mental science for five hours to a class of which the smallest attendance has been eight, the greatest twelve!—not a crowd, you see, but respectable, as our University lectures go, and considering the unattractive character of my subject. I do not aspire yet to rival Mr. Emerson or Mr. Lowell in drawing audiences. These five meetings have been in great measure experimental with me, since they are the first entire hours I have ever attempted to fill with undisputed talk; and for one of them I tried the experiment of reading from a prepared manuscript. Talking succeeds better. What I write usually contemplates an imaginary company of sages or experts, and requires to be read deliberately, and sometimes twice. Writing is, of course, talking to an imaginary audience; but the absent mediocre mind does not inspire in me any desire of communication. One of my class, a former pupil of mine, says that I have not yet given him any occasion to ask questions. There are, however, in my subject, as it is developed, temptation and room enough for questions; and I look forward to livelier times, especially when we get better acquainted. But, meantime, I am somewhat surprised at the ease with which the hour is consumed with continuous talk. All notes and manuscripts are a hindrance. With my mind full of the themes of discourse, the order and even the illustrations develop themselves, and in a manner apparently better suited to hold the listener's attention than any reading could be,—at any rate, any reading of what I could write.

This is in accordance with my original plan,—if it can be called a plan,—and my preparation was only keeping on the alert in reading and meditations, for whatever might be of service to the lectures. I did not even take notes, feeling sure that I should remember, and could refer to memory with more ease and profit than to a heap of manuscripts for whatever was really worth retaining. Writing and artificial memory are often, I think, in the way of a better sort of memory which holds what is worth retaining by more real ties. I did indeed take a few notes, but I doubt whether I shall find them of any service. They seemed at the time of more importance than they do now. Perhaps I attach the same exaggerated importance to what occurs to me to say now, and it is rather early to pass judgment on my preparation; five lectures are only one-eighth part of the course. I call the lectures "Expositions of the Principles of Psychology, from the Text of Bain."

To make this letter as egotistical as possible, or as a letter should be, I must tell you of what you may find in the current number of the "North American Review," an article on the "Limits of Natural Selection."[1] I read last summer, for my own pleasure and edification, a little book on this subject by Mr. Alfred Wallace; and in one of those moments of easy good-nature which, by the mere pleasure of their gracious majesties, see fit to impose burdens on other and less fortunate moments of our lives, I promised to the editor a notice of the book. I have broken such promises before: the other moments have rebelled, and insisted on their inalienable rights; but this time that great spirit, the sense of duty, which ought to rule over all, brought my leisure into subjection, established the divine right of the lazy promise, and put the pen into my hand, and, lo! what was conceived in the sense of punctilious duty and contracted obligation as a modest book-notice, expanded into the majestic proportions of a body-article, nigh thirty pages long, and was accepted as such, and will appear with all its damning heresies over my signature, without even the cloak of anonymousness to shield me from the indignation of outraged orthodoxy.

I forgot to say about my lectures that ——came to the first two. He has not come since: it may be on account of my explanation in the second lecture that psychology is more closely

[1] Philosophical Discussions, p. 97.

allied to the physical sciences than to metaphysics in its methods and motives; and my claiming for this science the right to take up heretical positions as hypotheses or questions of scientific inquiry, which are illegitimately held in philosophy or metaphysics as finalities, — though so long as scientific investigations are incomplete, as they always may be, these positions are practically finalities, but held in a wholly different spirit from a metaphysical dogma. I disclaimed taking sides in any other sense than as the side presents real problems, and suggests proofs of a scientific character. There is really a difference of method between the scientific adoption of an heretical position and the philosophical adoption or rejection of it. Philosophy passes like a judge upon its questions, as if, in practical matters, decision were quite as important as truth. Science takes them up as matters of curiosity or of possible future utility, and looks, at its leisure, into them. It acknowledges no burden of proof in its judgments, and is content to wait. But, as it happens usually that the heretic holds a possibly verifiable position, or one the evidence of which has not yet been completely explored, science comes to look with favor upon it, and this favorable view appears to the dogmatists of both sides as a really favorable decision. This attitude of science is very unsatisfactory to that hunger for knowledge, or rather for assurance, which is rather a ravening appetite than a discriminating instinct for proof, and is content to feed on fallacies, or will carry conviction by violence. Science contemns this. The rest it seeks is the remainder of knowledge, even principles which we do not yet know; and it holds what we do know as subject to our present ignorance (not a hopeless ignorance), and is hostile to the dogmatic attitude of either side, and to any finality in the present state of our knowledge on philosophical questions.

Don't suppose that I talked in this way to my class, or even exactly to the same effect. Imagine rather, in place of rhetoric, a painstaking, expository, much plainer style. I imagine that one great interest in Mr. Bain's system, on the part of some at least of the class, is in the issue that Mr. Martineau tries to make with him; but the subordinate, almost incidental value that some traditional metaphysical issues (like the ultimate nature of the connection of mind and matter and of cause and effect, and the dependence of life on matter) have in the view of the scientific psychologist, is with difficulty comprehended by those who approach the subject from a religious point of view. Dr. Lionel Beale, in his article in the present number of the "Fortnightly," on "the Mystery of Life,"— uniting a large culture and great acuteness with an interest in the question that is really metaphysical or theological, — accuses the scientific position that life or the properties of living matter are really subject to material laws, which, if known, would be a higher sort of chemistry, — he accuses this of being a dogmatic position; and probably it is so in the minds of many that hold it. They have the same weakness that the Doctor has. They transcend experience in trying to assimilate the regulative agencies of life and mind to the forces of matter, just as he does in trying to make them appear as different as possible. All his ingenuity cannot make it appear that the view he takes is not dogmatic, and even hopelessly so. His orthodoxy, his belief that life is not a possible chemistry, is unmitigated assumption in fact, however modestly put forward. As being essentially a finality, it leads to no further knowledge, and virtually denies the possibility of further knowledge. The heretical position, on the other hand, that life is, in some at least of its essential phases, a higher form of chemistry, when held with a confidence limited to scientific evidence, is only a following out of those suggestions and guidances of experience which propound the theory, and has, at least, what orthodox faith has not, the character of a working scientific hypothesis. The real *animus* of both sides is unscientific.

The one, from reverence (perhaps a misplaced one), taboos the grounds where the other, from want of reverence, wanders in the dark. The one protests against regarding life as *only* a higher form of chemistry, as if this theory in some way degraded it, rendered it less worthy of our reverence and regard. In such a protest is seen the real motive to the dogmatism, essentially unscientific, and, at bottom, irrational, that so perverts even an acute mind as to make it charge its own vices upon its opponents. It is this mixing up of two really distinct orders of ideas, ideas of moral dignity and ideas of causal dependence, running through the best thought of all times, that presents the greatest obstacle to scientific progress, not only in what relates to life and mind, but in every branch of science; for all was related to life and mind in the earliest conceptions of them. With what religious horror the ancient orthodox protested against the doctrine that the stars are not gods, but *only* earth and stones!

Dr. Beale claims that his prejudice does not prevent him from doing good service to science; but this is because there are problems enough outside of his sacred precinct. Science is not finished yet up to that line; but this does not prevent the invasions of hardier pioneers. We have just seen the monkey prejudice invaded in the Darwinian controversy. That men, being what they are, are descended from gods, is supposed to be a nobler conception of human nature than that, being the same creatures, they have struggled up from — well, even I don't like to say "monkeys" (partly because it isn't strictly true or probable), but I will say — the monkey's ancestors. This love of pedigrees and the attribution of moral dignity to them come from a just and useful sentiment when confined to rational limits. There would be a solid ground of assurance of a better future in the fact of a better past. We should have in it a type of the hope and faith in man's destiny.

A lady, . . . who I afterwards learned was strictly Calvinistic, assured me, the other day, that to believe in Darwinism would destroy all her hope for humanity. But I thought, and said, that there was some encouragement to be had in the progress men have made, according to this theory. Moral constructiveness, our æsthetico-moral nature, turns all history into mythology, and all science into mythic cosmology. It is the very heart of orthodoxy. The theory that there is a correspondence between moral ranks, or spiritual hierarchies, and the dependence of natural causes; that the first in the order of creation is first in order of moral worth; that history is a record of degeneracy; that lifeless matter is essential evil, — a theory received, it is supposed, by Plato from the East, — has, no doubt, been very serviceable by making men regard the past with reverence; and the absence of the sentiments to which it appeals, from the heart of the heretic, is perhaps, quite as often as any better cause, the origin of his heresy. Reverence, or the want of it, has quite as much influence on men's beliefs, or professions of belief, as proofs and disproofs have. It is only with the latter that science has any thing to do, except in that useful instrument of research, hypothesis, through which it sometimes presses hard on inveterate prejudice, as, I think, it does in Dr. Beale's case.

How badly I have kept my promise not to write a long or philosophical letter! But I have, at any rate, broken it spontaneously. This talk is not one of my lectures, and is not any part of my article, and was no part of my thought when I set out, — was not, at least, on the surface of my thought. Yet of what else should I talk, since you have all the news on your side of the water. The bits of private news about the great struggle which you sent me were very interesting. I imagine there must be an immense amount of diplomacy going on at the present moment, — a manufacture of opinion quite unscientific.

To Miss Jane Norton.

NOV. 20, 1870.

I have been much interested of late in my lectures, probably much more than my audience, though they show no lack of interest, and ought not to be expected to go beyond their teacher in zeal for knowledge. Still, my lack of experience and want of sympathy with the common or corporate spirit of an audience made me anticipate more than now seems rational from the spontaneity of the creature. An audience has a very passive consciousness. Doubts and questions are a private undercurrent in it, if they stir at all, — and it is difficult to bring them to the surface, the best minds have such awe of the inferior collective one. Still, I have had a number of interesting discussions with members of my class, in which the others seemed to be interested. On Friday, for instance, I was talking of sound and hearing, and questions about the significance of music forced themselves to the surface; and, for the time, we had the best sort of talk, — that of three or four independent minds, only too severely sensible. Our god, the collective *animus*, does not approve of any otherwise; and it is impossible to avoid the consciousness of his mute presence. He is so like an ox or crocodile, which, so far as it is active, acts on the lowest impulses, either lazy acquiescence or brutal excitement.

Absorbed in ideas, fascinated by them, we may imagine that this *animus* sympathizes with us. What it sympathizes with is our fascination, our interest. It gazes at what we gaze at. Whether it sees what we see, depends. Don't apply this, in a feminine way, to my audience in particular, but to the extreme difference of audiences in general from that wisest *animus*, the independent, individual interlocutor, — a difference which my audience merely suggests to me in contrast with their individualities.

I have ten very regular, attentive listeners, though I must confess that my consciousness of their number and individualities does not grow, but rather diminishes. I feared at the outset that I could not fill forty hours with what I had to say; but more than a third of the course has hardly begun to approach the heart of the subject.

My preparation for the lectures consists, I find, in all that I have ever read or thought about their subject. I depended, not unwisely, as I think, on what my memory could furnish, under the guidance of my text-book; but I was unwise in thinking that this repository would be available in preparation for extempore expositions.

So, latterly, after getting a vivid idea of what was required to meet the intelligence of my audience (whether an adequate one or not, the god only knows), I have written out my lectures. I have now a larger and more varied audience in my imagination than I used to write for, though its number is only ten. I expect to gain from it more than I give in exchange, as in every fair bargain. A disinterestedness that does not do this for us is uninterestedness, and deadens our powers, — our usefulness as well as our selfish enjoyments. I don't believe the stupid sentimentalist who demands effort without compensation, who thinks that disinterested actions are motiveless. Fascination, no doubt, allures us to heights beyond those to which selfish interest could impel us; but fascination leads us also into quagmires of misery. To be happy, then, one should distinguish rationally and, as I may say, selfishly between fascinating devils and fascinating angels. A bad idea, like that of throwing one's self over a precipice, or of suicide in any other way, may be as disinterested a fascination as the most fascinating virtue: but the one is to the rational mind that death or stupidity which has no power, and that no power can lead; while the other is rationally the selfish happiness, if I may so say, of the supremely blessed. To be led or drawn to happiness to which we are not impelled by antecedent motives is the freedom of our wills, or our freedom from selfishness.

This divides our higher from our lower natures. Beasts that perish may be fascinated to their ruin, as moths by a flame; but this capacity for being led beyond what pleasure or pain impels us to do is the characteristic irrationality of human beings, through which we may be led to ruin or to bliss. Ideas are the spirits that thus have the man in charge, and make him act out their wills, even against his own, and take possession of him, even though unwelcome guests. . . .

Though it is very true, as you say, that the tranquillity of old age often comes from a torpor in the nerves, yet it is generally dependent also on the growing supremacy of ideas in our lives. These have a different sort of influence on our wills from that of our sensibilities, and seem to be independent of the contrast of pleasures and pains, but can overwhelm them as modern armies with discipline and gunpowder could the old giants and heroes, or as mythic enchantments did in their time. It has always seemed to me a very wise observation of old Paley's that the child is never happy when not absorbed in pleasures; but that old age may be happy when free from pain. The brain has a longer lease of life than the senses, and finally comes to live in a remote past, even among the things of its childhood. Much of the happiness, the tranquillity of old age or of intellect, depends, of course, on the quality of our philosophy and experience, and, as you say, on unlearning much. The child thinks of heaven as a show or a refectory. Angels afterward people it, first strong and beautiful, then gracious and wise ones. To unite all these heavens in middle life, to keep the zests of childhood in harmony with the happiness that vigor and beauty and sympathy give to maturity, and to join to them the serenity of intellect, is to be truly happy in fortunate circumstances, if not to be great. Greatness is, however, too often any thing but happiness, though not a dull, depressing misery. It is often a tumult in which the heavens are at war with each other.

Our lives, though outwardly and apparently without such metamorphoses as insects, have them still internally. With the insect, the transition, though hidden and apparently abrupt, is yet really continued between the larva and the pupa, and from the pupa to the imago. And so the mind grows from feeding on the impressions and the pleasures of sense to a life of inward activity and refined enjoyment, and finally to the pleasures of thought and memory. Your human ideal — "a soul of perfect sensibility and perfect repose" — is not, then, to be met with once in a lifetime, but possibly in the stages of a whole lifetime. It takes a whole life to make a character; and happiness is not the result. Happiness is not a thing to be attained; but it may lie all along the way. This is what the old philosophers meant when they said that happiness is not a real or rational end, and that virtue only could be a real attainment, which, with circumstances beyond our control, might make the fortunate truly happy. Religion promises these fit circumstances, supposing, in its idealistic philosophy, that every hook must have its eye. But there are many unmeet meetings in the natural order of things, and no remedy for them; and neither happiness nor misery is anybody's desert, except so far as they are everybody's rational incentives. The human capacity for being led without these incentives is, therefore, the promise of improvement in the race, though not of heaven to the individual. Nevertheless, the two elements combined in your ideal of character are really combined in every source of refined pleasure. Ease and excitement, peace and passion, grace and vivacity, are synonymes of them, and include all pleasures or ends. By their combination, pleasures are refined as in music and in all the fine arts. Richness in musical tones and lustre in beautiful objects come from such combinations in the senses; and in this they resemble still more refined effects. But I have wandered through all these pages to come to the point where you finished your beginning, and bade me good-night.

I read last summer a part of the article by Mr. Morrison on "Subjective Synthesis;" but I never finished it, for the "Review" was removed from the reading-room before I came round to it again. What I read interested me, though I do not quite agree with it, — or I did not; and now I remember so little, or I have so imperfect an idea of the article as a whole, that I could not fairly criticise it. I shall look for it again, however, and give it a fairer reading. The news, also, in these exciting times, draws my attention away from abstract subjects. The news has just come by telegraph of England's excitement on the Eastern question, and announces Mr. Mill's protest in the "Times." If England really goes to war with Russia, will not the end of the world come next?

I never read Littré's "Life of Comte," and I doubt whether I should sympathize with his interest in the subject enough to enjoy it. I have more sympathy with what must be every patriotic French liberal's feeling about the present state of their country. I suppose that they must all share Thiers' illusions on this subject, which, I imagine, are not very different from what appeared to be ours, to European eyes, in the gloomiest period of our war. At the same time, the integrity of the French nation, or at any rate of its territory, does not appear to my perhaps prejudiced eyes as quite so important as did our national union. This question of territory is not separable from military glory. It is about changing a line of fortification and defence, instead of abolishing or avoiding one, as in our case.

Chauncey's University lectures seem to have been only partially successful. In commenting upon the general subject of education, or in answering particular questions, he was very instructive; as, for example, in his article on "The Conflict of Studies,"[1] and in one of his letters to Miss Howard.[2] In dealing also with a single pupil in his own study, he was in many ways an admirable instructor, — original, stimulating, fruitful. But for the systematic work of lecturing, and of handling an audience, he had marked defects, both mental and physical. Professor Gurney, who, as Dean of the College, had special opportunities of knowledge, has said something on this subject in a letter which is printed later on. In another letter, he says: —

... "You will have had a reminder, doubtless, that Chauncey delivered a course of University lectures, some years ago, on Psychology, based on Bain's smaller work, in one volume, on the subject. I did not hear any of them, for they came during my office hours. I suppose, however, from his talks at the time, and from the little I heard from auditors, that they were developments of what seemed to him fruitful topics in the text, and that they were not very successful, — as was, indeed, the case with most of those lectures. The year before his death, you will remember also that he took up in the middle of the year a course in Theoretical Physics, — based on the text-book of Sir William Thomson and Tait, — which had been begun by another, but had to be abandoned by him from finding his work too heavy. He had some ten clever Sophomores in the course; but his heavy artillery was mostly directed over their heads. They complained much to me (as Dean) of their inability to follow him; but Chauncey, with the best intentions, found it almost impossible to accommodate his pace to their

[1] North American Review, July, 1875; Philosophical Discussions, p. 267.

[2] *Ante*, p. 119.

short stride. His examination-papers, by the way, in this course, I remember as models of what such papers should be. Chauncey had as sound views on the subject of education, as fresh and original, and as little biassed by his own peculiar training and deficiencies of sympathy, as those of anybody I ever listened to, but he had no adaptability in practice."

It will, perhaps, also be interesting to read the account which a listener at Chauncey's lectures has given of them. A friend [1] writes: —

. . . "The audience at his lectures was very small, — not more than half a dozen regular attendants, and very few casuals. . . . They made a class of beginners in philosophy. The lectures were delivered in a monotonous way, without emphasis, and they failed to arouse interest.

"I think the explanation of this is to be found in the elementary character which he was obliged to give them, in order to adapt them to his class. In looking over the notes which I took at the time, I find that he began at the very beginning, and ventured to expect no philosophical training, and hardly even a knowledge of philosophical terms, in his hearers. In this sort of work, he had had, I suppose, no experience. A poorer man might have done it better. The class did not aid him much by discussion, — a thing for which he expressed much regret to me in private. But his monotonous fluency seemed, to those of the class who did not know him, to forbid interruption. He showed the utmost patience; but I do not think that he quite knew how to approach the class. . . . He did not talk over our heads; but he failed to interest us. You may think it strange, for you have undoubtedly seen him, as I often have, interest and instruct children and persons entirely without special training. But what he could do in conversation, stimulated by questions, and himself interested in the effect of his teaching or talking, he could not (or at least

[1] Mr. J. B. Warner, a graduate at Cambridge in the class of 1869.

did not) do in these lectures, where he had not one point to expound, but a system to cover, and that to a knot of persons who made little response but devout scribbling in their note-books.

. . . The picture which is vividly before me is of his face rather a blank, his eyes fastened on the desk below him and therefore appearing shut, his frame almost motionless, and his voice even, to a monotonous degree."

To show, on the other hand, the nature of Chauncey's influence over his private pupils, and something of his methods, I will quote a few passages from a letter of one who was under him, both in his public and private instruction:[1]—

"My acquaintance with Mr. Wright began in 1863, when I was in the Lawrence Scientific School. The course there, being adapted merely to the needs of a special calling, seemed too narrow for the objects I had in view; and, having heard of Mr. Wright as an able and learned man, I went to him, and at once decided to take lessons of him in physical and mental science. It was one of the most important and fortunate events of my life. He was an extraordinary teacher for any one who really wanted to study, — always ready with explanations and illustrations of difficult points, always patient and interested. Very soon my hours with him ceased to be mere recitation, and our time was spent more in discussing the points that the lesson raised than in repeating the words of the text-book. Before long I took up Logic, but I did not get a firm grasp of it, and at his suggestion soon took Hamilton's Metaphysics in its stead (following it with Mill's Logic), which we discussed very fully. I was exceedingly interested at once. The change was a wonderful one to me; and, with Mr. Wright's guidance, Hamilton became the great feature of that part of my mental growth. . . . The study

[1] Mr. Henry W. Holland, of Cambridge.

aroused and stimulated my mind as nothing had done before. Mr. Wright was so fair and full in his judgment; and his mental power so far exceeded that of any man that I have ever had the good fortune to know, that he might easily have kept me a mere listener; but his modesty and openness were such that he always treated my suggestions and criticisms as cordially as his own. . . . My lessons lasted only two years or so, but our relation as student and teacher continued to some extent during the dozen years of friendship that followed, for I never ceased to feel the power of his wonderful mind. He used to bring me his writings, or read them to me in his room, particularly of late years, welcoming any suggestion or criticism. . . .

"When he delivered his lectures on Psychology in the University course, they were not all fully written out beforehand; indeed, some were not written at all. He had quite as large an audience as could have been expected, considering the slight attention that the other University lectures received where any work was required from the hearers, — some fifteen or twenty, in his case, I think, rather unequal in philosophical skill, but all attentive and well in hand. . . .

"He had little society talk; but he could converse brilliantly at a dinner table or over the later cigar. He was, however, at his best in his own study, — with his gray dressing-gown on, and with his regularly filled pipe. There many men sought him, as I did, for information or suggestion; and those who came once seldom failed to come again."

To Mrs. Lesley.

CAMBRIDGE, May 7, 1871.

. . . After I finished my lectures, most of which I wrote after I had begun to give them (finding this the safest way), my pen suffered a great drought, and would shed no more ink except in the way of work, — until I began to think that I had lost all power of spontaneous effort. Three charming letters from my friends abroad, received during the winter, still remain unanswered.

Why is it that such an accumulation of short-comings is thought of as an excuse? I suppose it is that we prefer to be thought of as acting on principle though a bad one, and as generally weak rather than particularly wicked. But sickness is a plea I hate almost as much as selfishness, and, indeed, I haven't it to fall back upon solidly; for I have not been ill at all to speak of, — only *glum*, you know, or with an ailment spread out over many months, which consolidated into a week might have needed a doctor's care. . . . With me the spring is still medicinal, which shows that some of the gemmules of youth are in my constitution. I have for a week past resolutely performed a daily "constitutional" of ten miles, with great profit to my sleeping capacities. . . . What you say about your plans for Mary's instruction seems to me admirable, and I can conceive nothing that appears better than your proposal to have her taught topographical drawing; for the arts of the hand have so many uses that I have often thought that the training of it, even without reference to any special accomplishment or proficiency, ought to be a part of liberal education. And now-a-days, when so many arts of this sort are finding their way into the curriculum, like chemical manipulation and the use of philosophical instruments generally, there need be no fear of sacrificing general culture to any narrow utility by such a training. Besides, though men are, as Stuart Mill admits, superior to women in patient plodding of the brain, and certainly in the coarser use of their muscles, as in the stout bearings of burdens, — yet in delicacy, both of muscle and thought, women are doubtless equal, if not superior. Still, it should not be overlooked that the greater part even of genius, or at least of its success, lies in strength and patience, — for many geniuses have told us that their power was "a prolonged patience;" and it is very gratifying and the happiest augury, that Mary has grown to be so strong and ambitious.

I doubt a little, however, about this concurrent testimony of geniuses; for on this point they are not the best judges. They are generally too modest to like, more than other sensible men, to be thought singular; and, finding their work appreciated, they have imagined that others have the same delicacy of perception that they have. They forget that the judgments of criticism and unobstructed afterthought are much easier than those of invention and forethought; and wishing to correct the opinion of dullards, that the triumphs of genius are born without labor, they have exaggerated the importance of strength and effort as compared to skill. I once admired Dr. Johnson's definition of genius as large natural ability *accidentally* directed; but I am now convinced that directive skill, or delicacy of action and perception, is an essential part of it.

I may seem to you to have run quite off the track, since I was talking about Mary and not about Sir Isaac Newton. Still, I am not so far off as may seem, for I do not admit so wide a distinction between talent and genius as would-be geniuses assert in justification of their laziness. The widest difference is mainly this: that genius is led by its skill to apply its efforts successfully to the most difficult, and talent only to the least difficult, work. The first captures a fortress or carries a fortified position: the other makes long and laborious but little obstructed marches.

. . . I had not half told the news before these impertinent abstractions interposed themselves, "which require most plodding and long hammering at single thoughts." I was going on to say that I have a pretty definite (for me) plan of going abroad this summer for a visit, at least to England, and that I have dreamed that I may go in July. This is very far from the concrete engagement of a passage, and, judged by my projects generally, is very far from any sort of realization. Even now I hesitate in making the prediction, lest I abridge my future freedom by a *quasi* promise; since friends hold one another to virtuous courses, or to what they judge for one another the best, by insisting on consistency and by basing their respect for one another on what may be counted on, even to the fulfilling of intentions as well as the keeping of promises. The great majority of my friends and acquaintances in this community have been abroad or are going soon, so that the very obscurity that I love, the shade I instinctively seek from the glare of conspicuous singularity, ought to draw me abroad.

The Gurneys will not go this summer, for they have just moved into their new home, a very attractive house which they have lately built on the heights near Mr. Lowell's. The Norton house is let for two years and a half more to Alexander Agassiz. This looks as if their stay abroad would be lengthened out rather than shortened. . . . They passed the winter in the neighborhood of Florence, in a villa which was at one time, according to a tablet commemorative of the fact, the residence of Galileo, and may have been the place where the great philosopher was visited by Milton. What charm there must be in touching and seeing these material mementoes of great spiritual facts, — to watch the same moon rising over the same city of Florence, from the same point of view, where great thoughts were meditated! This, more than any other motive, makes me wish to visit England, from whose history I am chiefly descended. I grow more and more conscious every year that my most cherished thoughts and interests are of English origin. My blood, though English too, is nothing to them but their accidental road. All American interests and charms are in the future, or in a short past development prophetic of this future. They are not new powers or principles, but better opportunities for the old to work themselves out. They are not the struggle for the victory, but the realization of its fruits. For five hundred years, from the time when old William Occam asserted common sense and experience against the devoted and enthusiastic subtilties of continental and Celtic schoolmen, England has taken the lead in every great revolution in thought and practice, even down to Darwinism. Other nations have done much in carrying out and even in discovering in detail the principles of practice and science; but wherever a great victory had to be won for progress, and principles had to be established not only in experience but against authority, English genius has done it. If this be attributed to English freedom, it comes to the same thing; for English freedom was the product of English genius or common sense, aided, no doubt, by an insular position. Here progress has been substantial. They have kept old forms and names, but changed the things, while their unlucky neighbors, the French, have changed often the names of old abuses and absurdities, but kept the things, — fighting, they think, for progress, but really warring only against fetishes. Therefore, though eight generations removed from English soil, I am still an Englishman, and hope to touch the old ground of these battles again.

To find myself so near the end of a second sheet gives me renewed confidence in my pen, and faith in its rejuvenescence. I hope it may give you as much satisfaction. I shall try next a letter to Charles Norton; and then I shall put in ink and prepare for the print of the "North American Review" some rods I have in pickle for Mr. St. George Mivart, the English naturalist, whose book on "The Genesis of Species" I have nearly finished reading. . . . I never sent you or told you about my criticism of Mr. Wallace's book in the last October number, and as the "Review" has a rather limited circulation perhaps you have never seen it. After what some small critics said of it, I had little disposition to claim credit for it; but now that Mr. Darwin, in his last work, "The Descent of Man," has recognized its merits,[1] I have grown quite proud of it.

To Mr. Norton.

CAMBRIDGE, May 8, 1871.

. . . Hard work with the pen for several months, since I took to writing out my lectures as a precaution against accidental depths of depression, destroyed whatever resources of entertainment that instrument had in reserve for me; and I felt after the lectures were over that I should never make any spontaneous effort again in the way of writing. Time, however, and the reviving influences of spring, give play to slowly uplifting as well as degrading forces, and persistent devotion to "constitutionals" has overcome the long drouth of ink and animal spirits, and I am young and writing again. . . . What times ours are! Late events in France have frequently reminded me of your prophecy before the war, on the disturbances the socialistic element of modern society would produce in the future politics of Europe. The solidity of English genius seems to be the only hope of mankind, — even American mankind. The constant example of English good sense and substantial progress will keep England where she has been for five hundred years, — ahead in all that requires courage and good sense combined. The French accuse her of never fighting for an idea. What she never fought for is the outward sign, the word, — the fetish of an idea. She keeps old names and forms, but changes the things. The

[1] Descent of Man, Vol. II. c. xix. p. 319, note (Appleton's ed., N. Y., 1871). The article is referred to in this book more than once.

French keep the old abusive things, but change their names. English judges still sit on what they still call woolsacks, — monuments, says the French economist Say, of old financial folly. This folly she has no longer, only the name of it; while the communists of Paris are preparing to pull down the great fetish in the Place Vendôme. English conservatism is the only effective religion or guard against radicalism and empirical folly that remains in the world, — except, of course, gun-worship.

Whether the latter will save France this time remains to be seen; but there is hope of it, since the Germans have shown that gunpowder, spite of Teufelsdröckh, does *not* make all men equally tall, *morally.* The God of battles is not on the side of material advantages, except so far as moral superiority has secured them; else moral superiority would never have established any religion in the world, whether it be the Latin races' respect for forms, or the German races' respect for uses. This contrast in religious spirit of the formal and utilitarian faiths, of the fetish worshipping and the tool-using animal, is not, I imagine, so much due to original differences of race in Europe as to accidental relations of races to the current of civilization. Just as one savage will improve on another if he picks up or captures the other savage's fetish, thinking he can turn it to some rational use, or because it pleases his fancy, and having no other respect for it, or no such respect as to paralyze his energies, so Roman civilization improved in barbaric hands; not because of fresh blood, but under a fresh freedom. The torch of civilization has passed from race to race, —from the Aryans to the historic Persians, from the Persians and the Semitics and Egyptians to the Greeks, from these to the Latin races, and thence to the Germans; not simply because the older races have successively become effete or deficient in animal vigor (though this may have much to do with it, since the wealthy and cultured are seldom so prolific as the poor, and civilization doubtless tends to sap energy by perpetuating weakness), but also because the inquisitive, irreverent spirit with which barbarians approach civilization from without — their utilitarianism — has conquered in the long run the spirit of reverence, especially where reverence has rusted into Pharisaism or formal conservatism. The short-lived Arabic and Moorish supremacy was indeed the result of religious movements. But it was a *new* religion, and not the effete product of civilization; a proselyting spirit which brought these Semitic peoples into the same contact with civilization, and with the same freedom as inquisitiveness gave to the northern barbarians. When we contrast the Semitics and Aryans, race-differences become identical with the spiritual differences which in Europe proper were due to the accidents of history. No proper Semitic race ever maintained long a supremacy over Aryan neighbors. They are constitutionally too reverential, and have always been worshippers of fetishes, and have made the greatest advance in this direction, being the most persistent of word-worshippers, while the Aryans have respected tools and uses. We ought to be thankful, then, and confident that history has no necessary cycles, — since Utilitarianism has become the religion of England and Germany; and we should pity the poor French that they have no religion left but fear of hated symbols, or distrust of their own superstitions.

In this we see Natural Selection at work, the theory of which is the consummate doctrine of Utilitarianism. Spiritually, the Aryans and Semitics are distinct races, as men physically are distinct from apes. The German hates the Jew next to monkeys. But as, physically, men differ from and contend with one another (in skill of hand and brain, for instance) on the very same grounds that have given them supremacy over the apes, so, spiritually, Aryans differ and contend on the ground of difference which distinguishes them most widely from the Semitics.

Of course, I am speaking not of that narrow utilitarianism or epicurean doctrine which opposes, but of that which includes and utilizes all other devotions. Men can still climb trees awkwardly, when they have occasion, though they are no longer arboreal in their habits. The modern utilitarian English Aryan can still play for the uses of Church and State on the harp of David, though inharmoniously; can build temples and even burn incense, but he is no longer predominantly reverential. The reverential spirit in the true Englishman no longer takes possession of all thoughtful, meditative moments, like a conscience or supreme practical reason, either to elate or torture him into poetical fervors, as it did David. He uses his feet chiefly for walking; and utilitarian considerations stick in his thoughts and share with reverence his conscience. His reverence must harmonize with inquisitive common-sense and rational considerations of consequences. If it does so, there is no necessary bound to strength of conviction or even to heat of feeling, except in temperament. In Mr. Mill this is capable of great fervors. That Mill should be practically a sentimentalist, and at the same time the greatest prophet of utilitarianism, puzzles many, as I have lately seen in Mr. Mivart's book, — who commends his intemperate sentiments, but condemns his theories, — and as I have heard in conversation with persons who sympathize with his philosophy, but think his expressions of feeling either inconsistent or insincere.

Both the epicurean sensualist and the intuitional sentimentalist so far misunderstand Utilitarianism as to imagine that strong spiritual feelings cannot be moved by or in obedience to so weak a principle as utility; but really the practical strength of this principle depends on how much we regard or prize the ultimate standard, not on the fact that there *is* an ulterior standard for most rules of conduct, beyond the fact that we feel them to be right. So the actual practical strength of utilitarian morality comes to depend on how steadily we can think under strong feeling, or on how strongly we can feel with clear thoughts; and Mr. Mill exemplifies it in a high degree by what appears to his epicurean and to his transcendental opponents as an inconsistency. That he reverences the nature of women or his ideal of womanhood there can be no doubt, and little doubt that this comes in part from his inability to measure or clearly understand a type of mind so different from his own, — the intuitional. It would be only when he saw reason to doubt the guidance of feminine tact that this reverence would receive a shock, but the reverence and tact of the women from whom he has drawn his type avoid this; and as his own clear reason has unconsciously, as you suggest, furnished the guidance that he reverently follows, he worships unreservedly. But we all make our own gods, and then worship them, — no longer indeed out of wood or brass, yet still in our fancy; or, as Voltaire wickedly said, "God created man in his own image, and men have returned the compliment." Still, it is something not to worship another man's god slavishly; better still, not to worship, as Mill passionately refuses to do, a no-man's god, a nondescript block of the Absolute; best of all, to worship what we know to be real, though we overlook its defects.

. . . My dreadful negligence of Miss Grace's and Miss Jane's welcome letters would weigh heavily on my conscience, if I ever permitted such faults to come under its jurisdiction; but now that my inclinations are no longer the sullen rebels they were, I shall write conscientiously without fear of doing it perfunctorily. First, however, I must fulfil an engagement I have made, to deal with Mr. Mivart's book on the "Genesis of Species" for the next "North American Review." Since Mr. Darwin has recognized my last effort, I am encouraged, and defy Mr. Dennett and the "Nation," but only in the hope that I have improved my style a little.[1]

[1] Mr. Dennett, one of the editors of the "Nation," and also at that time the Assistant Professor of Rhetoric at Harvard College, had made certain shrewd criticisms on Chauncey's style in the "Nation," of November 10, 1870 (Vol. XI. p. 315). I give a part of it below: —

"Mrs. John Farrar speaks of a ride which she once took with her husband and Mr. Bailey, the Astronomer-Royal, in the course of which the two scientific men amazed her by talking for an hour together perfectly good English, of which she understood not a syllable. 'The effect was very curious,' she says, 'of hearing people converse in English without being able to comprehend what they said.' We suspect a majority of the readers of the present number of the 'North American' will, once in a while, have much the same feeling in reading Mr. Chauncey Wright's review of Wallace's 'Theory of Natural Selection.' The subject, too, is one more interesting to the general reader than any other in the whole range of science; and the dabbler in science may properly be condoled with on the difficulties which Mr. Wright's style interposes between the amateur student of Darwin and what even an amateur student easily perceives to be a very acute and able discussion of Mr. Wallace's arguments. That the style is evidently a good one, if the reader were only master of the writer's vocabulary, and that the essay is in many places intelligible even to the uninstructed, will increase, rather than diminish, our supposed reader's regrets and aggravate his botheration of mind. . . . It is fair again, inasmuch as we have said what we have about Mr. Wright's style holding his reader off from his subject-matter, to admit freely the difficulty, while suggesting the propriety, of an observance, whenever possible, of Joubert's precept for metaphysicians, that they should not, as too many of them have done, put common thoughts into metaphysical language, but should study, as almost none of them have done, to put their metaphysical thought into the language of common people. The day will be a good one for thought, literature, and instruction, when — decency being saved — the very last is seen of the practice, once prevalent and avowed, of writing for special classes and schools and coteries. By which general remark, we certainly mean no impertinence to authors like Mr. Wright."

To Miss Grace Norton.

JUNE 6, 1871.

. . . I have finished, in the mean time, an article of nearly forty pages for the "North American Review," against Mr. Mivart's book, and in the defence and illustration of the theory of Natural Selection.[1]

I might give you as a foretaste a few of the plums of the meditations which have so lately filled my mind; but I have too much respect for the individuality of a letter and for its true source in one's present imagination, however shallow, to fill it from the memory of past inspirations, however profound. If such had not been my pride, what epistles I might have copied and sent out to you last winter! I will say, however, that among the boldest positions I have taken against Mr. Mivart's theological science are the theses that the doctrine of Final Causes in natural science is not Christian, but Platonic; and that the principle of the theory of Natural Selection is taught in the discourse of Jesus with Nicodemus the Pharisee. Don't imagine, however, that I have given much space to such considerations. Most of the article is devoted to a discussion of the proper evidences of the theory.

. . . What public events, too, have altered the face of the world! I wish we could hope that the bloody peace just conquered in Paris would last; or that there were *cunning* enough in the supporters of the present order of things in Europe to forestall such revolutions by a wise as well as strong conduct of public affairs. But I don't despair of the millennium, or doubt absolutely that the human race may yet find out the secret of peaceful progress, and finally lose the character through which it has risen from animality by

[1] The Genesis of Species: North American Review, July, 1871; Philosophical Discussions, p. 126.

greater powers of destruction than belong to any other race. We cannot hope that any such change will come by the decay of evil passions, or through the influence of good sentiments, until a field for such a culture is prepared through the permanent conquest of strength by wisdom, — that is, by cunning: so that the king shall need no longer to depend on his dukes, or send them before him in bloody battles, and the statesmen have no more need of generals in governing, than men now have of their eye-teeth in securing food or captives. Till then, men cannot be made sufficiently Christian to keep the peace. It may be, or doubtless *is*, true that Paris has brought destruction on itself, because it was not Christian; but this is as little pertinent to a practical view of the matter as is the fact that its palaces were burnt because they were not fireproof. If it were a question whether the barbarism of to-day in Europe were best subdued by priests or schoolmasters, by preaching or teaching, such a fact as the irreligious character of the communists would be important to the statesman. But their ignorance is really the more important fact, since priests cannot reach them now, but schoolmasters may. Priests were themselves the schoolmasters, the teachers of the best learning, in their best and truly effective days. And the question is not so much between religious and secular instruction as between the effete and the effective; or what needs support from society, and what gives support to it. The latter, doubtless, still includes, and must always include, a more or less special culture; that is, a culture of feelings and habits, especially the social and practical.

But one of the chief difficulties with otherwise clear-sighted thinkers, on this theme, is that they are anxious about a substitute for the effete religion, which shall still be, as the old has been, a culture separated out from all the other enlightening and refining influences of civilization. They are searchers for a new religion, — for a new set of propped-up and protected institutes of culture, — for a new church; recognizing, as the old Romans did, by what was doubtless an early compromise in the formation of the state, two sources of authority in law, and two sets of laws, the divine and human. But new churches are essentially schismatic, and none can be catholic; and these thinkers, though earnest and liberal, are not utilitarian. Utilitarianism is indeed their natural enemy, as they instinctively know, though they have their attention distracted from its true position, which is that there is *one source* of culture and refinement, — namely, the best that civilization affords; and *one source* of authority in laws and customs, — namely, the needs of human security, progress, and happiness; and one priesthood, — namely, of the educated and refined, those who feel and understand most deeply the needs and conditions of human or social happiness.

I almost forgot to tell you that I was invited by the Committee of the Free Religious Association to address them in the anniversary week, just past, on "The Attitude of Science toward Religion," — or rather to follow the Rev. John Weiss, who was to make the chief remarks on this theme. They wanted one scientific man to speak, who was not a minister. I must not forget to add that I did not hesitate to decline the honor.

In declining, however, I felt bound to give a reason beside what modesty suggested, or at least a sentiment; and I said in effect, while disclaiming any special knowledge or other than a very subordinate interest in this subject, that I believed no necessary conflict existed between inquisitiveness and proper reverence, and that whatever free inquiry might effect towards destroying our respect for old doctrines of science or philosophy, which have received the sanction and support of religious authorities, there will yet be room enough for human improvement in directions in which reverence will still lead and teach, — at least the practical nature of man. But I preferred rather to subscribe to this article of faith than to expound or defend it.

Your picture of the view from the spot where, as you imagine, Galileo, seeing the same old moon rising over the same old city, thought his great heresy over, — is a sketch of one of the attitudes of science towards religion, which I might have expatiated on, if I had had the skill or courage to do it, though the theme is far from new. Few things could be more instructive concerning the present position of biological science than the series of such *independent* attitudes that the history of science presents. I have drawn a parallel, in my article, between Darwinism and Newtonism in their relations to the methods and demands of "experimental philosophy." This seems to me to be, on the whole, the better way, — better than the invidious reproach of religious authority for its series of blind oppositions and failures, or the glorification of science for its successes; since such a simple induction, or series of instances in the "chemical method," is apt to be fallacious when applied to such questions. For the latest claim against authority, in the name of science, is not more apt to be true on account of such arguments, — to which, indeed, charlatans are generally more ready to appeal than the true philosophers. The same sort of argument is easily invented by the other side. Thus, Darwinism might be put down similarly by showing how often the same heresy has previously undergone miserable condemnation, even at the hands of scientific authority. The only way is to analyze the instances, and, accounting for the success of some and the failure of others, to try the new by the principle of philosophizing thus established. "Sentimental relations with poor, dear Galileo" are, therefore, of little avail for the defence of new heresy. Many a village Galileo or Kepler has doubtless thought himself a martyr (and been one too) at the hands of village hierarchs and schoolmasters, who knew no better than he how foolish his ideas were, but only how obstinate and schismatic *he* was.

. . . It was pleasant to see Mr. Myers back again, so fresh and full of the most agreeable recollections of his journeys and visits. I have met him several times, and a few evenings ago had a very bright and pleasant call from him.

Of the article on "The Genesis of Species," Chauncey sent proof-sheets to Mr. Darwin; and in a letter to him, dated June 21, 1871, he wrote:—

"I send, in the same mail with this, revised proofs of an article which will be published in the July number of the 'North American Review,' sending it in the hope that it will interest or even be of greater value to you. Mr. Mivart's book, of which this article is substantially a review, seems to me a very good background from which to present the considerations which I have endeavored to set forth in the article, in defence and illustration of the theory of Natural Selection. My special purpose has been to contribute to the theory by *placing* it in its proper relations to philosophical inquiries in general."

This was the beginning of a correspondence with Mr. Darwin which continued up to the last year of Chauncey's life, and gave him much pleasure. Mr. Darwin replied to this letter, on July 14, with great cordiality, and asked leave to reprint the article in the form of a pamphlet. "I have hardly ever in my life," he writes, "received an article which has given me so much satisfaction as the review which you have been so kind as to send me. I agree to almost every thing which you say. Your memory must be wonderfully accurate, for you know my works as well as I do myself, and your power of grasping other men's thoughts is something quite surprising; and this, as far as my experience goes, is a very rare quality. As I read on, I perceived how you have acquired this power; namely, by thoroughly analyzing each word. . . . Now I am going to beg a favor. Will you provisionally give me permission to reprint your article as a pamphlet? I ask it only provisionally, as I have not yet had time to reflect on the subject."

On July 17, Mr. Darwin again wrote: "I have been looking over your review again; and it seems to me and others so excellent that, if I receive your permission, with a title, I will republish it, notwithstanding that I am afraid pamphlets on literary or scientific subjects never will sell in England."

To Mr. Darwin.

CAMBRIDGE, Aug. 1, 1871.

. . . My own ambition, my private interest in the fate of my article, is quite fully met and satisfied by your good opinion and kind expressions respecting it. I did not hope to have many readers, even here, who would have any genuine interest in the subject of the article, and not so many in England, where our "Review" has a very small circulation. If I had known beforehand what the article would come to on being written out, I should have determined to send it for publication to some English review, through which it would doubtless have met with a larger number of interested readers. But I undertook the work on rather short notice at the request of the editor of our "Review," and meant it at the start only as a book-notice. Somehow, it grew into the proportions and dignity of a body-article, and was accepted as such. I am only too well pleased that it should be regarded by you as worthy of republication and a larger circulation, and doubtless the editors and publishers of the "Review" will also be. I give permission, of course; but, as to the title, I am a little at fault. I do not well enough know the public scent. Titles of English books are generally more "sensational" than ours;

and, from what you say as to the cold scent the English public have for pamphlets, I suppose that nothing short of a somewhat sensational title will satisfy an English publisher. So I propose something like this: "Darwinism, being an Examination of St. George Mivart's Work 'On the Genesis of Species.'" . . .

I hope soon to publish a paper on the utility of the phyllotaxis, as you suggest.[1] I have already printed two papers on this subject, — one in 1856, in Gould's "Astronomical Journal," No. 99; and the second, in 1859, in the "Mathematical Monthly." A copy of the last was sent you by Professor Gray. In my new paper, I shall avoid as much as possible all abstruse mathematics, which I see has so obscured my thesis that it is only known to mathematicians.

The specialty of the phyllotactic fractions is *not* that they represent complete systems, so that, after a time, some leaf will come over the first one and be connected with the same vessels in the stem; this property would belong to any exact fractional interval; an exact proper fraction, after the number of steps represented by its denominator, and the number of revolutions represented by its numerator, would make a complete system, or bring the next succeeding leaf over the first. The peculiarity of the phyllotactic fractions is that the distribution is most rapid and complete *within* each set or system; that is, it is much more perfect than for other exact fractions. The incommensurate interval of the ratio of the extreme and mean proportion gives the best distribution of all; but here the system is infinite, — that is, no leaf ever comes exactly over an older one.

[1] Mr. Darwin, in his first letter, had expressed much interest in Wright's remarks on phyllotaxis in the article sent him. He stated also certain difficulties in the subject that had embarrassed him from his want of familiarity with mathematics, and expressed the hope that Wright would publish something more on the subject.

I have found among old papers a proof of my first article on this subject; and, for the sake of the diagram of this arrangement, I send enclosed a page of the article. The exact fractional intervals of the phyllotaxis have the distributive character of this most perfect arrangement to this extent; namely, that they determine, as no other intervals do, that every leaf shall fall in the middle third (or not beyond it) of the space between two older ones in which it falls. In all other exact intervals, there is crowding. Take, for instance, $\frac{4}{9}$, which does not occur in nature. Why should it not? The second leaf in this system would be placed very nearly opposite the first, or very near the middle of the space, and the arrangement is so far well enough; but the third falls at eight-ninths, $\frac{8}{9}$; that is, within $\frac{1}{9}$ of the first leaf, crowding up against it yet not near enough to get any advantage from connection with the vessels or sources of supplies which the first leaf has grown from. The fraction $\frac{3}{9}$, or the one-third system, would be better; for though the first and second leaves divide the circumference into one and two parts (the extremest ratio in the phyllotaxis), yet the third falls exactly into the middle of the larger interval, and the fourth is directly connected with the vessels from which the first leaf has grown.

Take the interval $\frac{3}{7}$ for another instance, which does not occur in nature. The second leaf falls, it is true, near the middle; but the third, at the interval $\frac{6}{7}$, is within $\frac{1}{7}$ of the first, crowding it unnecessarily, and has three times as wide a space on one side as on the other. In the phyllotactic intervals, the space on one side of a leaf is never more than twice as great as on the other. In all other cases, greater disproportions would occur in the distributions.

On September 12, Mr. Darwin wrote that the pamphlet was nearly ready, and that he would soon be able to send copies to Wright. "I have sent your article," he adds, "to some friends, and all have been *much* struck with it; but they say, and I agree, that several passages are rather obscure. Even if only a few scientific men will read it, I shall think myself well repaid for printing it; and I thank you very sincerely for your permission. . . . I am glad to hear that you are coming to England;[1] and I shall be delighted to see you at Down."

To the Same.

CAMBRIDGE, Oct. 11, 1871.

I have for some time past been so absorbed in the preparation of a memoir on the *uses and origin* of the arrangements of leaves in plants, that almost every other interest has been put aside; and I have delayed longer than I should, to acknowledge the receipt of the pamphlets you were so kind as to send me. The title-page is much more eye-catching than I anticipated; and altogether the pamphlet appears in a very taking dress. The printer's art may make up in part for defects in the style of the essay, which certainly is not of a pamphleteering sort.

. . . I presented to our Academy last evening my memoir on Phyllotaxy and other points in the structure of plants,[2]—which has become a much more elaborate essay than I expected. It is quite as long as the pamphlet, though the length is partly due to details and considerable repetitions, by which I have tried to give it a popular character. It was well received, and will soon be printed, when I will send you copies. The structure of plants has for a long time seemed to me as likely to afford one of the easiest, though by no means an absolutely easy, example of the use of the theory of Natural

[1] Wright had referred to this in his last letter as a possibility.

[2] The Uses and Origin of the Arrangements of Leaves in Plants: Philosophical Discussions, p. 296.

Selection as a working hypothesis; but I was not well qualified for working it out. I have not, for example, seen the Essay on Plants by Nägeli, to which you refer, and may not be aware of many of the difficulties of the problem; but I have not ignored any that I knew, and on points in physiology I have consulted Professor Gray. I have arrived at very different conclusions from those of that essay (if I can judge from your reference to it), in respect to the range of adaptive characters in plants.

With the resources of hypothesis afforded by the mathematical, mechanical, and physiological principles known to me, I have attempted the explanation of the special features of Phyllotaxy as present adaptations; also explanations of two genetic characters in plants, the general spiral and the whorl arrangements, as past adaptations; and have proposed to reduce the distinction of adaptive and genetic characters in general to a merely relative one. Regarding the latter as inherited features of past and outgrown adaptations, and conjecturing what some of these could have been, I have built an hypothesis across the chasm between the higher plants and sea-weeds. This sounds venturesome and paradoxical enough, much more so, I hope, than it will appear in the essay, where I feel the way along with at least some appearance of caution. . . .

On October 23, Mr. Darwin wrote: "It pleases me that you are satisfied with the appearance of your pamphlet. I am sure that it will do our cause good service; and this same opinion Huxley has expressed to me. . . . Your letter arrived just one day after the return of my two sons from America. They enjoyed their tour exceedingly, and, I think, Cambridge more than all the rest. I am sure I feel grateful for the extraordinary kindness with which they were treated."

And again, on April 6, 1872, he acknowledges the receipt

of the paper on Phyllotaxis: "I have read your paper with great interest, both the philosophical and special parts. I have not been able to understand all the mathematical reasoning; for irrational angles produce a corresponding effect on my mind. Nevertheless, I have been able to follow the general arguments; and I am delighted to have a cloud of darkness largely removed. It is a great thing to be able to assign reasons why certain angles do not occur, or occur rarely. I have felt the difficulty of the case for some dozen years. Your memoir must have been a laborious undertaking; and I congratulate you on its completion. The illustration taken from leaves of genetic and adaptive characters seems to me excellent, as indeed are many points in your paper. . . . I sent you some time ago a copy of my new edition of the 'Origin,' which I hope you have received."

To Miss Grace Norton.

MAY 24, 1872.

It was only a short time after my last letter that my father met with the serious accident from a fall, which, on account of his greatly enfeebled health, soon ended fatally. On returning to Cambridge, I was informed of the sad loss which had befallen you all.[1] . . . The impulse I felt to respond to the short note I received from Miss Jane seemed to me intrusive, rude, unfeeling. This instinct to regard language as a sort of lying device (dating back, perhaps, of its very invention — driving us back, as it were, to the dumb, inarticulate stage of our existence, when nothing but gestures and cries could utter our emotions) is, after all, a false instinct in a rational being, — to be yielded to only so long as it can master the more refined and genuine feelings which reflection

[1] The death of Mrs. Charles Eliot Norton in Europe, in February, 1872.

and speech really serve to express, — which they were not invented to conceal.

Much of the sting of mere animal and inarticulate grief is removed by the form the sorrow takes under the influence of reflection and the calmer, more cheerful emotions which grow up with it. Pure love and true respect, which make their objects as enduring and deathless as they themselves are, take much of the pain away from grief. Their objects are always invisible, whether in the living or the dead, and they suffer no shock except from deceit, or the discovered unreality of these objects, or from spiritual death. The painful shock which we must, nevertheless, feel when a dearly loved friend is cut off in the course of a useful, responsible, or honorable career, — which we do not experience when the work of a life is finished before the life itself ends, — this comes, I am convinced, from an association of the instinctive aversion we have for death, with the sympathies we feel for the purposes, the ambitions, the aspirations of a true and devoted life. It is difficult to imagine that such a breach in nature can be reconciled with faith in benevolent providence. We cannot, at such a time, believe that any thing can replace at all adequately the lost mother's love and care. But time and reflection dissolve this false association; not by that animal oblivion which still fears and shrinks from death, but by the survival and immortality of the real objects of pure affection, — in their past influences, in their essential worth, and in a reverent memory.

I have been a long time detained in Cambridge, but propose to go to Northampton to-morrow for a short visit to my brother. I was quite absorbed a few weeks ago in writing a rejoinder, so to speak, to Mr. Mivart's reply to my criticisms of his book. It is now in print, and will be published in the July number of the "North American Review."[1] I have sent a proof of it to

[1] Evolution by Natural Selection: Philosophical Discussions, p. 168.

Mr. Darwin. It is not properly a rejoinder, but a new article, repeating and expounding some of the points of my pamphlet, and answering some of Mr. Mivart's replies incidentally. I made haste, after concluding to write the article, to finish it and get it off my hands, so that I might be unimpeded in my preparations for the trip to England, — which is now fixed for the 2d of July.

CHAPTER VIII.

THE last letter ends with the announcement that Chauncey had taken his passage for Europe. He was little of a traveller, and this was the only time he ever went abroad: at home, he had never gone further west or south than a single rapid journey to Washington had carried him. An occasional visit to New York or Philadelphia, and his vacation rambles in New England, made up the sum of his journeying.

Of his visit to Europe there is no record of his own, except a letter giving an account of a night at Mr. Darwin's in England, and the mention of one or two details in a letter to Mr. Darwin himself; but Mr. Norton, who met him while abroad, has given me a few facts.

"In the autumn of 1872," he says, "Wright joined us in Paris. He had come abroad a month or two before, had made a rapid but pleasant tour through parts of Ireland and Scotland, and had spent a short time in London. Paris amused and entertained him, but to him it mattered little where he was, — Paris was as good as Cambridge. He carried on his own life of thought, his real life, in the same way in one place as in another. He sought no new acquaintances, partly because he found many old ones in Paris, — ourselves, Mr. and Mrs. Lowell, Mr. Rowse (with whom he was staying at the Grand Hotel), Mr. Henry James, Jr., and others. Before long he followed us to London, and here he was more interested in the great city. One beautiful October day he and I went together to Blackheath to see Mr. Mill, with whom he had had some correspondence; but Mr. Mill was at Avignon. I do not think he tried to see any one else. He met some interesting

Englishmen, especially Mr. John Simon, between whom and himself a strong mutual regard was established. But, before long, he got tired of Europe, and returned home.

"We came home the next spring, and from that time for the next two years and a half he was more than ever an intimate of our house, — always the same thorough, consistent, considerate friend."

To Mr. Darwin.

TAVISTOCK HOTEL, COVENT GARDEN,
LONDON, Aug. 29, 1872.

I hope to have the pleasure of calling on you within a few days, and before leaving London for the continent. I have, after a long but rapid journey with a party of American friends through Ireland and the North, been resting here for several weeks, or rather trying the anti-tourist plan of making acquaintance with London and its neighborhood; that is, taking time, instead of doing it by rapid journeys. This seemed like idling at first, but now I am satisfied with the plan; since it takes time to see any thing well, and especially so great a thing as London.

I was much struck by the suggestive views you give in your last letter[1] of the limits or definition of the effects that can

[1] On June 3, Mr. Darwin had written, thanking Wright for a copy of his article on "Evolution by Natural Selection," which "he had read with great interest." "Nothing," he says, "can be clearer than the way in which you discuss the permanence or fixity of species. . . . As your mind is so clear and as you consider so carefully the meaning of words, I wish you would take some incidental occasion to consider when a thing may properly be said to be effected by the will of man. I have been led to the wish by reading an article by your Professor Whitney *versus* Schleicher. He argues that, because each step of a change in language is made by the will of man, the whole language so changes; but I do not think that this is so: a man has no intention or wish to change the language. It is a parallel case with what I have called 'unconscious selection,' which depends on men consciously preserving the best individuals, and thus unconsciously altering the breed."

properly be ascribed to "man's agency" (or to the agency of free or intelligent wills, as the metaphysical moralists would name it); namely, that intended consequences only are properly attributable to this cause. This seems to me to simplify matters very much, and to be the common-sense view of the subject; and to be decisive with reference to the question of the origin of a language in any way essentially different from the origin of other customs or powers or structures in men or in other living beings.

A practical way of testing the matter would be to ask who are responsible or feel themselves to be responsible for the existence of any language; or who are to be personally credited with the invention, or for any changes or improvements, of a language, — excepting, of course, the inventions and improvements of scientific nomenclatures and those schemes of philosophical language which have been proposed; but even in these, credit is due for the proposition rather than the adoption or the actual existence and use among men of a form of speech. The test of responsibility is all the more pertinent, since it is agreed on all hands that responsibility or the feeling of it, is the evidence, or at least the mark, of so-called free, personal agency.

There is, however, one apparently serious objection to this test as a substitute for your view. We are held by moralists (not the metaphysical ones only) to be *responsible* for more than we *intend*. Therefore, personal agency extends beyond the intended consequences. We are responsible for consequences with which the non-existence of intentions can be charged, as well as for those which are intended. This happens when the existence of intentions which *ought* to have been ours would have altered the result. This objection, together with the mystical doctrine of theologians regarding the nature of the moral sense, gives rise, I am convinced, to that view of free or intelligent human agency which represents it as a line of cause and effect arising in an absolute beginning, thus introducing a condition or an element of causation peculiar and non-natural into whatever effects may be depended on it; and thus making these effects distinct from those that are strictly natural or due to unbroken lines of physical causation. I believe that this view is purely fanciful, or at least poetical; but that it is implicitly contained in, or lies at the bottom of, such objections as Professor Whitney's to inquiries and positions which are really dealing only with strictly scientific or physical problems, and are not concerned with the truth or falsity of the mystic view of causation, either in human or non-human agency.

But, to make this perfectly clear, it is necessary to consider what is strictly true in the statements that our responsibility extends beyond our intentions, that unintended consequences are therefore ours, and hence that our free agency concerns the beginnings rather than the ends of our actions. These statements, which are taken by the metaphysical moralist as absolute premises, *simpliciter*, are properly in need of qualification or explanation, *secundum quid*. They are concerned with the philosophy of moral or personal *discipline*, the question for what men as moral agents are rationally condemned or approved, punished or rewarded. Obviously, it is for many consequences of their actions which they may not have contemplated or intended, *provided* discipline tends effectively to bring such consequences, whenever important, under the purview of foreseeing and intelligent agency; that is, whenever intention *ought* to have been present and efficacious, or *can be made so by the requisite discipline.* But here the responsibility is a different thing from that sense of accountability that is appealed to as evidence of an absolute personal freedom, since responsibility is not really *felt* with reference to unforeseen consequences, or is not felt directly and specifically, but only through the obligation we feel to be better informed, more careful, or to submit ourselves to the guidance and hence to the correction of the better instructed, and to the ultimate authority on what is right or wrong.

Hence the sphere of human freedom and responsibility, though extending beyond what is actually foreseen as the consequences of our actions, is still within the limit of what might and ought to be known as the consequences of our actions; that is, either specifically foreseen, or implicitly contained in a moral principle, instinct, precept, or commandment. In other words, this sphere is limited to the objects and means of moral discipline. Its extension beyond the range of actually foreseen consequences has, therefore, nothing to do with strictly scientific or theoretical inquiries concerning that in which neither the foreseeing nor the obedient mind is an agent or factor, but of which the intellect is rather the recorder or mere accountant.

If the question concerning the origin of languages were how men might or should be made better inventors, or apter followers of the best inventions, instead of being how these inventions have actually arisen and been adopted, there might be some pertinency in insisting on the peculiar character of the choice to which changes in language are due. Moreover, an invention becomes or amounts to a change of language only when adopted by several speakers, or when it is more or less generally agreed to. It is this adoption with which selection is concerned. The inventions, which are, or may be, acts of individual or personal agents only, correspond to the variations in structures and habits from which selection is made in nature generally; and they survive and become customs of speech because they are liked by many speakers. They are thus, as you say, analogous to the variations in domestic animals and plants that are unintentionally converted by savages or semi-civilized peoples into permanent race-differences. Their adoption by the many speakers who fancy them, or choose them for any definite reasons, such as the authority of an influential speaker or writer, ease in pronouncing them, distinctness from other words already appropriated to other meanings, their analogies in sound and sense with other words, and similar reasons, — this adoption seems to me to correspond *very closely* to what you call "unconscious selection."

It appears to me probable that Professor Whitney had in mind, in denying that this is a case of "natural selection," the narrower meaning of the word "natural," as distinguished not only from systematic, intended, or artificial selection, but also from personal agency altogether; or was speaking from that view of natural phenomena, which, "binding nature fast in fate, leaves free the human will." This was the idea of his objection, which I expressed rather obscurely in a foot-note in my review of Mr. Wallace's book nearly two years ago. I imagine that he was also actuated in giving emphasis to the contrast of "nature" and "man" by his opposition to theories of an original natural language, and especially to Professor Max Müller's theory of roots, "the ding-dong theory," or the idea that invention in speech is governed by certain linguistic instincts, different for different races or groups of races, which affix general meanings *a priori* to certain sounds; and that his object was to insist on the *arbitrary* character of all the elements of speech, the roots of etymology as well as their developments. But perhaps I do him injustice by this supposition. Certainly, if he had more carefully considered the theory of natural selection, he would have seen that the theory, as it stands, more nearly accords with the linguistic views which he favors than with those of Professor Müller.

But the theory as it stands is not, it seems to me, inconsistent even with Müller's views, since it ascribes nothing and denies nothing to variations as a direct cause of changes in species or structures or habits or customs. It only attributes to them opportunities or the conditions for *choice*, and does not deny to them other forms of agency. Whether linguistic instincts, responsive to certain root vocables, govern the inventions, or rather the adoption of inventions, in any definite or general way, and independently of accidental associations, — or do not, it is certain that these inventions have such a range as to afford the conditions for a kind of choice that accounts for the diversities and continuous changes in languages derived from a common origin; and for this kind of choice it is obvious that men are neither individually nor jointly *responsible* in any proper meaning of the term. Whether in such choice they are bound fast in faith, or not, is a metaphysical question. But unless we distinguish man's proper agency from other causes in the way which you propose, we must fall into the greatest confusion with respect to other matters besides the origin of languages. Thus, man is a geological agent. He affects and alters unintentionally the physical forces and conditions of the globe. He changes climate even, and its consequences, by actions designed for other effects. Could there be any sense or true philosophy in attempting to establish in physical geology a clear line of distinction between such agency, and that of other forms of living creatures, like the coral animals, — or even that of lifeless physical causes, — in distinguishing between quarrying, for example, and the agency of frosts and storms, or between the transfer of materials in ships and carts, under the direction of seamen and carters, and the transporting agency of other animals and of winds and water currents? These distinctions would be of the smallest importance in geology, though they might be essential from a moral or legislative point of view.

But I have written what reads more like an essay than the letter I intended, though I suppose I ought to be held responsible for its unintended length. It will appear shorter, however, if we regard it as a brief of the case you have given me to work up, — and a more reasonable letter in view of the advantage writing has over talk, in continuous or consecutive discussion.

On August 31, Mr. Darwin writes his thanks for this "long and interesting letter," and adds: "I write now to say how very glad I shall be to see you here. . . . I trust that you will come and dine and sleep here. We shall thus see each other much more pleasantly than by a mere call, as you propose."

To Miss Sara Sedgwick, at Cambridge.

LONDON, Sept. 5, 1872.

I am not unmindful, as you will see, of my promise, — made a long time ago, as it now seems, and in the expectation of a very long letter in return, — to write you after seeing Mr. Darwin. It was some time after getting to these islands before I came to London. I turned tourist soon after landing in Ireland, and travelled with a party of Boston friends (who had a carefully matured scheme of travel), with whom I fell in on the very pleasant voyage we had in the "Olympus." We went through Ireland, leaving my first companion, Professor Langdell, to rusticate there, and across to Chester and Liverpool, and thence by the English lakes and the west coast of Scotland and the Scottish lakes, and through many interesting towns and cities, and by lots of monuments, ruins, and other antiquities, — all in the rapid way of the tourist, which for once I wished to try; and, as I am not doomed to do all Europe in that way, I am very well satisfied with this trial. The panorama is only vaguely impressed on my memory; but future recollections will doubtless serve to develop it into a more vivid picture than I now have or could sketch for you.

When I got to London, and parted with my tourists, a reaction, — or, I should say rather, an inaction, — came on, which, together with the inexhaustible interests of this town and its neighborhood, has kept me here a long time. But there has been so much of Boston here, so many of the best of our neighbors, that I have been very little alone, or at least have had but little feeling of loneliness, in my hearty enjoyment of the many interests which London has had for me. Many an odd or unexpected meeting with American friends has made the imagination familiar or not improbable, that I have only to walk a little way, or to call at some principal hotel, to be surer of meeting some Bostonian I know than I should in Boston itself. Thus, I met Mr. John Holmes one day on the Strand, and afterwards saw a little of him before he went to the continent. This was like meeting Cambridge itself. The last week, I spent several hours every day with Mr. Rowse, whom I luckily met in like manner when neighbors were beginning to be rare. We had many agreeable hours together. Such adventures and interests, together with my laziness, have kept me from seeking out friends belonging here; and so it was only yesterday that I made the little visit to the Darwins, from which I have just returned. A resolution to go to Paris near the end of this week, made with the help of Mr. Rowse, who went last Sunday, prevented my putting off the visit a little longer, so as to meet Mr. George Darwin, who is gone this week on a journey; and who was also absent in travels on the continent when I called at his rooms in London about a month ago. But the pleasure of meeting him again, though it would have added much to the satisfaction of my visit, seems little compared to the all but perfect good time I have had in the last few hours.

If you can imagine me enthusiastic, — absolutely and unqualifiedly so, without a *but* or criticism, — then think of my last evening's and this morning's talks with Mr. Darwin as realizing that beatific condition. Mr. Horace Darwin (whom I like very much, and mean to visit at his college in Cambridge before I sail for home) was at home; and I had several hours of pleasant discussion on various subjects with him, while his father was taking the rests he always needs after talking awhile. Who would not need rest after exercising such powers of wise, suggestive, and apt observation and criticism, with judgments so painstaking and conscientiously accurate, — unless, indeed, he should be sustained by an Olympian diet? I was never so waked up in my life, and did not sleep many hours under the hospitable roof. This morning, as the day was very bright, I walked through charming fields and groves to the railway station, most of the way with my younger host.

It would be quite impossible to give by way of report any idea of these talks before and at and after dinner, at breakfast, and at leave-taking; and yet I dislike the egotism of "testifying," like other religious enthusiasts, without any verification, or hint of similar experience; though what I have said must be to you a confirmation of what you already know. One point I may mention, however, of our final talk. I am some time to write an essay on matters covering the ground of certain common interests and studies, and in review of his "Descent of Man," and other related books, for which the learned title is adopted of *Psychozoölogy*, — as a substitute for "Animal Psychology," "Instinct," and the like titles, — in order to give the requisite subordination (from our point of view) of consciousness in men and animals, to their development and general relations to nature. So, if you ever see that learned word in print, you will know better than other readers when and where it was born! But you will not, I imagine, care so much about the matter of the conversation, which might be repeated, as about its incommunicable manner and spirit, which you will readily supply from your own imagination.

I also found Mrs. Darwin and her daughter very agreeable; and I repent now, as I have regretted all along, that indolence has kept me so many weeks from making acquaintance with so charming a household. . . . I had some idea of seeking out Professor Huxley, as well as Mr. Galton, Sir John Lubbock, and other fellow-disciples; but, not being in season to find them in London, or at home, I have yielded to the suggestions of indolence, and given up the project, at least for the present. . . .

This is the first letter that I have written home, having agreed with those friends who had any reason to expect such an effort from me that I would not do it, unless something more interesting or urgent than could be found in guide-books should warrant it. . . .

To Miss Jane Norton.

CAMBRIDGE, June 19, 1873.

During the winter and spring, I had been unusually well, and part of the time deeply absorbed in one of my essays. I think, however, that I never had a bluer day than that of my landing last November in New York.[1] I became then and there an undoubting convert to the climate theory of the difference between America and Europe, or at least America and England. As our ship steamed up New York harbor in the bleak, early morning, — depressed by the raw, icy air, I

[1] The accounts given by friends who saw him after landing in New York, and for some days afterwards, fully confirm the impression which this letter gives of the depression which attended the first hours of his return home.

was homesick for London, and would willingly have plunged back into its worst winter fogs, confident that I should not have found them worse than the exasperating, nerve-tormenting — otherwise-called exhilarating, stimulating — weather of our natal land. I believe my nerves to be natives of a foggy climate. It may have been, in part, the news of the Boston fire, which was the first tidings of home that came to us from the shore; except the climate, of which I was aware when nearly a day's sailing from land, — a certain look and feeling in the air and sky, which you must have experienced. A season's absence from their influence seemed to increase my susceptibility to them, though I am now, I believe, reacclimated. Our over-praised days in June, of which lately you must have had perfect specimens in Ashfield, — are they not like too large draughts of fragrant or sparkling wine? When well, one wakes in the morning fresh and invigorated, but soon becomes eager and excited by the overpowering day; and before noon one is ready to succumb to its stimulation, — that is, if one has nerves.

I had it in mind all winter to draw a letter from you about what you were seeing and doing in London; but much writing of another sort — not much, after all, yet enough for the usual effect — kept me from turning to the pen with any impulse of spontaneity such as inspires letters, or should do it. I see in Mr. Stephen's letter to the "Nation" that Mr. Mill was in London a short time before his death. I think Mr. Stephen's personal recollections[1] of him quite interesting; yet I do not know whether I really regret not seeing him last fall. I somehow never had the kind of interest in the personality of men whom I have admired for their works that many have, or at least never any strong desire to join my personality to theirs. It is not like seeing more nearly

[1] A letter by Mr. Leslie Stephen on "The Late Stuart Mill," in the "Nation," for June 5, 1873 (Vol. XVI. p. 382).

and intimately the man you have come to know, but is more like seeing his second, his intimate friend, his responsible agent, or even his scribe; though, no doubt, in Mr. Mill's case, I should have been charmed by the social side of the author.

I was a good deal struck with Mr. Stephen's account of Mill's habits of rapid writing and reservation of his thought till it was ripe for rapid utterance, and of his habit of walking great distances.[1] The fact, not mentioned in this letter, that Mill was a skilful botanist, may account, in part, for this habit; but doubtless his walks were the occasion of many a profound meditation. I can imagine him in his rambles, alternately detecting a fallacy in metaphysics and enjoying a new plant. In fact, some of the subtlest points in his writings, which I have passed lightly and listlessly over in reading, have come to me in their full force while walking. Think of any one's walking in America thirty or forty miles in a day without inconvenience! A walk of ten miles here is almost a feat for me, and five a considerable effort, though in London I made nothing of five. Muscular sensibility seems with us to take the place of muscular activity. The American appears to prefer a constrained attitude — his feet above his head — to a vigorous exertion of his muscles with his feet on the ground; and when he moves he prefers to fly, getting over the ground and the movement as expeditiously as possible. He may, with his instincts and nerves, ultimately develop wings, like a bat, and rest, hanging entirely by his heels, like that nervous animal, — a near relation, by the way, zoölogically, to the human species.

[1] Mr. Stephen had said: "It was his habit, I believe, to have every thing closely arranged in his head before putting any thing on paper. The actual writing was, therefore, extremely rapid. . . . Like some other distinguished writers, he was fond of taking long walks, during which his reflections were gradually moulded into a form fit for expression. Within the last year or two, he was still equal to doing thirty or forty miles a day without excessive fatigue."

It is getting very late, and I must reserve the rest of this letter for to-morrow. I spent the first few hours of this evening in a lively discussion with —— on the nature and significance of hallucinations. Whether to-morrow I shall give you the result of this talk, or catechise you on less abstruse matters, will depend on the mood of Spontaneity, that omnipotent but now sleepy divinity of the faithful letter-writer. Good-night.

Morning of Class Day, and no rain yet, nor sign of any. The traditions of the day, as well as the predictions of the weather office, are against hope. Meantime, the grass in Cambridge is dying, looking now as it sometimes does in August, in spite of artificial showers which one sees everywhere from hydrants and hose.

I am this morning, more than ever, provoked with myself for having missed "the much you had to tell, of all sorts of things." Half an hour's talk, — the contents of how many letters might have been compressed into it! . . .

I can well believe that coming home, after so long and in some respects grievous an absence, must have been a very sad, yet, by turns, a joyous experience. Sorrow, springing from tender regards of home, kindred, or friends, is not an emotion of so unmixed a pain that we shun the thoughts that inspire it, or seek to repress them. Imaginations of a painful and pleasurable kind alternate in this emotion, — offset and heighten each other. We turn from one to the other, from the depression of deprivation or loss, past or present, to the contemplation of worths remaining or restored to us, or still retaining an inward reality for us. Sorrow is a mixture having all the substance or weight of the pleasures and pains that compose it, but has the special qualities of neither. It is a chemical union of them, in which these qualities are neutralized, but in which weights are combined. Feeling has a substance, a depth, a weight with the will, which is not in its character, either as a pleasure or pain; but it is none the less a volatile salt of life, and is dissipated in time.

I hope the exertions and excitements of getting once again settled in your Ashfield home will not be found to have drawn too largely on the strength of any one of you. One feels such expenditures only some time after they have been incurred. But I imagine you, though resting, still preoccupied in gathering up old threads of association, bridging over, contrasting, or blotting out much of the interests and incidents of the long interval, — seeing, not without regret, that which has been so real fade into a dream.

I have been a good deal interested in England for a little time lately, — the England of the past and the present, — while reading M. Taine's graphic criticisms and interesting theories of English literature. His style gives the impression, which I have heard expressed, of his writing on a theory and adapting his observations to it. But it strikes me as a well-considered theory, founded on much previous sagacious observation, though the only part of his book which I feel quite competent to judge, his criticisms of Mill and the "Experience Philosophy," — as well as those on the same subject in his later work on "Intelligence," — seems to me weak. In these criticisms, he has obviously reached beyond the length of his tether, though he may be still quite sound in his views of English imagination, and its causes and developments.

Did you see any thing of Mr. Darwin last winter? I have heard nothing from or about him, except a statement in the newspapers last month that he was in Paris. This seemed to indicate unusual health and vigor in him. I did not send him my last essay in the "North American;"[1] for I preferred that he should be led, if at all, by his own interest in the subject to read it.

[1] Evolution of Self-Consciousness: North American Review, April 1873; Philosophical Discussions, p. 199.

Metaphysics is not his forte; and I feared to bore him, or at least desired not to compel from him either a judgment or a confession. I ought to have waited, and expanded the subject into a book, as —— suggested to me last fall in London, instead of publishing the sketch, which the article really is. But the editor of the "Review" demanded it, and I weakly gave it to him.

To Miss Grace Norton.

[JANUARY, 1874.]

Thanks for your notes on ——'s pamphlet. If you say you find it "easy to understand," I shall have something to say, when we meet, on the subject of understanding, — on the subtle distinction between understanding an author, or *why* he said so and so, what facts he had in mind, what divisions or distinctions he makes, or tries to magnify, in his subject, or what his motives were to the effort; and the understanding of his theory and of his statements in detail, with the degree of precision which analytic habits of thought demand. There is ease and ease — two kinds — in understanding. Mathematics is easy in one way, — cannot be misunderstood, except by gross carelessness; is no more vague than a boulder; is either out of, or in, the mind entirely. To make progress among a heap of boulders is, you know, far from easy, in one way; but it is easier than walking on water, or than clearing the rough ground by flight. It is easy to dream of making such a flight, and to have every thing else in our dream as rational as real things; and it is easy to be actually carried on the made ways of familiar phraseology over difficulties which we are interested in only as a picturesque under-view, but which do not tempt us to explore them with the chemist's reagents, the mineralogist's tests, or the geologist's hammer. But I am running on to say what I have promised to discuss with you in talk about this scientific understanding.

. . . My prime motive in writing, in disobedience to your commands, is my impatience to make known to you before the light of this bright day wanes, why you failed, as I at first did, yesterday, to see the black letters red.[1] I took a copy of the same blue book, on which I saw in the horse-car (and made others see) the black letters gleam with the color of gold; but, in the light that enters my sanctum, I could only see a faint dark red tint. The humiliating suggestion then occurred to me that perhaps the red curtains of the car-windows, though not golden in tint, might have contributed to the effect. If I had yielded to this suggestion, I should have punished myself unjustly. (*Peccavi*, let me add, ought to be only a general and comprehensive confession, or a presumption to be particularly applied only after judicial trial.) So I queried: What were *all* the differences of circumstances yesterday and the day before? I did not have to make a very long catalogue; only this: (1) Yesterday's light was brighter. This I diminished, but without the expected effect. (2) The book I saw the day before was a fresh one; its cover had not lost the polish of pressed paper, as a handled book soon does; the black letters had perhaps a smoother surface, and reflected white or surface light more perfectly. It was easy to restore this surface to the letters of my copy by rubbing them with a hard, smooth body, — the end of a knife-handle or paper-knife. This I did, — and beheld the letters gleam in the reflected daylight with a brighter hue of gold than I had seen before. Even the gaslight, in the evening, was sufficient to produce this effect, which I then took pains to guard from illusion by submitting it to other eyes.

[1] Wright had been surprised, one day in the horse-car, by seeing the large black letters of a title, printed on the dark-blue cover of a pamphlet, have the color of gold when the light struck them aslant; and he had endeavored to reproduce the appearance.

There are morals to be drawn from science as well as a science from morals. It is tame bathos, perhaps, instead of vague sublimity, to rest from scientific effort in the following reflection, — but I make it nevertheless: How much better for truth is patient induction and the use of judgment, than obedient deduction, humility, and submission to judgment? . . . Such patient, busy dealing with truth is sometimes falsely called humility. It is properly a reasonable pride; though if a metaphysician were to come down to it, it might be regarded as an act of humility. It is not humility to walk and climb when one sees clearly that he cannot fly; it is simply good sense. But of this anon.

To Miss Jane Norton.

MARCH, 1874.

Your note found me to-day in the midst of a metaphysical composition, and instead of distracting me infused a certain vigor of style into what I went on to write, — as I noted afterwards, or thought I did. Concrete inspirations, such as balmy air, or notes of inspiriting music, have this effect, as I have observed, of making abstraction more sure-footed.

No doubt, I shall gain for my composition (if it is not abandoned or completed before that time) an additional advantage of this sort by my coming down on Friday or Saturday — both will be free days to me — to the level of concrete magic and the entertainment of the children and their friends. At any rate, I shall be pleased to do what my art can for their pleasure on either day, and I will come to lunch as you propose. The only preparation which might be needed for some tricks is the "negative condition of darkness" of the spiritualists, or, at least, a light not especially appropriate to a sunny afternoon. But this, if necessary (and children have a savage's keenness of perception), may be had by closing the window-blinds in one of your rooms. It is only in the magical shower of bon-bons and the trick of the magnetized cane, and perhaps in certain card tricks, that two such powers of nature as a bright daylight and a bright child's sight would together be likely to defeat the powers of magic. In other tricks, however, which may be as good as a feast, I am, as you know, as powerful against light and sagacious observation as any Indian juggler.

To Mr. E. L. Godkin.

CAMBRIDGE, June 3, 1874.

I do not think that, in the talks of which you write, I mistook or misstated the argument in your article on woman's submission, in the way you suppose.[1] It was clear to me that you did not agree with Mill's theory (and without important qualifications I do not); and it was clear that the "fallacy" to which you wished to call attention was a fallacy of reasoning from his own assumptions, — namely, the assumptions that submissiveness in one sex and imperiousness in the other had become through ages of subjection heritable dispositions, which, nevertheless, legislation and opinion might alter or gradually eliminate. These assumptions seemed to you (and they seem to me) to involve the farther assumption, that such acquired qualities are sexually limited in their transmission; the one going down to the males alone and the other to the females alone, — or for the most part, — and passing, half the time, latently through the opposite sex, as from the maternal grandfather to a grandson, or from the paternal grandmother to a grand-daughter.

[1] The reference is to an article in the "Nation," of May 14, 1874 (No. 463), on "Woman Suffrage in Michigan." Some conversation with Wright relating to this article had been incorrectly reported to Mr. Godkin; who then wrote to him, in order to get at his views upon the points in question, and received this reply.

Now you think that such a mode of transmission is limited to natural (non-acquired) qualities alone; that is, to the natural or (relatively speaking) *fixed* distinctions of sex. You think that the contrary opinion would be, if true, "one of the most extraordinary facts in anthropology," and would need more evidence to substantiate it than appears in the case. "The non-transmission of paternal imperiousness to daughters would be a most extraordinary fact," you think, if we suppose this quality to be an acquired one; yet Mill has virtually assumed the fact without explanation. This is what I understood you to mean as the "fallacy" of the argument; and it might readily be admitted to be an omission of an important part in the exposition of the argument, — though not a very serious one in view of existing and published physiological evidence, or even of the not uncommon common-sense of unlearned but observant folks, on the subject of heredity. But I could not see the fallacy of this assumption, especially as it is true that "new characters often appear in one sex [both in men and animals], and are afterwards transmitted to the same sex, either exclusively or in a much greater degree, than to the other." (Darwin on Animals and Plants under Domestication, ch. xiv. Vol. II. p. 92, Am. ed.)

Under domestication (and no race has been longer or more completely under domestication than the human, especially the civilized branches), the secondary sexual characters are often found to be very variable, and "to differ greatly from the state in which they exist in the parent species." Now, it makes no difference in the argument whether we suppose the imperiousness of male men and the submissiveness of the female to be derived from a very remote animal race (as is most probable to the evolutionist); or suppose, with Mill, that these qualities were acquired, or at any rate increased, through the social conditions of barbarism. The fact is that the most fixed and the most uniformly transmitted physical qualities are not more governed by sexual limitation in inheritance than are the variations, whether normal or abnormal, which physiologists have studied.

. . . From the various facts recorded by Dr. Lucas, Mr. W. Sedgwick, and others, Mr. Darwin concludes that "there can be no doubt that peculiarities first appearing in either sex, though not in any way necessarily or invariably connected with that sex, strongly tend to be inherited by the offspring of the same sex, but are often transmitted in a latent state through the opposite sex." Analogous evidence from domestic animals is also given, — such as the unusual difference in size in the two sexes of the Scotch deer-hound, and the peculiar color of a variety of cats, called the tortoise-shell, being "very rarely seen in a male cat, the males of this variety being of a rusty tint."

But such evidence would perhaps have little force with those who are interested mainly in its bearing on the woman question. The purely physical character of these examples of inheritance, as limited by sex, would also rule them out of the case with many such judges, — unless, perhaps, the rather numerous and conspicuous cases of the psycho-physical peculiarity of color-blindness were admitted in evidence.

That some mental and moral peculiarities are inherited in men, as some are well known to be in domestic animals, would doubtless be admitted by disputants, who would, nevertheless, deny that there is any evidence of sexual limitation in the transmission of them; and who might, on the contrary, assume, in spite of the resemblance of them to corporeal peculiarities in being heritable, that they are not sexually limited in the line of inheritance, — seeing that "mind and matter differ by the whole diameter of being," and that the mind has no sex! Mr. Galton has done something towards clearing up the matter, by his researches on hereditary genius. It is certain, however, that the evidence in respect to the heritability of mental and moral peculiarities is much less clear in general, and especially in reference to sexual limitation, than that of physical peculiarities. But here Stuart Mill's fundamental assumption comes in for the explanation of this fact. Without denying the reality and importance (assuming them rather) of hereditary elements in the formation of mental and moral character, he ascribes a very large and important influence to *education;* including, in the meaning of this term, the unintended and unsystematic discipline of circumstances as well as the designed. The mental and moral characters are not born with the body of a man, and are, according to him, almost as much the offspring of teachers and society as of parents in the flesh. This assumption is probably near enough to the truth to explain why so little evidence appears in the human race, like what the mental and moral peculiarities of breeds of race-horses and dogs afford, in reference to the principles of inheritance.

But Mill seems to me to go altogether too far in this matter, and to attribute a disproportionate power to discipline, custom, and legislation; though it would be difficult to say what the true proportion of these influences to inherited ones really is, in the growth of individual minds and characters. I agree with you that the imperiousness of the man and the submissiveness of the woman are natural dispositions, or are fixed characters, so far as legislation can directly and designedly affect them, or so far at least as they can be immediately affected by any other legislation than that of Plato's Republic, — or where the state is a grand selective human breeding institution, conducted on scientific principles, and with unlimited powers. But I nevertheless agree with Mill that, natural as they are, they are still alterable, and have been altered by civilization. I do not think it improbable that savage conditions of society have increased these dispositions from what they may have been in a primitive human or more remote animal ancestry, and that civilization has again diminished them.

It has been noticed by more than one student of anthropology that civilization tends to assimilate the mental and moral characteristics of the sexes; and that, in moral characteristics at least, men have been more changed toward a common type than women. This anthropological observation agrees significantly with the more general biological fact, which I have quoted above; namely, that the male is commonly more variable than the female, and most variable in respect to secondary sexual characters. In the human race, the beard is a familiar illustration. It is wanting in most races of men, and is very variable in the bearded ones. Even allowing the full force which Mill seems to claim for disciplines, customs, sanctions, and institutions, when acting persistently, to modify inherited dispositions, — there would be no fallacy, but, on the contrary, very great reasonableness, in supposing these modifications to be sexually limited in their transmission; seeing that they are so limited in their direct effects on the parents. The male Scotch deer-hound has thus acquired, and is at the present time, from the want of his old training, actually losing, his abnormal superiority over the female in size and fleetness.

There is, however, one fundamental physiological fact accordant with your views, and pertinent to what women may do or become in the future, which Mill has almost entirely overlooked, and which late physiological writers on this subject have not sufficiently emphasized; namely, the difference of the human sexes in main or brute strength and courage, and its relations to mental and moral superiority. At first sight, this difference would seem, however firmly fixed or natural, to be only one among many cases of sexually limited inheritance, alterable by civilization, and not essentially related to primary sexual differences; or to be merely due to the savage's necessity of capturing, maintaining, and defending his spouse or spouses. There seems, however, to be a physiological relation of mere strength, or of unappropriated energies available for emergencies, which is more direct and essential, and is possibly sufficient to raise this difference to the rank of a primary one, or at least to an essential relation with the primary sexual differences; namely, its relation to child-bearing. Not only is the normal strength less in the female, but its resources are kept in reserve by a special check of constitutional habit during this period of life, except in gestation; for which occasions this general reserve, or restraint of force in all other directions, appears to be especially adapted. Whatever the ambition or energy of purpose in the woman may be, she cannot draw on her resources of main strength at much more than half the rate the idlest men ordinarily do. This conclusion is founded, so far as its estimate of quantity is concerned, on the ultimate physiological measure of expended energy, — the waste of the system, — and especially that determined by its gaseous exhalations in the form of the carbonic acid gas of respiration, the measure of oxygen consumed, which is, in the average, twice as great in the adult man as in the female (except in gestation) during the child-bearing period. This looks very like a natural check put on the ambition of the female, and a compulsion of nature, beneficent on the whole, which assigns her to her natural functions, however vehemently the individual's ambition may determine otherwise, or rebel against this lot.

Even Mill recognizes one point of inferiority in the mental power of women, which it appears to me is ultimately referable to this physiological necessity; and not, as he seems to suppose, to an alterable inheritance. He says, "The things in which man most excels woman are those which require most plodding and long hammering at single thoughts." This is analogous to the muscular strength manifested in the stout bearing of burdens. Darwin regards it as an admission of greater energy and perseverance in the man ; qualities which, with his greater courage, will (other qualities being equal) give him the victory in most competitions. But there is an ambiguity in the terms, energy, perseverance, and courage, which makes this conclusion far from clear or completely satisfactory. There is a moral as well as a physical courage, and a strength of purpose not altogether dependent on strength of nerves. The spiritual sources of untiring patience and perseverance are quite as important for the victories of genius as the available physical resources of work. But these, in turn, must set limits to the most urgent ambition or to the efficacy of the greatest spiritual strength. The woman, very likely, since she is most susceptible to moral and social influences, is apt to live more nearly up to the limit of her available strength. Whether this expenditure equals in effective amount, on the average, the average work which the consciences of men (less susceptible to spurs) call out from their uninvested resources, would be a very difficult problem. It is much easier to see that the most efficient patience and perseverance, or the genius, in which the greatest susceptibility to motives to work, and the greatest available resources of energy are combined, is most likely to be found in the man ; even supposing the mental machinery to be, on the average, as perfect in one sex as in the other. It was upon this last element of genius, its machinery, which is mainly a product of discipline, that Mill fixed his attention too exclusively ; to the neglect especially of the differences of sex in uninvested or available resources of mere energy or motor power.

Touching the suffrage question, I agree entirely with you, and not at all with Mill, and solely on grounds of public policy, — on which I conceive the right and justice of the suffrage to rest. If, instead of the more probable effect of long-continued civilization in softening the imperiousness of men, women could be made by it Amazonians, there might be occasion to conciliate them, and secure the state from anarchy by making them participate in the responsibility of its government. Or if, on the contrary, this basis of the suffrage — the anarchical basis, I call it — should become in the far future less important than it is now, the suffrage might become restricted to a much smaller body of electors than now; and individual women with the requisite qualifications, which would probably have no relation to sex, might be included in this body. On the first supposition, however, the Amazonians would probably conquer by a more primitive form of election than what they would have gained through the suffrage; a form of choice of rulers, which they would have by natural rights, or without political endowment, — namely, sexual selection. As imperious men would have become intolerable to them, that variety would become extinct, and power would have passed involuntarily from its unnerved hands. The qualities of imperiousness and submissiveness, which have for so many ages been associated constitutionally with sex, or been sexually limited in inheritance, would probably, in this not unparalleled case, still remain associated with sex; but would have changed the line of descent, — as supernumerary and deficient digits, color-blindness, and other peculiarities sometimes do.

Agreeing, as I do, with your main practical conclusions on the woman's suffrage question, there was no occasion for me to publish my dissent from one of your arguments, — or from your objections, rather, to one of Mill's; especially as the interested partisan does not distinguish with clear logic between an objection to an argument and opposition to the conclusion.

Excuse the great length of this letter; for being engaged

in the matter I was tempted to make clear, at least to myself, my views on the subject.

To Miss Jane Norton.

CAMBRIDGE, June 23, 1874.

Thanks for your whiff of Ashfield. I suppose that it must seem a much longer time to you. The shifted scene, the rattling machinery of the stage (by rail and the stage-coach in real life, — as well as at the play), count moments or hours for months and years; a longer time to you than to those whom you leave behind, or who, like me, keep memory in bonds of terrible subjection to the present. When let loose, or breaking away in one of these life-scene shiftings, what pranks it plays; with what sportive contradiction it drags its chain, — combining and confusing the true distinctions of time, shifting the costumes, stealing the gray robes of the sober long-past and putting them over the petticoats of the customary just-past, and decking out the old Then with the vivid motley of the Now. If memory were always so lively, it might be more serviceable; but not perhaps in just this way, which, though a lively movement, can hardly be called progressive. This display is interesting psychologically, as showing the nature of the faculty; just as dancing and athletic sports show the capacities of our limbs in their greatest, though least serviceable, range of action.

No doubt, sports are measures of capacities for work. The humor of an age is an index of its sober interests. The animals that dream are nearest man in intelligence, and dreamers among men are nearest the great poets. These pranks are moreover instructive, as showing, by contrast, what are the more common illusions of memory. Whatever conscience (the court of resident foreign ambassadors in us) may require of memory in behalf of prudence and considerateness, this servant does grudgingly; it is secretly in alliance with our individual weaknesses and unreason. The memory and the self are one in the flesh. Its black marks are more delible than the white. Pleasures last longer than pains in memory, or more of them last, because the selfish will practises memory secretly in the rehearsal of them. For the most part, we remember what we like, and are therefore grateful to memory, — the indulgent, the kind, illusive painter of the past, whose pictures are on the whole bright day-scenes, — or, at worst, tender twilights. I say, for the most part, and on the whole, notwithstanding typical instances to the contrary, which memory, no doubt just now on its duty, will be pleading to your consciences as proofs of its fidelity.

But it is unreasonable to expect that a wise court of Olympus will listen uncritically to the testimony of this Hermes in his own trustworthiness. Conscience does not really trust the crafty cup-bearer, but is always trying to surprise him by the accidents of life, — searching his pockets, setting the eloquence of the preacher against his persuasions, shifting scenes to catch him at his thefts. But this only incites him to his grander pranks and lies, — as you were observing in a sentence, and as I have been repeating through these pages, not exactly in rhyme.

You seem to doubt whether the memories of the blind are capable of such great revivals, or the rousing of great feelings by little thoughts and impressions, since they lack the associations of vision. I have no doubt they are so capable. Why not?

The world is always as large as the mind, and varied in as many individual objects or impressions as the interests of feeling can create in it, though these be only groups of touches and sounds. Or the unexperienced world is so much greater than the mind that it presses through narrowest crevices into the moulds prepared for it in our capacities for thought or feeling. Mr. Darwin quotes about Laura Bridgman, that, "when a letter from a beloved friend was communicated to her through the gesture language (by touch), she laughed and clapped her hands, and the color mounted to her cheeks." "On other occasions, she has been seen to stamp for joy." Here, touches alone gave a world large enough to rouse depths of feeling to which greater and graver depths doubtless answered.

At this point, I broke off my talk for lunch; and, after lunch and a talk with a friend from our table, who came to smoke with me, we were summoned by discharges of cannon to the festival scenes of the Dedication ceremonies.[1] I wandered without design in the crowd, or with the design only of escaping shortly back to the high, moralizing themes of this letter. But unjust fortune ruled otherwise. I espied classmates in a procession; joined them; was conducted with them to within a few benches from the speakers; heard every word, the prayer included; and learned afterwards that I had unwittingly joined the honored company of "the Committee of Fifty;" whereas many enthusiastic ladies, who had thought of nothing all day but to enjoy the things I despised, who had waited patiently an hour and a half of the hot afternoon for this purpose, were given reserved seats where they could hear nothing. The hall appears to have poor acoustical capacities; but does not seem worse adapted to the end of hearing than Providence seemed to be for bringing right ears to the hearing point. But perhaps devotion and enthusiasm are, in the arrangements of Providence, their own great and sufficient reward; and the occasion as a whole duly honored, may have more than compensated for the loss to its devotees of its details. Not to know what they lost may be a blessed ob-

[1] The dedication of the Memorial Hall at Cambridge, on Tuesday afternoon, July 23, 1874.

livion. I cannot tell how great an enthusiasm would have survived it. . . .

I have projected a philosophical dialogue with three interlocutors (to represent duly the varieties of the human mind), into which I propose to introduce the metaphysics I was writing some time ago, — about the time of your magical party for the children, — and all the various points of my recent studies in optics. It shall be called "Color and Form," and may include, among other things, some art criticisms, which I talked about with —— on Sunday. First scene, Sunset; second, a Laboratory, or Study by gaslight, with Huxley Perkins's Positivist Hymn.[1] I propose to explain in the person of my scientific sceptic why colors exist, and to make him confound the teleology of the æsthetic and religious enthusiast, in accordance with the judgment of my third interlocutor, who shall have good sense without subtlety, and shall keep the others down to the point of intelligibleness. I have not thought yet what names to give them, except A. B. C. Perhaps Greek names would be best. But shall they all be men? or shall the sensible one, or shall the enthusiast, be a woman? What do you think? If she be the sensible one, her decision might be attributed to personal preference or prejudice. If the enthusiast, it would be ungallant that she should be defeated by two men. I doubt if sex would not complicate the plot, and compromise the argument, as Mr. Godkin thinks it would in politics.

Perhaps you will help me in the dramatic arrangements. I think that, to begin with, a sunset is a happy thought. It introduces the colors so naturally. The scientific observer shall be looking at it between his legs, and the æsthetic religious enthusiast will disdain to do so. Shall I send the parts, as they are done, in the form of letters?

[1] This refers to an amusing piece in the "New York World," professing to be the account of the life and death of a positivist child.

To Miss Grace Norton.

JULY 14, 1874.

I fear the "conversational essay" will have to wait on conscience, too; for, in my thoughts about it lately, I have been going on with my speculative researches or theorizings in my head, not liking to arrest their growth by putting them prematurely in any form on paper; but "mewing their mighty youth and kindling their undazzled eyes at the full mid-day beams" of crucial tests and facts. Having settled several questions of physiological optics to my satisfaction, the last being "why colors exist," which includes in its answer why the delight in them exists, instead of giving this delight as the answer (a very subtile teleology, you see, — I hope you won't condemn it as "ingenious," as the unconvinced do), I have taken up another subtile question, to which the various momenta of my theories have led up; namely, how touch and sight alone, without the muscular sense, or how the nerves of the skin and the retinæ alone, give a perception of space, as I am convinced they do. This conviction came after the explanation; for I had previously believed, with most of the German and English physiologists, that tactual sensations, including the retinal, give only associated "local signs," without giving any idea, or any essential constituent of the idea of extension in objects. I was led, without making any hypotheses that were not probable antecedently and applicable to previous questions, to an explanation of how tactual impressions may be perceived immediately as more or less *distant* from one another; that is, independently of the changes consequent on muscular movements, or independently of the muscular sense, as well as of their own proper qualities and intensities. This explanation is very far from going back to that ignorant assumption of absolute simplicity, or immediacy in the perception of space or extension, which some metaphysicians have made in the teeth of physiological facts. I take, however, a shorter physiological road, and one that leads to a more immediate relation of tactual sensation to the perception of extension than that of local signs associated with movements. The effect of attention moving over a tactile surface, or from nerve to nerve in it, or the cerebral incitement or quantity of innervation produced by attention, gives a physiological datum in the perception of extension which has not been, so far as I know, yet taken account of. I do not consider it a merit of the theory in which I take account of this new quantity as an element in space-perception, that it seems to accord with common sense more nearly than the older one, for common sense is stupid in this matter. A power of trained imagination is indispensable in this most difficult subject, or an understanding which can not only emancipate itself from the stress of sense, but can even turn round and subjugate sense combinations to its analysis, or see how we see, without visualizing and thus duplicating the process.

There is endless confusion, it seems to me, in the still more abstruse questions of metaphysics about object and subject in perception, on account of the lack in thinkers of that analytic imagination, or abstractive understanding, which can possess itself of the dissolved yet distinguished elements, instead of the broken pieces, of sensuous images, and can put them together chemically, so to speak; or can take up a movement in perception as it individually exists, dissecting it out both from what causes it and from what follows it. I wonder whether you get any adequate idea from this most inadequate sentence, or are duly impressed by it with the difficulty of exposition I shall have to contend with in setting forth my theories.

Science has compelled psychologists to the so-called empirical theory of perception, but has not yet, for the most part, trained their imaginations to the adequate comprehension of empirical idealism, to which I believe they will have to come.

Idealism is a "discipline," rather than a theory; or is true only to an understanding subtile enough not to grossly suppose an external world to be demonstrated, or the question of its nature in any way affected, by striking the ground with a walking-stick. But this theory is in need of a little clearing up as it stands. Its positions are somewhat dislocated, from its contest with metaphysics. It has hitherto made too emphatic its incidental opposition to metaphysical substance in matter, and has become itself metaphysical by positing a substance of consciousness. Empiricism has driven philosophy from both these positions. The real and essential battle of idealism is then against the transference of the introspective duality, or distinction of subject and object in consciousness, to the line of physical causation in perception; or is against the confusion of the physical conditions of perception with the object of it, and of the psychical conditions with the subject as introspectively distinguished.

About this time last summer, I discussed with Professor Wyman the substitution of new terms in physiology for the metaphysically confused terms, "subject" and "object;" proposing to call what depends in consciousness on internal conditions "encephalic," instead of subjective, and what depends on external ones "eccephalic." I held that an hallucination is objective, though encephalic, and that its illusory character does not make it a subjective phenomenon, or an imagination, as is sometimes supposed. The accidental or after-images of vision, and other illusory appearances, are sometimes called by English writers "subjective," by a still cruder use of these vague words. The true and false in judgment, or the real and unreal in consciousness, is not a distinction coincident with the introspective division of mental states into subjective and objective. One may either truly or falsely remember and imagine, and either truly or falsely perceive and act. The true and the false, or the real and unreal, of waking and dreaming, are not the two worlds (as they are somewhat poetically called) of the duplicate or reflective consciousness. Although it is proved by all experience that an objective phenomenon of encephalic origin, like a dream, is illusory, yet this is not an identical proposition, or its truth is not involved in the meaning of its terms. That subjective phenomena are all encephalic is empirically known; and the converse of the proposition, or that all encephalic is subjective, is not true.

The aid I hope to get from the form of the conversational essay is, of course, the motive I have for turning dramatist. But this form brings its own peculiar difficulties, which is the reason, I suspect, why it is not more often used. All that I have put on paper are certain headings of subjects. The dramatic arrangements are still in the shell, while the main themes are some of them still moulting. But do not suppose that I shall send you these lucubrations as substitutes for letters. I shall probably write long prefaces to each part in way of letters, as authors always do, making a great flutter about the new-fledged things, gratulations that they have survived the dangers of callow youth, and deprecations of injurious criticisms.

To Miss Grace Norton.

JULY 29, 1874.

I have just tried my butterfly nature in search of summer sweets. I spent Friday night at Blue Hill with the Putnams. On Saturday, I flitted to Portsmouth, going in the evening on a picnic, up with the tide, on the banks of the Piscataqua, and floating, after tea, down the tide in the moonlight very romantically. On Sunday, Mr. Emery and I walked or crawled to York, visited our friends, the Brookses, of Cambridge, absorbed the beauties of the place by sunset, and returned by moonlight, —

a round trip afoot of more than twenty miles. Mr. Emery is an excellent travelling companion, devoted mainly to the business afoot. . . . We only settled on the walk one important question, which Clifford Watson, at the picnic, had propounded from his experience in boating. We, or at least I, concluded that the question was to be decided by moral, not mechanical, causes; and I generalized that in the moral world difficulty increases success, instead of diminishing it, as in mechanical efforts; and that the problems of boating were threefold, or depended on three classes of *momenta*, — the purely mechanical, the physiological, and the moral, the several advantages of which have in practice to be duly adjusted; a very *owl-wise* settlement of the practical question!

On Monday, I had no disposition to walk, but took wing again, and alighted on the way back at Magnolia, where I found my young friend, Meggie Lesley, and several other friends. Mrs. Lesley was gone away for a visit of a few days. Yesterday brought me back here to the old grub-chamber, a still living, full-grown, full-blown, and, perhaps, full-flown *imago;* whether thus ephemeral, or whether I may go farther, is as yet undeveloped in my moral consciousness. Invitations to Mount Desert, to Northampton, to Florida Mountain, and, neither last nor least, to Ashfield, are prophetic of a longer winged life. . . .

Why do you want me to spell color with a "u"? If it is only a prejudice, I have one opposed to it, and will compromise by not insisting on your leaving the "u" out. Let it be one of those orthographical varieties that are the very spice of spelling, which else had scarcely enough of flavo(u)r. I should prefer to leave it so, rather than to quote, count, or weigh authorities against you. I think, however, that the best that can be said for colour, flavour, honour, and the like, is that they preserve some of the ancient liberties of English speech. I can conceive of one use, besides, in the two forms;

namely, allowing a division of meanings between them, as synonymes often do. Let deep, pure, or "saturated," as opposed to pale or insipid colors, flavors, and honors, be spelt with a "u." There would then be a utilitarian, as well as æsthetic, reason for keeping both forms. It is much easier to understand why colors exist than why they are so named and spelt; that is, we can get nearer the root of the thing in the uses of life than to that of the word in the usages of speech.

I do not feel so confident about your problem, "Why do *we* exist?" . . . Not that I believe there is any essential mystery in the nature of things, other than what an idle question-asking habit gratuitously imports into them for the sake of won der, — a rather dry and superfluous fodder for that divine sentiment! All the ends of life are, I am persuaded, within the sphere of life, and are in the last analysis, or highest generalization, to be found in the preservation, continuance, and increase of life itself, in all its quantities of rank, intensity, and number, which exists — "for what," do you ask? Why, for nothing, to be sure! Quite gratuitously. Does any one seriously expect to be answered in any other terms than those in which the question could be rationally framed? Are any ends suggested out of the sphere of life itself? If not, this is an aimless curiosity. Interrogation is reduced by it to the point which one may answer thus [Here follows an interrogation point with the mark of exclamation across it. — *Ed.*] . . .

The *social* value of questions is, indeed, a matter we might overlook in a too serious purpose to find their answers. The social value of the weather is nothing to theirs; and insoluble questions have a permanent value of this sort. Religions are founded on them.

Still, in the interest of sober inquisitiveness, it might be worth while to root out some of these questions for the sake of others more genuine. Let the questions of the uses of life, then, be put in this shape: To what ascertainable form or phase of life is this or that other form or phase of life valuable or serviceable? If we fail in this direction, we need not be quite non-plussed; for no form of movement in life is without a value in itself. It is not pleasures alone that would go on, if they were permitted. Pains and griefs hug themselves sometimes, and think they have the same right to last: and the nobler ones even win the will over to their conservation. I am more than half persuaded that most, if not all, of the puzzles of metaphysics, may be reduced to unconscious puns, or unseen ambiguities in terms. Now, "life" means in common discourse two things very different, but easily confounded. We sometimes mean by "life" what is comprised in the plans, purposes, inquisitions, and aspirations that make ambition and the zests of curiosity and anticipation so large a part of the conscious life of youth. Well, if for any cause (an indigestion, for example), the strength and zest that went in search of these goods of life happen to fail, we say we have tried life, and exhausted its resources! It has no more value for us. We are ready to die! If we meditate suicide, it is not our duty to others, nor the rights others may have in our lives, that should restrain us. We are more irrational than to merely forget the claims of conscience. We suffer from a mental indigestion. We have not solved the ambiguities of words. The *life* we would attack is not the culprit. The kind of dying which a wise moralist would enjoin is the death of the unsatisfied anticipations, curiosities, ambitions, which, fixed as habits, still linger, and distress the soul, since the strength and zest have failed which could give them further fruition. But these forms of life die without sacrificing one's usefulness or duties to others, or without cutting off a host of resources which come in old age to make "life" quite tolerable. "As to exhausting life objectively," the wise moralist would add, "that is sheer illusion, even if you happen to be an Alexander. Gain back the nerve, the strength, the zest, and you have gained back the world with its inexhaustible resources. But the true philosophical way is to look on life as it is, as somewhat broader than the fading pictures, plans, and purposes which you have mistaken for it, and as consisting in more than that set of inveterate habits which you call yourself. The death you should desire is the death of those desires, which, like all unsupported or no longer satisfied impulses of habit or instinct, have become pains. Work in other channels, and thus immolate yourself, and you will not find an end of life desirable. Life in this wider sense is neither good nor evil; but the theatre of possible goods and evils. There is no choice between it and death, not because their claims are equal, but because real, unillusioned choice lies wholly within the sphere of life. The will is constrained between this and that form of life, and is never impelled to real unconsciousness. We desire sleep, it is true, but, rationally, in only two ways, neither of which is unconsciousness; namely, first, the falling asleep as an immediate end or pleasure in itself, and, secondly, sound sleep as a means to the anticipated end of a refreshed and invigorated waking. All the rest is beyond our choice, a matter of fate and automatic change, or else of frenzied action under the influence of illusion, — the illusion that death resembles sleep in any thing for which sleep can be desired. There is never any real choice between a state of consciousness, however painful, and unconsciousness, — no real movement of the will that way, — though there is an illusory superficial resemblance to unconsciousness in vague anticipations of more pleasurable conditions than those we seek to escape."

The penalty, I suppose, for disobeying these wise directions, is to be judged foolish. I agree with this wise councillor that life in general exists for nothing. The impossibility of really wishing for annihilation, or for real unconsciousness, is, however, no evidence to me, as it is to the mystics, that there is no such thing, or that the fates, of which my choice is no part, have not this condition in store into which to turn me, as automatic changes in life put me into a soundness of sleep in itself undesired, however pleasant the way to it or the refreshment of waking from it may be.

To limit the question of rational ends to the sphere of life is to bring a host of questions to light touching the dependence of one form of life on another, which to the moralist as well as the naturalist promise more than the gratification of a prurient wonder at insoluble mysteries, and are more than topics of social incitement.

Now, the question why colors exist is just one of these. If colors are of use for any thing beyond the delight they inspire, then this delight may be subservient thereto, since it engages the will in the exercises and disciplines which are serviceable to their use. One of your poets has said, —

> "If eyes were made for seeing,
> Then Beauty is its own excuse for being."

I do not know that I quite understand the logic of this, if any was meant. . . . There is an ellipsis in the reasoning, which I propose to supply. The play of all the faculties of an animal is adapted to developing them to the point of their serious usefulness; and delight in the mere exercise is what sustains a faculty in its immaturity, and makes it grow. Other motives come in afterwards, and more immediately relate it to its real uses, or serious purposes, in life. Now, this is also curiously the case with colors (or, perhaps, I should spell them here *colours*) that is, the most simple or pure ones, — the red, the green, and the violet of the spectrum.

But what are these colours? The opticians say that they are three specific, but usually mingled, effects on the sensibilities of retinal nerves, produced, in the highest degrees, by ethereal tremours of three certain definite wave-lengths; but also produced, in lesser degrees, by other tremors within narrow limits from these. The nerves of the retinæ have in general been made (apparently for some purpose) especially sensitive to wave-lengths extending altogether over scarcely a quarter of the whole range of actual ethereal tremors, and even less than this amount with the color-blind, who are insensible to pure redness. The three primary colors are produced in ordinary eyes from similar, but subordinate, emphases or concentrations of sensibility, and doubtless exist for a similar purpose. Now what can this purpose be? It is now known that the eye is not the perfectly achromatic instrument it was once supposed to be. All the various tremors of different lengths and different refrangibilities from any point in a white object are not brought by the lenses of the eye to the same focus, or to a point, but are concentrated along a short line of depth in the retina; feeling red at the greatest depth, green in the middle, and violet at the front end. Or they would feel so, if separately and successively attended to, instead of combining their effects, as it were, chemically, in our consciousness of whiteness.

Now, Helmholtz supposes that the nerves at various depths are especially sensitive to wave-lengths, which, in ordinary circumstances of adjustment, would be brought to a focus at or near these depths. To give the turn to the problem which I propose, the hypothesis may be stated thus: Three transparent nervous screens, at slightly different distances, contain nerve corpuscles that are *but little* sensitive to wave-lengths, differing much either way from those which are ordinarily brought to a focus upon them. That is, these corpuscles are but little affected by the light, which is scattered, passing through them, but out of focus at their several distances, and which comes to a focus at, or nearer to, depths in the retina where appropriately sensitive corpuscles are situated. Dispersion — or the non-focalization, at a point, of all the rays of white light from any point of an object — is a cause of imperfect definition, or indistinctness in the minute parts of an optical image. It is also called in dioptric instruments chromatic aberration, on account of the more conspicuous evidence of it shown by the colored fringes about white objects. This defect of dioptric instruments, which is essentially the lack of perfect definition or minute precision in images, is partly remedied by compound lenses called "achromatic." Though the eye is provided with lenses of different materials, it is far from perfectly achromatic; dispersion is remedied, however, or provided for in them by a much neater way. A paradox; namely, that what renders the defects of refracting instruments so conspicuous (the colors shown in them) is what avoids the effect of dispersion in the eye! Colors were invented by Nature to avoid the confusing effects of dispersion; to produce definition by *limits in sensibility*, subordinate to the general limits, which make possible a selection of the physically well-defined movements of light out of the confused.

Light is, in general, so feeble a force that a considerable range of its undulations had to be called into the service of vision in order to affect the nervous tissue adequately, and to bring into sufficient contrasts the lights and shades by which the forms of objects could be discriminated. But such a range involved the defect of dispersion, or want of definition: and to provide for this defect ordinary vision was divided into three parts, each with a range of sensibility for which the defect of dispersion was insignificant; while these parts in their combination still retained sufficient intensity in the total effects of light. Definition is also secured in a less ingenious way at the centres of our retinæ, or at the yellow spots. The middle portion of the spectrum rays are at these parts transmitted with greater relative intensity than elsewhere, or the extreme rays are here partly absorbed. In the eyes of many birds and reptiles, absorption of light by minute colored globules of oil, placed at the front extremities of many of the rods and cones (some of them red and some yellow), appears in a similar manner to limit the range and the consequent dispersion of the rays which affect these nerves.

The invention of the three colours is, however, the most ingenious application of physics in vision; and all the three ways, namely, specific subordinate sensibilities, general absorption or narrowing of the range of refrangibility, as in the yellow spots, and specific absorptions, as in the eyes of birds, are better adapted to the purpose (considering the materials in which the vital opticians had, and have, to work) than the device of compound achromatic lenses would be.

The eye as an optical structure is not only in fact, as Helmholtz has shown, a bungled work compared to that of the mechanical optician, but is necessarily so from the nature of its materials and formative causes. Its defects as a mechanical structure are, however, provided against by its perfections as a nervous and muscular apparatus. If it could have been rendered perfectly achromatic, or if all effective wave-lengths could have been brought to perfect foci, these would have required a perfect sensitive surface or nervous screen, perfectly shaped to receive the image thus defined; and colours, or different kinds of sensibility, would not then have been needed for definition of form. (Would they have existed?) The retina is really not a geometrical surface, and could not be effectively made so (like that of a daguerreotype plate), but is a transparent body having some small thickness even in its sensitive parts, within and about which the image, or a luminary series of images in different colours, is formed. And the perception of color is the separation by the sensibilities of the retina of these laminæ of concentrated light, from the different light of different refrangibilities, passing through and mingled with them.

The fact that we delight in colors, not only in childhood but far into life, seems to be good evidence that these specifically limited and narrow ranges of sensibility in the three sets of nerves is partly the result of habit and discipline; the value of which to life *in general* is obviously in the uses of distinct vision. The pleasing effects of complementary colors is a direct disciplinary play of these faculties of discrimination. Beauty is *our* motive to exercises, the natural ends of which we discover only by philosophy, — by that philosophy which is founded on a study of physics and natural history.

. . . What a narrow, selfish, childish, and egotistical philosophy is that of the poets and sentimentalists, who look on life as a play-ground which they think their Maker has laid out for their delectation: whereas it is for keeping their race a-going (or was), whatever the use of that may be. There is one among that sort of philosophers, who has caught a glimpse of this great natural truth in what his disciples call "Newman's principle," — an important half-truth. "You will not be happy," he says, "unless you are virtuous; but you will not be virtuous, if you seek for happiness." No wise utilitarian would be disposed to question this as a psychological fact; but none would accept the paradox as an ultimate theoretical principle of morals. And there are not wanting illustrative parallels to it in the natural science of life. Nature puts the most important functions of life in charge of automatic and instinctive agents, which have their own most vigilant and effective motives. These are sometimes so independent of the will that even a favoring interference of this general governor disconcerts the special agent, and frustrates the common purpose. Thus, we sneeze much more vigorously against our wills than with their aid; which, if too eager to promote the action, may actually suspend it, or prevent it altogether. The same is true of an acquired nature or habit. If we, or our reasons, distrust any one of our acquired dexterities, and attempt by attention to help it out, we are apt to put it quite out of kilter, or to paralyze its proper efficiency. Every habit (and virtue, as Aristotle taught, is a habit) is its own motive, its own "excuse for being," — or one of its excuses. The pains of disconcerted or frustrated habits, and the inherent pleasure there is in following them, are motives which nature has put into our wills without generally caring to inform us why; and she sometimes decrees, indeed, that her reasons shall not be ours. So that, practically, we find ourselves acting the more reasonably and more for the real ends of nature, in proportion as these are not our immediate motives, but give place to more completely devoted, single-purposed, and therefore effective powers, or to instincts and habits; which we should, nevertheless, as reasonable beings, subject theoretically, or in our philosophy of life and duty, to the test of the good they subserve in the economy of life.

Utilitarianism needs to be supplemented, in order to meet misunderstandings, by a Philosophy of Habit, and to lay down among its practical principles that, since motives are effective, not in proportion to their usefulness or reasonableness, but rather to their singleness or instinctiveness, therefore it is reasonable to foster and to rely practically on the force of proper habits and just, natural inclinations. In the serene and unopposed play of these, — and especially in their concord or harmonious play, — there is a source of happiness to the agent, which the sentimental moralist mistakes for the real, or natural, end of virtue, but which belongs to it only as a habit, or as a body of mutually supporting or concordant habits; and is quite distinct from the happiness or well-being to which as virtuous or reasonable habits and inclinations they are or should be adapted. Dignity is a weight with the will, or an effective source of happiness, which these powers of habit and instinct gain from their mutual support or harmonious action, and from their persistent influence, and which would be the natural result of accordance with the harmonious real ends of life. It is to questioned and artificial rules of life, and to the morals of legislation rather than to the instincts of the individual conscience, that the utilitarian test is of greatest practical importance. Nature has not waited for human reason to discover or to test all the instincts and disciplines best adapted for keeping the surviving races of men in the most flourishing condition; just as she did not wait for physiological science to disclose the uses of color, but secured them in her economy by making them the delight and one, apparently, of the most important ends of vision, though really one, as we have seen, of its most important means.

At the beginning of the last letter there is some account of a visit to Portsmouth with Mr. Woodward Emery. Mr. Emery, then and now a member of the bar in Boston, was Chauncey's chum at Cambridge during the last years of his life. He has kindly given me a sketch of the habits of his friend at this period, from which I copy the following passages: —

"My intimate acquaintance with Chauncey Wright is confined to the last two years of his life. . . . He rarely went from home; his wants were few, and his tastes simple. There was so little variation in his daily life that the description of one day may suffice for all. He rose late, breakfasted heartily, and, lighting his cigar, sauntered to his lodgings, — always amiable and ready for a chat by the way. He rarely worked hard in the forenoon, passing his time in reading or in conversation. The afternoon was his time for exercise, of which, however, he was not very fond; yet he could endure a hard walk very comfortably. I have walked with him twenty miles between afternoon and bed-time. Dinner was his chief meal, and he fully appreciated the merit of a well-appointed and well-spread table; at the same time, it is rare to meet one so indifferent to a poor one. The table seemed to bring out his unrivalled conversational powers, and he would talk for hours with interest and animation.

"He labored best and performed the hardest work at night. He fairly bloomed, if I may be allowed the expression, in the night; and it was far into the morning when he sought his bed. . . . His habit of work was always a fearful strain upon his nervous system; when once he began to write out his cogitations, — thoughtfully constructed always before he touched pen to paper, — nothing interested him or broke the thread of continuous effort until it was determined by its natural end, or by his own physical exhaustion; meals, sleep, and exercise were alike forgotten, or partaken with utter irregularity. Otherwise, simplicity and regularity were the rule of life with one who was more regular than most men I have known, more simple than any."

To Miss Grace Norton.

AUG. 12, 1874.

I went last Tuesday week to Mr. Shattuck's, at Mattapoisett, for a visit of a few days, — a visit long ago projected. It was a very agreeable one, extending to nearly a week. The Rev. Dr. Rufus Ellis and his daughter were the other guests at first; after them came Professor and Mrs. Dunbar, of Cambridge, and their daughter. It was a pleasant as well as edifying variety in life to be so long with these sensible as well as conservative and religious people. Mr. Ellis, you know (or perhaps you don't), was my first instructor in theology, and he is said to have been the main adviser in sending me to Cambridge. What a scoffer I should have become, probably, at Amherst or Williams College! It has been many years since I have had with him any real talks. I did not tell you,

I think, that I met him first this season, shortly before, at Magnolia ; but we did not get deeply there into religious conferences. . . . I have always found myself quite in easy relations with sensible, orthodox[1] people, though a little surprised sometimes at the freedom I feel and take. They entertain sharp but honest doubts without annoyance, and do not impatiently brush at them with vagaries like the so-called "liberal" sentimentalists. I did not quite convince Dr. Ellis, I think, that his sense of indestructible vitality, even at the lowest ebb of strength, spirits, and purpose, was not good evidence that he was going to last for ever, though I charged his personality with being only a set of inveterate habits ; but I was interested to find that he, with other conservative thinkers with whom I have talked, regarded this evidence as good only for the individuals who feel it. This tenet may spring from an unconscious proselyting spirit, — an indirect compulsion of one by leaving one out in the cold. Our freest, longest talks were on a drive to New Bedford, and in walks through that old town.

. . . I did not quite desert science on this visit, but mastered Dr. Gray's little book on "How Plants Behave," and found illustrations of it in numerous flowers of the place, among them fine specimens of orchis in the woods. I had just read in Mr. ——'s discourse, as to how teleology was a much misundertood science, and did not treat of the use one thing is to another, but of the service each is to the universe (to "the glory of God" perhaps he meant, according to your quotation from the Catechism). But I am curious to see an instance of the successful treatment of scientific things that

[1] Chauncey uses this word here, not in its specific local sense, [*e.g. ante*, p. 64], as intimating the doctrine of the Trinitarian Congregationalists, — once the established church; but with the more general meaning expressed just before, where he speaks of his friends as conservative in their opinions. They were all Unitarians.

way. I quite agree that a true teleology does not include such facts as that the beauty and perfume and sweetness of flowers are serviceable to us, or even to insects; but is deeper than this in its scrutiny of ends, and finds in the colors, odors, sweets, and, above all, in the particular structures of flowers, means to the end of perpetuating their lives or the life of their species. Dr. Gray, in his late notice of Mr. Darwin, praises him for restoring teleology to its true place. A better statement of the question of Final Causes than I thought of then, or in my "statement" to you, now occurs to me. The Final Cause of any thing is that very thing, when it is or can be considered as conserved or reproduced by that essential part of its action or effects which perpetuates the life of which it is a part. Is it not singular that this definition has just reminded me of what I read long ago about Aristotle's definition of Final Causes? I never quite understood that, and find, on turning to the Encyclopædia, that it is in these words: "The *final* cause of the thing is that very thing in its completeness; as a statue when made." The *material*, *efficient*, and *formal* causes of the statue are, according to the illustrations of Aristotle's four causes, — severally, the marble, the sculptor, and the particular shape or individuality, or the what-it-is-in-itself-ness of the statue.

These subtilties of classification are not worth much; yet, as there is a resemblance between Aristotle's "final cause" and what I have just drawn from natural history, I am tempted to see how close the agreement can be made without making too ingenious an interpretation of the words in search of clearer meaning. "That very thing in its completeness" does not seem to me sufficiently distinguished from its formal cause or particular determination, which is sometimes called its type. Should we not say, rather, that the properties of any thing by which it is the agent, though indirectly, of its own production or of the reproduction of its sort, belong to and define it as an end or final cause? The "completeness" meant is, perhaps, in the round of its self-restoring or self-preserving agency as a species. Conceived in the mind of the sculptor, the statue is the "purpose" for which he works. Or, as being the embodiment of that which determined the sculptor's purpose and labor, it is a final cause. The *round* of agency through which a thing realizes its sort, or realizes the conditions of its existence, may be called, if Mr. —— wishes, a universe, — its universe as a final cause, — but not, if he pleases, *the* Universe. Don't hold me responsible for the useless subtlety of trying to save to science this highly respectable name, Final Cause!

But let us pass now from statues and flowers to men and women. You say that while you do not believe the noblest end of life to be "serviceableness," in the ordinary meaning of the word, — "whatever it may be as an aim" (proximate end?); yet you still less believe that in the last analysis we should find the ends of life in the preservation, continuance, and increase of life itself. I agree entirely with you about "serviceableness" as an end; that is, serviceableness as such: for this would be a foolish confusion of the essence of means with ends; though, as one of "a Christian's" delights, and blissful habits or virtues, it doubtless makes part of the noble "perfectness" of individual human existence. This "perfectness," which you contrast with the preservation, &c., of life, I meant to include in what, as I recollect, I added as the *quantity in worth, dignity, or rank* in the increase of life; its quantity in intensity and number being other parts of it as a final cause. What do we really mean, understandingly (not emotionally), by the words "perfectness," "dignity," "absolute worth"? The mystic, who finds God in the inward perfectness he dreams of in himself, thinks it the end of the universe; whereas, I think its dignity is limited to that spiritual mechanism of the human flower which is most purely and concentratedly serviceable to that *whole* life of mankind which reproduces and embodies it. Dignity, as I think I defined it in another connection, is a weight with the will, or a power as a motive, which depends on the mutual support that what we therefore call our virtues get from one another, and from all the motives of life in their most complete harmony and consistency. Mysticism is so stupid and spiritually self-engrossed that the better self, which it ought to contemplate as a particular representative of the endless solidarity of human life, is thought of by it as the individual mystic's immortal part. Mysticism is so blindly self-engrossed that it cannot understand Utilitarianism, but supposes this doctrine to mean a service of the higher or the virtuous inclinations of our nature to the lower, or merely to the gross well-being of human life. Utilitarianism does not mean this, though this is a *part* of its meaning. The lower, *so far as* they are the conditions of the higher; the appetites, *so far as* they are also essential to the preservation, continuance, and increase of life; the passions, *so far as* their singleness or instinctiveness is serviceable to the whole, — are, in a stricter sense, ends, or final causes even, than is that perfectness of virtue which is its own reward. So far as the happiness of virtue depends on its being a fixed habit, as it does in the egotistic regard of the Pharisee, — so far it has no more worth, dignity, or perfectness than any instinct or any other habit in itself. But, so far as any habit, on the other hand, is not opposed by equally strong and persistent motives, but is in wide and strong alliance with others, which, with it, are therefore named "reasonable" or "virtuous," it is an integrant part of a system of dispositions which, as superintending, so far as it goes, the whole of the conditions of human life, and leading to the conservation of the whole, itself included, is what we call *conscience*, and is pre-eminently a final cause in human nature.

Now, utilitarians have consciences as well as the sentimentalists. Their philosophy concerns itself with the conscience of conscience, with its truest harmony, or with its reasonableness, with the accordance of every thing in it with the least doubtful of its behests. "Nature," says Cicero, "has inclined us to the love of mankind; and this is the foundation of laws" (*fundamentum juris*). This is both the rational and the disciplinary foundation, the ground and the efficacy of laws; since fear becomes a moral power only by its sanction; and even those laws which we may be said to observe instinctively, or as ends from the start and in themselves, are instinctively associated with the love of mankind, with the wish for the greatest good of the greatest number. On this wish hang all the law and the prophets.

The *reliance* of utilitarians on their philosophy, which (in consideration of their acknowledgment of the essential value of instincts and habits, though not of the ultimate authority of these) gives you so much surprise, — this reliance is not different from what the disciples of any other creed have on a philosophy that professes to be the *guide* of life. It is not a reliance on the ability of the individual reason to review, in the light of fundamental principles, the whole range of possible moral actions. It is not even a reliance on the whole *reflective* experience of mankind, as transmitted in customs and traditions. The reliance of experiential philosophers in general is not on the ability of each investigator to verify, by experiment and observation, what he nevertheless has good reason to accept as true laws of nature, and as really verifiable; nor is it on the completeness of what has been already ascertained experimentally. It is a reliance on *its method*, whenever or wherever any method is needed. But the reasonableness of many enjoined customs and rules of life is of a negative sort, — the non-existence of any thing truly obligatory that is really seen to be opposed to them. This proves their harmlessness at least, so far as we can see; and, wherever they seem to have a foundation in instinct (like the horror of suicide or murder), there is a positive presumption that they are somewhat more than merely harmless injunctions. Yet, in this, they have to the utilitarian nothing more than a presumption of obligation; for inherited instincts are not always right, or useful to present conditions of a progressive form of life. They may have made the whole transit from what *ought*, to what *ought not*, to be obeyed, though still remaining instincts in our nature, like fear and rage; or even though in the individual will they may have the pervasiveness and the permanent sway of a rational principle. The large part which the authority of teachers and force-sanctioned laws have in our moral life affords, indeed, a presumption against the trustworthiness of instincts in general; and, when a seemingly instinctive inclination receives sanction in customs and early discipline, it is often difficult to distinguish how much training has added to nature: for the consciences of savages differ from ours in both respects; and more discipline is needed for some of our youths than for others.

What utilitarianism *distrusts*, therefore, is the authority of mere strength or earnestness of moral feelings or injunctions, when set up as a reason for conduct. But this does not mean an habitual distrust in the utilitarian of his own conscientious feelings, nor a doubt of them leading to the abrogation of their actual authority or weight with his will. Earnestness is a proof of conscientiousness, not of the rightness of a conscience, or is the measure of efficacy, rather than of rectitude, and is often much greater in respect to mere superstitions and rules of etiquette than to the most certain of moral principles. For earnestness is oftener the result of that love for mankind which takes the form of reverence for teachers, or of following the supposed divine in human examples, than of that love for mankind which should (but, unfortunately, not always does) guide the reason of the leader and teacher.

This distrust becomes a positive rejection, on the part of this philosophy, of any authority in the earnestness of a feeling, when this is brought into the judgment, or rational trial, of a rule of conduct in any real dispute concerning it. In any real dispute about the wisdom or rectitude of a moral rule (not about the motives of a moral agent), utilitarianism takes the reins of judgment into its own hands, then actually asserting what is always its prerogative, the supremacy of its tests over all authorities, — tests supreme, so far as they are seen to go, even over the universal instincts of men; since only so far as these can be seen, or else presumed to be allied with the love and service of mankind, can they be justified; and utilitarianism sits in permanent judgment over all law-*making*, over all devices of expediency, whether these be deductions from laws, or exceptions to the existing and acknowledged rules of duty. Its reliance on the forces of habit and instinct is not for rational guidance, but for practical efficacy; yet these are so important to its aims, that they are not safely to be disregarded, or unnecessarily opposed, or weakened by substituting for them habitually the calculations of expediency. The mystic who mistakes for the final causes of the universe that better part in himself which, as the representative of all human interests, is a final cause of the universe of human life, dreams in his conceit that he is God, and that stars and flowers, as well as statues, exist for him and for his equals in immortality. He lays down his life, if at all, for the furthering of his own inward bliss (as he dreams), or for heaven; instead of for the furtherance of nature's care in life for the whole, in which, sooner or later, he must disappear. . . .

"Sanity and insanity *are* more closely interlaced" than you have believed. Between them, as conditions of mind, there is not a wide gulf, nor even any sharp line of demarcation. We do not generally need to be enjoined to admire the beautiful or to loathe the ugly, though discrimination may grow by instruction even in respect to what deserves these names; nor do we generally mistake pleasures for pains through too close a proximity of one to the other, spite of the close relation between them, imagined by the Socrates of Plato. But we have to be always on our guard against *irrationality*, which does not require a permanently diseased brain for its habitat. . . . Taking figures of speech literally is perhaps one of the commonest forms of insanity. . . .

To desire as an end, or for its own sake, what in the order of nature is a means, like going to sleep, is not irrational; but to mistake this means for its end in nature, or to suppose this end to be the happiness which we have in the means, is fatuity. To think we have perfected in sound sleep the pleasure we have in falling asleep, and then to suppose that unconsciousness in general, or that of death in particular, is perfect bliss, is doubly irrational. . . .

. . . The human heart is a gallery of the future, illuminated by the light of its instincts and experience reflected from pictures and images of the future and the universal. As the repository and agency of all rationally conceived ends, it is the only rational final cause to itself, however serviceable it may be incidentally to other forms of life or living beings. The uses of other forms of life to the human are not final causes, though the uses of any forms of life to the universe would properly be final, if it were *true* that the universe is served by them in any other way than to make it up, or to be among the threads that are woven in its endless combinations, — its *formal* rather than its *final* causes.

Touching "classification," . . . I don't think the word "classification" is used very distinctively or serviceably when it is not restricted to the results of more or less cool attention to the grounds of the divisions we make in things, or to the sphere of the active sense of the word. The *ego* and *non ego* are classes of phenomena, it is true, considered as divisions made by consciousness, and not as primordially involved in it; but to consider them as such is so disrespectful to both that most intuitional metaphysicians prefer to call them divisions in substance, though this comes perhaps to the same thing; since, as Fichte says, "Attributes [or phenomena], synthetically united, give substance [are synthems,[1] I should say], and substance analyzed gives attributes [marks or characters]." Again, to call that division of things or persons which we make because we like or approve some, and dislike or disapprove others, more or less, — to call that a classification, or even a real division, and not rather a feeling merely in us about them, is to force these stiff, logical terms out of their sober proprieties. I don't dispute that in any sense "classification *is* judgment." It is the converse that I dispute, and especially that an *intuitive* judgment is an *analytical* classification, or classification by characters. And all I assert is that descriptive classification or characterization indicates weak feeling, — mainly, an intellectual interest, — or that you don't much love the subject; and I ventured from the point of view of intuitive or æsthetic judgment to say that such a throwing of a fellow-being to the logical dogs is severe, being a trifle worse than damning with faint praise.

It was not from any actual fear, however, that you had been describing me in your English letters (as you do to myself) as a man who never asks a question, or as a man just as queer, only just the opposite of Mr. ——; it was not from any such fear that I put myself in his place (the place of the characterized), but because in fact I sometimes *do* ask questions, though not very often in the social, interrogative form. Grammatically they are statements, rhetorically they are ironical, — that dangerous figure! Socrates is thought to have

[1] In another place, Wright had said: "Syntheses; — *synthems* is a better word, which I borrow from the Greek to express the passive sense of syntheses, — as poem stands to poesis."

made large use of irony in his discourses, but more especially in his questions, — mocking the show of logical acuteness, and letting himself get defeated in the battle of questions and opinions to show (when he cared to show it) how well his common-sense and his convictions, when they were clear, survived such exposures and assaults; and how logic, though the life, is not the armor of convictions. If Mr. ——'s questions were only ironical, now, they might have the force of statements; as ironical statements have the force of challenges and questions: so perverting is the use of irony! I think that, on the whole, half-true categorical paradoxes are the deepest probing questions, especially if no irony is suspected. They rouse the real convictions of your interlocutor, if he has any, or discover the fact, if he has not, much better than the open sincerity or even the irony of questions. Do not ask, for example, whether the moon is made of green cheese or of earth, nor waste time in canvassing the probabilities of the two hypotheses only to prove everybody's ignorance; but maintain the probability of the least plausible. That will bring out the best reasons for the other; which is better, I think, on the whole, than to discover the uncertainty of both. The weak side of Socrates was his contempt for the merely most probable. Modern scientific doctrines are many of them of this sort, which is something, — provided "the most probable" does not mean merely the most believed, as it does, independently of systematic induction.

One is exposed, to be sure, by this form of ironical inquisition to more injurious suspicions of trifling with truth than even Socrates was; and there is perhaps a safer way. Mother Goose was, indeed, a profounder philosopher; and philosophers have generally, in effect, followed her method rather than that of Socrates. For, as one of the ancients has remarked, "there is nothing so absurd as not to have been asserted by some one of the philosophers." Categorical nonsense — what you cannot believe — both entertains and edifies; and is honest, withal, and not unsocial like irony. Tickling arouses a reflective attention, and institutes a scientific exploration and a mapping of mental *terræ incognitæ.* One discovers — not what Socrates taught, "how ignorant we are" — but how knowing, in such trifles of experience as might escape a common philosopher's reflective notice. One gets well grounded at this school in common-sense, which is the faculty that never seriously doubts any thing, yet differs in different minds as to what is thus exempted from question. The philosophy of Mother Goose comprises all that is certainly *common.* There is no hope for the child who seriously questions the assertions of this great teacher. The plainest irony will never arouse in later years its slumbering powers of reflection. If it begins with doubting her statements, it will end by accepting the more plausible ones of dishonest people. Have you ever noticed that Mother Goose never asks questions, except, perhaps, indirectly, — or leading ones, like this? I have no doubt that you have, and do therefore despise all that are questions in form.

The mystics, from Pythagoras down, have taught a doctrine which is the sacred head or obverse of this sterling one. They held that "nothing concerning the gods, or divine doctrines, is to be doubted." "Nothing is to be doubted as to its unconditional possibility, or as possible with God," is the response of science. The unintelligible cannot be doubted — nor believed. And it is only about probabilities, the *conditionally* possible, — what is likely, not merely possible, that questions are legitimate or answers useful, for any but social and religious purposes. Beyond the court of science, and the jurisdiction of the probable, creeds are social badges of differences, which, to be rational, should be peacefully and lovingly maintained. Within this court, even *axioms* are only "the most probable." They have no peculiar sanctity, and must lay aside their priestly robes, or bear to have them defiled. Axioms in science have no "benefit of clergy," but are tried like all the rest by the laws of induction. . . .

The now established doctrine of natural history, or biological science, — that genetic or inherited characters, and their variations, are not always fitted, even in the average, to circumstances of life (and are exactly fitted only by accident), and that the amendment of this defect is not, in general, to be found in the individual life, — opposes itself to the mystical doctrine that such ill-fittings are prophetic. The remedy for the ills that follow to the individual life is to be found only in the more vigorous development, and the prevalence in it of such powers as *are* adapted to its circumstances; or else by such command as is practicable of circumstances that are found by an intelligent examination of our natures to be fitted to them. Our natures are, it is true, prophetic, so far as by making themselves known to us in recognized past examples, and by thus defining for us their true circumstances or conditions of development, they lead us as reasonable beings to seek for these. No wonder that in Goethe — whose genius found no parallel in history, and was abetted by a powerful scientific inquisitiveness — it should at first have thought itself prophetic, and sought its destiny by suicide. But he also had the sense to wait, and the will to *make* the circumstances to which in old age it became so easily adjusted. No doubt, the adjustment between our natures and circumstances is mutual. If we live long enough, the "mystic sense" in us, unless too fondly cherished, may die first. "If every one lived to be old, no one would believe in immortality," was said, near the end of her life, by a free-thinking but hard-working and devoted woman.

In the last letter, Chauncey gives some account of a meeting with his old friend, the Rev. Rufus Ellis. Dr. Ellis, in the letter from which I have already made one extract, has referred to this same interview, in a passage which I will insert here. In doing so, I retain some expressions of opinion which may at least emphasize the catholic and kindly estimate formed by Dr. Ellis of one with whose conclusions, in some particulars, he so widely differed.

"I removed," he says, "to Boston whilst Chauncey was in Cambridge; and, as one never sees the nearest persons so much as those who are occasionally near, I saw but little of him during his University life. . . . More than once we met during the summer vacation days, — once especially for more days than one, and I found what he had become. It was a strange experience, and yet I suppose not an uncommon one in these days, — sad in so many respects, if this must be regarded as an abiding or final state; but the promise of a very sweet dawn seemed to be wrapped up in the darkness. I remember a day's drive with the philosopher who, as a boy, had been my parishioner, and how from the beginning to the end of it we talked about the highest religious themes, — God, duty, immortality. Once it came to my mind, What does our driver — a simple colored brother and Methodist deacon — think of all this? but I saw that, happily, it was Sanskrit to him. To one who looked only at the appearance, and rested on the surface, the minister was talking with a man who from having been his Sunday-school pupil in childhood had 'developed' into a full-grown infidel. And certainly as to the affirmations of Christian faith he was singularly lacking; but a few moments' conversation with him would have convinced any candid man that here was one whose religion it was to have no religion, and that whatever he was, he was by the grace of God. I could not but be sorry, profoundly so, that he had not been so mastered by the Divine Master as to have been filled with religious faiths and hopes, and thus furnished with the very facts which were to him so essential; but the light in him was so pure and steady that he seemed to me all unconsciously to have been enlightened of the One True Light, and his perfect candor and sweetness were more than what we call natural. He did not talk for victory, but as one who sought for truth, and rejoiced in it. There was no pause in his *moral* faith; and had I been the prophet I ought to have been, and witnessed as clearly as might be for the kingdom of God as Christ is revealing it in our world, I could not have asked for a more promising hearer of the good tidings. As it was, it seemed to me that we came nearer together; and, whilst I have sometimes come away from converse with men of immaculate orthodoxy, and most scrupulous in all ceremonies and ordinances, with a feeling that between them and me there was a great gulf, and that their religion and mine were essentially different, I was conscious of nothing of the kind when I returned with Chauncey from our day's voyage out upon the fathomless and shoreless ocean of religious speculation. We had the same city in view, and its Builder and Maker is God. I cannot doubt that the heavens which seemed closed above him on earth are open now, and that being of the truth he hears the Teacher's voice. I could see as we talked that the dogmatism of those who are known as advanced thinkers was as offensive to him as the dogmatism of the religionist; and, that whilst he hoped to find out what was right by learning what was useful, he recognized a motive power above and within all consequences, and had, however unnamed and unmapped, his realm of holy mystery, and was guided, however unwittingly, by the divine counsel. 'A dangerous man,' does some one say, 'and able to deceive the very elect;' but such was not the effect of his life and conversation, noticeably not upon the young, with whom he was so great a favorite. He destroyed no man's, no child's faith; but was fitted to show to all who would discern the signs of the times, what it is that some who seem to be irreligious are waiting for, 'as they who wait for the morning.'"[1]

[1] While Chauncey was on this visit at Mattapoisett, the daughter of his host secured the taking of what is called his "mental photograph;" and she has most kindly sent it to me. I am sure that Chauncey's friends will thank her for the leave I have to print here this amusing paper, which is at the same time so characteristic. The patient, it will be remembered, while undergoing this process, is seated at a number of written questions, and writes his answers. "I remember Mr. Wright," says Miss Shattuck, "perfectly as he wrote the answers, and seemed to take pleasure in thinking them out."

AUGUST 9, 1874.

1. Your favorite color?
   Ans. The complementary.
2. Your favorite flower?
   Ans. The red, red rose.
3. Your favorite tree?
   Ans. The Great Elm.
4. Your favorite object in nature?
   Ans. Vistas of mountains.
5. Your favorite hour in the day?
   Ans. 11 to 12 P. M.
6. Your favorite season of the year?
   Ans. Days in June.
7. Your favorite perfume?
   Ans. Incense of Havana.
8. Your favorite style of beauty?
   Ans. The animated.
9. Your favorite poets?
   Ans. Shakespeare and Tennyson.
10. Your favorite prose authors?
    Ans. Stuart Mill and Charles Darwin.
11. Your favorite character in romance?
    Ans. Plato's Socrates.
12. In history?
    Ans. The real Socrates.
13. Book to take up for an hour?
    Ans. The one one feels inclined to read.
14. What book (not religious) would you part with last?
    Ans. The one no one would care to borrow.
15. What epoch would you choose to have lived in?
    Ans. The most modern.
16. Where would you like to live?
    Ans. In the most familiar place.
17. What is your favorite amusement?
    Ans. Metaphysics.
18. What is your favorite occupation?
    Ans. Mathematical problems.
19. What trait of character do you most admire in man?
    Ans. The disposition to be just.
20. What trait of character do you most admire in woman?
    Ans. Thoughtful sympathy.
21. What trait of character do you most detest in each?
    Ans. Brutality and vanity.
22. If not yourself, who would you rather be?
    Ans. Nobody.
23. What is your idea of happiness?
    Ans. Undisturbed, easy occupation.
24. What is your idea of misery?
    Ans. Distracted *ennui*.
25. What is your dream?
    Ans. Of flying.
26. What is your favorite game?
    Ans. Solitaire.
27. What do you believe to be your distinguishing characteristics?
    Ans. Ignorance and modesty.

To Miss Grace Norton.

AUG. 18, 1874.

When I say that any thing is not true, I generally mean that I think the statement inadequate, inexact, or even logically misleading, — a naming of what is true, perhaps, but a darkening, not an illuminating naming. I am often wholly engrossed in the interest of the *form* of truth. What does not tally with the balance of accurate statements seems, in my dissatisfaction, of little or no account, or to belong to the confused infinite of what we do not at all know. This Socratic disposition is apt to disregard the feeling for truths which, though inadequately embodied in words, are yet not the less — are perhaps even the more — deeply interesting.

But I also have the feeling which made Socrates, as he testifies in the "Apology," very annoying to those with whom he discussed; namely, that there is no merit in any really known truth, however sacred to any one, greater than clearness and adequacy of expression. Many truths are, perhaps, better worth knowing than those which may have acquired this merit; but their worth is not really attained without it, though often involved in our personal worth, — in our experience, insights, and latent powers of giving birth, or external form, just proportions, and objective value to truth.

In discussions about abstract matters, in which one's views are as inseparable from one's self as our features are, the dialogue sometimes seems to me like that of the half-enchanted people in the "Tempest," — each seeing and talking unintel-

28. If married, what do you believe to be the distinguishing characteristics of your better-half?
    Ans. To wish to be married to another man, and therefore unhappy.

29. What are the saddest words in the world?
    Ans. Those beginning with D, — as death, debt, diseases, dishonor, and all the d—d *dises.*

30. What is your aim in life?
    Ans. To secure the most trustworthy means of happiness.

31. What is your motto?
    Ans. The greatest good of the greatest number.

ligibly about a different unexplored world. So I never *aim* at attacking any persons, though doubtless I seem to, since you so judge, — no real persons at least, or even imaginary ones, that could possibly stand for any real ones I know. Much less am I inclined to say to any one, as you suggest, "I think you are greatly mistaken;" for I think that the saying of this, though conventionally a civil or perhaps gallant way of conducting a discussion or closing it, does not lead to that end of discussion which seems to me desirable when I get into it. I think, on looking back by the light of your letter upon the *mood* in which I wrote mine, that I could not make entirely clear to you, far less justify to you, what it was, — what idiosyncrasy of nature it came from, but, as it seems, did not fairly represent. It seems to me now a curious mixture of that which Dr. Walker alluded to in characterizing his friend —— as having "an irritable intellect," with an unsteady, flickering desire for friendly discussion, — not a desire for apparent conquest in discussion. . . . The letter, or essay, was a sort of preaching, not at all considerate, as I now see, — but not, as I venture to hope, essentially more disrespectful than that kind of literature is apt to be, although turned in an opposite direction. This style does not *apply* truths, or mean to apply them, but only *utters* applicable truths on general themes. . . . From the opinions of no persons that I know do I pretend to comprehend the personality in its springs so well as to be much surprised at the unexpected in what they may say or do. *What is said* by another, I am often disposed to cavil at, but not at all as charging thorough misconceptions or culpable confusions in any way peculiar. I am sure I have not imagination enough to adequately grasp or to sympathize with or assume for myself temporarily the mental history and life of another, so as to lead out of these to what might seem to me a better way of looking at things. I have only imagination enough to feel that I have not enough for this.

Impersonality seems to me to belong to the very essence of truth. To quote texts and criticise *what is said*, doing this without malice and without wilfully perverting its obviously intended meaning, and to test statements by the only tests that are valid, namely, what both parties believe clearly, or accept without question of fact or meaning, — is not to my feeling a personal attack. . . . Perhaps that was the effect on my style of the mood I was in. I had on Sunday, at Miss ——'s, just such a mood, and drove ——, in a discussion on art, not exactly to refusing to speak to me further, but to the perception, I imagine, of the true cause. It was, I suppose, a mad perversion, through emphasis, of an enthusiasm for exactness and systematic understanding, which forgets for the time the rights of persons.

To Miss Jane Norton.

Friday evening [September, 1874].

. . . I went [to Magnolia] for only a day's visit, — the last day, as I had heard, of Mrs. Lesley's stay there. I had missed her on a previous visit, and had put off the second till the last moment. But my coming induced her to linger two days longer by the sea, — perfect days of autumn weather. We drove to see the Gurneys at Beverly on Saturday; and all the short time at the seaside seemed, while it lasted, to be a season off from Cambridge times and circumstances.

But now these have had their revenge, and put those days off into telescopic distance and minuteness. As usual, when I come back to Cambridge from long or short absences, I come to it like a clod to its native earth, with all motive impulses expended and satisfied.

Before I went away last week, I got my head full of "facts for Darwin" from the stores of knowledge in Mr. Sophocles, touching the gestures of the Eastern peoples he had known;

and especially the gestures of the head, which I have long speculated about in relation to optical theories. These facts fitted on to my older observations and speculations (and even a "Magnolia" perspective gave me one good related point of optics). I have now written it all out in a letter to Mr. Darwin; adding three new points on expression that I have picked up this week, — two of them from Mr. Lowell, on the gestures of the Italians. I read to him on Wednesday all the rest I had set down. So you see I have not been idle, nor left entirely without explanation the appearance of coldness towards the attractions of Ashfield. I suppose that now, having got the matter all down in black and white, I shall gradually harden my heart towards it; so that when we meet I shall look upon it and treat it as a weak enthusiasm, — as old people look upon athletic sports. It is well that I did not sooner quench my thoughts in ink; for it seems to leave me without resource to turn to.

What satisfaction there must be in the habit of reading! The power to give one's self up graciously to a book is the wealthiest habit, I imagine, that one can acquire. It is fulness itself, or an endless and ever-ready resource. To make books is to have one's hive robbed. Now, I attack a book as a bee does a petunia, not reaching its honey delicately, as its regular customers, the night-moths, do; but biting into its nectary, or breaking in like a burglar. Yet the bee is accounted by moralists the more virtuous insect; the rule in the moral world being, since all fall so far short of perfection, to award praise where praise is most needed as a motive, rather than most fit or deserved in an absolute way. Still, I think bees and ants (as well as their Author) are much misunderstood by moralists; they love the excitement of their brisk business, and stand in no such need of praise or social support for a motive, as the lazy, unproductive people do who are sent to observe and imitate them. The *rationale* of rewards and punishments has to do with the use of them, and involves essentially the short-comings of the agent, or the feebleness of motives to actions, as well as the absolute value of the actions themselves. Hence, hymns of praise seem to the practical utilitarian a sort of fetish worship, or else hyperbolical, — misleading either way, as matters of reverent belief. — The chief end of morals, however, seems to be to afford topics for my letters!

To Mr. Darwin.

CAMBRIDGE, Sept. 3, 1874.

In a late talk with Dr. Gray, he expressed so much interest in certain points of observation and inquiry which I have lately made on the gestures of the head, that I am encouraged to think they will be of sufficient interest to you to warrant my claiming your attention for them. I was led to this subject by my great interest in your principles of expression and a desire to trace them out in new directions, but principally through coming unexpectedly upon the matter from what at first sight seems a remote line of investigation.

For clearness, I ought first to explain this briefly. Many years ago, the problem of the physiological cause of the intensification of the sunset colors, produced by looking at them with the head inverted or much inclined on one side, interested me, and I found that the effect was not due to the position of the eyes, but to that of the images in them, since the same effect is observed in paintings of sunset by inverting the pictures instead of the head; and, later, I observed that reflections of the colors in a horizontal mirror, or in the surface of smooth water, gave the same result. I then roughly generalized the hypothesis that any distortion of a view, by withdrawing attention from the interpretation of forms, sizes, and distances, or from mensural perception, gave prominence, at least, if not greater intensity, to the consciousness of colors as mere sensations. This was in accordance with the recognized principle in psychology that perception and sensation are in inverse relations to consciousness, — "inversely proportioned," as Sir W. Hamilton expresses it; or, as I prefer to state the fact, the consciousness of a sensation as a sign is accompanied by a diminished consciousness of it in its special quality and quantity as a sensation. The application of this principle to the explanation of the phenomena considered was apparently confirmed by a fact which I learned from an artist; namely, that certain defects of form, where colors are not employed, as in crayon portraits, are discovered by artists by inverting their pictures! For a long time I vaguely associated this fact with the above theory; but I have lately come to think that the true explanation of the heightening of colors and that of bringing out small defects in form by a change or distortion of aspect are different though analogous explanations; and this difference seems to promise a useful point in the difficult psycho-physical problem of mensural or space perception.

But I must not stop to explain this here. To pass directly to the matter in hand, the next fact that came to my notice in this connection was an observation by a gentleman, which I got from him in talk a few months ago. When a boy, he noticed and called his father's attention to the fact that the servant girl, in arranging the furniture of a room or the table, inspected her work critically, not by looking straight at it from various points of view, but askant, and in walking by it. "Was this," he asked, "because the side vision is keener than that of direct looking?" "Not at all," the old gentleman answered, "for, if I wish to see exactly what time it is, I look straight at the clock; so," — with his eyes directed straight at the clock, but with his head decidedly though unconsciously inclined to one side. On telling this story to a friend, and mentioning in connection with it the habit of artists of observing their work sidewise for the effects of finishing-touches (one artist, celebrated for his crayon portraits, whom I know, has a mirror at his right into which to glance for the effects of touches; and lately I read in an English novel how the heroine, being busied with the final touches of a drawing, glanced sidewise at them), my friend remarked that a woman, in examining the fitting and other points of another woman's dress, will turn her head first to one side and then to the other, stepping backwards, and around the object of her inspection.

These facts led me to think that there is a serviceableness or advantage in the side-glance and a meaning in it, besides the sheep's-eye of shyness, or the movement away from direct vision from the desire to conceal the look. A dog, such as the one whose picture you give in Chapter I., under the topic of "Associated Habitual Movements in the Lower Animals," watches for things he is on the alert for, or when in uncertainty about what is going to happen, as when waiting for a gesture of command from his master, — with his head turned so as to raise one eye above the other. But the intentness of watching in simple expectation is effected by direct and level vision, as in the pointer. It occurred to me that, in the case of a woman, as a dressmaker, inspecting another's dress, the movement of the head is possibly in part a true gesture, or expression of critical interest, as well as a really serviceable movement; and that, as a gesture, it is derived from the serviceable habit, in accordance with your first principle of expression.

I was then led to look for the exhibition of this gesture as a true unmixed one, or as depending merely on association, and as the gesture of critical interest or consideration. Not only are the eyes often half-shut in abstraction or meditation, but the head is often inclined on one side; and an instance of the lateral movement of the head is incidentally mentioned by you where you illustrate the movement of the eyebrow in recollection, — the case of the "young lady earnestly trying to recollect a painter's name, and she looked to one corner of the ceiling, and then to the opposite corner, arching the one eyebrow on that side." Two of my friends show in a very marked manner — so marked that their acquaintances, to whom I have mentioned it, recognize the gesture at once as a characteristic one — the gesture of slow lateral movements of the head from side to side with pauses between, in giving serious attention or consideration to what is said. One of these gentlemen is a professor of law in Harvard University. The other is a grandson of a distinguished professor of theology in the College, of half a century ago, who had the same characteristic movement; and many now living who remember the grandfather are vividly reminded of him by this characteristic in the grandson. Other instances have occurred to my memory of this habit, which does not seem to me so rare, except in the degree of its manifestation in these two cases, as to be properly called a trick-gesture.

Without giving here the speculation I have pursued on the primary serviceableness of these movements, I will come at once to the matter to which all the above is preliminary. You state, on the authority of Dr. Lieber and Mr. Tylor, that the Turks express *yes* by a movement like that made by us when we shake our heads. This seemed to me, when I first read it, very strange, and it lay as a doubt in my mind until, on independent grounds, the shake of the head began to have to me the new significance which I have indicated; and the hypothesis then occurred to me that, in a derived or secondary meaning, it might signify a deliberative or cautious assent, or else an acquiescent deliberation, — besides having the meaning of pure categorical negation it has with us, and the meaning of disapprobation, anger, or threatening it has (as I have ascertained) throughout the East, with the Greeks, Turks, and

Arabs, or Semitics generally, and also had in the East in ancient times. I fortunately bethought me, at this point in my speculation, of an authority who turns out to be a much better one than I had imagined. Professor Sophocles — whose scholarly works, and especially his "Lexicon of Byzantine and Patristic Greek" and his "History of the Greek Alphabet," have given him a great reputation with European philologues — is a native of Greece. His boyhood was passed at his birthplace on one of the slopes of Mount Pelion; and his early youth, in Egypt, at the celebrated ancient monastery at Cairo, of which the superior was his uncle. His education was finished in this country, at Yale College, from which he came to Harvard as a teacher of Greek many years ago. He has been Professor of Greek, Ancient and Modern, here for fifteen years; and has twice returned since he has been here, for short visits to Greece and travels in the East. But, in spite of all this, I did not at first think that his memory was to be trusted as to the negative fact, on which he has insisted strongly, namely, that the Turks do *not* signify *yes* by a shake of the head. It was only by accident, in a second talk with him on this and related subjects, that I found he still retains several characteristic expressions of his native country, and unreflectively makes use of them, with an instinctive sense of their meaning. For instance, he informed me that he frequently finds himself making the Greek sign of simple objective negation (the equivalent of *οὐ*); namely, nodding the head upwards. The cluck which accompanies this gesture among the Greeks and Turks is also used by him sometimes, as I learn from an officer of the College who sees him much oftener than I do. I have got a valuable hint from him as to the fundamental meaning or primary association of the cluck. I had previously noticed, unreflectively, the upward nod, — attaching no significance to it, though the accompanying half-closure and downward looking of the eyes indicated clearly enough the dissent he was expressing. If I had reflected on the gesture, I should have regarded it as a trick, — a very familiar one to me, as I recognized on his making it and explaining to me its meaning and its origin in his early habits. Another seeming trick was also familiar to me, but is now explained as the common Eastern gesture of beckoning or invitation; namely, moving the hand towards the body with the palm turned inward, but downward, instead of upward, as with us. A gesture which I had never seen him use unreflectively, but which, as I have since learned, others have seen in him, he explained to me as the Eastern equivalent of snapping the fingers to express contempt, and more abstractly to express minuteness, and secondarily nothing or negation, — namely, touching the upper front teeth with the thumb-nail, and then snapping it away, as if throwing away a bit of the nail.

Remembering that you had found no interpretation for the cluck, which is made by withdrawing the tongue suddenly from adhesive contact with the upper teeth and front palate, I cautiously asked Professor Sophocles, thinking that, as a philologue, he would have ingenious theories on the subject, what, independently of any theory, his sense of the primary meaning of the cluck was, or whether he attached any other meaning to it than that of simple negation. He immediately answered that it meant smallness, being the smallest of vocal sounds; and he proceeded to compare it to the gesture with the thumb-nail, which he said also meant nothingness or mere negation. We afterwards thought of similar verbal combinations of expression, as in English, "Not a bit," "Not a jot;" or, in French, *ne – pas* or *ne – point.* He says that, among the common people of Greece, as with the shepherds he knew in the mountains, it is common to illustrate stupidity or clownishness in any one by saying of him that he answered a call from a distance, as, "Have you seen my sheep?" with, — and here the upward nod and cluck are given. The clown should have answered, to make himself understood, by the verbal negation, which in ancient Greek was *οὐχί*, and to which the modern negative is similar. The upward nod and the cluck are the equivalent of the pure objective or matter-of-fact negative; namely, *οὐ*, or its modern equivalent, but is never used with the particle *μή*, which expresses the subjective negative; namely, doubt, disapprobation, warning, or threatening. With this negative, the shake of the head is the only head-gesture. Mr. Sophocles has often seen Turks shake their heads in anger, and to express threats or strong disapprobation; and this gesture, he says, is universal with the Eastern peoples he knows. This was the case also in ancient times. The passage (Matt. xxvii. 39), "And they that passed by reviled him, wagging their heads," is paralleled by the passages in Psalms, noted in Reference Bibles; namely, xxii. 7, "All they that see me laugh me to scorn; they shoot out [protrude?] the lip, they shake the head;" and Ps. cix. 25, "I became also a reproach unto them; when they looked upon me, they shaked their heads." The word in Matthew, translated "wagging," is from *σείω*; and *κατασείω* "is in sign of disapprobation," according to the Lexicon.

A rapid shaking of the head is a common gesture towards children to express disapproval or warning; or by them to express dislike or refusal, and seems to be a very natural one; and, as the equivalent of the subjective negative *μή*, is not only natural, but also much more extensive than appears when we do not thus limit its meaning. In this meaning, the origin you propose for it, as well as the origin of *μή*, becomes the more probable. The repetition and rapidity of the shake appears to give emphasis to its meaning, as reduplications do in the etymologies of vocal signs; for example, to express perfect past actions. Mr. Sophocles explains the apparent non-comprehension of the shake of the head by the Arabs on the Nile, as observed by Dr. and Mrs. Gray, by their interpreting the shake as a threat or wagging, or as an expression of disapprobation, and by their not seeing the applicability of the gesture with this meaning to the particular occasions.

The gesture of objective negation, the upward nod for *οὐ*, appears to belong equally to the modern and to the ancient Greeks. Liddell and Scott say *ἀνανεύω*, I nod up, is the equivalent in token of denial of our shaking the head. It is opposed to *κατανεύω*, which expresses both the gesture and the meaning of simple affirmative. Both gestures belong to the modern Greeks as well as to the Turks. Mr. Sophocles has often seen Turks in their *cafés*, listening to narratives of travellers, as of merchants from the West. Etiquette forbids them to interrupt the speaker by words ; but they express their interest and assent very conspicuously by close attention and by continually bowing their heads with great gravity. If any thing is said, however, to which they are unwilling to assent, they throw their heads straight back. He assures me that he has never seen them under such circumstances shake their heads. It would not follow that, under other circumstances, they might not use this gesture, and for other purposes than to express anger or disapprobation, though it seems probable that the gesture is not used for simple affirmation.

I have concluded, as to the value of Mr. Sophocles's testimony, that, though it is that of a memory of long-past scenes, and without conscious or designed observation, yet, as coming from his instincts or habitual impressions, it is better than the record of a naturalist would be, who might have misinterpreted the recorded gesture.

In ancient Greek, *ἀνανεύω* and *κατανεύω* are in direct antithesis, and are the names of the gestures as well as of their meanings. *'Επινεύω* was also used as an equivalent for the latter, though not, Mr. Sophocles says, as a name for the gesture; but, according to the Lexicon, it expresses the nod of approval or command. *Ἀπονεύω* had for a secondary meaning "to refuse by shaking the head." Mr. Sophocles quoted to me from memory a curious passage in an early part of the Acharnians of Aristophanes to the following effect, — but I have not verified it: A Greek countryman is examining one who is really a Greek, but pretends to be a Persian ambassador. To a question concerning the intention of the Persian monarch, the sham ambassador answers by an upward nod. Stage direction, *ἀνανεύει*. To the next question, he answers with the downward nod, indicated also by a stage direction, *κατανεύει*. The countryman then says: "He nods like a Greek. I will question him further." This, as Mr. Sophocles remarked, may indicate that in these gestures the ancient Greeks and Persians differed.[1]

Now I was led to all this curious inquiry, as I have said, by a wish to discover the source of discrepancy between the authorities you quote on the affirmative meaning of the shake of the head with the Turks, and that of Mr. Sophocles; and I have conjectured that such a gesture may mean with the grave and reticent Turk either a deliberative assent, or an acquiescent consideration, or an emphatic expression of one or both of these states of mind. The original serviceableness of the movements from which such a gesture might be derived I take to be as follows: When any thing is seen in a natural aspect, or with direct and level vision, — anticipation, or expected and ideally determined looking, may interfere with true objective perception, and produce illusion in respect to slight features of form, or slight changes in form from movement. I call this an effect in perception of *ideation*. To avoid illusion from such an

[1] The passage referred to begins at line 109 in Ribbeck's edition of the play.

effect on minutiæ and "to see how it strikes the eye," the artist examines his work askant, or by inversion, or by reflection from a mirror; or the watching animal will revolve its head so as to incline the medial plane of vision. The critical state of mind accompanying this serviceable movement will by the directest association tend to produce it, even when the service is very slight, or is of no account; so that the movement becomes a true expression of this state of mind from the very start, and will be a voluntary one whenever sympathy prompts to the expression of critical interest; as when politeness makes us attend to what is pointed out or submitted to our inspection. It will be made conspicuous, as in the preacher, whenever this state of mind urges to the expression of itself with emphasis, as in solemn asseveration.

I may remark here, by the way, that according to the observation of a very intelligent English lady, long resident with us, who has lately returned from a short visit to England, emphatic expressive movements of the features and head are much more common, especially among women, in America, than in the same classes of persons in England; apparently, because etiquette does not forbid it here so strictly. The greater animation both in action and in fixed expression of the average American countenance, as compared with the English, has been remarked by others, and I have myself noticed it. We may believe that one of the most direct effects of civilization, or more properly of cultivation, is to make the subjects of it, and especially the subjects of self-culture, seek to difference themselves as much as possible from the manners of the uncultivated, with whom emphatic bodily expression is a prominent characteristic, derived from the savage. The very spirit of refinement, and the end of fine art, appear to be the avoidance of vulgar emphasis; and to reach the desired effects of it indirectly, by the composition in expression of congruent accessories which are individually weak and are the stronger in combination from the beauty of novelty and distinction.

The speculation from which I started on this line of research — namely, as to the cause of intensification in the colors of sunset, when seen by inverted or much distorted vision, and which I for a long time failed to separate by its distinctive marks from the speculation just mentioned, on an effect of *ideation* — has now assumed for me a new and very great interest. The explanation I have now reached is analogous to the above, but is physiological. Colors are, I believe, not merely reduced from special attention by abstraction when the vision is engaged in mensural perception, or on perspective signs and marks, but are actually not produced in consciousness with the same degree of intensity, I think, for the following reasons: I extend the word "innervation" from its present physiological use, to denote not merely the incitement of motor nerves from the nerve-centres; but also that of the nerves of tactual surfaces, the retina included, or the action of attention on such nerves in mensural or space perception. This action of innervation wakens up, I suppose, all the nerves of such a surface; so that single and separate nerves cannot, on account of this division of nerve force, be externally excited to such a degree as when most of the nerves are asleep or inactive. The intensity of a sensation does not depend on the number of nerves affected. The lesion of a single nerve may produce the most intense and all-absorbing pain. Tickling is such an intense sensation; in it, single isolated nerves or small groups of nerves are externally excited. "The precise point to be touched in tickling must not be known," as you remark. That is, the surface tickled must not be in use for space perception; which, as I suppose, involves the internal activity, innervation, or incitement of all the nerves of the surface. Such an attention to any surface as tickling one's self implies, is a perceptive use of that surface; so that, as you also remark, "a child can hardly tickle itself, or in a much less degree than when tickled by another person." This is, I think, because nerve force or nutrition cannot in such a case be concentrated so as to produce intense action in single nerves.

Now I apply this theory of tickling to the passive perception of colors. I suppose the mind to be withdrawn from attention to minute perspective marks by an inverted or distorted vision; and although the colored lights fall continuously on extended parts of the retina, yet, I suppose, single nerves are accidentally more excited than their neighbors, and draw nerve force or nutrition to themselves. In other words, I suppose nerve force or nutrition in passive sensation to be in unstable equilibrium, and to tend to points in which it is accidentally first excited; whereas, in the mensural perception of minute space differences and marks, the innervation is uniform and steady. And so I was led to suppose that the intensification of inverted sunset colors is a sort of tickling of the retina. I suppose "innervation" to prevent or check the intensity of impressions in this case, just as "ideation" prevents or checks minute objective perception in other cases of direct and level or ordinary vision.

I studied a few days ago, at the seashore, the effect on an ordinary perspective view of an inverted or much inclined vision, with reference to effects independent of color which were first brought to my notice as objections to this theory. I found that judgments of distance were not, in the gross, diminished, but were, if affected at all, rather increased on the whole; yet the parts of the vista were roughly grouped, as in a landscape painting compared to a natural scene. Thus, the foreground of grass and shrubs by the shore, the water between them and a distant island, the island itself, and the open sea beyond touching the sky, seemed, compared to the continuous natural perspective, so many successive and separate flat plains of the picture. In this case, it was clear that the minute perspective judgments of ordinary vision were much enfeebled.

It had long before occurred to me that painters, who, until lately, in aiming at making their pictures most natural in aspect, have used, instinctively, less pronounced colors than those of natural scenes, have done so on account, I conceived, of the inherent imperfections of the perspective marks and signs of their art, and in order to keep the two kinds of vision in harmony with one another. If I am right in this, the more recent style of painting in vivid colors is in error, unless the beauties of color and atmospheric illuminations are the ends aimed at, as appears to be the case in some of Turner's paintings. But, in this case, the careful and minute rendering of forms, practised by the same school of realists in art, would be an inconsistent aim; though it might be justified on other grounds than those put forward, — on opposite grounds, indeed; namely, not of following nature, but imposing what is virtually a new convention, a self-imposed restriction, or condition, within which greater and greater perfection may be sought.

But the most important bearing of this theory, and to me the most interesting, is in consequences touching the empirical theory of space-perception, into which, however, it will not do for me to extend this letter, already, I fear, too promiscuous and too long.

I have just received a curious confirmation of the above theory of affirmative head-shaking from Professor Lowell. He said that, during his late visit to Italy, he frequently noticed (in Southern Italy, he believed) a shake of the head like our negative one which has an affirmative signification, but appears, as he remembers it, to express deliberative assent rather than simple affirmation. This confirmation was the more valuable, since it was given by him before I had fully explained the points of the above theory, or more than put the problem before him. He suggests, since the population of Southern Italy is a mixed one, and as the Saracens lived there for a considerable time, that this gesture may have come from the East. He also mentioned — what I had before heard described — the habit in the common people of Italy of expressing anger by a rapid shaking of the head. But this gesture is, I suppose, more likely to come from the habits of childhood, or from innate dispositions, than by tradition from the East.

To this admirable letter Mr. Darwin wrote a prompt reply on September 21; but, owing to some error in the address of his letter, it did not reach its destination, and was returned to England from the dead-letter office. Mr. Darwin then forwarded it again on January 29, 1875, remarking, in a postscript, "It is by no means worth forwarding; but I cannot bear that you should think me so ungracious and ungrateful as not to have thanked you for your long letter."

Mr. Darwin had said: "I have read your letter with the greatest interest; and it was extremely kind of you to take such great trouble. Now that you call my attention to the fact, I well know the appearance of nervous moving the head from side to side when critically viewing any object; and I am almost sure that I have seen the same gesture in an affected person when speaking in exaggerated terms of some beautiful object not present. I should think your explanation of this gesture was the true one. But there seems to me a rather wide difference between inclining or moving the head laterally and moving it in the same plane, as we do in negation and, as you truly add, in disapprobation. It may, however, be that these movements of the head have been confounded by travellers when speaking of the Turks. Perhaps Professor Lowell would remember whether the movement was identically the same. Your remarks on the effects of viewing a sunset, &c., with the head inverted, are very curious. We have a looking-glass in the drawing-room opposite the flower-garden; and I have often been struck how extremely pretty and strange the flower-garden and surrounding bushes appear when thus viewed. Your letter will be very useful to me for a new edition of my Expression book; but this will not be for a long time. . . . I dare say you intend to publish your views in some essay; and I think you ought to do so, for you might make an interesting and instructive discussion."

To Miss Sara Sedgwick.

[1874.]

It will give me great pleasure to join in the delight the children will have in Mr. Trowbridge's honest and natural magic. The choice of time seems happy, and refers, I presume, to the religious instruction of the children; for the science of electricity is, you know, an explosion of the "theological theory of thunder." If time remains after the exhibition, why shouldn't we have the reading of a Greek tragedy by way of corrective and relief? "Œdipus at Colonos," in which the hero is warned by Zeus, in peals of thunder, of his approaching exit to Hades, would be an appropriate choice. We might thus restore to poetry what is taken from dogma.

To the Same.

Dec. 18, 1874.

I am sorry to be unable to deceive your young friend this evening, but shall be consoled, if he will at some other time submit to my impostures.

It is difficult, without experience, to appreciate the satisfaction of the juggler, — a small divinity in his way. There is no love of power more natural or instinctive than that which we instinctively refer to the *divus;* namely, the desire to excite fear and wonder. And so I am sorry again that I have not discovered or invented, either in magic or science, any new miracles for Christmas, to serve for interlude or afterpiece to the play; but I shall have the nobler satisfaction of sympathy with the children's performances, — in imitation of a later and finer, or more humane, attribute of the *divus*, or more truly of the *diva*, — whose I am very truly.

CHAPTER IX.

WE reach now the last year of Chauncey's life. I do not know whether it will seem to others as it does to me that some of the letters of this year have a peculiar and even tender interest, from a greater number of allusions to himself and his own early life than was common with him. But, certainly, there is here a full measure of that same serene, easy, playful, long discourse, with which we have now grown familiar, — the utterance of a mind that seemed to be always on a vacation.

In his speculations on conduct, here as well as elsewhere, those who knew him well may occasionally find some pathetic reminder of a defect. He had, I think, insensibly permitted the scientific habit — that habit which, as he himself has acutely said, refuses to acknowledge any burden of proof — to creep into the region of conduct; unobservant, in his own case, of those laws of life by which conduct of some sort is forced on men, and even inaction is made to count for action. His disorder was not that of Hamlet, where enterprises of great moment sicken from too much thinking: it was the more subtle difficulty of a mind, healthful and vigorous in its speculative activity, which is content to have no enterprises at all, and to decline the unremovable burden of ordering its own life. He had suffered little, except in one grievous particular, from the goads of experience; and he knew little of the hard exigencies of practical affairs, or of the strifes, the griefs, the longings, and the needs of the passionate seeker after moral perfection.

But, meantime, this cool tranquillity of intellect was very favorable to clear thinking; and out of it has come that body of discussion upon the high subjects with which the thinkers of his generation were most busy, — which has seemed to his friends so solid, so simple, and so fruitful.[1]

To Miss Jane Norton.

JAN. 5, 1875.

All the incidents of the New Years of my boyhood, which recur to my recollection readily, were very pleasant, I believe; and yet, like nearly all the rest of what has found lodgement in the garret of my memory, have a tinge of melancholy. This, I think, is not an indication at all of the surrounding love and kindness, or the reverse, in the circumstances of childhood, but is in accordance with a constitutional peculiarity.

I hold and have maintained with you, I believe, that memory is one of the most fallacious of our faculties (if a power so fundamental, the essential mind itself, is properly called a faculty), when not checked by other records or by rational criticism. The fallaciousness is not so striking as that of the single senses, perhaps, because its fallible testimony is in general not so important as that of the eye or ear to present interests. Yet the things remembered are not just and truly proportioned pictures of the past, but incidents which were impressed on account even of their abnormality, and through the predominance of feelings which temperament determined, rather than the actual and normal surroundings of life. I do

[1] As to the correctness of his results, there must, of course, be a variety of opinion; this is a matter which has to do with premises, as well as methods of reasoning. But, if I may judge from my own case, those who differ from Wright can hardly have a wholesomer exercise than to read him.

not account, however, that youth or woman unhappy, unlucky, or less level with the realities of life whom melancholy has marked for her own. He may, if not too deeply marked, be even happier in the early renunciation of all expectation or wish for happiness. This abstraction, "happiness," is objectively a dream, and has no simple, single, answering feeling or passion in our natures. Its meaning is realized only in the concrete; in the particular desires, purposes, and passions, which happen to have their way, unopposed by others equally strong, or by untoward circumstances. The wish for a happy New Year is from this point of view an affectation. What we really, simply, and sincerely wish is the furtherance of the particular projects in the contemplation of which the present happiness or realized interests of the human mind so largely consist.

It is not to a general happiness through the year that we immediately aspire. The rational Promethean human mind is composed of hooks and eyes for the particular felicities of the morrows, the indefinitely recurring mornings of life and strength. "Good morrow" is a genuine wish, a sympathy with the real efficients of activity and happiness.

You write to this effect in what you say of the paltry value of the good resolutions of this season. I go farther, and assert their positive injury to the moral nature. Their reinvigorating effect on one's morality is like that of a stimulant that calls out an energy which it does not replace. Though meant for a future, they only serve a present occasion, most likely at the expense of the future, and are very damaging to conscience. The true moral strategy is to surround one's self with objective safeguards and incitements, and not to trust these raw recruits (these seasonal resolutions that are only spasms of enthusiasm in an enfeebled will), which may desert at the first occasion of real need. It is not wisdom, but conceit which relies on them. . . .

I have continued the warfare which I had begun, when we parted, against the æsthetic imagination, — against the word "imagination," as used by æsthetic writers, not against what they denote by the word.

I had in a club-talk, a few days ago, a good illustration of the misleading influence of this misnaming, and of the pretence of explanation which namings often involve, when they are, at best, only true classifications or divisions; the name unhappily connoting attributes that are not the real grounds of the classification. The *a priori* philosophy surreptitiously introduces itself into theories of art and genius through such misnamings, — though my chief objection to this use of the word "imagination" was on account of its being already appropriated to a precise scientific meaning; a meaning whose limits and precision are disregarded in the æsthetic use of the word. Such words as "wit" and "humor," or even "fancy" (though not this as in any true antithesis to what should be meant by imagination), are unscientific terms, and æsthetic writers are at liberty to wander at their own sweet wills within the limits of vagueness which these terms cover. But for the other count, — the misleading character of the theory implicated in "imagination" as the name of the poet's faculty (his *faculties*, one should say, for his equipment is not in one single point or faculty alone): I had asserted that Kepler's third law, "that the times of the planet's revolutions are in the sesquiplicate ratio of their mean distances," did not imply so much invention on his part, nor (as was more properly the case) so much learning and discipline in mathematics, as some of his earlier, untrue hypotheses; which, because they proved false, are now called fanciful. My opponent said that this true hypothesis is properly referred to the inventor's "imagination," because it was in accordance with the nature of things (!) As if this omniscient but long-time dumb faculty were a natural algebraist, and knew *a priori* the meaning of sesquiplicate. Here you see a natural consequence of the fallacies of naming. My friend had gathered from this false naming that somehow there existed a faculty in us which is independent of the disciplines and tests of experience, and guides us rightly in our imaginations when freed from the disturbances of capricious fancy. Our familiarity with what to Kepler must *a priori* have seemed as fanciful as many of his failing hypotheses, being thus mistaken for imagination in him, becomes proof of the want in any one, so thinking, of the faculty or faculties so badly misnamed.

The fact that there is a heap of truth in the inference so drawn only makes the matter worse. Experience itself, and not any faculty independent of it, is what makes the imagination work more steadily toward the truth in some minds than in others, or on certain subjects better than on different ones. Thorough acquaintance with what is already known or accomplished on any subject guides the guess or device, especially in a negative way; or leads to the speedy rejection of many inventions, which *a priori* are just as good as the true ones.

But this experience is often in the *intuitive* mode of mental apprehension, or is not distinctly, reflectively, or discursively apprehended. Our judgments of inventions as they arise in imagination are in the form of common-sense judgments, though founded none the less on experience, and in fact on the inventor's own experience.

This is especially the case in æsthetic judgments. They are in the common-sense shape, or are judgments for which the reasons or grounds do not distinctly appear in thought; the very subtlety of which, indeed, is impaired by habits of analysis. So that an artist with theories is generally the worse artist for them. Now, the man of genius, whether poetical or scientific, has greater capacities with given opportunities to gather this sort of experience, and the fertility of his imagination is correspondingly greater than that of common minds; but it is not in this fertility—it is not in imagination at all—that his characteristic excellence consists. It is in the tests he can immediately apply from experience either through his culture or superior spontaneous observation; or where these fail (as they generally do, with reference to any great originality) it is in his patient self-directed study and his power of prolonged application, or in the efficient motives to these, that his superiority lies.

But artistic or poetic genius requires for its full determination some further qualification of this definition. Such a genius has, I think, either originally, or by early discipline, greater voluntary power over modes of feeling. Feeling plays a greater part both in the spontaneous and in the controlled imaginations of such a mind than is common. Now, it is a universal fact in psychology that in a state of passion, or simple, definite feeling, the ideas, images, and expressions that are congruent with such a state arise alone. All irrelevant fancies are excluded by it. This therefore serves as a test or standard, analogous to the objective standard of experience in which the waking eye or ear governs the dream of thought, suppressing all that is irrelevant to clear perception; and we are said to perceive the *truth* or the *reality*. This "truth" of imagination, though analogous to that accordance, that *agreement in significance*, of thought with experience, of the universal with the particulars of experience,—in which truth really consists, though analogous to such truth in being a controlled or rectified fancy, is yet more properly called the "*fit*," the "becoming;" or when it is a revelation by the poet or artist of that in the harmony and justness of expression, which the common mind cannot attain without his aid, it is properly the *beautiful* or the *fine*. The ancients honored this name, "the beautiful," more than we do, and thought it an equal of the true. With us, the word has acquired a less serious meaning, and a taint of sybaritism; so that serious, moralizing art critics, to assist the appearance of levity in their favorite study, and with a just sense of the moral worth of beauty, have abused the name of truth. But allowing their aim and study to be called "truth," or "truth of imagination," it is no more properly an essential element of an internal faculty to be called imagination, and distinguished from fancy, than proper truth is an attribute of imagination in clear, objective perception. In neither case does the imagination contain the test of truth. It is rather rectified by the real standard. In poetic or artistic perception, capacities of simple, sincere, unaffected feeling is the rectifying standard. In outward perception, the standard is in our waking senses. In both cases, the imagination *becomes* true. In itself, it is no other than the fancy, and is neither true nor false *a priori;* though more likely false than true, when very fertile, and not governed by the excellences of mental equipment, which have been unjustly attributed to it. That which is misnamed "imagination" is the capacity of taking in truths from experience, not that of evolving them from within, in any other sense than implicit or common-sense judgments are from within;—unless we include also in this faculty connections of feeling with expression, so far, at least, as these, without discipline, may go.

You demanded, in our talk on this subject, what name I would substitute for "imagination," when speaking, for example, of studies which are said, with real meaning, "to educate the imagination." You objected to "cultivating studies," because of its pretension; and to "the sentiments," as smacking of affectation. Feeling, I know, is a favorite word; and lest pretension and affectation should approach too near, or lay rude, sacrilegious hands on what is so foreign to their nature, let us say the studies we seek to define are those that require, and, when genuinely pursued, develop through exercise true capacities of natural feeling.

Or let us say that certain studies educate, refine, and furnish with appropriate materials the natural feelings or the genuine sentiments of the man. The word "liberal" would hardly do, and is affected by both technicality and vagueness. But what if one cannot find an equivalent expression to take the place of what is, on other grounds, objectionable?

Terseness is a good quality in a phrase; but when it is at the expense of periphrasis elsewhere, or compels a writer like Professor Tyndall to import the German *Vorstellung* in order not to get confused with æsthetic writers, it is proper for the latter to take a lesson in lexicography.

But my talk has run too continuously on from our last debate; and true feeling would perhaps have put more vividly before my imagination the change in your interests and circumstances. Metaphysics might do as a diversion from your cares at home, but may not so well season your relaxations. Still, I find a new problem in your letter, — that on belief in dreams. Dr. Maudsley somewhere says that the development of incipient diseases are sometimes anticipated in dreams, and, he thinks, naturally from the altered proportions of our feelings in sleep; for symptoms scarcely perceptible in the presence of vivid waking sensations may assert themselves enough in sleep to govern the dream. And I may add that ideas, not unfounded in our experience, and really true, but opposed to some waking conviction or decision of our judgments, may assert themselves in dreams, and attach themselves vividly to interests which will give them weight in waking reflections; especially if we are in the habit of recalling dreams. But in this case the true ones remembered are as likely to be in the same small proportion to the false as in the case of rarely recollected dreams. The sensitiveness of certain conditions of ill-health is perhaps a more frequent cause for concern at dreams than race-peculiarities, nationality, temperament, or even habit. But into what a didactic vein I have fallen!

The following memorandum of a conversation with Wright, on "Living according to Nature," was taken down by one of his friends in January, 1875: —

It is permissible to use the word Nature as the name of the harmony of things, but it is not permissible to confound the harmony in the whole, the laws of nature and the invisible orders both without and within us, — to confound the law of causation, whose formula is, "If thus, then so," with the harmony we seek as moral beings, which without our seeking would not, and does not, exist. This (cosmically considered) lesser, but (morally considered) greater, or more important harmony sounding in our very ears, always alluring, though never actually or invariably regulating, like proper laws of nature, the agency of moral beings, is, in its completeness, an ideal harmony. What are properly called the laws of nature pervade the (cosmically speaking) lesser harmony; for we are parts of fate: our lives are also made up of the inevitable, when looked at from the cosmic scientific point of view.

The mistake of mystical philosophy is to suppose this lesser harmony to pervade also, or to be a part of the cosmically greater. This is Plato's realism. The laws of this harmony are of a wholly different order, *different in meaning*, out of the other's sphere, neither contradictory to nor in conformity with those of the scientific cosmos; though involving them as the laws of living structures involve those of matter generally, or as the laws of mechanical structure involve those of its materials and surrounding conditions. Mechanical structures, living structures, artistic and moral structures, are all fittings to ends; and these, though not absolute accidents (since nothing in the cosmos is absolutely accidental), yet relatively to any discoverable principles of the cosmos, are accidents. Now, the conditions which determine these several forms of fitness are in the cosmos, but the ends are not, — except so far as human imaginations preconceive them, or as the actualities of constructions in living forms in art and in moral character are their embodiment. Being embodied more or less perfectly according to the standard of what can be conceived, they seek, or stimulate to action (by a law which is one of the cosmic ones), for their perpetuation and for their perfection; according to the abstract or ideal standard of that which they alone are, or which exists alone in them.

But this ideal standard has its determinants partly in inherited dispositions, and still more in those which early religious training induces. M. Antoninus was not a profound thinker upon what had made him what he was or felt himself to be. Innate predispositions to perceptions and actions, which, *if right* in their directive agency, are in accordance with reason, — that is, with the results of experience and observation, — are not thereby made a standard, or at any rate an independent standard, for self-culture. The way to follow Nature is to observe the means which, in accordance with the cosmic laws or conditions of Nature, and of human nature, are found to be conducive to self-sanctioned ends in the higher social or moral life of man, or in his reflective social nature; *naturam observare* is the way *naturam sequi.* This research observes the conditions of necessity, the laws of inevitable sequence in cosmic nature, and seeks to join to them the ideals of life in such manner as will realize or make actual these ideals as perfectly as possible in outward action. In this relation, Nature is not a teacher, but only a part of the lesson, and is a guide only in the sense in which a mountain-pass is a guide; namely, the limits within which our efforts are saved from total failure.

While, therefore, it is not permissible, in respect to the harmony of ideal ends with the outward activities of life, to confound it with those laws of universal nature that are not to be obeyed, since they cannot be violated; yet the theoretical fault of this confusion is in some sort compensated by the practical value and force it has had with many minds of the poetical type. To imagine an ideal to be embodied somewhere or actualized, and to have an independent existence which, instead of being determined by reason, — that is, experience, — is what determines it, and especially determines the innate, intuitional, or spontaneous reason, seems to be a very natural tendency of the human imagination. Reverence, or at least the poetical form of it, demands that power and goodness or moral harmony should exist *in actu*, in a being in real nature, as well as *in posse* or ideally. Historically, this tendency has been of the greatest service to moral advancement. The Nature appealed to as a standard has been, in fact, a realized abstraction, an imagined embodiment of moral convictions, whether called the will and the laws of the gods or of universal nature or of common nature, or called a harmony which is objective or actually external to the idea of it. But, while theoretically wrong, its practical effect as against the superstitious reverence for idealized realities, dead forms, institutions, and sanctions, has been immense. Natural rights were pragmatically real, so long as divine rights remained so. The Nature still deserving our worship is the harmony of an elevated ideal standard, pragmatically opposed to the claims of traditional institutions and sanctions.

To the Same.

FEBRUARY, 1875.

. . . I have meditated for a long time a machine for setting down thoughts, which should only involve the easiest play of the fingers, without subjecting to servitude the arm or the body, and would be as easy of manipulation as the deaf and dumb alphabet, but more expeditious. No doubt *thoughts*

— even the thoughts of the foolish — are of sufficient dignity to hold in subjection and rightfully claim the service of all the muscles. But true Christian democracy teaches that mercy is above commandment; and that the dignity shown chiefly by the latter is one not sufficiently shown otherwise.

To Mr. Darwin.

CAMBRIDGE, Feb. 24, 1875.

Your letter of last September, after its long wanderings, reached me at length through Dr. Gray in time to serve as a Valentine, and gave me much pleasure, of which not the least part was the release I had from the discipline of a doubt whether my long letter of last summer was properly mailed or ever reached you.

It seemed to me, and this was my chief motive in writing, that a letter to one interested especially in some of the many points of investigation which lay loose in my mind, would serve to give them a greater degree of coherency, while preserving for me more freedom than was compatible with the more vigorous requisites of an essay. I have found that writing in any other style is apt to crystallize one's meditations into opinions too fixed for clear, open thought. I was quite willing to submit them, however, as comparative crudities to so friendly a critic, and I am much gratified that you found so little to object to in the letter.

I had thought a little upon the point you make that the two motions of the head, that of denial and that of inspection, are widely different, and had conceived of their grading into each other in the expression of the mixed mental states. I have since made a sort of geometrical analysis of them as extremes of a series of movements. Thus, placing and holding fixedly the tip of the forefinger on the top of the head, the head can only move on an axis through this point and the turning-point in the neck. This is one extreme, — the gesture of denial, refusal, warning, &c. By placing the finger successively on the forehead, the tip of the nose, and the chin, the axis of rotation is successfully brought forward by stages toward the horizontal direction it has in the most neutral of critical considerations. But already at the forehead there is a decided element of consideration introduced into the gesture, according to my instinct of interpretation. Professor Lowell is unable to recall distinctly the character of the movement, like our negative, which he saw in Southern Italy, and learned to understand as an affirmative one; but he is so far interested in the question that he has offered to make inquiries of Signor Monti, an Italian gentleman, a native of Sicily, who formerly taught the Italian language in this College. If, as I hope, he gets the true gesture from him, I will preserve and transmit to you as accurate a description of it as I can.

Very lately, while reading for the first time in my life the Memorabilia of Xenophon, in translation, I came to a passage near the beginning of Chapter iv., Book 1, where Socrates gives an interesting statement of the argument from the appearance of design for the existence of the gods; and I was struck with this sentence: "Is it not," he asks, "like the work of forethought . . . to make the eyelashes grow as a screen, that the winds may not injure it [the eye]? *To make a coping on the parts above the eyes with the eyebrows, that the perspiration from the head may not annoy them?*" It was with the latter query that I was most struck; for it was a new suggestion to me, and seemed truer than the first. I found that the idea of this use was in the minds of several of my friends; but whence they derived it, they could not tell, whether from literature or direct experience. One gentleman, formerly much devoted to athletic exercises, told me that, in rowing, the perspiration was often annoying from running into the outer corners of his eyes. His eyebrows are rather thin and short. Dr. W.

James, Instructor in Physiology in the College, who went with Professor Agassiz on his first expedition to South America, says that he spent several hours a day in a part of the expedition fishing in the Amazon, under a scorching sun; and that the sweat, running from his forehead and drying into a brine, irritated his eyes excessively, so that he was obliged to bathe them frequently in the river. Fishing under a broiling sun in a tropical stream seems not far removed from the conditions of existence of primeval man. I thought that if you had referred to this use of the eyebrows, I should have remembered it; but I made a cursory, though fruitless search for it.

I have lately read, by the way, the principal additions and corrections in your edition of the "Descent of Man;" and your less qualified adoption of Mr. Wallace's views on the use of the lay of the hair on the gorilla's fore-arms gave me another hint toward the little speculation on uses, which I venture to propound at the risk of making another long letter. The survival of the *panniculus carnosus* in the human forehead and scalp (the latter partially rudimentary), the development of the corrugator muscles, the survival, or perhaps even the development of the eyebrows, and the length of the hair on the head, — all seem to me related to the denuding of the forehead, which doubtless was by sexual selection, or for ornament. The *arrangement* of the hair on the foreheads of most hairy animals, and in the eyebrows as well as in the eyelashes (which do not serve, as Socrates thought, for screens against the wind), seems to be adapted to keep the rain and perspiration out of their eyes, or to serve for shedding water. Now, the loss of this use in the hair on the forehead would have been a considerable expense for beauty, if the correlative adaptations made for it below and above, in the retention or increase, perhaps, of the hair on the brows, and the increase of length in the hair on the head (to serve as a parting thatch for shedding rain, in place of the old shingles), had not taken its place, and laid the foundations for later developments of beauty. The prototypes of the long hairs, or vibrissæ, in the eyebrows of some families, perhaps served the same use; I have met with an instance of this occurring in three successive generations, at least. But the eyebrows are sometimes curly, and may serve (as a friend suggests, who has curly ones, and is one of the three who have had vibrissæ) to catch the perspiration and rain, which strokes of the hand would remove from time to time. It occurred to me that, in the same way, a negro's woolly mat might serve to catch a tropical shower, and hold it till he has an opportunity to shake it out. Perhaps the *panniculus* of the scalp served for this latter purpose. The reversal of direction in the hair bordering the forehead in some monkeys may be for a similar service; the above suggested use of the *panniculus* could be experimentally determined in this case. The cowlicks on the foreheads of many children may be relics of, or reversions to, a similar normal arrangement in the straight-haired varieties or races of primeval men. The vibrissæ of the brows, especially in curly ones, would have served in former times as gargoyles; as in the nose they apparently serve for joining drops, and extending the conducting and evaporating surfaces of the nasal passages, thus promoting the circulation of the lachrymal ducts.

Other features serving the same important end in vision, of shedding water, I have hinted at above; namely, the muscles which produce the transverse and vertical furrows of the forehead. Their non-appearance or slight development in childhood indicates the lateness of their acquisition by the race. That these furrows have been serviceable as drains or watercourses, taking the place of arrangement in the hair formerly on the forehead, is not inconsistent with the uses of the grief-muscles which you seem to me to have fully made out. To compress the eyeball in the more energetic action of the corrugators, and to shade the eyes from excessive light by their lesser action, seem to be unquestionable uses. That they should also serve this other use, and that their development has largely depended on this use, are, to me, none the less credible and even probable views.

The inquiry as to which of several real uses is the *one* through which natural selection has acted for the development of any faculty or organ, or stands and has stood in the first rank of essential importance to an animal's welfare in the struggle for life, has for several years seemed to me a somewhat less important question than it seemed formerly and still appears to most thinkers on the subject. The reasons you give why sexual selection should have had much to do with several of the features, of which I have spoken, I still believe are perfectly valid. The uses of the rattling of the rattlesnake, as a protection, by warning its enemies, and as a sexual call, are not rival uses ; neither are the high-reaching and the fore-seeing uses of the giraffe's neck rivals, but are in the most intimate conspiracy to the same effects. Furthermore, it seems to me presumable that in a long course of development, even in cases of highly specialized faculties, existing uses have risen in succession or alternately to the place of first importance, as in the various uses of the hand. This principle of a plurality of existing uses involves a very important influence in secondary uses, whether these are incidental or correlative acquisitions, or are the more or less surpassed and superseded ones. They seem to connect in some cases the action of natural selection with the inherited effects of habit and exercise. An animal may, for a comfort or convenience, which bears but little reference to its essential welfare, be indirectly furthering, through exercise, certain faculties which, though rarely called into exercise in functions of prime importance, may nevertheless have, or may come to have, such functions. Thus, the constant or frequent use of the corrugators for forming vertical furrows and draining the forehead into the lachrymal ducts, or down the nose, or drawing the brows together for shading the eyes, may have been a preparation of them for their rarer but more important surgical service of quickly correcting the circulation of the eyes, and thus keeping the vision keen in conditions of exposure to danger.

There is nothing in this principle which is really new or different from what you have set forth in your works, except the emphasis or prominence I am inclined to give it. The value of a plurality of coexisting uses in making the principles of natural selection and that of the inherited effect of habit co-operate in a larger number of cases and to a greater degree than could otherwise happen, ought to raise the principle from the rank of a scholium to that of a main theorem in the development doctrine. At least, my present interest in one of its possible illustrations makes the matter seem so to me. It is, no doubt, a very interesting inquiry how any given organ or faculty is specially related to essential conditions of an animal's existence; but it is not so important to the theory of natural selection as it would be if the efficacy of this process depended solely or generally on a single or permanent relation of this sort. The aid, too, which sexual selection gets (and gives) from such an association with habits and natural selection, or through a plurality of uses, is worthy of consideration. I do not conceive the question whether, in a given case, the coloring of an animal is protective or sexually attractive, is a question of alternatives, of which only one can be true. Sexual selection may in one case take up what natural selection has laid down, as in lengthening the hair beyond its value as a thatch for keeping the rain from the forehead and eyes. Or this agency having perhaps elaborated in another case the woolly mat of the negro, the hair may then have curled still closer than the task demanded, from its value in holding water; and then, later, sexual selection would return to the artificial cultivation of the African savage's coiffure.

Among the multitude of topics in my head last summer, one, for which I had no space from the length of my letter, related to a class of gestures used in reflection, meditation, and, I may add, continuous thought or speech under distracting circumstances. To some of these gestures you refer when you say, "Why the hand should be raised to the mouth or face in deep thought is far from clear." I came to this question from the speculations of which I wrote; and I hope—since it would make this letter too long to do so now — to discuss it with you some other time. But I may state here one general conclusion which I had reached. The service on which many gestures seem to be founded appears to be to prevent the attention from wandering, by turning it to something upon which it can readily be kept, and from which it can as readily be recovered. This prevents its wandering too far into the swamp of vague, uncontrollable feelings, such as those of self-attention, visceral sensations, and the reflexes from involuntary movements. The great sensibility of the face, especially about the mouth, seems to me to explain the gesture to which you especially refer; and even the pressure of the hand on the forehead appears to relate rather to vague sensations in it, thus controlled by the hand, than to any direct effects of the pressure on the action of the brain. But the full justification of these conclusions is a long argument, into which I will not here enter.

I send, in the same mail with this letter, a number of the "Nation," which contains a couple of "Notes" by me about books on evolution. They begin at the foot of page 113.

In this letter, Chauncey expresses the purpose of writing again to Mr. Darwin; but in the six months of life that remained to him he did not do it. Mr. Darwin's latest note to him was written in reply to this, on March 13. He says, "I write to-day, so that there shall be no delay this time in thanking you for your interesting and long letter received this morning. I am sure that you will excuse brevity, when I tell you that I am half killing myself in trying to get a book ready for the press. I quite agree with what you say about advantages of various degrees of importance being co-selected and aided by the effects of use, &c. The subject seems to me well worth further development. I do not think I have anywhere noticed the use of the eyebrows, but have long known that they protected the eyes from sweat. During the voyage of the 'Beagle,' one of the men ascended a lofty hill during a very hot day: he had small eyebrows, and his eyes became fearfully inflamed from the sweat running into them. The Portuguese inhabitants were familiar with this evil, as I well remember from a ridiculous incident: they immediately brought a woman who was suckling a baby to squirt milk from her breast into his eyes; but he ran away in dismay! I think you allude to the transverse furrows of the head as a protection against sweat; but remember that these incessantly appear on the forehead of baboons. . . . I have been greatly pleased by the notices in the 'Nation.'"[1]

To Miss Grace Norton.

JULY 12, 1875.

The charm of the first days of the vacation in Cambridge is a theme which I believe I have several times summoned the muse to set forth through me; but *stilts* were the only aids she

[1] Wright's correspondence with Mr. Darwin may well draw attention to his powers as an observer. A friend who saw much of him speaks of "the personal observation and investigations of the facts of science which he was all the time carrying on with great interest during his later years, and of which there is but little direct expression in what he wrote for publication. Perhaps," it is added, "the notices of him have hardly emphasized the mention of his great abilities in this direction sufficiently to give an adequate impression of them."

ever lent me, as Miss Jane, whom I invoke to keep me from mistaking such aids for wings, will testify, if you will not take my word for it. And so, in plain prose, I say that the change is almost as complete from the busy days of Commencement and the Centennial[1] as a journey and a complete change of scenes and associations could produce; so that the fortnight since you left us seems almost as long to me as it ought, of course, to seem to you. I met a Professor in the college grounds last evening luxuriating in the cool moonlight and the solitude, and truly grateful in his heart to the multitudes who have fled from the College, leaving it to silence and to such as him. They take all the trouble, he said, of journeys, and of providing uncomfortable accommodations for themselves; and leave behind them comfort and the fullest, richest accommodation to him, for which he feels much obliged.

A part of this feeling no doubt comes from the easy, serene, and full, but unforced occupation of the vacation; though the calm outward circumstances keep very perfect harmony with these, at least in the beginning. But though untrammelled, unstimulated spontaneity is the Buddhist's bliss, its progress, as his philosophy recognizes, is towards sleep. Not this sleep, but somnolescence, is the true philosophic end, as we agreed, I think, last summer.

One is sure to find, at this season, the crabbedest resident in a civil mood. It is under such circumstances that I go to see our old friend ——, feeling sure to find him in his most social humor; though I have not yet called on him this season.

. . . .

I have nothing to write about, — not a thought for which to beg audience or hospitality of you, and no disposition to

[1] The celebration of the taking command of the American army by General Washington, at Cambridge, July 3, 1775.

enter on any of our old debates. In fact, my disputatiousness has lately exhausted itself in my last three communications to the "Nation;" the very last being a renewal of my old warfare with Spencerism, written since you left us. Utilitarianism even would fail to put me on the defensive; since I have had my say on it against Sir Henry Maine.[1] I am in my present mood quite willing to allow that the rules of right are founded in the nature of things: without insisting on any explanation of how they are so founded or discovered; or what the things are, the nature of which shows the right, and should be followed. Still, in accepting this mystical formula, I think it no more than fair to reserve the right of a positivistic inquisition and interpretation of it when we come to a serious discussion.

. . . .

Mrs. Jacobs's house is closed, and I am proposing to myself to go back to Mrs. Wood's boarding-house, for the vacation, where I expect the companionship of Professor Lovering and Mr. John Fiske, for a part of the time at least. I had a very pleasant, long, and philosophical afternoon call from Mr. Fiske on Saturday, and found him quite open and unprejudiced in his appreciation of Spencer.

But what a lot of gossip I have found for a letter which had nothing to say, or only friendly greetings to bear. Yet even a friend is an egotist, and true altruism is a conversion and reflection, not a sacrifice of self-regard; an identification, not an opposition of interests. And a friendly reception implies some endurance of egotism, if not much interest in its beggarly garb of gossip. The amount, or rather the depth, of this medium of gossip is unlimited, objectively, reaching even to the numbering of the hairs on one's head, to say nothing of the ideas within. And its pertinency extends to the range of illumination which the light of sympathy diffuses through the circumstances of life.

[1] A Note in the "Nation" of July 1, 1875, at p. 411.

To the Same.

JULY 18, 1875.

. . . It never occurred to me before that our prospective treatise on "Manners" would be, so far as my contributions would determine its form, a branch of the utilitarian philosophy. It would be a great triumph if I could get you to indorse a utilitarian account of such manners as the votes of all refined and sensible people approve, — the true lawgivers in this branch of morals; an account which would show that their justification is wholly in effecting the greatest happiness of the greatest number, — notwithstanding that the refined and sensible would mostly be unaware of any such principle of judgment, would be simply conscious of having no superstitious regard for the *authority* of manners. The true character of common sense is not to interfere with the due poise of the considerations that determine its judgments by handling them with the force of analytic attention. Reverence, however, not less than irreverent analysis, interferes with this poise; and to be free from superstition is, therefore, the supreme merit of such a judgment.

. . . .

One remains a boy longer in philosophy than in any other direction; though this has its drawbacks, since manners even in philosophy — modes of thought and feeling, even about the most abstract subjects — are early fixed, and the danger of a late maturing in philosophical opinions is that such heterogeneous combinations, such deformities, as dogmatic scepticism, come to pass.

. . . .

—— wants to reconcile, or to have somebody else reconcile, views that are in conflict in his mind; and because men like Lewes pretend to do this, he admires them, very uncritically, I think. Lewes, in my opinion, is a very shallow thinker, who is making capital out of a strong general desire to have the two philosophies reconciled.

. . . .

On Friday evening, I saw —— again, and introduced the subject of the "duty of belief," as advocated by him in the "Nation." He retracted the word "duty." All that he meant to say was that it is foolish not to believe, or try to believe, if one is the happier for believing. But, even so, he seemed to me to be more epicurean (though he hates the sect) than even the utilitarians would allow to be wise. He is by temperament opposed to what is known as epicurean; and, mistaking pleasure to be only the passive pleasures of life, he misunderstands what this philosophy really teaches. To him the perfection of moral action and belief is in heroic conditions of life; and a creed adapted to these, however rare they may be in fact, is to him the true creed, covering the whole range of life, and prescribing a rule for the extremes of human action; whereas, he thinks an epicurean could, according to his philosophy, do nothing better *in extremis* than commit suicide. And so I had to argue over again the irrationality of suicide on epicurean principles; the necessary illusion of it as an end, or a means to any end; in short, to prove to him that the suicide is sane only on heroic principles, which, as being responsible for such insanities, had to provide imaginary motives against it.

He quite agrees that evidence is all that enforces the obligation of belief, and that it does this only in virtue of its own force as evidence. Belief is only a matter of choice and, therefore, of moral duty so far as attending to evidence is a volitional act; and he agreed that attention to all accessible evidence was the only duty involved in belief. On the other hand, I allowed that he was not the only sinner who misuses the word "duty," which ought to mean only those principles of conduct, and what follows from them, which recommend themselves to all rational beings, or at least to all adult, rational, *human* beings. And, further, I allowed that unproved beliefs, unfounded in evidence, were not only allowable, but were sometimes even *fit, becoming, or appropriate* to states of feeling or types of character which are deserving of approval, or even of honor. This fitness does not however amount to an obligation of duty. So far we are agreed, and he retracts.

. . . .

A Rebus for the children. What does "S E E 8 o" spell?

To the Same.

JULY 25, 1875.

I see that you make "selfish" synonymous with "spontaneous." Now the noble divinity Spontaneity is any thing but selfish, — except as children and poets and lovers are selfish.[1] His are actions without reflection, or what depends on reflection, — like the dictates of Duty — or of anybody else. He is, it is true, sometimes selfish, or inspires selfish acts; but oftener, in good people, he favors every duty but that of thinking of and doing to-day, in cold blood, what a glow of enthusiasm or generous feeling prompted under his influence yesterday, — like writing a poem. But Spontaneity is generally credited, and I think rightly, with a certain

[1] Chauncey was fond of humorously deifying "Spontaneity." The reader of Plutarch may recall a passage from the "Life of Timoleon," where it is said: "And having built a chapel in his house, he there sacrificed to Good Hap as a deity that had favored him, and devoted the house itself to the sacred genius." Mr. Clough, in his revision of the earlier translations of Plutarch, appends at the word "Good Hap" this note: "*Automatia* in Greek; almost equivalent to spontaneousness. . . . His instinctive and apparently unreasoning decisions had been attended with such happy results as to make him unavoidably refer them to something out of himself, to some preternatural guidance."

elemental force, inchoate, undetermined in direction, but making its own course among accidents, like a torrent. Such is the play of children and the young of all animals. This, however, is in itself mere activity; and something of Spontaneity, its best part, is in the quieter flow of a lesser energy in the channels of habit and natural instinct, such channels as afford the least obstruction, or give to energy the least of the character of work or of energy converted to use by purpose. Don't think this to be of necessity selfish; for to think so is to pervert the word "selfish" to what I have observed to be a peculiarly feminine meaning. . . . To be selfish does not mean to please, or to be level with, one's self merely; but to do this at the expense of somebody's more or less well-founded rights, or at the expense of generous feeling, at least, in one's self. But unphilosophical women are, I have observed, apt to be miserly of this latter expense; to suppose that every generous impulse is obligatory, simply because it is generous. But generous principles, not impulses, are alone obligatory even to the best, and must conform to the higher laws of justice. A disposition to absolute and universal sacrifice, or altruism, leaves, in theory, nothing to sacrifice any thing to; and is, of course, in practice, never realized. All that is realized is a morbid, irrational self-accusation of selfishness. . . .

You ask if letter-writing is still odious to me. I think it is, but so that the good of it, the Promethean endurance and philanthropy of it, is set off on high artistic principles against its evils, the vexatious stupidities of the Cadmean invention.

To the Same.

AUG. 2, 1875.

I go to-morrow to Portsmouth, and on Wednesday to Magnolia, there to visit for a day or two Mrs. Lesley and her daughters, — my once little friends. Whether I shall get back in time to reach you on Friday, or not till Saturday, I leave to Spontaneity. . . . The weather here is so cool to-day, and has been for several days, that it seems absurd to go down to the Sea on account of comfort, or for less than some spiritual advantage, such as Friendship or Truth; for which I have spelt it with a big S. . . .

I hope the "Nation" will publish this week my incidental notice of Spencer's "Persistence of Force" in an article on "German Darwinism."[1]

I have been thinking and writing more or less to the point on æronautics, but have not got far into the subject yet.

Chauncey mentions in the last two letters an intended visit to the Lesleys at Magnolia, — on the seashore, near Manchester, Massachusetts. Of this visit, Mrs. Lesley writes: "His last visit to us was at Magnolia, only a few weeks before his death, when his deep composure, his perfect self-control, and his splendid conversation restored to me any impression that might have faded of my earlier intercourse with him. Day after day he wandered on the shore with Mary, discoursing to her of wonders in sea and sky and air. How carefully he explained, how considerately he waited for her comprehension, how glowingly and enthusiastically he pointed out successive wonders!"

To the Same.

NORTHAMPTON, Aug. 22, 1875.

. . . Shall I then attempt to celebrate the glories of Ashfield, and especially of the last day of my visit? Or would it not be more in keeping with my inveterate habits of thought to account for the seeming inconsistency of my deserting your

[1] The Nation, September 9, 1875; Philosophical Discussions, p. 398. This was his latest printed article.

paradise, and staying so long here, — in this very centre of dog-day weather?

While I meditated on the irrationality of such a proceeding (or non-proceeding), the sensible effect of the weather got ahead of any rational considerations upon it. I have not cared to move (spontaneously) since I came; and numbers of little reasons have bound down to the ground by small threads my great sensible purpose to get back to sea air. I roused myself, however, so far this morning as to take a short tramp with my nephew Fred, a boy of thirteen, to the summit of Mount Holyoke. The air had a whiff of Ashfield in it; and the always beautiful view was varied at a later hour by picturesque clouds and distant showers along the great valley and over the hills. I mean now to go to Cambridge on Tuesday.

It seems much more than a week since, last Tuesday morning, I set out on the stage-top, with the driver, in a drizzling fog. I was reduced to interesting myself in the talk of the driver with a former schoolmate of his, just returned from the Far West on a wedding journey with his bride. Think of my being seriously interested to catch and remember the points of humor in this talk! But they were not memorable, and have all escaped me. Only the serious fact remains, that a large number of Ashfield youths — the more energetic of them — are scattered widely; some gone to larger towns, and some to the far Western settlements. This was a glimpse of the process which has been going on for more than two generations in all the lesser towns of Massachusetts. And I was reminded of a theoretical consequence of this fact, — one of my pet speculations, — which a lately settled Northampton physician, an old schoolmate of mine, long resident in the hills, entirely indorses; namely, that the physical deterioration of Massachusetts populations, resulting in so large a proportion of persons afflicted with nervous and mental disorders, is due, not merely to hard fare, but to the selection and removal from the population of those best able and most determined to better themselves by emigration. This is, of course, a normal fact, or universal social law, so far as the relation of the country to large towns is concerned; though in England, and other parts of the world, it is not, of course, carried so far as it has been with us.

. . . .

A rather interesting bit of youthful reminiscence occurred to me the other day. A part of an herbarium which I collected in my boyhood, and which I had supposed entirely destroyed by a fire many years ago, had come to light in the garret among the things saved from the fire. My examination of it was a partial exemplification of a position I held in a talk with Miss Jane a few (by the Almanac) days ago, on the illusions of our memories of childhood,—a singular impression, on comparing memory with these documents, of familiarity and strangeness combined. The herbarium, or this remnant, is in a good state of preservation (probably saved from the insect teeth of time by the smoking it got), and seems creditable for a boy; but the botanical names, written in an unformed hand, and other points of strangeness, almost made me doubt the identity of this youthful collector with your correspondent; and a considerable number of the plants are perfect strangers to me now, though, of course, very carefully examined by their descriptions then.

As a converse experience, I took up the current number of a Northampton weekly newspaper late last evening, and, glancing at its literary matters, saw, under the heading "Educational," a short piece on "The Memory." Reading the first sentence, it had to me a strange familiarity; and then I discovered that the piece was an extract from my Todhunter article,[1] and that my name (not that of the Review) was

[1] The Conflict of Studies: North American Review for July, 1875; Philosophical Discussions, p. 267.

appended. "This is fame!" I said; but, as the family had all gone to bed, I had to wait till morning to show them how a prophet had been recognized even in his own town.

. . . .

. . . But all that I have said is not celebrating the praises of Ashfield, — unless it be by a theme which might appear to you to appear to himself to be one of its transient and departed glories. Nothing but poetry, I am sure, could sound the true praises adequately; and my muse is not equal to that, though in my youth she also undertook it. Late in youth, however, in a mood of scientific reformation and repentance, I burned up all my performances of this sort (and they were considerable in amount), destroying them more effectively, it seems, than the fire did the botanical labors of boyhood. Now, only for narration, exposition, description, argument, any thing didactic, — are the quills I wield. To throw a new light on old objects, — "a light that never was," &c., — this I only emulate in abstract matters. There *is* a sort of resemblance between philosophy and poetry. In neither are the objects or themes matters of novel interest: in both, it is the vision, not the object, that is brought with fresh novelty to consciousness; and novelty in the object is only an aid or accessory to sight, — a new light, not a new task for it. Philosophy is poetry in the abstract, — "the vision and the faculty divine." And poetry is philosophy in the concrete. And Ashfield, with its walks and talks, its drives and discussions, is both! Could I say more?

In the last letter, Chauncey refers to a conversation, at Northampton, with a physician who had formerly been his schoolmate. This was Dr. Thomas Gilfillan,[1] formerly of Cummington, who had lately returned to his old home, and whom Chauncey had not met for many years. Dr. Gilfillan's account of this meeting will interest those who remember

[1] See p. 14.

Chauncey's quiet, easy ways among his intimates: "In the summer of 1875," he says, "he made his last visit to his early home. We met again after nearly thirty years of separation. How quietly he would drop into my room of an evening for a chat! Taking from his pocket his corn-cob pipe, and the stem and tobacco, he proceeded to mount, load, and light it, insisting that a corn-cob made a most superior pipe. He smoked, and as he smoked he talked; and amid the pleasant fumes of his homely pipe we chatted, — sometimes of old times, sometimes of science, sometimes of medicine; often we drifted into or over many subjects; but, whatever the subject, the amount of information he would bring to bear upon it was wonderful. His memory seemed to have grasped the most salient facts, and to hold them ever ready for his use. He was at home on medical topics, — familiar with the newest and most approved remedies, their use, effects, and even their methods of preparation.

"These were happy evenings; and, as they passed, I could see more and more of the old friend, as he was of old, so like and still so different; but, though years had wrought such changes in him, he was the same quiet, companionable friend as in days gone by. He, too, seemed to enjoy his stay with us, reluctant to see its end. Several times he named the day for his departure; and still its evening would find him in my room, with his friendly cob pipe, smoking and chatting. He seemed to linger, loath to leave, as though he had a premonition that this was the last time. We parted but a few short weeks, and then the silver cord was loosed."

To Miss Jane Norton.

CAMBRIDGE, Sept. 1, 1875.

—— has convinced me that letters ought to begin like talk. I have paraded all my reasons against it, and surrendered the point. I stayed in Northampton until this week, when by a desperate effort, on Monday, I tore myself away, and came to Cambridge.

This was a true case of fascination, — out of the realm of the simply agreeable and rational, — and I believe I understand now what the attractions of Northampton are to the summer visitors who stay there. These visitors very generally appear in the character of invalids. The place is medicinal, the climate sedative. A few days, or doses, of it, induce complete inactivity, a semi-paralysis, which benefits the nervous patient by compelling rest, bodily and mental. The scenery is charming and a rational attraction. All besides is fascination; that is, a *drawing*, or holding, without reason or excuse, or even in spite of reason and against one's will. How lazy those are made by it, who are not acclimated, is seen in the fact that, to induce them to ascend Mount Holyoke, the charms of its matchless view are powerless. Elaborate steam machinery is provided to carry them all the way up the tremendous height of three hundred feet (not very steep), all the rest of the entire nine hundred feet being accomplished in common carriages. Six or seven times the height is an easy feat for pedestrian tourists, in stimulating mountain air. I do not think that I was hurt by this treatment, though I was not in much need of it.

The later days were much more pleasant than the first, and added rationality to my stay. I was too lazy to write even a postal card (what I never did) to say that what struck me in the article in the "Springfield Republican" that I sent to you was the reference to Mr. Tennyson's own judgment on his "Queen Mary," and the accordance of this judgment with the view which ——, alone among the critics, had expressed regarding the motive of its interest; the accordance of this judgment also with Miss ——'s as to the artistic merits of the poem.

The marriage question discussed by Mr. Gladstone was interesting, but did not suggest to me our talk. I think we agreed that the State, or all outside influences, whether civil or religious, legal or moral, could wisely exert over marriages only a *veto* power of a well-defined character, laid down in black and white. Reason, or rather the analytic reason, is but a rude guide of life; there can be but little *positive* wisdom in any system of laws; and the happiness of life in minutiæ depends upon very much that is not common in our judgments, or laid down in any defined wisdom; these are not competent to deal with such questions. Wisdom herself, if I may use so realistic an expression, — or the power of judgment, and not merely wise counsels, — must be imparted when possible; or men and women *will* make marriages of a piece with the general tenor of their foolish lives.

I do not think that we ought to idealize the marriage state to the extent of expecting that two weaklings, however skilfully matched, could make themselves strong by the union, nor do I believe that any censors (much less any system of censorship) could compass the skill of true match-making, except negatively in well-defined prohibitory rules, — though some obstacles thrown in the way of marriage, not materially different from what now exist, would have the effect to make the parties give more thought to the rational side of the subject than their natures or fancies incline them to do. As to any ill effect upon posterity of the present freedom of marriage unions, no law-givers, no private counsellors, are at all equal to the subtle skill of nature, shown in the survival of the fittest; which, though a rough remedy for evils that wisdom, if it existed, might forestall, is one which wisdom has not yet equalled. The ancient state of Sparta, whose law-givers undertook to do the work of nature in selection, perished in consequence; and nature selected those ancient communities whose principles of freedom and humanity to the weak seemed opposed to her Dracontic laws. *Not to help* natural selection is the human way, strong in its weakness, of gaining the favor of this fatal power; and not to legislate is often the wisest principle of legislation. Not to judge for one's neighbor, not to advise even for a friend, but rather to present grounds of judgment and advice, is often the wisest rule of personal influence. For what do we know? Does wisdom exist? And if not, — are we to be misanthropes or despairing philanthropists? This would certainly prove that wisdom does not exist in us, but rather that the conceit of it has made us judges. To those whose past life is predominantly practical and executive, whose first question is "what to do about it?" who feel called upon first to act, and secondly to act wisely, the special Delphic answers are these radical ones: "Know first, and act only on real knowledge; beware of opinion." — "Keep knowledge at nurse as long as possible; cherish its grounds, reasons, and questions; draw conclusions only when the necessity of decision compels." And the Delphic wisdom would, I think, also say, in criticism of a later oracle, "Let not your love of your neighbor mistake itself for a knowledge of him." — "Treat him, morally, as a specimen, not as an individual. As an individual, like or dislike him, according to the bent of your nature, yet strictly within the limits of justice." — "Don't mistake an æsthetic preference, on the one hand, for a moral judgment; nor let generous feeling, on the other hand, corrupt either justice or good taste." — "The Golden Mean, as a rule of duty, is more level with reason than the Golden Rule, though perhaps as a sentiment it is less effectively beneficial in the unreasoning mass."

But perhaps you are mentally charging me with the supreme conceit of dealing out Delphic wisdom much beyond what is written or delivered by the priestess. My defence is that this wisdom is only of the negative sort, about "what not to do," in which the moral institutes of wisdom chiefly consist, and to which the common experience of life mainly contributes; and if I have fallen into my old way of preaching, — why, this, I hope, will be a pleasant reminder of old written talks of the sort.[1]

To Mr. Norton's Daughter, Sara.

SEPT. 1, 1875.

On going yesterday to Shady Hill to call on your father, I was most agreeably introduced to the interesting little animal-plants which you so kindly and thoughtfully sent me. Last evening I read about them in Mr. Darwin's book; and this morning, after they reached my room, I gave a dead fly to one of them, and while writing other letters I have been watching the sun-dew close upon it. Only a few hair-like arms have yet laid hold on the fly, though the rest are slowly heading towards it. The sun-dews are not so lively as animals which have minds, but seem, according to Mr. Darwin's account, to be almost as sensitive and intelligent, though they don't appear to know it. I suppose that it takes so long for them to act that they have at the time no energy to think. They seem so well provided with intelligence for their wants, that they do not need any minds to gather more for them.

Instead of catching a new fact every day to remember and think about, a fresh fly once a week to digest is all they get or want from the world they live in, besides water, air, and a little earth, — and sunlight and warmth. Not many wants! Don't you wish you were a *Drosera rotundifolia*, — such a fine name to have, too, — to which a fly is as welcome as a letter, or more so? They only feel, probably, if they feel at all, just as you do when you get nearly or quite asleep, and

[1] This is the last of the letters to Miss Jane Norton. I preserve, upon a later page, Chauncey's expression of admiration for this gracious and noble woman. She died in May, 1877.

a fly lights on your nose; only with your arms you would brush it away, instead of folding it in them so fondly as the Drosera seems to do. The Drosera seems to love flies; but really does not care for their minds, and has not any sympathy or pity for them, I think, — not having any mind of its own.

When I was in Northampton lately, I found some dried pressed plants which I had preserved when a boy, and among them was a pitcher-plant, a sort which also catches flies and drowns them with other insects, and is thought to live on them, though it does not digest them like the Drosera and the Dionaea. There ought to be some pitcher-plants in Ashfield, in the swampy places; for I remember finding some in a swamp among the hills, not far from Ashfield, many years ago; they are also called side-saddle flowers and huntsman's caps. Their botanical name is *Sarracenia purpurea.*

It will not be long before we shall meet again in Cambridge, and then we will talk more about your nice present, for which I thank you very much.

To Miss Grace Norton.

SEPT. 1, 1875.

Among illusions, not "my own idiosyncracies," is one arising from not clearly dividing associated accidents from essential characters, when in the synthetic operations of imagination we have joined them together, — as what we are saying or have said to a friend, on the one hand, with their personal traits and individual characters, on the other. Imagination, the so-(mis)called faculty, the "faculty divine," is distinguished from common powers of the sort by an instinctive apprehension of what truly and essentially belongs to its objects, which, in common minds, only reflective comparison could separate from accidents; and this power so guides invention that the poem is recognized as a true representation by others besides the poet; but every one other than the ideally perfect poet is under the illusion that the thoughts and interests between the lines of his own composition are conveyed by them more or less distinctly to his readers; and this illusion obtains most in letters, since correspondents are never to themselves what they seem to us. Indeed, one of the charms of intercourse is in the riddles thus presented. Discussion is often not so much for the sake of truth or decision as for the discovery of individual traits and causes, infinitely various, and the reading of these riddles. . . .

Our solicitude about posthumous reputation is just as rational, when truly disinterested, as about a contemporary one. One's reputation is a trust to keep and transmit, if it aspires to be more than a claim to present advantage; and solicitude about its future is not, therefore, any thing different or less noble than one's present devotion to its excellence. To be sure, it makes no difference to the dead what is thought of them, or into what hands their names and fames may fall; but it makes a vast difference to the living, — mere idealists though they all are, — who act with reference to the future, the permanent, and the universal. It is a present sense of a fitness for which we are now responsible, rather than any future sense, which is concerned.

It is a great advantage in spoken words that the impress of them in the world is for the most part a sound vanishing in the air, the vehicle only, not the storehouse, of thoughts incorporated in the mind or becoming the thoughts of another, or at best the momentary embodiment of social sympathies. If phonantographs were common, would they not be worse than weeds, — *dirt*, indeed, which we would expel furiously? And written words are rivets and chains by which our freedom is fettered, our moods pinioned, and our Protean lives set in false because fixed postures. . . .

I haven't yet read Professor Clifford's article, but do not recognize in his scepticism, as you quote it, a novelty in philosophical opinions. It is very like that of the very ancient pre-Socratic sceptics, but looser in thought than a well-trained modern thinker ought to be. The truths of geometry and mechanics are abstract or conditional truths, not true at all as descriptions of what actually is or ever has been, except by the rarest accident, since the conditions supposed in them, like drawing a perfect circle or straight line, or the postulates demanded in their enunciation, are never exactly realized. If Mr. Clifford supposes, or thinks it legitimate to suppose, that there was ever a time when an infinite intelligence could not have comprehended the actual orders of the world in complex formulæ, involving the abstract truths of geometry and mechanics, as we now know them, or would have found it more impossible than now, he surrenders the whole ground of scientific speculation on the subject. He needed not have been so particular in designating the superseded laws, but might as well have admitted miracle at once into his speculation, as the orthodox do, — and for the unseen present as well as for the unrecorded past. If one speculates in science at all, it must be from some grounds; but it is not necessary to assert dogmatically that these are indefeasible. Science does not deal with the unconditionally possible or impossible, or with what the orthodox call "the possible with God," but follows out consequences from what is known, surrendering speculation rather than these grounds. To come in conclusion to the admission of miracle is a wasted journey; why not admit it at the start? A law that is good for a moment is good for infinite time, unless it be presumably — on the ground of higher laws, not of mere uncertainty — an alterable law.

I had, a month or more ago, a hot dispute with —— about Stuart Mill's position on this very subject, which he conceived to be the same as Clifford's. Dr. —— took sides with me, in distinguishing between Mill's doctrine, that inconceivability in the negative is not a legitimate proof of absolute truth of fact, — and the doctrine of Clifford, as I understood and still understand it, viz.: that this test could be disregarded in a scientific speculation, in rational inference, — as if reason had not its *laws*. *Confusion* may not have any laws, perhaps, or any ascertainable ones. ——, after calling Mill and his doctrine many hard names, had to admit that this distinction noted an important difference.

I stayed in Northampton even longer than I intended when I wrote. It was one of my excitements to plan every day for going the next, though this grew tiresome after I was reduced to complete sedateness, and the weather got a little cooler. I reached Cambridge on Monday evening. The proofs of my long-delayed article on Darwinism had been waiting for me here a week, and the publication was thereby still more delayed. I am thinking a little of a short visit to Mr. Thayer at Mount Desert.

This visit to Mount Desert he never made. On September 2, he wrote to me: "Think of my staying at Northampton for a fortnight in August! I found, on returning, a card from William Ware, a fortnight old, calling on me to join him in the journey to Mount Desert. . . . If I do not get from you any discouragement, I propose to go down by the Bangor boat on Tuesday next, the 7th." On Tuesday, he had packed his bag for the journey, but sat talking in his room until it was so late that it would require some exertion to reach the boat in time; whereupon, much according to a common habit with him, he concluded not to go. We, at the other end, knowing nothing of this, expected him, and when he did not come still looked for him by the next arrival. In a few days, however, instead of welcoming my friend, I opened the Boston paper to read of his sudden death; and the date of the paper was the day of his funeral.

I cannot better tell the details of his death than by quoting from a letter of this same date, in which my kind friend, William Ware, first told them to me: —

"BOSTON, [Tuesday], Sept. 14, 1875.

"You will, I suppose, before this reaches you, have learned all that is to be told about Chauncey's death. It so happened that I myself heard of it only last night. I went early this morning to Cambridge, but, as I learned from Mr. James,[1] he had already been taken to Northampton. His brother came down yesterday, and I presume the funeral will take place there to-day. Except St. John Green and Hooper, whom I have not seen, no one of his friends was in Cambridge but Mr. James; he went at once to the house on Sunday morning, but it was too late. It seems that his landlady found him sitting over his writing, with the gas still burning, at some late hour on Sunday morning, and was leaving him undisturbed, thinking he had fallen asleep. A sound of distress attracted her attention; and, finding him insensible, she sent at once for Dr. Driver, near by. He arrived immediately, and said at once that there had been some kind of attack, and that another was coming on. This was indeed the case. They laid him on his bed, but before Dr. Wyman, who had been sent for, could arrive, he was gone. The impression seems to be that the first attack must have been early in the evening.

"He had been very bright and well, and there was nothing to give warning that all was not right with him. Mr. James said that about a week ago he spent an evening at his house, and he had never known him more delightful, — talking in his best vein, not about things and ideas but about people, giving astonishingly minute characterizations of them. Innocent, mild, kindly, sympathetic, pure-minded, — these were the

[1] Mr. Henry James.

words Mr. James used about him; and, in speaking of his relations at the Nortons and his admiration of Miss Jane, he quoted his saying that he would rather have her personal approbation than all the fame of this country and Europe. It was a great satisfaction to hear Mr. James's appreciative talk, and to have all his lovely and amiable ways brought up; and I could not but hope that Mr. James was mistaken, of late at least, in thinking that he had been so miserably unhappy. I had hoped that for the last year or two things had been less difficult with him. He has certainly seemed, as I have seen him, quiet and serene. . . . Mr. James said that his face was perfectly white and very noble to look at."

On the night before he died, he was perfectly well, and stood in the door-way talking cheerfully and kindly with his landlady (the daughter of Mary Walker), and her colored friend, Mrs. Jacobs, with whom he had boarded. This was at about ten o'clock on Saturday evening, September 11. The college vacation was not yet over, and most of his friends were away; even his chum, Mr. Emery, was absent for the Sunday. The apartments consisted of two bed-rooms and a common study; on Sunday morning, at about seven o'clock, he was found in his study in the manner which is described in Professor Ware's letter; and he died in half an hour, with no sign of consciousness, the physician and his friend Mr. Green being present. No definite cause could be assigned for this sudden death, even after a post-mortem examination.[1]

[1] The examination was made by Dr. Thomas Dwight, of Boston. Dr. Dwight informs me that the membranes of the brain were much congested, and there were appearances which indicated that a certain amount of congestion had existed for some time; but the cause of death was not ascertained. He adds: "The brain weighed fifty-three and a half ounces, which is above the average, but not remarkable. The frontal portion was uncommonly developed. In studying the arrangement of the convolutions, I found an anomaly, of which there was at the

He was taken to Northampton on Monday. But few persons from a distance were able to be present at the funeral on the next day; yet his faithful and dear friends, Mr. Norton, at Ashfield, and Mrs. Lesley, at Magnolia, had learned of it in time to come. He was laid in his father's tomb, in the old graveyard where so many of his ancestors for two hundred years had been buried. The tomb is by the roadside, looking over the great meadow, — that reaches round to his father's door, a mile away, — and across the distant Connecticut, to the long, even brim of the Pelham hills that bound the eastern horizon. It is the same large and tranquil scene which lay before his eyes when they first opened upon this world of wonders.

time but one instance recorded in literature; namely, a bridge of brain tissue extending over one of the chief fissures, that of Rolando. Whether it is of any real significance, our knowledge does not permit us to say, but it was certainly remarkable. . . . The anomaly was observed in the brain of a Dr. Fuchs, who was a clinical professor at Göttingen. He was, of course, an educated and intelligent man, but I am not aware that he was in any way remarkable. The case was described by Rudolf Wagner, in a work of which I think the title is *Vorstudien zu einer wissenschaftlichen Morphologie und Physiologie des Menschlichen Gehirns*. It is in two thin quarto volumes, and contains good plates: it is at the Boston Public Library. Hetchl, of Vienna, in the *Wiener Medizinische Wochenschrift*, of October 13, 1877, describes six additional cases which he has observed, and alludes to two by Teré, one of which he considers doubtful. The arrangement of the convolutions in the temporal and parietal lobes of the brain of Mr. Wright was remarkably simple."

CHAPTER X.

After the foregoing pages had been for the most part prepared, I received from Professor Gurney, in Europe, a letter giving his recollections and impressions of Chauncey. It reached me just as I was pondering the matter of a general summing up of the qualities of our friend; but after reading it I have had no wish to say any thing more; and so I will add it here, with a few notes, as the best ending of this book:[1] —

"Rome, 1877.

. . . "Though we were classmates, I knew Chauncey but slightly in college: our real acquaintance began in the autumn after our graduation, in 1852. Then I lived for a few weeks in Cambridge; and he, Chase, and I fell into the way of spending our evenings together. By some freak of memory, one of these evenings remains still distinct in my mind, although all

[1] Mr. Gurney, having graduated with Wright in 1852, was a tutor in the College from 1857 to 1863; Assistant Professor of Latin from 1863 to 1867, of Philosophy from 1867 to 1868, and of History from 1868 to 1869; from 1869 to the present time he has been the University Professor of History. From 1869 to 1876, he was also Dean of the College.

Mr. Gurney sends the letter in a rough draft, and with some expressions of misgiving as to the form of it. Illness and much occupation, he says, "have caused this letter to drag along, until it has lost all unity, and become a somewhat unwieldy mass of reminiscences and reflections, with many repetitions; yet I have neither the time nor the spirit to recast and rewrite it. The rheumatism, I dare say, has got into the joints of what I have written." And he goes on to give me a very wide power of amendment. Although I quote this, out of justice to Mr. Gurney's own literary conceptions, I feel sure that the reader will thank me for making no considerable changes.

the others are a blank. I can still see the room, — and almost the formulæ of Taylor's theorem, over a point in which the talk began, — as Chauncey sat discoursing to me till morning upon the metaphysical conceptions underlying the methods of fluxions and the Calculus. I mention this only because it illustrates to me how like in mental habit was the young fellow of two-and-twenty to the man of two-and-forty. That evening was the prototype of thousands we afterwards spent together; and had I, twenty years later, raised the same question, the chances are that he would have unconsciously reproduced in all essentials the same thoughts and in the same order. The tenacity, by the way, of Chauncey's hold upon all the results of his past thinking was marvellous, and showed, if I may say so, how organically connected was his whole structure of thought. 'You remember,' he would say, 'the definition I evolved of this, — or the law I formulated of that, — in such and such a talk with you,' — and the conversation, it might be, had occurred five or ten years before.

"I said just now that it was by some freak of memory that I recalled so vividly one particular evening. Doubtless, however, the exceptional distinctness of it is due to my brain being already excited by a fever, which obliged me to return to Boston after a few weeks' stay in Cambridge; and it was five years before I went back to Cambridge to live. In the course of these five years, *the Club*, as you remember, was established, in whose earlier and more literary days Chauncey played so important a part.[1] During these years, I saw much less of our friend than you and several others did who lived in Cambridge. But besides meeting him in the Club, of which the head-quarters in those days may be said to have been in his rooms at Deacon Brown's on Bow Street, I occasionally went out to spend an evening with him there. The talk, as well as I can now remember, always ran in much the same

[1] See pages 39 and 40.

channels. As the evening wore on, from whatever point the conversation started, it was sure soon to become a stream of psychological or metaphysical speculation on Chauncey's part.

Cave hominem unius libri, says the proverb; which had probably a more frequent application once, when books were rarer. At any rate, Chauncey was the only striking illustration that has come in my way of the immense amount of nutriment that an original and meditative mind may draw from a single author. Sir William Hamilton, at this period of Chauncey's life, held for several years substantially the same place in his intellectual life that was afterwards occupied by Mill and Darwin.[1] You will still remember how refreshing it was to us in

[1] In a letter of Mr. Darwin E. Ware, from which I have already quoted, he says: "The lateness of the development of Chauncey's tastes and powers in the direction of philosophy, considering the aptitude he afterwards displayed, is quite remarkable. While in college, mathematics, the physical sciences, and natural history absorbed nearly all his attention. In these, he was recognized in the class as without a peer or rival. His capacity for philosophy, I think, was not then suspected by others, or even, as I believe, by himself: there were those in his class who showed a deeper interest in metaphysical studies. The notes of Sir William Hamilton contained in Dr. Walker's edition of Reid, that was used as a college text-book, tempted here and there a fellow-student to go further, and examine whatever of Hamilton's writings were then accessible. Late in the Senior year, I remember that Hamilton's essay on the 'Philosophy of the Conditioned,' published in 1829, in the 'Edinburgh Review,' was to him an unknown chapter in the history of speculation. A few years after, he was not more familiar with the simplest problems in geometry than with the whole of Hamilton's philosophy down to the nicest attenuations of definition that pervade it.

"The only subject related to philosophy in the course of the college exercises, which, as I remember, deeply interested Chauncey, was the question given out by Dr. Walker as the subject for a forensic, — whether the faculties of men and animals differ in kind or degree. Dr. Walker was then the Professor of Philosophy, and preached in the college chapel. His powerful influence was on the side of the transcendental school. It shows

our college days to pass from the text of Reid, with his homely, practical way of applying his common-sense to metaphysical problems, to the notes furnished by Dr. Walker from Hamilton's edition of Reid, almost obtrusively precise, acute, and learned. It was like turning your eyes from the motions of a sturdy ploughman to those of a trained athlete. The taste then acquired for Hamilton was soon afterwards more fully gratified by the reproduction in this country of nearly all that he had then published, and the College Library copy of Hamilton's edition of Reid supplied the rest. Later, after Hamilton's death, came a fresh interest and new material from the publication of his lectures on Logic and Metaphysics. Though Chauncey, in after years, abandoned all that was peculiar in Hamilton's system, as for instance his explanation of the origin of the so-called necessary truths, I doubt whether any other philosophical author would have aided his development in so many ways. Our friend all through his life, so far back at least as my acquaintance with him runs, was utterly averse to reading. All that he required from books, and all that his nature allowed him to obtain from them, was stimulus and direction to his own thoughts from the questions they raised, and to a less extent from the solutions they offered. Now, Hamilton, from the superabundance of the stores of learning which he brings forth upon all things, great and small, in the history of philosophy, was exactly suited to meet this want of Chauncey, while

how normal to Chauncey's mind was the philosophical system he afterwards espoused, developed, and taught as a master, that, in harmony with it, and notwithstanding the instruction given him in recitations, lectures, and sermons by a revered teacher, he, with the greatest earnestness, maintained that this difference was one of degree, and not of kind.

"I think his interest in philosophy was not greatly aroused until after 1856. For in this year, while we roomed together, he was reading Whewell's 'History of the Inductive Sciences,' and was deep in the *Novum Organum* of Bacon, whose aphorisms concerning the province of science and the interpretation of nature were constantly in his speech."

the easy mastery that he has over his learning and the new setting which he gives to others' thoughts save him from becoming pedantic and tiresome. Chauncey's relation to Hamilton in those days was in a way like that of a devout Christian to his Bible. Not that he was ever given to accepting the plenary inspiration of any one; but when he was in full sympathy with a method in philosophy, and felt a thorough respect for its representative, — as was then the case with Hamilton, and later with Mill and Darwin, — he was never weary of going back to the texts, so to speak, to find food for meditation. and starting-points for new developments and applications of his philosophical principles. One might truly, I think, carry the suggestion a step farther, and say that Chauncey's intellectual adherence to a system sometimes took a tinge of personal loyalty to its founder, which inclined him to be forward to defend, at least against followers of a different school, even the *obitèr et incuriose dicta* of the master. If, however, his judgment was ever unconsciously biassed in particulars by his regard for one thinker, or his strong disregard, if I may say so, for another, the intellectual foible was more than offset by the modesty and simplicity of character it revealed. Though in pure philosophical power he was quite worthy to rank with the first, and grew with years into a fitful consciousness of his own worth, his spirit led him always, as a matter of course, to subordinate himself to the recognized representative of his philosophical faith. In spreading this gospel, his labors almost always took the form of exposition, defence, illustration, or new application of that representative's teachings, however original, subtle, fruitful, might be the contributions to the system which he thus furnished. The same loyal spirit showed itself in a different way in his contemptuous disregard, of which I just now spoke, for certain thinkers, not of the same modest type, who seemed to him over-hasty and over-eager to differentiate themselves into a new school.

"But, in reviving my remembrance of Chauncey during the early days after he left college, I have unwittingly been following the development of his mind into later years. Another book which, in his way, he read much at that time was Whewell's 'History and Philosophy of the Inductive Sciences.' This gave him such knowledge as he needed for his speculative purposes, of the development of science, just as Hamilton incidentally did of the progress of philosophy. Brande's Cyclopædia served him as a ready repository of the scientific or other data he might happen to need in his meditations. I remember, too, his being interested in List's 'Political Economy' in those early days, and the ingenious manner in which he used then to defend the theory of protection to domestic industry.

"In the spring of 1857, I went to Cambridge to live, and from that time, as you know, was on terms of the greatest intimacy with Chauncey. Not very long after my migration, he moved from his old quarters in Bow Street to Little's Block, in which my rooms were; and, for eight or ten years, there were few days in which we did not spend several hours together. It was about this time, I think, that he began to teach philosophy in Professor Agassiz's School; and the pleasure he took in this occupation for several winters was very great. It gave him a fresh motive for going systematically through Hamilton, with whom he was already so familiar; and it furnished him with the audience which alone was needed to make Chauncey's happiness in following out his trains of thought complete. Not very far from this time, I should place the earliest of Chauncey's review articles that I definitely remember, based on Blodgett's 'Meteorology of the United States.'[1] These, too, were the days of the *Septem*, — the little knot of men who

[1] The Winds and the Weather: Atlantic Monthly, Vol. I. p. 272, January, 1858.

passed so many pleasant evenings together in Little's Block, — but whose motto, in the pentameter verse of one of their number, has something tragic in it, when I think of the one dark thread in our friend's life, — *quod placet his fas est, quod placet hi faciunt.*[1] How much Chauncey enjoyed those evenings and that society!

"It must have been in 1859 or 1860 that Chauncey first felt the influence which was to be more powerful than any other in giving direction and color to his intellectual life. This was the publication of Darwin's 'Origin of Species.'[2] We read it and re-read it aloud together, and talked over it and the reviews that appeared of it interminably. The ground had been prepared for the seed by Chauncey's interest in theoretic geology, and the argument for the sufficiency of causes now in operation to explain past changes in the condition of the earth; by the discussions which had gone on for years in Cambridge between Agassiz and Gray concerning the true nature of the terms 'genus' and 'species;' and by the fruitfulness, already shown, of the historical method in dealing with social phenomena. I think I am not mistaken in putting the publication of Maine's 'Ancient Law' — my interest in which was shared by Chauncey — very near that of the 'Origin of Species.'[3]

"Up to this time, however, the abstract theory of evolution

1 On a photograph of this little company, the following lines were written: —

> "Foederis en juvenes socios sancti aspice septem;
> Quod placet his fas est, quod placet hi faciunt."

It is unnecessary to say that the motto was hardly a serious one. There was another reading, not wholly approved,— "quiddam placet hi faciunt." This had the merit, such as it is, of hinting powerfully at the slang English phrase, — then a familiar one, — of which the last line was an adaptation. *Ante*, p. 343.

2 The first English edition appeared in 1859. On February 12, 1860, Chauncey says that he has just finished reading the book. *Ante*, p. 43.

3 The first English edition of the "Ancient Law" was published in 1861.

had not found favor in Chauncey's mind. In illustration of this, I recall, years previously, a talk with him about the 'Vestiges of Creation,' into which, I think, he had barely dipped, and how lightly he regarded the thesis itself, as well as the arguments.[1] I remember, too, how decided were his leanings for Cuvier as against Geoffroy St. Hilaire, and how destitute of attraction for him had been the nebular hypothesis. To his mind, no theory of evolution would have commended itself on *a priori* grounds; but the cumulative argument, based on observation and experiment, of the 'Origin of Species,' in harmony as it was with his own habits of thought, carried with it complete conviction. A real explanation, so far as it went, had been furnished as to the manner in which the organic world had come to take its present form; and, more and more, as time went on, it became the predominant intellectual interest of his life to study the problems, physical and metaphysical, which the acceptance of this explanation presented.

"Not only was the direct influence of Darwin on Chauncey's scientific views thus great, but hardly less curious and important was the reflex influence upon his purely speculative opinions of the questions in which he was now most interested and the methods employed in their solution. There was no sudden change; for Chauncey's opinions had been too well considered, and were too organically connected to admit of any serious modification, except that which comes from a changed attitude of the mind as a whole. Such philosophical conversion, in a serious, powerful thinker like Chauncey, proceeds so gradually, that one who is in constant intercourse with him is almost as unconscious of the process as of the imperceptible changes that come with time in the expression of a face. As I look back on those years, however, I can see

[1] Mr. Sheldon, his teacher at Northampton, had discussed this book with his pupils; and it may be surmised that Chauncey retained the unfavorable estimate of it to which he was then accustomed.

that Hamilton was less and less resorted to, except for his learning and on points of which the treatment is not affected by fundamental philosophical conceptions; and that Bain and Mill came to furnish the topics of his thought. I put them in this order, because I think it the chronological one of his intimacy with them. The interest in the inductive and semi-physiological treatment of the old psychological problems which led so unpractised a reader through Bain's two thick octavos, ponderous in every sense, was an indication of whither he was drifting in his philosophy. I remember that Professor Winlock was laid up for several weeks by lameness at about this time, and how great satisfaction Chauncey had in inducing him to read Bain, and in discussing with so acute a man Bain's statements and solutions.[1] Bain, however, was a

[1] Professor Winlock, Director of the Observatory at Cambridge, died no less suddenly than Wright, and but a few months earlier. The same number of the "Nation" (June 17, 1875) which contained a sketch of Winlock by Wright had in it, also, Mr. Lowell's sonnet: —

"Shy soul and stalwart, man of patient will
Through years one hair's breadth on our Dark to gain,
Who, from the stars he studied not in vain,
Had learned their secret to be strong and still,
Careless of fames that earth's tin trumpets fill;
Born under Leo, broad of build and brain,
He watched, while others slept, in that hushed fane
Of Science, only witness of his skill:
Sudden as falls a shooting-star he fell,
But inextinguishable his luminous trace
In mind and heart of all that knew him well.
Happy man's doom! To him the fates were known
Of orbs dim-hovering on the skirts of Space,
Unprescient, through God's mercy, of his own."

It is startling to think of Wright's reading these lines not three months before his own most sudden death. One who recalls certain points of resemblance between the two men, and the nature of Wright's own astronomical calculations, finds an application of the sonnet to him in more respects than one.

specialist, and not a philosopher; and, after his facts had been fairly taken up by Chauncey's mind, his volumes went upon the shelf as books merely of reference. It was Mill who succeeded Hamilton as Chauncey's constant, cherished philosophical companion; and the tie grew stronger and stronger to the end of Chauncey's life.

"Analytic as Hamilton's method is, up to a certain point, he then stops short, declares that bottom has been reached, turns his face in the other direction, and proceeds to build up on the foundation of his ultimate truths of consciousness — buttressed by the veracity of the Creator of consciousness — a system of philosophy which can be shaken, he thinks, only by a scepticism that, with consciousness and its Creator, shall engulf the universe itself. How stoutly Chauncey originally held by these doctrines, I have the more reason to remember well, because, having been greatly interested in Mill's Logic in my Senior year and subsequently, I spent afterwards many long evenings in discussions with Chauncey over it and the philosophical doctrines it presupposed. In these, I need not say that I was always driven to the wall. Thus, up to the time of his interest in Darwin, it was Chauncey's synthetic powers that were most called into play in his philosophy. From that time, the analytic element became the more potent, and bit by bit the old foundations crumbled away. Occam's razor,[1] which Hamilton found so useful in lopping off superfluous causes from previous systems and in producing the trim neatness of his own, was used by Chauncey with more and more ruthless consistency, until nothing was left standing in the mind that was not rooted in experience. Experience of phenomena gave both the content and the form of knowledge; the ground and the sanction of moral judgments; the limits of the universe in its intelligible, credible relations with man.

[1] The maxim, "Entia non sunt multiplicanda praeter necessitatem."

"I have dwelt at this length upon the development of Chauncey's philosophical opinions, because he was in a sense peculiar to himself among all the men I have known, 'a being breathing thoughtful breath;' and because I believe that I am the only friend who was continuously intimate with him during the whole period of their development, and also sufficiently interested in such questions to lead him to discourse upon them freely. During the last half-dozen years of his life, after my marriage, I saw him, to be sure, less constantly; but, happily for me, he always kept up his habit of reading to me what he had been writing, and of talking over the philosophical problems that were interesting him. I was thus kept fairly well acquainted with the thread of his speculations to the end.

"Let me try now, however imperfectly, to give form and proportion to my impressions of Chauncey's character and mind. One so seldom attempts to bring to a focus the myriad impressions which lurk in the memory, that the best image one can hope to bring out will seem very rude to those who were familiar with the original.

"One would naturally begin with the physique, — so sound, so massive, so inert, and yet capable of so much effort and endurance! His body was like an engine that, if sufficiently stoked with sleep and food, however irregular the intervals, was always in condition to do what was required of it. Heavy as were the draughts he made at times on the reserves of his constitution, the springs of its strength long seemed unfailing. Save one ugly attack [in 1863], I can recall no ailment of his, great or small, during the many years of our daily intercourse. Especially notable was his exemption from all nervous discomforts, like headache. His sleep was profound beyond that of childhood. He always kept excessively late hours, but slept steadily from seven to nine hours, be his hour of going to bed what it might. He formed these habits in the days when, at

Mrs. Lyman's, Mary Walker was ready and glad to give him his breakfast at whatever hour he presented himself; and, with characteristic phlegm, he adhered for life, without regard to the obstacles that boarding-house keepers or friends might throw in his way, to a disposition of his hours that suited him. So deep was his sleep, that you could pull him out of bed in the morning without fairly rousing him. For the first hour or two after he got up, he seemed to feel an owl-like strangeness in the bright world about him; and it was only by degrees that he recovered full possession of his faculties. He dreamed little; and his only recurring form of dream was that of flying, or rather floating in the air, a little distance above the ground. After the complete repose of these nights, by about twelve or one o'clock in the day, he began life again perfectly fresh, no matter how late his hours had been, nor for how long a time late hours had been kept. The sluggishness that accompanied the soundness of Chauncey's body extended to his senses, with the exception of that of sight. This was marvellously keen, as well as alert: the others were content to respond when called upon.[1] Given a sound body, a sluggish temperament, and a mind always occupied on some purely intellectual problem, one might, I fancy, anticipate the chief features of Chauncey's character, if one failed to do justice to its finer qualities. Calm, gentle, unassuming; ready to be pleased; demanding little of his friends; as pure as a woman in thought and speech; fond of children, and unwearied in giving them pleasure; free from passion to a defect; never selfish, though at times, from preoccupation of mind or from lack of imagination, not wholly considerate; deficient in ambition; devoid of jealousy and envy; perfectly honorable and perfectly amiable;—there stand out in the memory of his oldest friends, as the last impressions of his character,

[1] An exception should also be made of his sense of touch, which was hardly, if at all, less delicate and quick than his sight.

the same large features, great simplicity and great dignity, which would have struck an observer meeting him for the first time.

"One is impressed, in going through life, with the disparity among men in the use that is made of their Christian names. Some seem to lose them in childhood, and outside of their own families are known only by the family name, with or without a prefix, according to the degree of intimacy. At the other extreme stand those who have in truth a 'given' name, and with whom men slip easily and unconsciously into the use of it. One seldom sees so notable an illustration of this gift for creating easy relations as in our friend. When one considers how formidable to most men such an intelligence as his in itself would be, it speaks volumes for his simplicity, sweetness, and modesty of character that he should have been known as 'Chauncey' by all who came much in contact with him.

"Of this intelligence, which made Chauncey so marked a man, let me end this long letter by trying to give you my impressions with a little more method than came naturally in speaking of his philosophical development. Marvellous as that intelligence was, — quite unmatched, indeed, within its own great range, in my experience of men, — its limitations were very sharply marked.

"Chauncey's intellect was very little fed through his emotions; and to the beauties of nature, of art, and of literature, his susceptibilities were neither quick nor cultivated, — striking and novel as were his comments at times on such matters, from acuteness of observation or force of intellect. With little relish for literature as literature, with little call for any class of facts that would demand much reading or a resort to foreign tongues, — whatever aptitudes he possessed for acquiring languages remained entirely dormant. History, except as occasionally a fact caught in conversation or chance reading might furnish him a peg on which to fasten some thread of political or social speculation, had little interest for him.

"On the other hand, no fact concerning the mind itself or the material universe came amiss to him. Each at once fell into its proper place, determined by its relations to other facts already known; and, thanks to this web of natural association, it was seldom that what he had once acquired slipped out of his memory past recall. Hence, although he was no reader, as I have said, and not a student in the ordinary sense of that term, the amount of his knowledge was prodigious. The workings of Chauncey's mind might well have suggested to Plato his doctrine of reminiscence; for one could easily fancy that the universe and its laws had been once mirrored in his mind in their completeness, and that experience and meditation were simply bringing out into consciousness the dim lines of the image they had left. The acquisitions of several men whom I have known have excited my admiration; but in the case of no one but Chauncey have they caused wonder. However vast the other structures, one knew the processes by which they had been reared, and could reckon, if I may say so, the number of days' work which had gone into them; but of Chauncey's knowledge one could only say, *crescit occulto velut arbor aevo*. . . . You who knew Chauncey in his boyhood, when the foundation of his scientific acquisitions were laid by your excellent teacher at Northampton of whom he has often spoken to me, can doubtless recall the beginnings of his scientific knowledge; but when I became intimate with him, at twenty-five, his easy mastery of the principles of all the physical sciences and of psychology, the only subjects about which he ever much occupied himself, made his knowledge then seem as complete and round as it was fifteen years later. The increase that came with time seemed, even to one in constant intercourse with him, rather a process of development and expansion than, as in the case of most men, one of accretion. He worked in no laboratory; neither botany nor geology drew him into the field; when he took up a book, it was only on a subject that interested him, and it was usually simply to look over the table of contents, and to read a page here and a page there to give him what was characteristic in the author's treatment of his theme; yet so thoroughly did he possess his subjects in their principles, so fully had he worked them out in his meditations, that, the place for every new fact being always ready, the new fact was sure to reach him as if through the air. Though a specialist in no scientific subject, — for he early gave up all continuous study of mathematics, — few specialists could have failed to find an hour's talk with him fruitful in furthering their investigations.

"When scientific acquisitions so great had been made, as it were, by the way, without resort to the apparatus of books or instruments with which men commonly lay siege to their subjects, without the usual persistent application of months or years to the mastery of one, the question could not but arise in the mind of a friend of Chauncey, — What distinction might not this man achieve, if, enamoured of a science or stimulated by ambition, he should concentrate his powers within a narrower field? The better one knew Chauncey, however, the more clearly one saw how completely so exceptional a mind carried the laws of its workings within itself. His temperament was too sluggish, his interest in discoveries too purely philosophical, to allow him to make his mark as an investigator, — in spite of the subtilty and fertility of his mind in devising experiments, when he desired to satisfy himself upon a doubtful point. For continuous work in the field of theoretical physics, for which his mathematical ability and his large scientific imagination, seemed especially to fit him, I do not remember that he ever showed any inclination. Work of this kind would have involved an amount of drudgery to which

Chauncey would have hardly subjected himself, except from a keen interest in solving a particular problem. He showed his power to cope with such problems when they came in his way, but he did not seek them for their own sake. In a word, Chauncey's mind did not work under the discipline of the will. It was not indolent: few brains indeed worked more incessantly; but it always shrunk from uncongenial work, and all effort with him that was not spontaneous was uncongenial.

"Few powerful minds had less of the artistic element, in the ordinary sense of that term, than his; yet the character of the satisfaction he found in making his mind a mirror of the intelligible world — the world of law without him and within — is best illustrated, I think, by the delight that the eye sensitive to material beauty finds in gazing at a lovely prospect or noble work of art, and the mind in analyzing the charm. He lived indeed in an intellectual paradise, in which all his powers found full activity, and were free from all constraint; nor was the friendly ear, which was his one need more, often lacking into which to pour the results of each day's meditations. Was it a paradise, or was it rather a Circe's garden, which sapped a feeble will, and beguiled him from the tasks that might have opened up some unexplored corner of the universe, or have given mankind a Wright's law, and himself a name? I cling to the paradise theory; but I may be biassed by the consciousness of all that I have enjoyed and gained from the manner of life he led. Some of the external conditions of his life one would have wished changed, notably his mode of bread-winning. The computations which, for many years, he made for the Nautical Almanac, — as not demanding from him more than two or three hours' work a day, and making no draughts on his thinking power, — furnished in one sense an occupation as favorable as could be imagined for a mind that desired simply leisure for speculation; but, unfortunately, the temptation to him was irresistible to crowd the work into the last two or three months of the year within which it was to be finished, and to try to reduce himself during this period to the insensibility of a computing-machine, working from noon until two or three o'clock in the morning. For a time, the prospect of perfect independence for nine or ten months sufficed to carry him through this yearly period of purgatory; but, in the course of years, he found stronger stimulants necessary to support him, and was betrayed into the one serious failing of his life. Had he escaped this reef, and had his pecuniary position been a little more easy, there is little in Chauncey's lot that I can look back upon, and wish it had been other, — he being the man he was, and so little capable of conforming himself to alien conditions of life.

"Our qualities are dogged by their defects as inevitably as our substance by its shadow. As in Chauncey's mind trains of thought went on incessantly, with as little effort of will apparently as most men put into their day-dreams, so his will had too little power in controlling them when control was needed to make them most effective. A lack of sympathetic imagination in the most amiable of men — a deficiency which was, perhaps, an indispensable condition of such a life of solitary thought — went far to rob him of the pleasure which he prized next to that of thinking, the pleasure of finding a response to his thought in others. Neither as a teacher nor as a writer was Chauncey successful. I could name a pupil or two, indeed, who found him the most stimulating of instructors; and, as we know, some of the best minds in the world have prized his writings. Still, we must admit that, as a rule, pupils whom Chauncey himself would have pronounced competent, and readers whom he would have been the first to call intelligent, failed to appreciate him or to profit by him. He lacked the first condition of a successful teacher, whether by voice or pen, — the power of catching by sympathy the wants of his audience; nor did he possess at all the sensitive flexibility of mind which makes so large a part of the literary gift. His writings were more like simple transverse sections from the web that was ever unrolling itself from the loom of his busy brain than like pieces woven for the occasion, in which a particular effect was to be produced by proper combination of the material at his command. I fear that my illustration may not seem a very pertinent one; but it presents itself naturally to me, as I recall the process of composition of the bulk of his published essays, and many more that never went beyond his friends. He wrote with pencil, usually in a notebook, and when he was in the mood of composition wrote pretty steadily all day and far into the night. He was too precise in thought and expression to need to correct much or to revise what he had written; and I can hardly recall an instance of his rewriting, or rather reshaping, an essay, short or long. The starting-point was usually some fruitful reflection that promised to reward development; and from this point he would proceed on what was really a voyage of discovery, though in waters that were in general familiar to him. What he wrote during the day would probably be read to me, or the friend that was nearest, the next day, and talked over in a way. The end often came quite as much because the afflatus had ceased, as because a natural conclusion had been reached. What he thus produced were rather studies than finished work. They aided him to make his own thought clear to himself, but were little fitted to impress that thought upon others. Original, solid, suggestive, as they always were, from the very manner of their production, they lacked proportion, relief, perspective. It seems a hard thing to say of our Chauncey, the most simple, modest, and unconscious of men, that he never knew how to sink himself in his subject; yet just here, in the lack of quick instinct to discern how the minds he was addressing would be affected, and in the lack of discipline to accommodate the workings of his own mind to their needs and not unreasonable demands, lies the explanation that an intelligence so rich and powerful, so eager to give of its abundance, has not left the world more in his debt. He fell dead at the very noon of intellectual life, as he would have wished to do, at his desk; but, from the qualities of which I have spoken, I doubt whether he would ever have been appreciated properly as a thinker, outside of a small circle of readers, had his life been prolonged ten or twenty years. I cannot recall any suggestion on his part that he ever contemplated, even for a moment, any more considerable or continuous book than such essays as he contributed to the 'North American,' the 'Nation,' and other journals. It would have continued to be, as it had been, by detached studies, and by the effect of these upon thinkers who had the ear of the world more perfectly than he that his influence would have been felt and would have grown.

"Not a little of Chauncey's pleasure in the last years of his life came from the society of younger men than himself, undergraduates, advanced students, and junior instructors in the University largely, who sought his company as well for his amiable, companionable qualities of character as for the perennial flow of that wise talk in which he delighted above all things. Nothing could be more stimulating to young men full of intellectual life than Chauncey's range and vigor of thought and boundless stores of scientific knowledge. Not a few clever men must feel that they owe more to him than to any other intellectual influence in their Cambridge life. To Chauncey these young men supplied a need which he felt more strongly as he grew older. He craved intellectual companionship, at the least an intelligent auditor, for the thoughts with which his mind was always teeming. The old friends in Cambridge on whom he could count for interest and sympathy in his speculations were of necessity few, from the nature of the subjects with which he chiefly occupied himself and, in a measure, it must be confessed, from his invincible tendency to keep later hours than those could do whose duties began earlier in the day than his; but, of these younger and more thirsty souls, a great University town furnished an unfailing supply, as men came and went. The relation had its danger, however, as well as its pleasures and advantages, as one sees, I think, even in Plato's ideal picture of Socrates. The reaction of too constant contact with minds less powerful or less mature will make itself felt in the soundest heads and the sweetest natures. Certainly, in Chauncey's last years, one sometimes caught a glimpse of almost arrogance of manner in dealing with an absent opponent, and of something like contemptuous absoluteness and emphasis of language in expressing or criticising opinions, of which I cannot recall a trace in the days of my own greatest intimacy with him. The disturbance of his nervous system by physical causes was doubtless the source of this nascent foible, as the too predominant association with less ripe minds tended to foster it; but I doubt whether it had often, if ever, come to show itself in Chauncey except in the form of indignation at the condemnation of purely intellectual judgments on moral grounds. With his interest in the controversy over Darwinism in its manifold phases, he had occasion often to be angry and sin not; but, in earlier years, it would have been his mirth or his pity that would have been stirred, rather than his wrath.

"Chauncey was so purely intellectual and his intellect so predominantly scientific, with most precise canons of evidence rigidly applied, that it was hardly possible that he should do full justice to natures of a different type, into whose judgments the feelings are always filtering. He was so devoid of all desire to make up his mind on speculative points upon which the evidence left his judgment in doubt, so content to leave such matters unsettled, — those of the greatest equally with those of the least moment, that he could not at all understand the state of minds impatient of uncertainty and eager for a decision, at least upon all important questions. Chauncey, in other words, was by intellectual temperament a sceptic, in the best sense of that term, an on-looker who is interested neither to prove nor to disprove, but to judge; and, when there is insufficient material for judging, to hold his mind in suspense, — a suspense, however, which contains no element of pain. Upon his chart of the Universe, the *terra incognita* of the not-proven that stretched between the firm ground of the proved and the void of the disproved, included some of the chief beliefs to which mankind has clung; but it should be said also that he admitted the entire rightfulness of the claim of Faith to take possession of any portion of this territory, provided she did it in her own name: there might even be much solid and goodly land there, and not mere mirage of tradition and the emotions; he denied only that it lay within the range of man's experience, and therefore of knowledge in the sense in which he understood and used that term.

"Chauncey had given too much thought to the processes by which impressions on the senses are converted into knowledge not to be interested in the psychology of illusions. The satisfaction which he took in performing juggler's tricks arose hardly less from the pleasure of analyzing the workings of the minds that he was deceiving than from the enjoyment that he knew he was giving his friends. He took up the practice of juggling quite late in his life, but became surprisingly skilful in it for an amateur. His power of observation, and still more his capacity for holding a complex impression or series of impressions steadily in thought, until the relations of the several elements of it to one another became clear, were never better shown than in his analysis and reproduction of some of the most difficult of Hermann's tricks, after seeing them performed once or twice. The same faculties were brought into play that would have been employed on a complicated problem in mechanics, and the process of thought was hardly less methodical. I have often regretted that a mind so well fitted by gifts and training to explore that border-land of abnormal phenomena, where physiology, psychology, and imposition meet, was never seriously tempted to do so. But that adventure seems to exercise no fascination upon the heads which are really strong enough to undertake it: those who attempt it return either subject to the sorcery, or with merely conjectural accounts of what they have experienced. Chauncey, like most scientific men, was satisfied with a rough, qualitative analysis of what he conceived the charm to be, though he would have recognized that only a thorough quantitative analysis would set at ease the mind of the world at large, and persuade it that no uncanny ingredient entered into the business.

"In commenting upon Chauncey's character and conduct, I find myself always going back almost at once to that powerful intellectual machinery which was ever weaving his own experience and that of others into theories of Life and the Universe. Yet this does injustice to him and to me. It is not the philosopher, but the friend, that comes so often into my memory, — more often, indeed, as time passes than when he first departed from among us. That noble head recalls not so much the massive brain as the sweet smile and the eyes that brightened with enjoyment of every touch of humor. The playfulness of his manner stands out as distinctly as the sedateness and dignity which it lighted up so charmingly. What simple dignity his manners had! Like those of another friend (Dennett), likewise cut off in his prime, with literary gifts as exceptional as Chauncey's in abstract thought, his manners had that stamp of innate nobility which makes, instead of learns, the rules of good-breeding. The manners, I need not say, were but the expression of the qualities within. The perfect simplicity of his character, the inconsistency of it with the very idea of an *arrière pensée*, gave a singular attraction to the complexity and profundity of his thinking; but not less admirable was the reserve that never obtruded itself nor gave an opening for obtrusion on the part of others. My wife reminds me how ready he was to condescend in explanations to scientific intellects of low degree; but Chauncey had that genuine superiority, both of mind and character, which is never conscious of differences of degree. It is worth noting, however, what power he possessed, from his perfect mastery of his subjects, for making difficult things plain when he recognized what was a person's need; but an explanation meant to his mind a reference of a particular case to a general law, — the more perfect, the higher the generalization; and he paid his pupils the unconscious compliment of supposing that they could keep pace with him, unless they constantly warned him to the contrary.

"It was pleasant to see in so masculine an intellect as Chauncey's such thorough appreciation and enjoyment of women, and all that is most characteristic and fine in women. He was certainly catholic in his taste among men; but, as I run over in my mind the women who found a place in his regard, I am struck with the sureness of his instinct for what is charming, refined, and feminine. The friendship of such women was the strongest of testimonies, were testimony needed, to a singular rectitude and purity of soul in Chauncey, and to the native delicacy of spirit and absence of all personal claims, which make such relations cordial and easy. Like the friendship of children, which he always inspired, it gives a certain stamp as of sterling quality to the character. The praise of these would have been to Chauncey's ear the final word of commendation, and I will add no other."

INDEX.

25

INDEX.

A.

ABBOT, FRANCIS E., 54, 107, 123 *n.*, 147; letters to, 55, 76, 100, 108, 123, 140.
Accuracy in statement, 300.
Æsthetic judgments, 324.
Agassiz, 43, 367.
Aim in life, 300 *n.*
Altruism, 186.
American Academy of Arts and Sciences, chosen Fellow of, 42; contributions to, 42; discussions in, 71.
American Association for the Advancement of Science, 88.
Animal plants, 353, 354.
Annihilation, 276.
Astronomy, early interest in, 7, 14.
"Atlantic Monthly," 83.
Aristotle, 177, 286.
Art, 190, 197, 198.
Aryans, the, 222.
Ashfield, 84, 88, 89, 95, 345.
Atheism, 133.
Audiences, 207.
Authority, 113, 229.
Anthropology, 257–265. See *Darwin.*
Axioms, 108, 109, 295, 296.

B.

BACON, LORD, 30, 364 *n.*
Bain, Alexander, 178, 179, 197, 202, 369.
Beale, Lionel, 204.
Beautiful, the, 194–198, 277, 281, 325.
Bees, economy and symmetry of cells of, 42; architecture of, 42.
Belief, 96, 100–103, 129, 130, 141, 204–206, 342.
Biology, 296.
Blind, memory of the, 266, 267.
Botany, 14 *n.*, 347, 354.
Brown, Addison, recollections, 28.
Burden of proof, science acknowledges none, 203, 320.

C.

CALVINISM, 114, 118, 206.
Cambridge, 2, 99.
Cary, Professor G. L., recollections, 26, 27.
Causation, 73, 108.
Character, ideals of, 210.
Cheever, Professor D. W., recollections, 27, 28.
Childhood, 39 *n.*, 209.
Clarke, Isaac Edwards, recollections, 13
Clarke, Mrs., letter to, 8, 11.
Classics, small knowledge of the, 19, 20, 23.
Classification, 43, 292.
Clifford, Professor, 356.
Club, the, 39, 40, 174, 362.
Cognition, 124–133.
Colors, 268, 273, 274, 277–281, 304, 314–316.
Comte, 166, 186, 211.
Conception, 59, 129.
Conscience, 180, 196, 288, 289.
Consciousness, 111, 128, 129.
Cosmogony, 16, 177.
Cowlicks, 334.
Creation, 111.
Curtis, George William, 89, 144, 166.
Cutler, Professor Elbridge J., 199 *n.*

D.

DARWIN, CHARLES, 30, 220, 239, 253, 303; correspondence with, 230–236, 240–246, 304–318, 331–338.
Darwinism, 206, 219, 229, 345, 363 *n.*
Death, 86, 237, 275.
Dennett, Professor, 225, 383.
"Descent of Man," 205, 220, 248, 333.
Discussion, advantage of, 124, 300, 355.
Disinterestedness, 208.
Dreams, 299 *n.*, 327, 372.
Duty, 114–118, 297.
Duty of belief, 342.
Dwight, Dr. Thomas, 359 *n.*

E.

EARNESTNESS, 290.
Education, 120, 168, 212-215, 216.
Elections, reforms in, 146-152.
Ellipse and Hyperbola, Properties of Curvature in, 42.
Ellis, Rev. Rufus, 284, 285; recollections, 19-21, 297-299.
Emerson, R. W., 30, 87, 143, 147.
Emery, Woodward, 272; recollections, 283, 284, 359.
Empiricism, 270, 271. See *Experience-Philosophy*.
Ends of life, 274-277.
England and English genius, 218, 219, 220, 253.
Europe, voyage to, 239.
Eyebrows, use of, 332, 338.
Evidence, 96, 103, 342.
Evolution, 85 *n*, 368.
Evolution by natural selection, 237. See *Natural Selection*.
Evolution of Self-Consciousness, 46, 253.
Experience-philosophy, the, 46, 124, 129, 270, 271, 289, 381. See *Positivism*, *Knowledge*, *Utilitarianism*.

F.

FAITH, 103, 381.
Farrar, Mrs. John, quoted, 225.
Feeling, 194, 252, 326.
Fichte, 293.
Final causes, 226, 286, 287, 292.
Fisher, George H., recollections, 25, 26; letters to, 28, 32, 33.
Fiske, John, 340.
Freedom, 74.
Free-will, 70-75, 110, 241-246.
French genius, 220.

G.

GALILEO, 218, 229.
Genius, 216, 217, 324, 325.
"Genesis of Species." See *Mivart*.
Geology, 176.
Geometry, 356.
Gestures, 304, 305, 331, 332, 337.
Gilfillan, Dr. Thomas, recollections, 15, 16, 348, 349; quoted, 346.
God, 96, 133-135, 297.
Godkin, E. L., 174; letter to, 257.
Good resolutions, 322.
Gould's Astronomical Journal, 232.
Gray, Professor Asa, 286, 331, 367.
Greatest good of the greatest number, 118, 300 *n*.
Green, N. St. J., 32, 358.
Gurney, Professor E. W., 33, 34, 53, 87, 107, 137, 189, 192, 212, 218, 302; recollections, 361-383.

H.

HABIT, 282.
Hamilton, Sir William, 30, 55-63, 82, 119, 120, 214, 363-366, 369, 370.
Happiness, 210, 282, 322.
Hare's Electoral Scheme, 148-152.
Harvard College, 2, 148, 157.
Heat, 177.
Hegel, 179.
Helmholtz, 278, 280.
Hoar, E. R., quoted, 148.
Holland, Henry W., recollections, 214, 215.
Holmes, John, 247.
Holyoke, Mount, 9, 346, 350.
Howard, Miss Catherine L., 90; letters to, 91, 94, 119; recollections, 120-122.
Human agency, 240-246.
Human progress, 226-228.
Huxley, Professor, 235, 249.
Hypothesis, 206.

I.

IDEAS, fixed, 170, 179.
Idealism, 132, 270, 271.
Ideation, 312, 314.
Imagination, 323-327, 354.
Immortality, 65, 86, 101, 102, 121, 122, 134, 135, 237, 285, 297, 381.
Indefinite, the, 80.
Infinite, the, 57, 80-82.
Inheritance, 167-169, 257-263.
Innervation, 314.
Insanity, 291, 292.
Intuition, 105, 106, 126-128, 195-197, 324.
Ireland, Miss Catherine I., letter to, 53.
Irony, 293-295.

J.

JAMES, DR. WILLIAM, 332, 333.
James, Henry, 358, 359.
Jugglery, 11, 178, 256, 319, 381.

K.

KANT, 106, 164.
Kepler, 323, 324.
Knowledge, 73, 77, 104, 124–133, 141, 204–206, 300, 352, 356, 381. See *Experience-Philosophy*, *Positivism*.

L.

LANGDELL, PROFESSOR C. C., 22, 23, 246, 307.
Language, 236, 240–246.
Laws of the universe, 132.
of nature, 177.
Law School, 33.
Leaves in plants, uses and origin of arrangement of, 42, 234.
Lectures, University, 2, 157–159, 174, 175, 200–204, 207, 208, 212–215.
Lesley, Professor J. P., letters to, 38, 67, 75; recollections, 64–67; mentioned, 53, 54, 88, 143, 166.
Lesley, Mrs. J. P., her Memoir of Mrs. Lyman quoted, 18, 19; recollections, 34–36, 139, 345; letters to, 37, 42, 157, 164, 175, 215; mentioned, 143, 192, 302, 360.
Letter-writing, 28, 344.
Lewes, G. H., 341.
Life, 177, 204, 274–277, 281, 283, 287. 296.
Light, experiments in regard to, 255.
Light, 279.
Living according to nature, 328–330.
Logic, 214; reform in, 162, 163.
Lowell, James Russell, 41 *n.*, 83, 107, 316, 318, 332.
Lowell, Mrs. Charles R., 21, 40, 41 *n.*
Lyman, Mrs. Joseph, 18, 19, 34, 38 *n.*

M.

MAINE, SIR HENRY, 340; "Ancient Law," 367.
Manners, 341.
Mansel, 61, 85 *n.*
Marriage, 351.
Martineau, Rev. James, 85 *n.*, 178, 179.
Materialism, 66, 178.
"Mathematical Monthly," contributions to, 41, 42.
Mathematicians, 54, 67.
Mathematics, Wright's study of, 15, 23, 28, 45, 75, 254, 356, 363 *n.*
Maudsley, 327.
Maxims, 352.
Memorial Hall, dedication of, 267.
Memory, 124, 201, 265–267, 321, 347, 362
Mental photograph, 299 *n.*
Metaphysics, 84, 120, 204, 275, 299 *n.*
Migration, 346.
Mill, J. S., 30, 82, 84, 101, 120, 130, 131, 142, 152–156, 165, 166, 211, 216, 223, 224, 250, 251, 257–265, 356, 370.
Mill River, 9, 10.
Miracle, 43, 176, 356, 357.
Mivart, St. George, 219, 224, 226, 230, 237.
Modern ideas of morality, 171.
Modern types of moral excellence, 169–174, 181–185, 186–190.
Molasses candy, why it grows white from working, 91–94.
Moral greatness, 171, 181–185.
Moral nature, the, 178–185.
Moral sense, 118.
Morality, 46, 97–99, 180–185, 281. See *Utilitarianism*.
Mother Goose, The Philosophy of, 39, 39 *n.*, 294, 295.
Mount Desert, 44 *n.*, 46, 84, 89, 357.
Müller, Max, 162, 244.
Myers, James J., 230; recollections, 199, 200.
Mysticism, 288, 295, 296, 328.

N.

"NATION, THE," list of contributions to, 85.
Nature, 37, 153, 177, 328–330.
Natural selection, 71, 191, 202, 222, 226, 230, 235, 237, 240 *n.*, 332–336, 351, 352.
Nautical Almanac, 2, 31, 70, 86, 122, 137, 376, 377.
Nebular hypothesis, 46, 176.
Necessary beliefs, 129, 130.
Necessity. See *Free-will*.
Newcomb, Professor Simon, recollections, 70, 71; letter to, 71.
Newspapers, 169, 170.
Newton, 229.
Nomenclature, proposed new, 71–73. See *Ideation*, *Synthems*.
Northampton, 3, 9, 10, 99, 350, 357, 360.
Norton, Charles Eliot, 53, 137, 139, 219, 360; recollections, 82–84, 89, 90; letters to, 84, 87–89, 97, 99, 107, 114, 148, 169, 191, 220; his sketch of Wright, 1, 11, 17; death of Mrs. Norton, 236.

Norton, Miss Grace, 95, 137, 139; letters to, 95, 152, 157, 178, 186, 200, 226, 236, 254, 269, 272, 284, 300, 330, 338, 341, 343-345, 354.
Norton, Miss Jane, 95, 137, 139, 359; letters to, 99, 135, 142, 144, 165, 207, 249, 256, 265, 302, 321, 330, 349; her death, 353.
Norton, Miss Sara, letter to, 353.
Noumena, 104, 131, 132.

O.

OBJECT. See *Subject*.
Optics, 255, 269, 277-281.
Occam, William of, 219, 370.
Old age, 209.
"Origin of Species," the, first reading of, 43, 367; discussions of, 71, 367; mention of, 236, 368.
Orthodoxy, 285 *n*.

P.

PASSION, noble, 181.
Peirce, Professor Benjamin, 122.
Perception, 269-272, 312, 314.
Perry, John T., recollections, 26.
Phenomena, 131, 132. See *Noumena*.
"Philosophical Discussions" referred to, 1, 30, 42, 46, 67, 202, 212, 226, 234, 237, 253, 347.
Philosophy, 27, 100, 141, 167, 179, 203.
Phonantographs, 355.
Physical theory of the universe, a, 46.
Phyllotaxis, 42, 42 *n*., 66, 232-236.
Plato, 30, 299 *n*., 328.
Pleasure, 195-198.
Poetry, 10, 11, 12, 299 *n*., 348.
Points about an Axis, most Thorough Uniform Distribution of, 42.
Political economy, 172-174, 186-188.
Politics, 171-174, 192, 193. See *Women, rights of; Elections, reforms in*.
Positivism, 95-97, 102, 103, 140-142, 145-147. See *Experience-Philosophy, Knowledge, Utilitarianism*.
Posthumous reputation, 355.
Post mortem examination, 359 *n*.
Postulates in science, 108.
Power, the supreme, 109-113.
Preaching, 103, 135, 140.
Prejudice, the way to meet it, 135, 136.
Prismoidal formula, 41; extension of, 41.
Probability, 294.
Property, 172-174, 186-188.
Psychozoölogy, 248.
Psychology, advice as to the study of, 119, 120.
Putnam, Lieut. Wm. Lowell, 48.

Q.

QUINCY, MRS. JOSIAH P., recollections, 21, 40, 41.

R.

RADICALISM, religious, 147.
Reading, 303.
Realism, 162, 328.
Relations, knowledge of, 104.
Religion, 97-99, 100, 103, 114-118, 141, 142, 170, 185, 189, 190, 227.
Responsibility, 241.
Reverence, 206, 228.
Rowing, 273.
Rowse, Mr., 247.
Runkle, President John D., 41; recollections, 122, 123, 137 *n*., 142.

S.

SALTER, CHARLES, 191, 199, 200.
Scepticism, 152, 178, 381.
Science, 113, 141, 176, 203, 229, 256, 356.
Sedgwick, Miss Sara, letters to, 246, 316.
Selfishness, 186, 208, 343, 344.
Semitics, the, 222.
Septem, the, 366, 367.
Serviceableness, 287.
Sex, 85 *n*., 153, 257-264, 268, 336.
Shakespeare, 299 *n*.
Shattuck, George O., 284.
Sheldon, Professor David S., Chauncey's teacher, 13, 14, 368 *n*., 374.
Slaves, fugitive, 38, 50, 51.
Sleep, 276.
Solar system, 176.
Socrates, 152, 185, 293, 295, 299 *n*., 300, 332, 333, 380.
Sophocles, Professor, 302, 308-312.
Sorrow, 86, 237, 252.
Space and time, philosophy of, 55-63, 76-82, 103-107.
Space-perception, 269, 305.
Spencer, Herbert, 61, 340, 345.
Spontaneity, 339, 343 *n*., 345.

Stephen, Leslie, 250, 251.
Stewart, Dugald, 119.
Style of writing. See *Wright, Chauncey*.
Subject and object, 270, 271.
Suffrage. See *Woman's Suffrage*.
Suicide, 342.
Sympathy, 179.
Synthems, 293 *n.*

T.

TAINE, M., 253.
Teaching, 140. See *Wright, Chauncey*.
Teleology, 268, 269, 285, 286.
Tennyson, 299 *n.*
Terms, use of, 112.
Time, 176. See *Space*.
Thayer, James B, 1, 2, 13, 29, 30, 33, 43 *n.*, 142, 192, 357; letters to, 29, 357.
Theology, 67–70, 96, 109.
Thomson, Sir William, 67, 177, 212.
Topographical drawing, 216.
Tranquillity, 209.
Travelling, 164.
Trowbridge, Professor John, 318.
Truth, 300–302, 325, 326, 356.

U.

UNCONDITIONALLY limited, the. See *Indefinite*.
Unconditionally unlimited, the. See *Infinite*.
Unconscious selection, 240–246.
Uses in natural selection, 332–338.
Utilitarianism, 46, 178, 185, 222–224, 228, 282, 287–291.
Utility, the principle of, 192–198.

V.

VACATIONS, 43 *n.*, 338, 339.
"Vestiges of Creation," 368, 368 *n.*
Virtue, 282.

W.

WALKER, DR. JAMES, 363 *n.*
Walker, Mrs. Mary, 38, 49, 50, 359, 372.
Walking, 251.
Wallace, Alfred, 176, 191, 202, 219, 333.
War of the Rebellion, 47–50, 211.
Ware, Darwin E., letter to, 37; recollections, 43–46, 363 *n.*
Ware, Professor William R., 53, 307, 358.
Warner, J. B., recollections, 213.
Wealth. See *Property*.
Weather predictions, 74.
Whewell, Dr., 364 *n.*, 366.
Whitney, Professor W. D., 240 *n.*, 244.
Williston Seminary, 19.
Winds and the Weather, 83, 366.
Winlock, Professor Joseph, 369, 369 *n.*
Wishes, 322.
Woman's suffrage, 151, 257, 263–265.
Women, rights of, 152–156, 159–164.
Words, "good" and "bad," 112, 113; ambiguities, 275.
Wright, Ansel, 3, 4, 236.
Wright, Ansel, Jr., 13; letters to, 52.
Wright, Chauncey, birth, ancestry, and family, 1–4, 12, 13; Class-Book Life, 4–7, 14 *n.*, 19 *n.*, 23 *n.*; his first name, 5, 373; school-days, 5–7, 13–15, 18, 19, 21; first letter, 8; early habit of writing verses, 10–12, 348; wit, 10 *n.*; youthful studies and speculations, 7, 10, 14–17, 347, 354; temperament, characteristics, personal habits, 5–7, 10, 14, 15, 17, 18, 21, 22, 25–28, 31, 34–36, 43–46, 50, 51, 53, 64–66, 70, 83, 89, 90, 95, 120–123, 137–139, 199, 200, 214–216, 220, 239, 246–249, 250, 251, 283, 284, 320, 371–383; personal appearance, 24, 25, 44, 45, 382; love of children, 35, 36, 39, 142, 372, 383; leaves school, 18; employed in his father's store, 18, 20, 21; scholarship, 19, 20, 22, 23; college life, 21–30; becomes a computer on the Nautical Almanac, 2, 30, 31; his habits of work on the Almanac, 31, 122, 199, 200, 376, 377; his means of support, 31, 33; essays read before his club, 39, 40; teaches at Professor Agassiz's School, 2, 42, 366; invited to lecture at Harvard College, 157, 158; becomes an instructor in the College, 212; visits and travels, 37, 43 *n.*, 84, 88, 89, 95, 142, 152, 164, 165, 175, 217, 218, 239, 240, 246, 247, 272, 273, 284, 302, 345, 346; habits of study and reading, 15, 22, 45, 375, 376; habits of writing, 100, 200, 378; powers as a thinker, 45, 230, 231, 321, 362, 363, 382; mental

development, 45, 46, 363, 364 *n.*, 364–374; his sketch of his brother, Lieutenant Wright, 47 *n.*; health, 50, 137–139, 199, 249, 371; his appreciation of women, 383; as a teacher, 212–215, 377, 383; intercourse with younger men, 379, 380; style of writing, 225, 378; account of his visit to Mr. Darwin, 247–249, see *Darwin;* powers as an observer, 338 *n.*; death, 357–359; post mortem examination, 359; burial, 360; estimate of his intelligence by Professor Gurney, 374–383.
Wright, Elizabeth Boleyn, 4.
Wright, George F., 12, 13; letter to, 16; death of, 85; letter to his wife, 86.
Wright, Lieutenant Frederick, 13; letters to, 48–52.
Writing, 355.
Writing-machine, 330.
Wyman, Professor Jeffries, 271.

Cambridge: Press of John Wilson & Son.

www.ingramcontent.com/pod-product-compliance
Lightning Source LLC
Chambersburg PA
CBHW051520100726
47898CB00005B/1518
9783337136284